MW01264667

Blowin' in the Wind

Barbara Vortman

BARBARA VORTMAN

*Thomas ~
Keep Writing !*

Blowin' in the Wind
Copyright © 2016 Barbara Vortman

All rights reserved. No part of this book may be reproduced or transmitted in any form without permission of the author, except by a reviewer who may quote brief passages in a review.

This is a work of fiction. Names, characters, places, and incidents are the products of the author's imagination or are used fictitiously. Any resemblance to actual events, locales, organizations, or persons, living or dead, is entirely coincidental and beyond the intent of the author.

ISBN:1533641447
ISBN-13: 978-1533641441

For My Husband, Jeffrey,
who gives me the courage to follow my heart
and march to my own drumbeat.

ONE

My hands held the drumsticks, tapping the rhythm, but my heart and my head were someplace else. I leaned over and whispered to Louie, "We're losing them. Let's take a break."

As I hit the final beat of the song, Louie schmoozed into the mic, "Okay everyone, we're taking a short break. But don't you worry, we'll be right back."

I set my sticks across the snare drum head and rushed past a gaggle of girls who were headed for the restroom to gossip and repair their lipstick. In the kitchen, bent over with my head stuck in the refrigerator, I searched for something to quench my thirst.

A sudden voice boomed, "Looking for something, or just trying to cool off?"

Bobbing up, I bumped my head on the freezer compartment. I'd been caught. "Just looking for a drink," I said, rubbing my temple.

At other gigs I wouldn't give it a second thought, but this was a Negro sorority and I wasn't sure how they felt about white people helping themselves to their refreshments.

Turning, I looked up into the dark eyes of the fellow I'd been watching all evening. He was taller than I'd thought—well over six feet—almost a full foot taller than me. Compared to the dusky surface of his broad face, my skin was pale as a bleached out towel. His tightly curled black hair was cropped close to his head. My dishwater blond hair hung like limp twine, unable to hold a curl in spite of a perm and torturous nights wound in bristly rollers. We were complete opposites and I couldn't take my eyes off him.

Reaching around me, he pulled two Cokes from the back of the refrigerator. "Want a glass? Ice?"

His smooth dark skin and short hair both reminded me a little of Harry Belafonte and he had the same strong melodic baritone voice. I half expected him to break into a calypso tune.

1

"Thanks. Bottle's fine," I squeaked.

He pried off the cap and handed me the bottle. "Been with the band long?"

I felt my face grow warm. He'd noticed me. The heat rose higher. Of course, he'd noticed the only white girl here and a drummer. That's not something you see every day. At least he'd brought up the right topic. I could talk about music with anyone who showed the slightest interest.

"We've been together since last year when we were freshmen." I thrust my hand toward him. "I'm Melanie." My mother had always told me the way I stuck my hand out reminded her of a dog trained to shake. I was never as graceful and ladylike as she wanted me to be.

He glanced at my outstretched paw. Did he think I was an uncultured hick? His lips parted in a broad smile as he grabbed my hand and shook it vigorously. "Moses Carter. Pleased to make your acquaintance."

I smiled and nodded, my brain completely empty of words.

The throbbing beat of a gritty song pounded against the other side of the kitchen wall. Casting a puzzled look at Moses Carter, I left to investigate. Someone had put a stack of 45s on the record player and the crowd was digging the music. Their fingers snapped and their toes tapped. Several girls grabbed their dates by the arm and pulled them to the dance floor. Bodies swayed and hips bumped to the primal beat.

As the persistent tempo grew more intense, the crowd formed a circle around a fleet-footed couple who kept pace with the quickening rhythm. The girl had kicked off her shoes. Her partner grabbed her by the waist and hoisted her to his hip. With the precision of a well-tuned machine, she bent her knees, swung behind him, dropped to the floor and continued moving her feet without missing a step.

The last chord faded and I clapped and hooted along with the crowd. When I turned, I bumped smack into Moses Carter. I felt my face glow as red as a Columbia Records' label, not just from the heat and excitement of the dancing, but from embarrassment, too. Or maybe it reflected the glow of his beaming smile.

"You appreciate rock and roll, too, I see," he said.

"I grew up loving this stuff. At night, I'd find race stations out of Chicago or Detroit that played Negro music—" The minute the words were out of my mouth, I felt my face turn ten shades of purple. I tried to formulate an apology that wouldn't push my foot even further down my throat, but he laughed. Was I funny or just dumber than a stump? I couldn't stand to find out. "Break's over. Nice meeting you," I called over my shoulder and rushed back to my drums.

Louie nodded and said, "Harbor Lights" and brought his clarinet to his lips.

"Can't we play something more lively?" I whispered. The first notes sounded in my ear.

We'd had the argument before. Louie had said, "Rock and roll isn't for trained musicians like us. It's for kids. And this is a formal dance, not a silly sock hop."

Louie had been wrong. The kids here craved the vitality and energy of the latest music. They'd caught the beat and danced without restraint. They were cool.

I'd taken classes in music theory, composition, piano, even voice. I was familiar with everything from the chants of Gregorian monks to the piano jazz of Thelonious Monk. I loved it all, but I was a drummer and rock and roll stirred me like no other music. It was my future. Someday I'd be a star. Then I'd be cool, too.

From my vantage point on the small stage, I could view the student center's entire ballroom. Red and pink foil paper hearts dangled from the ceiling and glittered in the dim light. Most of the girls had their hair fashioned in smooth up-dos tamed through the magic of hot combs and chemicals. The snug bodices of their organza gowns revealed their smooth, dark shoulders and pinched their waists. The dazzling co-eds wrapped their lithe arms around the necks of their tuxedo-ed dates and the couples swayed to the music. As the girls danced their voluminous, poofy, multi-layered skirts twirled about the room like pastel parasols.

We'd gotten this gig on a fluke. The Silvertones, so popular on campus even white organizations hired them, had canceled the week before because their piano player had mono. My band, The Dreamweavers, was the last resort to fill in at the Delta Sig's Valentine's dance. Some people had already cut out, no doubt bored with our lame musical offerings.

My eyes returned to the tall good looking fellow I'd met in the kitchen. He was dancing with a pretty girl. In perfect synchronization they moved effortlessly across the floor, his smile lighting the way. Yet her eyes darted about seeking a more interesting place to settle. He was just a prop she'd invited to enhance her own good looks.

I closed my eyes a moment and envisioned his muscular physique hugged by his crisp white shirt and charcoal gray sports coat. *Ding!* The cymbal clanged off beat and my eyes flew open. He turned at the discordant sound which no one else seemed to hear. The girl in his arms was a fool.

A few days later as I walked toward the library a voice called out, "Hey! Melanie!"

I turned around. There he was, Mr. Tall Dark Handsome striding toward me with a delighted look on his face. Or maybe that was my imagination. I'd seen him bestow that same easy smile on everyone at the dance, as if each person was special.

He quickly caught up to me and said, "Remember me? Moses Carter."

Remember him? The image of his face had popped unbidden in my head a half dozen times since we'd met.

"Of course. Hi." I tried to sound casual but I was nervous as a thirteen-year-old at her first eighth grade dance. "How are you?"

"Good. Are you on your way to class or do you have time for coffee?" He pointed toward the student union across the street.

"Sounds good. I have a little time. My next class is at eleven."

As we crossed the street, I realized I'd been hasty accepting his invitation. Most people didn't approve of mixed white and colored couples. Coming from a small town where gossip was the favored pastime of the majority of females, I should've known better than to put myself in a situation that would cause tongues to wag. But this was college. Surely people here weren't so narrow-minded.

Moses Carter held the door open like a gentleman and we walked into the crowded cafeteria. I'd spent lots of time there in the past so I knew where my friends would be sitting. I knew, too, that the Negro kids always sat at the tables clustered in the southwest quarter of the room. Where would Moses and I sit?

He interrupted my worries, "How do you take your coffee? Or would you rather have something else?"

"Oh, black, thanks." I waited off to the side while he went to the counter and bought our drinks.

Cups in hand, he nodded toward the window at the far end of the room. "That table over there okay?"

Crossing the cafeteria, I felt every eye in the Negro section sizing me up. Some of the girls leaned in, their heads almost touching, and whispered. I couldn't make out what they were saying, but I could tell by the sharp hisses it wasn't complimentary.

Carol and Joannie from my music composition class waved from a table in the middle of the room, signaling me to join them. Then they realized I was with a guy, a guy with skin almost as dark as the coffee he carried for me and, as I rippled my fingers in their direction, they looked away. Soon they were whispering, too, like the colored girls.

Moses Carter and I reached the empty table by the window and he smiled as he set down the cups. Was he trying to cover his feelings about everyone's curiosity or hadn't he even noticed? I attempted to smile, too, but was so uncomfortable it probably looked like I had gas.

Once we were seated, I ignored the stares and focused on our conversation. Moses was relaxed, friendly, confident and apparently oblivious to the blustery air of speculation surrounding us.

"Where are you from?" he asked.

"Middleton. It's a little podunk town a couple hours north of here. About a thousand people. How about you?"

"Other side of the state. Flint. A bit bigger than where you're from. Around 200,000 people."

I'd heard of Flint, of course, but didn't really know where it was and I couldn't imagine life in a city so big. I struggled to think of something to say.

He broke the silence with another question. "You always lived in Middleton?"

I told him I pretty much grew up there, except for a few years during the war when my dad was stationed in Texas and we lived near the base.

"My dad was in the army and we lived by the base when I was a little kid, too," he said. "Of course, I don't remember much about it."

My memory of those early years was dim, too, so that conversation didn't go anywhere.

"Do you have brothers and sisters?" I asked, wanting proof that we weren't so different from each other.

He had three sisters and a brother, all older. Not quite the same as my two brothers and sister, all younger, but close enough.

His dad had worked on the line at General Motors. Moses' voice grew thick, like something blocked his airway, as he told me what happened. "He worked hard every day of his life. Made sure we had everything we needed even if he had to go without. Then one day a couple years ago, he came home from work with a headache and went straight to bed. A little later he shouted 'Birdie', what he always called my mama. Before she even reached their bedroom, he was gone. A stroke."

Moses chin dropped to his chest so I couldn't see his eyes. I struggled to think of something to say. What would I want to hear if I had to tell someone my father was dead? How would I even bear to talk about it?

"I'm sorry," I whispered.

He lifted his head and said, "Thanks. What about your folks? What does your dad do?"

"My dad owns a television and appliance store," I said, trying to keep from showing the pride I felt. Maybe Moses and his father had been close, too, and my good fortune might make him sad. I didn't want him to think I was snooty because my dad owned his own business. "But he used to work in a factory, and he built the business up himself. It's not all that big because we're in a small town. It's not like we're that well off or anything," I babbled, afraid Moses Carter would think I thought his family was poorer than mine.

Instead, he laughed and said, "My dad did alright. G M was a good living and now my mama gets part of his pension."

I wasn't sure what a pension was and, only later, I realized that his father probably had made more than mine could ever hope to.

"You major in music?" he asked.

I nodded and swallowed the last gulp of my coffee.

"Planning to teach?"

"If I have to I'll give private lessons to support myself until I start making records." I held my breath. My family always told me I was crazy for hoping I could be a music star. I'd shared my dreams with few other people and certainly no strangers. Would he think I was crazy, too?

He shifted in his seat and leaned forward, elbows on the table, cradling his cup in his hand. "Your band made any demos?" he asked as if my plan for the future was real, not a pipe dream like everyone else thought.

"The other Dreamweavers' dreams aren't in harmony with mine," I answered. "Bob, Mike and Louie like playing older dance music and classical. They're planning to teach high school band. But that's not for me. I mean, I like kids and all, but once I'm through school I'll be ready to strike out on my own and form my own band. I already have the name picked out—The Gingersnaps."

The din of rustling papers, scraping chairs and raised voices distracted us as students prepared to leave for their next classes. Did I dare skip mine? We were just getting to know each other and I didn't want it to end. Moe grabbed my cup and napkin and stood. "Guess it's time for you to get to class."

I pulled my jacket on and picked up my books."Thanks for the coffee."

He didn't ask which hall I was going to or offer to walk with me. Instead he headed for the side door while I went to the front of the building. Just like that he walked out of my life.

The next day on my way to my music composition class, I remembered that Carol and Joannie had seen me in the student union with Moses Carter. Who knew what they thought? Maybe they were prejudiced against Negroes. What if that one cup of hot coffee chilled our friendship?

I slid into the seat next to Joannie and whispered, "Hi.'" She smiled. Carol, who was sitting on the other side of her, leaned forward and asked, "Did you finish the rondo? Can I see it? I'm stuck on the transitions."

The instructor banged on his desk for attention. I nodded to Carol and mouthed 'see you after class.' Apparently they'd forgotten about Moses Carter like he'd forgotten me.

The next Tuesday after my nine o'clock class I was sliding my way down the ice-glazed sidewalk when I saw him. Even though he was bundled in a heavy overcoat, and over-sized earmuffs pinched the sides of his head, I instantly recognized Moses Carter. Risking falling; endangering life and limb; and courting potential humiliation, I rushed toward him. Please don't let him turn around and see me running after him like a dog trying to catch a pickup truck. Slow down. Act nonchalant.

"Moses Carter?" I called.

He turned. He smiled. I could breathe again.

"Hi. I thought I recognized you. On your way to class?" The high pitch of my voice betrayed me. Anyone could tell I was a phony. Pretend as I might, he must have known I hadn't just casually bumped into him.

"Nope. I'm done early on Tuesdays."

"Oh, um, uh, well, I have a bit of time before my next class. How about I treat you to a cup of coffee since you did me the favor last week." There. That sounded right. It wasn't a date or anything, just me returning a favor.

We sat at the same table and this time I asked Moe about his major.

"Finance," he told me. "I'll probably get a job in banking or insurance. Nothing so glamorous as your future."

Ordinarily his choice of career would seem as dull as milking cows, but thinking of Moe in a business suit, working in an office in a big city, intrigued me. Would he work with white people? When Mom and I had made our annual shopping trips to Grand Rapids I hadn't seen many colored folks except the ones who cleaned the bathrooms at Herpolsheimers or cleared the tables in Wurzburgs' tea room. I think all the men in business suits were white, but then I hadn't paid much attention.

Our conversation eventually turned to music and I learned that he'd played clarinet since fourth grade and picked up the sax in high school. He grinned and told me, "I got pretty good if I do say so myself. But I don't have much time to play now. Just jam with a couple guys in the dorm now and then to keep from getting rusty."

His score on the fascination scale shot way up. I think I actually batted my eyelashes as I gushed "I'd love to hear you play."

His laugh boomed so loud people at the other tables stopped talking and looked at us. What stories would they conjure up about the big dark man laughing at a red faced girl? I'd spent half my life with a flaming face, not rosy cheeks that made people think I was cute and coy, but the color of a bad sunburn. I blushed over everything, and nothing, leading people to conclude all the wrong things. The staring students probably thought I was embarrassed to be with him. I didn't care what they thought, but I wished I could get inside his brain and discover what he thought my red face meant.

When it was time for me to go to class, Moses Carter walked me to the door. Standing outside shivering in the blustery wind I asked again, "So, will you play your saxophone for me sometime?"

His answer was better than I'd hoped. "I don't know about playing the sax for a music major and future star, but I'd like to have coffee with you again."

After that, we had a standing "coffee date" every Tuesday morning.

When Moe and I were together I ignored the nasty looks glaring from both white and dark faces near us. Now and then a hateful whisper would waft above the din and wend its way to my ear—"nigger lover", "white bitch."

Moe's face remained impassive and he kept right on talking so I wasn't sure he'd heard the remarks. Did he think I hadn't heard?

When he talked about his family, especially his mama, I felt a twinge of envy. I could picture their kitchen, crowded with family and friends.

"It's like there's a revolving door at our house," he said. "You never know who'll be dropping in."

I could smell the soup—chunks of tender beef, pungent bits of garlic and onions, orange carrot coins—simmering in a large enamel pot on the stove. I could taste tart homemade lemon pie and fluffy light biscuits. I heard laughter climbing to the rafters. I wanted to try black-eyed peas and collard greens. To feel his mama's arms welcoming me in one of those hugs she freely bestowed on everyone. To know his life.

I tried to make him like my family, too, but my stories were no match for his. Unlike his mama, my mother wasn't very friendly and she was always bugging me about something. I didn't want to say much about Dad even though he was funny and there were so many things to like about him. How could I talk about my father when Moses Carter had lost his? My stories about my family fell flat. We were ordinary.

Moe and I talked a lot about music. He never once made fun of my dreams. "If it's what you want, you can make anything happen," he told me and related his parents' story to prove his point.

Early in their marriage, they had been sharecroppers in South Carolina. After the war, they moved to Michigan in search of a better life. He proudly held them up as an example of success through faith and hard work. My own parents were hardworking and hadn't exactly come from a soft life, but the picture he painted of his parents' struggles was so desperate it was hard for me to grasp. The distant, melancholy stare veiling his eyes spoke of all they'd suffered. Their pain was forever woven into the fabric of their family heritage.

By comparison, I had it easy.

Schoolwork was a safe topic, like talking about the weather. Something we returned to whenever the conversation got too heavy or too personal. Moe tried to enlighten me about finance and business.

My dad's business and I had practically grown up together, and

I'd tellered in the local bank the previous summer, but it was all so small town. Everyone knew each other, deals were made on a handshake, sometimes customers bartered crops or livestock instead of paying cash. My mother, who hadn't even finished high school, kept the books for Dad's store. On one page of her account book she wrote down the income and on another the expenses and always hoped the total of the first was bigger than the second. Dad placed orders with the salesmen who came by every few weeks to tout modern appliances and the latest Hi-Fi. The store's advertising consisted of hand-drawn posters (many by my little sister), a small ad in the Middleton Weekly News, and word of mouth. Even at the bank, an application for a loan was only a short page with the approval dependent on what Mr. Johnson, the bank president, personally knew about the applicant.

Moe told me the things he was learning about corporate business. The complexity, the legal aspects, the divisions of work: one person responsible for researching products, another negotiating deals, another tracking supplies. It took someone with a master's degree to oversee the bookkeeping. There were ledgers and statements and balance sheets and all kinds of reports. It was beyond my comprehension, but Moe was eager to become a part of it.

"I'm not sure how," he confided. "There are some Negro-owned businesses and we're making progress getting into white companies. I can't wait to get started on a career like that."

Just like I believed drummers would play a bigger part in rock and roll, he believed Negroes would have more opportunities to work alongside white people.

When I complained about my classes he sympathized. "A lot of those subjects might not seem important but you get more out of life when you learn new things. All my life I was told learning is the key to success. I heard it at school and in church and, most of all, at home. My Granny only finished fourth grade but she was curious as a cat. If she didn't know something, she asked. She was always taking a peek at our schoolbooks and taught herself just for the sake of knowing things."

My parents didn't think book learning was so important. They preached that working hard, being honest, and honing skills on the job would take anyone far in life. I wouldn't have been in college if my Grandmother Moroskavich hadn't paid for it; one more reason people thought she was too snooty for our small town.

I didn't see how learning the names of Civil War battles would help me in life, but Moe really believed it so I wanted to believe, too. I became more determined to earn decent grades, even in the classes that had nothing to do with music. I'm not sure why, but I didn't want to disappoint Moses Carter.

I'd never had a boy tell me so much about himself and truly listen to what I said. Whenever we talked I learned something more about Moe and sometimes I uncovered things I didn't know about myself.

I ignored the frosty stares and whispered comments from both races. Why couldn't a Negro and a white person be friends? I knew it couldn't be anything more than friendship so what was the fuss? Let those bigots talk. This was 1960, not 1860, and we were in college, not some hick town. I was open-minded and not ashamed to have coffee with a colored boy.

Each week our brief coffee hour ended too soon and left me thirsting for more.

TWO

Spring burst forth with a frenzy. Buds popped from tree branches, crocuses fought their way through waterlogged soil, robins flocked home from their southern vacations, and children ran out of houses like escapees from a prison in the Siberian tundra. Everyone shed boots and heavy wool coats and put on light jackets and sparkling smiles.

All campus organizations hosted spring dances and, in spite of our stodginess, The Dreamweavers played a gig every weekend. We were never first choice, but our affordability meant we were always hired. The thrill I felt playing the drums, especially when the audience expressed appreciation, sparked my enthusiasm like lightning setting a parched prairie ablaze. Whenever I had spare time, I practiced drum patterns by accompanying the latest records played on the rock and roll stations. The drumming was pretty much the same on all of them. I still preferred the old timers like Gene Krupa and Louie Bellson whose solos were an important part of every song their bands performed. Someday drum solos would be featured in rock and roll music, too, and I'd be ready.

I was ready to burst forth myself and flourish like the bright yellow forsythia that grew rampant and wild in my grandparents' yard. But first I had to go home for the summer where my mother would try pruning me into the shape most pleasing to her. The continual repetition of our arguments and the tedium of small town life meant I was in for a long dull summer. A summer without the exhilarating reprieve of Tuesday morning coffee with Moses Carter.

I'd just finished packing my things on the last day of my sophomore year when the intercom buzzed. The voice of the desk girl squawked, "Guests in the lobby for Melanie." The code 'guest' meant it was either another female or an adult. When we had a 'visitor,' it was a boy and we knew to put on lipstick and fix our hair.

I'd had very few 'visitors' over the two years I'd lived in the dorm—a couple of dates which led nowhere and the guys in the band. Louie, Mike, and Bob were real squares. I'm surprised the desk girls didn't announce them as 'guests.'

Excited to see her for the first time since Easter. I dashed down to meet my mother. I knew we'd undoubtedly be at each other's throats within a few days.

Letting out a squeal, I ran across the lobby and grabbed my dad in a hug. "I didn't expect to see you! Who's watching the store?"

His ears reddened as they always did whenever I hugged him in public. "I been in business long enough to take a day off now and again for important stuff like opening day of trout season." He paused a full measure rest. "Or, bringing my daughter home for the summer." Ba-Dum Tsch!

I led my parents up three flights of stairs to my floor. Stepping into the hallway, I called the warning, "Man on the floor!" even though it was moving day and one of the few times males were allowed in the girls' rooms. My roommate had left earlier, so all the boxes, suitcases, and paper bags sitting next to the stripped bunk beds belonged to me.

Dad let out a whistle. "Whew! Rita, I told you we should bring the truck. How we gonna get all Mel's durn paraphernalia home?"

Usually my mother rolled her eyes at his joshing, but she was busy opening drawers and checking under the bed to make sure I wasn't leaving anything behind. In an instant I reverted from an independent twenty-year-old to a nine-year-old and not a very bright one at that.

Dad hefted the biggest box; I took a smaller one; Mom grabbed a suitcase; and, huffing and puffing, we carried them out to the parking lot. Dad opened the Ford's trunk and because he was the only one in the family with sufficient geometry skills he took charge of stashing things. We made two more trips. After giving the room one final look, I locked the door, dropped the keys at the reception desk and followed my parents outside.

Moses Carter stood next to my parents' car.

I lurched with surprise and almost dropped the box of records— my precious albums and 45s.

He held a saxophone. Spotting us, he lifted the mouthpiece to his lips and began to play "Johnny B Goode". People stopped loading cars and saying good-byes to listen. Some probably didn't recognize

Chuck Berry's song played on a sax rather than a guitar, but I knew it right off. It was the kind of music I'd listened to from the time I was thirteen and would sneak out at night to Dad's radio shop where I'd mess around with the Motorola looking for the race stations out of Chicago.

Moe's head moved back and forth to the tempo. On the brass keys, the fingers of his right hand tickled out the melody. The music was loud, urgent, expressive and raw. When he finished playing, he clicked his heels together and gave a little bow.

Since we'd first met I'd pestered him to play for me, but he'd made excuses until I thought he was afraid his playing wasn't good enough. How wrong that had been. What a farewell gift.

I clapped my hands and called, "That was great! Why have you been keeping all that talent a secret?"

He grinned at me, broke down his sax and packed it into its case.

Dad busied himself rearranging the trunk and back seat for the third time. Mom stood by, arms crossed, hands grasping opposite elbows. Her nose wrinkled as if she smelled cooked cabbage that had overstayed its welcome. Was she irritated by Dad's fussing or that I hadn't packed everything in boxes neat enough to fit the allotted space? Maybe she thought I shouldn't have brought all this to school in the first place. Her look of disdain probably had more to do with the rowdy music. And the saxophone player.

Rather than waste time trying to decipher the impenetrable workings of my mother's brain, I motioned Moe closer. "These are my parents. Mom and Dad, this is my friend, Moses Carter."

Dad thrust his hand forward and pumped Moe's up and down. "Nice meeting you. You sure know how to make that thing honk." Mom dipped her head and forced her lips into a tight smile.

"Thank you, sir," Moe answered. Releasing his grip on my father's hand, he turned and nodded to my mother. "It's a pleasure making your acquaintance, ma'am."

"Likewise," she muttered without an ounce of sincerity. "We'd better go, it's a two-hour drive." Her voice was as clipped as a summer lawn.

Moe handed me a slip of paper and mumbled, "Here's my address if you have time to write."

I gave his arm a little slap. "I promise I'll write if you promise to write back." He rewarded me with the irresistible grin that always left me wondering why no girl had snapped him up.

As soon as we were on our way, Mom turned in her seat and asked, "How do you know that colored boy?" In spite of her effort to sound like she was making casual conversation, her voice was as accusatory as Perry Mason's implicating one of Hamilton Burger's witnesses.

No Negroes lived in our small town, but my mother shared the same prejudices as everyone else in Middleton. Whenever we'd driven through the colored section of Grand Rapids, she'd said things like "Look at those dirty little pick-a-ninnies splashing in that mud puddle." The first time I heard her say it, I laughed, too young to know it was a slur. Later, I burned with shame. How would she feel if someone called me a dirty bohunk? Watching the evening news on television she'd shake her head over a crime committed in the city and say, " If those jigaboos would get off their lazy butts and get jobs maybe they wouldn't be robbing honest folks." She never made a comment like that when the bad guys were white. She often snapped off the radio in the middle of one of my favorite songs and sneered, "How can you stand that jungle music?" as if the music was tawdry and I was indecent. And now she had just been introduced to a pick-a-ninny, jungle music playing jigaboo by a daughter who called him her friend.

I wanted to say we'd met at a dance. It was true, but not the way she would take it. Bringing my hand to my mouth, I stifled a giggle. Maybe I should say he's my boyfriend. She'd flip her lid.

"He's a friend I met through band," I said. It wasn't a hundred percent accurate, but at least in her mind it would seem one hundred percent innocent except for maybe the friend part.

I hadn't wanted to start my summer break with an argument, instead I'd started it with a little white lie. How many times had I tried to keep peace with my mother only to get caught in a disheveled nest of deception flung together with inaccurate bits and pieces? Was this the beginning of another one?

"Are there colored girls in your dormitory?" she asked in her I'm-just-interested voice. I knew she was trying to figure out how many Negroes I'd befriended. Maybe she was afraid their color would rub off on me.

"Yes, a few. They're all nice girls." I stared out the window trying to think of another topic to divert my mother from this race thing. Why should she care who lived in the next room or who I was friends with? It wasn't like I was going to invite them home.

As he often did when things got tense, Dad rescued me. "Mr. Johnson stopped by the store yesterday. Said he's glad to have you back at the bank on Monday. One of the tellers up and quit a couple days ago."

"Really? Who?" I asked.

He tilted his head up and looked at me through the rearview mirror. "That chubby one. What's her name?"

Mom snorted. "Wouldn't surprise me if they come up short. People don't quit a good job like that unless they're up to no good."

"Maybe Dorothy decided to move back home. Her mother was sick last year, maybe she's worse." My remark ended the conversation. I smiled to myself. See, Mom, not everyone has ulterior motives. She might have actually been making a sacrifice for her mother.

We rode the rest of the way home without talking.

Sharing a room with Darlene again was the pits. She'd gone from my cute, pesky kid sister to a moody, half-crazed twelve-year-old. She changed her clothes a dozen times a day and left her discards wherever they landed, often on my side of the room, which she'd claimed for herself and only reluctantly gave up. Her collection of teddy bears slumped haphazardly in the corner near my bed. Cootie and Mr. Potato Head, games she'd outgrown, still took up valuable space, as did her stacks of books and art supplies. I reached under my bed and pulled out several of her shoes, random pieces of clothing, a hairbrush and her Magic 8 ball.

"Will my slobby sister ever learn to keep her junk off my side of the room?" I asked, twisting and turning the ball while Darlene rolled her eyes and slammed her fists into her hips.

"Don't count on it," the ball advised with uncanny accuracy.

Darlene had covered the walls, including over my bed, with magazine photos and eight by ten glossies she'd mailed away for—Ricky Nelson, Fabian, Paul Anka, Frankie Avalon—all the pompadour-sporting singers teen girls swooned over. She played their sappy records about puppy love and teen tragedy over and over until I wanted to throw up.

One evening I finally snapped. "Can't you listen to anything better than that?"

"This is better than that crazy jungle music you like!" she screamed, turning up the volume. I shook my head. She was the very imitation of our mother.

My brother, Junior, had given up and joined the army after a year of working odd jobs since graduating from high school. He was away at boot camp, otherwise he would've engaged all of us in combat right there at home. The bully's favorite pastime had always been picking on someone. I didn't miss his relentless teasing and the uproar he instigated whenever he was around. Maybe the army would straighten him out.

Our younger brother, Randy, had just graduated from high school. The very next day he started a job with the county road crew. Every evening, he came home covered in dust, tar and sweat and dumped his work boots in the kitchen. The boys' bedroom, which he now had to himself, looked like an atomic bomb had exploded in it. Stunk, too. He left the tub in such a scuzzy mess I had to scour it with Ajax before I could take a bath.

"Can't you make that slob clean the tub?" I complained to Mom.

"He works hard and shouldn't be expected to do women's work, too," she said.

I disagreed with her theory on the division of labor, but her ears went deaf whenever her parenting techniques were questioned.

In spite of the dirty bathroom and extra laundry, I was proud of Randy for getting up every morning and working so hard. He'd always taken the easy route avoiding anything causing exertion except for football, and even there he hadn't put himself out much. He must have really wanted the motorcycle he was saving for.

Work at the bank provided a welcome escape. I didn't mind standing all day in the teller's cage because no one knew I'd slipped off my heels and waited on customers in my bare feet.

"No stockings? That's disgraceful!" Mom chided as I left for work.

"Nobody can see my legs, and besides, I have a tan so they look just fine!" I shouted at her. I'd coated myself with baby oil and iodine and let my fair skin sizzle to a bright red under the summer sun in order to speed up the tanning process. A couple weeks' pain beat wearing stockings and a garter belt all summer.

Everyone used the local bank to take care of financial business and at the same time socialize with neighbors. Often they confided in me as they took out their money. "I'm sending my daughter a bus ticket so she and the baby can come home. I always knew that husband of hers was a no account scoundrel." "I'm saving up my egg money so I can buy a new couch." "Tinkered all I can with that damn tractor, now it's deader than a skunk on the road. Going to the auction to see if I can get me something reliable."

I heard their secrets, I saw their pay checks, and I knew how much they paid for their cars. I even knew that Mrs. Mason, the president of the Ladies' Guild of the Mortonville Community Church, opened an account with money from selling her deceased mother-in-law's wedding rings. She asked me how she could ensure her husband wouldn't find out about the account or the rings.

Of course, I'd never reveal what I learned about someone's finances. That would be unethical. And my refusal to blab drove my mother up the wall.

Sometimes on week-ends, I needed to get away so I ran off to my grandparents.

Grandmother Moroskavich, who lived in town, served lemonade on her patio while the muted strains of Mozart and Bach played in the background. I often wondered why she hadn't moved back to the city after her husband and her son, my real father, died in the fire. She should be where she'd have friends who would go with her to concerts and plays and art museums. Instead, she'd withered alone for almost two decades in her big fancy house. Everyone whispered about her stinginess, but she'd paid my college costs and convinced Mr. Johnson to hire me at the bank. Still, during my visits, we struggled with stilted conversation and awkward silences. I squirmed and hemmed and hawed, as unsophisticated as the rest of the small town yokels.

Dad's folks owned a dairy farm ten miles from Middleton. As soon as I stepped onto the wide porch surrounding the front and one side of their house, Oompa and Gaga greeted me with hugs and kisses. Gaga stuffed me with home cooked food, favorites she made just for me. She regaled me with tales of my aunts, uncles, cousins, everyone in the family, even her dog Brownie. I was comforted, loved, encouraged, and accepted every moment I spent with her. Their house was my real home.

I dropped in to see my best friend Pearl every couple of weeks. A year before, I'd been her maid of honor and now she was a happy little housewife, thrilled at the prospect of motherhood. She complained about her condition like legions of pregnant women who'd gone before her proudly bearing their discomfort. "Look at my ankles. They look like those giant kielbasas Mr. Grabinski used to enter in the county fair. And this heat! I can barely breathe."

I feigned interest in booties and bottles, but Pearl's life had taken such a different path from mine I had little to add to the conversation. After a while, I lost interest in planning her baby shower so Mom jumped in and took over. It was right up her alley. The way she doted over Pearl, knitting tiny caps and sweaters, giving advice, and relating stories of childbirth, you'd think she was the one who was Pearl's best friend.

As I suffered through the tension and boredom of summer in Dullsville, my music languished. I tried getting my old high school combo together, but Ron was the only one still in town and he'd traded his clarinet for new tires for his Impala. When I practiced, Mom or Darlene shouted at me to cut out the noise. I had no one to play with. I stashed my kit in the basement and, except when giving lessons to a couple kids, I didn't play for the rest of the summer.

The second day I was home, I'd written a letter to Moe, but I tore it up. It was too soon. There was nothing to say. I waited a week, then wrote another. I reread it several times but it was so flat I couldn't figure out how to make it better. Tuesday mornings at coffee I'd chattered like a chipmunk, but now I could barely think of anything that might interest him. What did he care that Pearl was pregnant, or that I spent my days taking people's deposits and cashing their checks? He was far away in Flint. It might as well have been Mars.

I pondered over the closing—Yours truly, Melanie Sedlak; Sincerely, Melanie; Your friend, Mel; Affectionately, Melanie; Love—I finally opted for Hoping to hear from you soon, Melanie.

I finally licked the envelope and sealed in the mundane words and the empty spaces where I'd been afraid to write my true feelings. Then I ran to the post office for a stamp before I changed my mind.

A few days later, Mom met me as I came through the door after work. "There's a letter for you," she announced, as if a Pony Express rider had traveled hundreds of miles over the desert to reach me with a vital message before his horse collapsed. Her eager curiosity irked me. Was I that pathetic that no one would bother writing me a letter?

I brushed past her into the dining room and retrieved the envelope resting on the middle of the table. She followed and peered over my shoulder waiting for me to share information. Didn't she know it was a federal offense to snoop in other people's mail? I waltzed up the stairs leaving her standing there with her nose out of joint.

Once in my room, I kicked off my shoes, pulled off my skirt and blouse and slipped into bermudas. Sniffing the armpits of the shirt I'd worn the past two evenings I decided it would do one more day. I plopped down on my bed and scrutinized the envelope. Moe's bold handwriting filled most of the front with my address. I carefully tore open the envelope and pulled out a sheet of notebook paper.

> *Thank you for writing. It sounds like you have a busy summer. I understand what you mean about it being hard to live at home again with younger siblings although I don't have that problem since I'm the youngest in my family. Two of my sisters, Ruth and Lydia, are married and out of the house. My brother Jeremiah is in the army so I won't see him this summer. My sister Naomi works the early shift at Hurley Hospital and I'm on second shift at Buick so we hardly see each other.*

He wrote a little about his job on the line and mentioned that he'd gone to Ann Arbor over the weekend to see a buddy. He signed the letter simply. *Moe.*

I reread the brief letter several times, wishing it was longer, wishing it sounded less formal and more like Moe, wishing he was talking to me in person. It definitely was not the torrid epistle my mother imagined. Still, I locked it in the jewelry box Grandmother Moroskavich had given me for Christmas, in case Mom's curiosity got the best of her.

All summer Moe and I exchanged weekly letters. One afternoon, I caught Mom holding the envelope from Flint up to the window to catch the light. Her nose almost touched the pane as her squinted eyes strained to make out the writing inside.

"See something interesting?" I accused as I walked up behind her.

She jumped, dropping the envelope like it contained the polio virus. Her hand flew to her cheek which flamed red. Regaining her composure, she cleared her throat and said, "That colored boy is the only one who writes to you. Don't you have any white friends? You aren't dating him, are you?"

It was the question I knew she'd been dying to ask all summer. Just to rile her up, I wanted to say something ridiculous like Moe and I were madly in love. But she was already flustered and upset. I was a big fat disappointment to her. She thought I should have a handsome, steady boyfriend by now. A white one. While I was at school, she'd enclosed engagement and wedding announcements from the Middleton News in her weekly letters; a not very subtle hint that I was behind schedule and would end up a dry old maid if I didn't get busy and hook a man. The only degree she wanted me to earn in college was an M. R. S. She wondered what was wrong with me that I never had a real boyfriend. Something I'd worried about too, although I'd never tell her.

I bent down and snatched the envelope from the floor. "My friends are my business," I spat.

"Melanie, I'm just concerned about you. I don't want you involved in something you can't handle."

"Who says I'm involved in anything?"

"Certainly there are lots of nice boys at school. Maybe if you'd wear a little makeup and get your hair cut and dressed a little nicer..."

"There you go again," I shouted. "Always trying to make me into you! Well I'm not you. I'm me. And I'm glad. When you were my age you were on your second husband and had three kids. Is that what you want?"

Her hand smacked me across the cheek so hard I stumbled against the dining room table. Grabbing my shoulders, she glared into my eyes. "I want things to be easier for you. I want you to marry a nice boy. Being friends with this colored boy will only cause you trouble."

I shook free from her grasp and ran out of the room. As I fled up the stairs she called after me, "Someday you'll understand."

I already understood. My mother would never be satisfied with me.

Neither of us spoke again about Moe. An uneasy truce settled between us as we prepared for Pearl's baby shower. In silence, I helped her write out invitations. At Woolworth's, with little discussion, we chose pink and blue napkins and paper plates, nut cups, and a paper stork for the dining room table. On the Sunday afternoon of the shower, I trimmed the crusts off slices of bread which she then spread with chicken or ham salad. Gaga arrived with a beautiful three-layer cake and the three of us chatted about how happy we were for Pearl. Nothing like a baby to bring women together, although I couldn't help feeling my mother's wistful wish for a baby in my future.

On the hottest day in August, Pearl's husband Larry called from the hospital to tell us the baby had made his appearance an hour earlier. Mother and child both doing well. Mom and I hugged each other and went to Dancer's to purchase a blue romper with embroidered bunnies.

Whenever she could get away from the store, Mom hightailed it to Pearl's house where she cuddled the little critter and bestowed child-rearing advice. She changed diapers and talked my friend through her breastfeeding worries. Pearl's own mother had long ago crawled deep into the booze bottle and now barely knew little Larry existed. I was happy Mom was there for Pearl.

Besides, it took the focus off my spinsterhood.

THREE

On Labor Day, my mother drove me back to school for my junior year. Struggling to keep from showing how eager I was to get away from home, I said little on the two-hour drive.

I collected my room key from the front desk and was surprised to learn Patti had dropped out. Roommates for the past two years, we'd gotten along well enough even though we didn't have much in common. She had hordes of friends; I was more of a loner. She'd treated our dorm room as a place to stash her stuff and to sleep while she spent her free time with friends or breaking some poor schmo's heart. Still I thought she should have told me she was getting married. It's not like I expected to be a bridesmaid, but an invitation wasn't too much to ask of someone I'd lived with for so long.

My enthusiasm over having a room to myself shattered when I unlocked the door and stood face to face with Diane. She was a bit chunky with an enormous mess of frizzy brown hair which looked remarkably like a robin's nest that had been caught in a windstorm.

"Hello," she chirped. "I hope you don't mind having a freshman for a roommate. I took the top bunk, unless you want it. We can trade."

I introduced myself and my mother and started to unpack. When Diane left to use the bathroom, Mom opened her closet door. "Too bad she's bigger than you or you could share clothes. Hers are a lot cuter than what you wear."

After she helped me arrange my things the way she thought they should be, I walked her to the parking lot and waved good-bye. She didn't hug me, let alone shed tears like I'd seen other girls' mothers do. Still, I felt empty as she drove off. I drifted back to the dorm like a rudderless boat.

Needing a purpose, I stopped to try the key in my mailbox. The rhythm of my heart quickened. Moe had left a message for me. *Welcome back! I'll be at our usual table tomorrow after my nine o'clock.*

The next day, I was at the student union a few minutes before ten. Grabbing a coffee I made a beeline across the room. I stopped short. Several students clustered around the table—our table. Outfitted in new clothes, their faces shining with eagerness, they all talked at once. Freshmen, for sure. The mingled smell of Aqua-Velvet and Aqua-Net hung in the air like a bank of cloying smog. The entire room overflowed with new students. Khaki and plaid attired future frat boys crowned with crewcuts playacted being cool. Coeds in skirts and bouffant hair shrieked greetings to each other. "Margo! I missed you since orientation!" "Oooh, I love your hair!" "Shelley!"

I felt a hand on my arm. Suddenly I no longer heard the cacophony blaring around me. I only heard Moe. "Sorry, forgot how crazy this place is the first week. Wanna go someplace else? I've got a car this year."

As I slid over the wide leather seat of the '56 Bel-Air I felt a secret thrill. It was almost like being on a date. But that was ridiculous. We were just friends. Moe drove downtown to a Greek diner on the corner of Main and Michigan Avenue.

The place bustled with businessmen on coffee breaks and smartly dressed women sipping tea before setting out on shopping sprees. Their eyes followed as we walked to a booth along the wall and sat across from each other. A woman who looked remarkably like an older version of my mother raised her eyebrows and whispered something to her companion. I pretended not to notice the cluster of waitresses glaring at us and the older one pushing the youngest in our direction.

"What can I getcha this morning?" the girl mumbled without looking at us.

Moe flashed his most charming smile and boomed, "Two coffees, please. One with cream, the other plain." His enthusiasm failed to soften her.

"Sugar and cream's on the table," she whined. "That all you want?"

"I'll have a cinnamon roll," I blurted. Maybe if we ordered something to eat, they'd get over having a mixed race couple in their white restaurant.

"Make that two," Moe ordered. Although she had refused to look at us, he focused on the girl's eyes. He'd often looked at me just as directly, but I'd never seen him look so boldly into the face of another white girl. The Moe I knew was always polite, even deferential. Now he hadn't even said please. He seemed to be challenging her.

The waitress scribbled our order and scurried away. In a flash, she was back with the coffee and rolls. She slammed them down on the table. I picked up my cup and took a gulp. The coffee burned my throat. Why hadn't that waitress even brought water to our table?

A bit of frosting from the cinnamon roll clung to the side of Moe's mouth and I wanted to reach over to brush it away. I'd pictured him a thousand times over the summer, but now he looked different, older. His shoulders were broader and his shirt pulled tight across the muscles in his upper arms. His jawline was stronger, too; the soft flesh had become firm giving his chin more definition. Staring, I realized he was no longer just a college boy. He had become a man. His hair, which he'd always worn closely cropped, had grown into a tight, fuzzy black halo. I resisted the urge to reach up and touch it to see what Negro hair felt like.

We both started talking at once, eager to reestablish the connection that three month's separation had disrupted. In an unspoken pact, we decided to skip our next classes. I babbled on about the bank and Pearl's baby, trying to sound as if my summer hadn't been all that bad. I didn't mention how bored I'd been, how my mother constantly nagged me, how I'd missed him.

Like me, he related bland details of his summer, ordinary stuff he'd already written about in his weekly letters. It was as if we were bobbing on the surface of a vast lake, afraid our lungs would burst if we dove deeper to explore our real lives teeming below.

The waitress slouched over, ripped the bill from her pad of paper and laid it on the table.

"We'd like refills, please," Moe said staring at her as if daring her to refuse him. She slumped away and returned with the pot.

His reticence ebbed and Moe opened up. "I guess I shouldn't complain," he started. I couldn't think of a time I'd ever heard him complain.

The impending confession promised intimacy. I leaned forward to catch every word and every nuance of expression as he revealed the truth about his summer job.

"I was one of the lucky ones. Lotta guys couldn't find work this summer. My uncle's a union steward and he got me in at Buick. Good pay, almost three bucks an hour. I even got used to the monotony. Eight hours a day, in a stinkin' hot room, on hard cement, lifting eight pounds off the conveyor. Lift, twist, set, turn, lift, twist, set, turn..."

My body could feel the repetitive motion. It was like the drills I'd practiced on my drums over and over until I felt myself moving to the pounding beat even in my sleep.

"It went on and on," he said. "You couldn't even scratch your nose without throwing off the whole line. Then that jerk, the line boss, would speed up the conveyor and laugh like a hyena while we busted a gut trying to keep up. For two hours after every shift the noise of the machinery left me deaf."

"Sounds gruesome," I commiserated, thankful that my job at the bank had been more varied and air-conditioned.

He slammed his cup down on the table with such force I snapped my head up like a startled deer. The muscle in his cheek twitched as his jaw tightened. "The worst of it was the supervisors treated us like peons. They got a charge out of calling us names and giving us extra work. You were always the target if you weren't white."

The truth shocked me. He'd been treated worse because of his color?

"That's not fair!" I argued. "Couldn't you complain to someone? What about your uncle?"

He snorted at my ignorance. "Uncle Jess warned me. There wasn't anything anyone could do about it. The bosses expected us to grin and shuck like lackeys. Said we couldn't take a little friendly ribbing. Only it wasn't friendly. Some of the older guys could barely stand by the end of the shift. We were treated worse than stray dogs."

My lips trembled so I could hardly speak. "Did they, did you, were you beat up?"

"No. All my life I was taught how to act around whites. Not that any lived in our neighborhood or went to my school or my church. When we had to go to a white business, my mother made sure we were clean and dressed in our best clothes and stood up straight. We spoke only when spoken to and called white folks sir and ma'am."

He paused and stared blankly at the table like he was trying to make out a fuzzy newsreel from the past. "I remember Mama standing a long time waiting for all the white folks to be waited on first, even the ones that came in after us. We had to stay next to her without making a sound no matter how long it took before she could pay, even if it was for only a yard of material or a spool of thread."

I couldn't believe what I was hearing. Dad always said, "The customer is right, even when he isn't." He treated every person who came into his shop with respect and fairness. Didn't matter if it was our parish priest or Pearl's father, the town drunk. And in the IGA it wasn't unusual for people to let someone with just a couple items go ahead of them in the checkout. Would they act the same toward a colored person? Dad would. I wasn't sure about anyone else.

Moe sighed. His head drooped. "I knew enough to mind my own business, put up with crap and do the best I could so I'd be left alone. Most of the time it worked."

Straightening, he pulled himself from the booth and picked the bill off the table. I followed him to the counter where the older waitress stood behind the cash register. He handed her the tab and a dollar. She lifted the bill from his hand, pinching the edge between her fingers as if his blackness would infect her. She laid a quarter from the cash register on the counter. Moe picked up the coin and moved back to the booth where he left it as a tip—a third of the bill—for the girl who had snubbed him. The bell over the door clanged as we left.

"I will never go in that place again," Moe said.

Even, if I could have thought what to say, I was too choked up to say it.

Neither of us talked on the ride back to campus. Letting me off in front of the student union he said, "Guess we should stick to this place for our coffee meetings. Thursday at ten?"

The rest of the day, my brain wouldn't let go of what I'd learned about Moe. I had no idea his childhood had been like that. There were no Negroes in Middleton so I'd never thought about them. When I was in high school, I overheard the librarian talking on the phone. "We don't allow them in our town," she'd said. "Well, no, they're never shown any of the houses here. They couldn't afford it anyway." I didn't know who she was talking to, but it wasn't hard to figure out who she was talking about and why there were only white people in our town.

I thought about the dark time in my life when I'd run away to Memphis. Lots of Negroes lived there. I got used to seeing them on the bus and in the stores, and I walked to Beale Street to listen to their music. Signs were posted everywhere—"white only", "colored only." The Negroes sat in the back of the bus or stood so white people could sit. They called me ma'am even though I was just a girl. Back then I wondered why people thought it was okay to have coloreds cook and serve their food, but it wasn't okay to sit at the same table and eat with them. Attitudes here weren't different, just kept hidden. But if I saw it, I'm sure every Negro did too.

My chest tightened as shame flooded over me. Why had I kept myself separate from the Negro girls in my classes? I smiled and said hello to them, even talked with them, but I'd never asked one to join me for a Coke or to study together or go to a movie. I'd never been in a colored girl's dorm room or invited one to mine. I didn't sit at their table in the lunchroom. My only Negro friend was Moses Carter. Was I a racist, too?

The next day on my way to my advanced music theory class, I ran into Bob Brooks. After a brief exchange he announced, "Mike dropped out. We're without a sax player."

My mouth flew open. The shocking news turned me into a stammering fool. "Wha? What? Mike? Mike dropped out? Why? What happened?"

"Not sure. Story has it he moved to San Francisco."

"But he had only a year til graduation. Did he transfer? Get a job?"

"I don't know any more than you do. Louie thinks we oughta disband. It's a tough load with classes, marching band, orchestra. And next semester he'll have student teaching. So, no sax player no Dreamweavers."

My ears burned at the words. I grabbed his arm. "We can't just give up because Mike left. I know a guy who plays sax. He's really good." The idea had appeared like a genie popping from a bottle. A thrill buzzed through me. What a magical, marvelous plan.

"You don't mean that Spangler jerk, do you?"

I shook my head. Richard Spangler believed he was God's gift strutting around campus like a crown prince surveying his realm. He'd challenged and won first chair saxophone in concert band two weeks into his freshman year. No one challenged him after that. His discordant personality set the entire music department off key.

"No. This guy isn't a music major, but he's really good. I could ask him."

"I'm game. Why don't you bring him around tomorrow to try out? Six work for you? I'll let Louie know."

The next morning I fidgeted through my nine o'clock class, tapping my pen and doodling all over the cover of my notebook. My nerves threatened to snap. How long was the teacher going to drone on? We weren't stupid; we could read the syllabus he'd handed out. Apparently he didn't think so because he went through it item by item. Blah, blah, blah. He checked his watch, determined to keep us the entire fifty minutes. Much to everyone's frustration, the filibuster worked.

As soon as he released us I ran out the door and sped to the student union. Our usual table was empty, but the place was filling fast. Should I run over and claim it before someone intruded on our spot? Tempting fate, I ordered coffee, black for me, cream for Moe, and carried the brimming cups to the table. As I waited, pesky thoughts of the incident at the diner crept into my brain and settled like field mice coming inside for the winter. I didn't want Moe to think all white people acted that way. What should I say? My face had turned red as a stoplight, betraying my emotions. Did he know I was embarrassed over the bad behavior of the waitresses? Or had he thought I was ashamed of being with him?

"Hey!" his voice broke into my worries. "Thanks for the coffee. Next one's on me." He pulled out the chair, sat down and flashed his dazzling grin. I let out the breath I'd held. There was no way I'd stifle my pleasure by mentioning the diner.

Ignoring the boisterous commotion rising from clusters of students, we settled into our familiar pattern of patter. We compared class schedules and teased each other over whose was the most challenging. It was no contest. His classes were clearly harder than mine, except maybe for Botany which I'd signed up for because I needed a science elective. I'd figured learning about flowers and trees wouldn't be too hard, but when I'd seen all those Latin names in the textbook I'd freaked.

Was it a coincidence that both our schedules had a free hour from ten to eleven every day? Had he left that time open, as I had, hoping it would mean we'd see each other more often?

Tension seized my neck muscles as I told him about our runaway saxophonist. Then, as if a brilliant solution had popped into my brain, a light bulb shining brightly above my head, I yelped, "Hey! You could join The Dreamweavers! Why didn't I think of it before? It's perfect!" I practically screamed about my sudden inspiration.

Moe laughed. Had he seen through my ruse? He shook his head.

"Me? No, I don't have time. You'll find someone else."

I stuck my lower lip out in what I hoped was the cute seductive way I'd noticed the popular girls use. "It doesn't take that much time," I cooed. "We only rehearse once a week and we don't have that many jobs. Maybe once or twice a month. C'mon, it'll be fun."

Moe kept shaking his head. "No, really, I can't."

I employed every feminine wile my mother had arduously instilled in me from age two on. I tilted my head and batted my eyelashes. "Pleeease," I sweet-talked. "You're the best sax player I know. Just come to meet the guys. That's all I ask."

Moe raised his hands in surrender. "Okay, okay, I'll go to see what it's about. That's all I promise."

That evening I was fifteen minutes early. Clumping back and forth across the tiles in the Maybee Hall lobby, I willed the clock on the wall to match my pace. After a long time, I heard a whir and a click as the hands shifted forward, adjusting to the new hour. Had Moe changed his mind? Had I been stood up? Where was he?

Resigning myself to owning up to Bob and Louie that I didn't have a sax player after all, I reached for the handle of the door leading to the stairwell. Suddenly the lobby door whooshed open and Moe dashed in. "Sorry! Took longer than I expected to get here from east campus."

"It's okay, I just got here myself."

He followed me upstairs to the rehearsal room. Louie looked up from the piano and gasped, "What the?" He stared as if I'd brought a skunk into the room. Bob's mouth flew open and just as quickly clamped shut.

"This is Moses Carter," I said ignoring their reactions. "He's the sax player I told you about."

Moe smiled and extended his arm. Louie turned away. Bob hesitated, then shook Moe's hand. Out of the corner of my eye, I saw Bob wipe his hand on his pantleg. I wondered if he was even aware he'd done it. Had Moe noticed?

"I see you brought your instrument," Bob said. "How about playing something for us."

Moe set his case on the desk, opened it and assembled his sax. He put the reed to his mouth to moisten it, then trilled a few scales. "What would you like to hear?" he asked.

Louie shrugged and Bob said, "We play mostly swing and jazz. You know, stuff people dance to."

Moe played "Harlem Nocturne" with such ease you'd think he was born for it. The tone was mellow, sweet and lush as a warm summer breeze.

Bob and Louie stared at each other, eyebrows raised, as Moe switched to a medley of Johnny Mathis songs, easy-going danceable tunes.

"We play rock and roll, too," I interrupted. "Play something for them."

Instantly Moe switched to "The Twist" and then a few bars of "Blue Suede Shoes." Nothing like Chubby Checker and Elvis to fill the dance floor. He played with such gusto sweat beaded on his forehead. I danced across the floor calling out, "See! I told you he was good."

As Moe took apart his sax and fit the pieces into its case, Bob said, "We're working on our rehearsal schedule. Melanie can let you know."

Moe started, "I'm done with class by noon on Monday, Wednesday and Friday. I have a—"

"He said we'd let you know." Louie's only words since crying out "what the" hung over us.

Moe snapped the latches of the case shut, the loud click shattering the silence that had followed the contentious remark. Bob and Louie busied themselves with their sheet music.

Moe's voice rang, "Thank you for allowing me to try out." He murmured to me, "I'll see you later," and left the room.

I screamed at Bob and Louie, "That was rude! You should have asked for his schedule. How can you set up rehearsals if you don't even know when he's available?"

"We aren't setting anything up," Bob said. "He's not in the combo."

"But, but," I sputtered.

"We don't want him," Louie said.

I flinched. "How can you say that? You heard him play. He's great."

Louie glared at me. "No coons in our band. Tell Sambo he's out."

My muscles tightened, especially my heart. I turned to Bob and begged, "You don't agree with him, do you?"

Bob shrugged. "Sorry, Mel. He doesn't fit in."

"Fit in!" My face was hot as fire and I felt like I would burst, spilling all my pain on the floor. "I'll tell you who doesn't fit in. Me! I'm not a racist bigot like you two. Moses Carter is my friend, which is something you'll never be!" I stormed out of the room giving the door a forceful shove. As it slammed shut, the rattling of the glass panes provided little satisfaction.

All night I sputtered and fumed about the way the guys had treated Moe. What should I tell him? I couldn't repeat the hurtful things Louie had said, but what could I say about why they cut him out? He knew they were impressed with his playing. Even a blind bat could see how the music had affected them. I tried rehearsing a speech that would spare the details and assure him I didn't feel the same as those two jerks. Nothing sounded right and when the time came I'd probably just blurt out something stupid. I gave up, deciding to wait until I saw him in person.

The next morning I hurried to the student union, bought our coffee and headed for our table. As I approached, it dawned on me why no one else ever sat there. The tables on the left were filled with Negro students, those on the right with white. The room was clearly divided and our table sat smack in the middle, squarely on the color line. I set the cups down and sat in the chair on the colored side opposite my customary seat. The lively chatter around me dimmed.

Moses Carter, carrying two cups, walked up. He sat across from me and grinned without commenting on our new seating arrangement. An undercurrent of buzzing whispered around us. Didn't they ever get tired of speculation and gossip?

I lifted a cup to my lips to avoid starting the conversation I dreaded. I took an enormous gulp. The liquid burned the roof of my mouth and scorched my throat. I coughed and choked, my eyes watered. It was the perfect performance for drawing extra attention. Moe pulled a handkerchief from his back pocket and handed it to me.

I wiped my eyes and cleared my throat. "Thanks. I think I'm okay now."

He smiled. "Your friends didn't care much for me, did they?"

I shivered. Nothing like getting right to the point. Oh well, it was better than dancing around afraid to talk about what had happened. "They aren't my friends!" I squawked louder than I'd intended. "I'm sorry they acted that way. I had no idea they were such..they felt.."

"You don't have to apologize. I could tell right away they didn't like me. John Coltrane himself could've tried out and they wouldn't have taken him."

A tear slid down my cheek and dripped off my chin. I honked into Moe's handkerchief and looked directly into his eyes. "Not everyone is like them. If I'd known I'd have never had anything to do with them. I quit the band."

He leaned forward. "You quit? Because of me?"

"Of course I quit. I told them you're my friend and they're a couple of racist bigots!"

He reached across the table and rested his hand on mine. At his touch, I felt a startling rush of electricity. There was a lull in the noise from the tables nearest us as the other students detected the intensity of our conversation. Or maybe they were curious about this public display of—of what?—affection, caring, friendship? My head felt as inflated as a bagpipe, but I still heard their whispers begin again to buzz around us. They apparently knew what this gesture meant even if I didn't. Maybe I should just ask them.

I stared down at our hands—his large, strong, dark; mine, small, weak, pale. So different and yet the fit was perfect. He quickly withdrew his hand and bowed his head like a bashful child embarrassed at being singled out in class.

"I'm sorry," he murmured.

I shook my head. "No, it's okay. I didn't mind." I wanted to add, "please do it again."

"But I know how much your music means to you. Your dream is to play drums."

I felt the red emblazon my face from neck to temples. He was sorry I'd quit the band, not sorry for holding my hand. How stupid of me to think it had meant something.

"I'm not giving up," I recovered. "I'll form my own band. Hand pick the right players. And you are my first and only choice for saxophone."

"Thanks for the vote of confidence. I know it'd be fun, but I'm really swamped this semester. I have a lot going on right now. You'll have to find someone else."

He looked at his watch and shot out of his chair. "No time to drink all this extra coffee or we'll be late for class. See you Monday." He gathered up the cups and headed for the trash can, calling over his shoulder, "Good luck. You'll find the right people."

I stumbled out of the building, so disappointed I couldn't bear going to botany class. I slumped back to the dorm, crawled into bed and pulled the covers over my head. The lecture on haploid and diploid phases of embryophytes was the least of my worries.

A far off whisper called to me in my dream, "Melanie, Melanie."

In my semiconscious state between sleep and wakefulness, I struggled to identify the source. The image of my mother, coaxing me to wake, quickly vanished. She'd often called to pull me out of sleep, but her voice was harsh, demanding, not soft and hesitant like this one. Forcing my eyelids open I peered through the tiny cracks I'd created. Diane's bird nest-topped head hovered over me.

"I'm sorry," she chirped. "Are you okay? It's almost time for the cafeteria to close and I didn't want you to miss supper."

My eyes flew open and I bolted upright. "What time is it?" I grabbed the alarm clock from my nightstand and stared at the hands. 6:20. How had I slept all day? Marching band practice was at seven. Our first performance of the semester was during tomorrow's football halftime and Mr. Beretta had a strict rule: you miss practice, you don't play. I jumped off the bed, grabbed my purse and my drumsticks and rushed down to the cafeteria. Making my way down the meal line, I bypassed the entrees and filled my tray with portable food: a roll, an apple, a hard boiled egg and a cookie. After cramming the food into my skirt pocket and my purse, I deposited the empty tray at the dishwashing window then ran off to the football field, devouring the makeshift supper on the way.

Most of the band members were already in place when I ran onto the field. I was the last percussionist to arrive, so the others had claimed their instruments, leaving me with the one no one wanted to play. From the moment I pulled them on, the straps of the glockenspiel bit into my shoulders.

My resentment grew as we worked through our routine. Few notes were required of my instrument and the snare drums had a really cool solo I wanted to be a part of. Even the cymbals were more exciting.

Our program was basic because none of us had played together since spring and there were lots of freshmen who needed to get up to speed. After a couple runs-through, Mr. Beretta ordered us to the bleachers for a critique. He asked for a show of hands of those willing to cover the pep band section during the game. My hand shot up. Maybe there'd be a chance for me to show my drumming skills. Mr. Beretta called the woodwinds back to the field to practice their part.

I focused on the saxophone players. Which one could I recruit for my new band? As soon as Mr. Beretta deemed them adequate, everyone scurried off the field so I didn't have a chance to talk to any of them.

The next afternoon, I dressed in my uniform and left for the football game. Halfway there I looked down at my shoes and realized I'd forgotten my spats. Mr. Beretta was insistent that we all wear brown oxfords, freshly polished, and then cover them up with those silly white nuisances. Whose brilliant idea was it for us to wear some goofy fashion item from another century? I scrambled back to the dorm and searched high and low, tossing clothes and books, even my pillow, willy-nilly.

Diane watched wide-eyed. "What are you looking for?" she asked when I paused from my frenzy.

"My spats! Where in heck did I put them?" I screeched.

"Oh!" she gasped. "I put them in your purse. I know I told you. I'm sorry."

I grabbed the purse I'd thrown on my bed and snapped open the latch. There they were, neatly folded right on top, my glistening white spats. If Diane hadn't looked so pathetically guilty, I would've grabbed her under her double chin and wrung her neck.

Out of breath from running all the way, I climbed up the bleachers and plopped down behind the pep band drums. Every musician scowled at me for being late. I picked up the sticks and tapped on the drum head, while my lungs and feet competed for the title of most aching body part.

Turning, I scanned the upper bleachers where the Negro students gathered to watch the game. Was Moses Carter one of them? Every chance I got, I searched the stands but didn't see him. He hadn't come to the game because surely I would have been able to pick him out of the crowd.

Eventually, I got into the rhythm and spirit of the pep band's task. When our team scored a touchdown in the second quarter, I launched into an impressive buzz roll, which few heard over the cheering crowd. Closing my eyes I imagined the roar was for me, but my name wasn't Go Broncos.

Our halftime show went off without a hitch, except for the clarinet player who'd forgotten his spats. I happened to walk past him after the game and heard a woman who was probably his mother remark, "Well, anyway, we were able to pick you out of the band even from where we were sitting." She laughed and he grinned at her even though his face was red as a rooster's comb.

The Broncos eked out a win and the jubilant students streamed out of the stadium, headed for pizza shops and Dairy Queen to celebrate. I hobbled on blistered feet back to the dorm where a hot shower and an evening with *Introduction to the Plant Kingdom*, chapters three through six, awaited me. What a drag.

Over the next two weeks, I paid more attention to the examination of the species *musicianus prospectus* than to the specimen slides my botany teacher presented. I needed a new band and this time I wasn't going to make a mistake.

The freshman music majors, with their long hair, casual clothes, and confidence bordering on cockiness, were hipper than the older students. Transistor radio cords snaked across their shoulders from shirt pockets to single earpieces connecting them to the latest rock and roll tunes. Of course, I had a transistor radio—two of them in fact. Having a father who owned a radio and TV store, I was privileged to have all the latest gadgets, but I never dreamed of walking around campus or going to class with a radio blasting in my ear. The earpiece was intended to allow a person to listen without disturbing anyone. It was distracting to see so many people wearing what looked like hearing aids. Older folks probably thought rock and roll had permanently damaged the ears of all those teen-agers. Still, the radios were a good indication that these kids appreciated the latest songs.

Juniors and seniors were invited to assist with band tryouts so we could hear the new students and hone our critiquing skills. Although a percussionist, I offered to sit in on tryouts for saxophonists, bass players, and jazz pianists. I would find musicians for my new band. Once, I sneaked into the vocal department's rehearsals thinking I might add a songbird. After hearing the beautiful tones coming from the sopranos, I changed my mind. Better I should be the only female on stage.

To figure out their musical aspirations, I engaged the students in conversation. High school music departments need have no fear of being unstaffed; most of the students planned to become band or choral directors.

One kid told me, "'Bout the time I graduate, Sister Immaculata should be ready to retire. I was her favorite. Her protege. I'll just waltz right in and take over as Annunciation's musical director. I've got plans..." I stifled a yawn, nodded, and escaped as soon as I found an opening.

Some dreamed of performing with professional symphonies, which would be nice if you didn't mind playing for old people. Then there were a few who felt like I did. Rock and roll stardom was the prominent feature of our futures. I focused on them.

The time it took to search out the perfect partners for my band drastically altered my schedule and I had to cancel a few coffee dates with Moe. When we finally got together we continued to take seats on the opposing sides of the color line. After a while the inquisitive stares and gusty whispers slowed to a dribble of curious looks and few comments. I wondered how many of the students thought there was something between us. Having coffee wasn't like going on a real date. Not that that would ever happen.

"I had no idea how hard it would be to choose guys for my band," I moaned. "Most of them are good musicians, but I'll bet they won't settle for having a girl in charge."

"Don't sell yourself short," Moe said. "You're good on drums. You know your stuff. You're older. How many of them have been to Memphis, or cut a record?"

He'd made my resume sound more impressive than it was. My stint in Memphis was as a sixteen-year-old runaway. My one and only recording was basically a demo with my part barely audible. Maybe I had a few years on the others, but I felt like a kid who had no idea what she was doing.

"You don't understand," I argued. "You don't know what it's like to be a girl. People don't give us the respect we deserve. They think we're dumb bunnies who belong in the kitchen. They think men are the only ones capable of being leaders. To them, women are second class citizens."

I looked up from the coffee I'd been absentmindedly stirring.

Moses shook his head and chuckled. "No, I don't know what it is to be a girl." He left the rest unsaid. I felt my face turn sixteen shades of purple.

"I, I didn't mean—I meant—I'm sorry." My stammering proved I was a dumb bunny after all.

"You've got a good sense of what people are like. You'll recognize the ones that think that way." How could he think that after I'd been blind to the attitudes of Bob and Louie?

"Thanks," I said. "I guess I'll just have to use my woman's intuition."

We both laughed harder than my witty remark warranted.

That evening, I drew up a list of top contenders for my band. Then, just for good measure, I made a list of second choices even though I was sure I wouldn't need it.

Over the next few days I discovered the second choice list was a necessity and in the case of the guitarist a third place contender was called for.

"I don't have time," the first pianist said. "I give private lessons three afternoons and Saturday mornings. College isn't cheap."

"I know," I said, "but it won't take long for us to make a name for ourselves and then we'll have enough paying gigs to make up for your lost students."

"Sorry, I need a steady income. Don't have time to make it big just yet."

I argued a little further, but I knew it would take time for us to make money. It was already too late to snag a Homecoming gig and, at the rate it was taking me to put together a group, we'd miss the Christmas dances, too.

I arranged to bump into Johnny Bartz outside the piano studio after his ten o'clock class. "Hey," I said. "I remember you from try outs. You're the one who likes rock and roll. Remember, I told you I know Jerry Lee Lewis?" It was chancy bringing up my friendship with Jerry Lee from my Memphis days. He hadn't had a hit in quite a while thanks to the scandal over his marriage to his underage cousin. Still, there was no one who could pound on the piano like Jerry. Johnny Bartz wasn't impressed.

"I'm looking for a new piano man for my combo. Interested?"

He seemed unimpressed with my offer, too, so maybe that was just his demeanor. "I might be. When do you rehearse?"

"We can be flexible. Fit into your schedule," I offered.

He agreed to meet the band on Saturday morning. Now the pressure was on me to find more players. Drums and a piano did not make a rock and roll band.

I approached my number one choice for guitar next. He laughed and said, "Thanks for the offer, little girl, but I'm already spoken for. Heard of the Hesitations? Yep, that's me. Good luck, though."

The Hesitations! I'd heard of them all right. They were a group out of Grand Rapids and already making a name for themselves. Their record had received a good bit of radio play. I wished their band needed a new drummer.

My second choice declined, too. He saw himself as a Segovia rather than a Duane Eddy. He recommended Marvin Fleck. I hadn't considered Marvin, but he jumped at the chance and I thought I might be able to bring him along with enough practice.

Brad Stone was the only one on my number one list who agreed right away. He was good on the saxophone, could play clarinet and a little trumpet, too, and was eager to join a band. My heart fell to my feet when he said yes. There went my excuse to persuade Moses Carter to be my sax player.

FOUR

"Our first rehearsal is Saturday morning. Are you absolutely, positively, one hundred percent sure you don't want to be our sax player?" I knew better than to ask Moe for the hundredth time, but a girl can hope. I could offer Brad a spot as trumpet player.

Even though Moe and I had agreed to meet every day between classes it hadn't worked out. I'd been busy finding band members and he'd canceled a couple times. If only he'd say yes, I'd not only have a great musician, we'd have more time together.

He slowly shook his head and stared into his cup. "Sorry Mel, I'm too busy. Besides, you told me you have a guy who knows a heck of a lot more about music than me."

"Too busy? C'mon you hafta take a break once in awhile. Don't be such a slave." I clapped my hand over my big fat mouth, making my stupid remark even more obvious. Would I ever learn?

A laugh rumbled from deep in Moe's chest. "Woman, you crack me up."

A blush crept from the base of my neck to the top of my head. He isn't mad at me! He thinks I'm funny and cute even when I say dumb stuff. And he called me woman.

"Classes and homework take a lot of time, but there are other things, too." The set of his jaw told me he was as serious as he'd sounded.

Over the past couple weeks, I'd blabbered about my trials and tribulations getting a combo together; it was all we'd talked about. He'd listened and offered ideas and kept telling me it would all work out. I never once asked what he did in his spare time. I'd imagined him chained to his schedule, classes all day, studying all night. Did he have a girlfriend? I'll bet that was it. Any girl would want a fellow like him.

"What do you do in your spare time?" I asked, not sure the words came out sounding as casual as I wanted. Not sure I wanted to hear the answer.

"A bunch of people I know are starting a new group. Sort of like SNCC or CORE."

What language was he speaking? What was a snick or a core?

"What's your group called?" I asked, hoping to garner a clue.

"We haven't decided on a name yet. We're looking into affiliations."

"Oh, like a fraternity?"

He shrugged and took a sip of coffee. The conversation was going nowhere. I was too ignorant to think of even one reasonable question to ask.

"When do you meet?" I tried.

"Different times. We're looking for a permanent space."

Why was he being so curt? Was he joining some secret society? Or didn't he want me to know about his social life? Could it be he thinks, like everyone else, Negro groups aren't a white girl's business?

He stood and tucked his books under his arm. "Gotta get to class. Good luck with rehearsal." He left without walking me to the corner like usual.

On Saturday morning, even though I was fifteen minutes early, I heard piano music coming from the rehearsal room. I walked in, surprised to see Johnny Bartz flawlessly pounding out The Drifters' "There Goes My Baby" He stopped playing and greeted me, "Just warming up."

I nodded. "Sounds good. We should put that on our playlist."

"Do you have a copy? I'd like to see how many of the songs I already know."

"Um, I don't have it with me," I answered, not admitting there was no list because until that morning there was no band.

Brad Stone and Marvin Fleck walked in carrying their instruments. Brad set his sax case on a desk and looked at the rest of us. His eyebrows pulled together in a frown. "What the hell is this? We're all freshmen except you, Melanie. I thought you said you already had a band. You guys ever played together?"

Marvin and Johnny shook their heads and all three glared at me like I was the biggest double crosser since Benedict Arnold.

"Look guys," I gushed. "I was in a band, but they didn't want to play anything new. Besides, not one of them was as good as you are. I wanted a fresh start with the best. That's why I hand picked each of you."

They rolled their eyes and snorted. Maybe I'd laid it on too thick. I put on a bright smile and wheedled, "C'mon guys! Let's play a couple songs and see if we're a fit."

They continued to stare.

"How about "There Goes My Baby?" Do you know it? Brad? Marv?" I begged.

Johnny turned back to the piano and played the opening chords. I slid onto the stool behind the drums and picked up the beat. Marvin strummed on his bass guitar.

Brad's saxophone hung around his neck like a big brass candy cane. I held my breath waiting for him to pull it to his lips. But he didn't. Was he going to leave? A vision popped into my head: Moses Carter heroically stepping into Brad's place.

Then Brad's foot began to tap and he wailed, "doo doot doo doo" He pulled the sax to his mouth and echoed the rhythm he'd just sung. We took turns calling out lyrics. The pace of our playing quickened until it reached a fever pitch. As a finale, we all burst into laughter. We were a rock and roll band.

It was such a blast jamming with the guys I was bummed we had to give up the room to a string quartet. In the hallway, we set a time to meet again. The boys agreed to think over the name I'd chosen. Not that I would let them pick a name other than The Gingersnaps. Maybe I'd have to tell them the story behind it—how my friend Ginger and I had made a record in Memphis and the terrible thing that had happened to her.

Racing back to the dorm, jittery with excitement, I crossed my arms and tapped my biceps repeating the beat of the songs we'd rehearsed. When I got back to our room, I was disappointed Diane wasn't there. I had to tell someone about the new band. I wandered down the hall to the bathroom intent on striking up a conversation with other girls, but they were busy sharing their best techniques for teasing hair. I could feel my own mop getting limper as their combs swished through their manes creating haystacks and rat's nests. As they smoothed the snarled strands into poofy hairdos, I slipped out of the lavatory, away from the misty fog of hairspray, and slumped back to my room.

I plunked down at my desk, pulled out my botany notes and tried to study. Within minutes I was back at the end of the hall, crammed into the phone booth.

"Walwood Hall, please," I told the girl at the switchboard.

As I expelled the breath I'd been holding, the connection was made and the voice of Walwood's operator boomed, "Walwood. Who do you wish to speak with?" I winced at his grammar.

"Um, uh.." I sounded more moronic than he did. Maybe I should hang up. What was I doing, calling a guy? "Moses Carter—"

He cut me off before I could say please. My hands shook and I thought I should slam the receiver on the hook and forget about the whole thing. It seemed like forever before Moe answered.

"Hello?" His strong voice humming through the phone line made me shiver.

"Oh! Hi! It's Melanie. I hope I'm not bothering you or anything."

"Hey. I'm glad you called. How was rehearsal? Things work out okay?"

I'd been tense as a guitar string tightened to the snapping point; now I fell limp against the wall and finally relaxed. "That's why I called. I couldn't wait for Monday to tell you." I rattled on about the morning's experience. He listened and whenever I took a breath interjected comments like "that's great," "glad to hear it," "sounds neat."

I finally wound down and felt like a doofus for yakking his ear off. "So, what are you doing tonight?" I asked. Oops! I'd really stuck my foot in my mouth this time. He must think I'm nosy about his private life. What if he thinks I'm on the make? I shook my head to erase the foolish thoughts. He probably has a date with a nice Negro girl.

"I'm going to a SNCC meeting. We found a spot at the Second Baptist Church."

"Oh, that's nice," I mumbled.

"How about you? Got a hot date?"

"Yeah, with my botany book." As soon as I said it, I wished I'd made up something more interesting.

"Wanna come to my meeting? I've got room for one more in my car."

"Are you sure? I mean, are white people allowed? Do you have to be a member?"

I heard his faint chuckle before he answered. "Open meeting. You've been curious about what I do in my spare time. Now's your chance to find out."

Yikes! He does think I'm nosy. I should turn him down, but I can't. I want to know what this snick is. And if he has a girlfriend I bet she'll be there.

"Thank you. I'd love to."

"Good. We'll come by for you at 6:30."

"It's a date!" Phooey. Now I'd really stuck my foot in it. No wonder he hung up so fast.

I dashed back to my room and pulled half my wardrobe out of the closet. What did people wear to snick meetings? Was my lime green sheath too dressy? Clam diggers? No, he said the meeting was in a church. Women shouldn't wear pants in church even if they aren't attending a service. I'd never been in a Baptist church. Maybe I was supposed to wear a hat and gloves. What if they had some sort of church service first? What should I do? Catholics can't go to services in other churches. I should have told him I had something else going on tonight. What was I getting myself into?

I finally pulled on my old reliable beige shirtwaist and black Capezios. I'd take my black cardigan along in case it got chilly. Running a brush through my hair, I wished I'd paid more attention to the discussion in the bathroom. Strings of dirty-dishwater blonde hair hanging limply from crown to shoulder wasn't exactly the beauty image I wanted to portray. I slicked Bonne Bell apricot lipstick over my lips and smacked them together on a Kleenex, blotting most of the sheen away.

At 5:30 I went down to the cafeteria. I picked at my supper, afraid that later I would throw up everything I ate. Moe was picking me up at the dorm. He would have other people with him. What kind of stir would it cause when he came in and asked for a white girl? Everyone would think we were going on a date. They'd think he was my boyfriend. They'd freak out.

When I went to the sign-out box in the lobby, a cluster of girls surrounded it. Didn't anyone stay in on Saturday night? We each found our cards to list the time we were leaving and where we were going. I stared at my card. What should I write on it? Maybe I should pretend I was going to the library. It wouldn't be the first Saturday evening I'd spent there. Then with a stroke of genius propelling me I neatly printed *church*. It wasn't a lie. I'd be back long before closing and no one had to know where I had been. I went outside to wait for Moses Carter. Another disaster averted. That is if no one noticed who was picking me up.

Moe pulled up as I reached the curb. He turned off the car, probably intending to get out and open the door for me, but I pulled the passenger side door open and jumped in before he had a chance. He flinched like a dog startled by a backfire. His eyebrows pulled together in a frown as he bent forward to restart the car. Did he think I had poor manners? Or had he guessed the real reason I'd met him outside?

As he drove away, he cocked his head toward the back seat where three Negro students sat shoulder to shoulder. "These are my friends, Joe White, Vivian Pratt, Willie Jackson.

I turned in the seat and smiled, "Hi, I'm Melanie Sedlak."

Vivian leaned forward and used the line most students asked to break the ice, "Where you from?"

"Middleton, about 80 miles north of here. How about you?"

"Deetroit, east side."

One of the fellows—I'm not sure which was which because they looked alike—leaned back behind Vivian and said to the other in a whisper we could all hear, "So, we're stuck in the back of the bus while whitey takes the front seat."

My hand flew to my mouth stifling a yelp. I tried to act nonchalant as if I hadn't heard. I glanced at Moe. His jaw tightened; I could almost hear his teeth gnash. Vivian pushed back against the seat, separating the two boys. Moe gunned the motor and his car careened around the corner. He sped into the parking lot behind a little red brick church. Slamming the gear shift into park, he turned off the ignition and opened his door. I jumped out of the passenger side, leaving the door open for the others; but they all exited on Moe's side.

Vivian rushed around the back of the car and grabbed my arm, "C'mon, we meet in the basement."

As she tugged me away, I heard Moe speak through his still gritted teeth. "Don't you ever say anything like that again to a friend of mine."

I didn't catch the rest of what was said because Vivian had pulled me through the back door and down the basement steps. Scowls shadowed the faces of the three guys as they came down the stairs a minute later. Joe and Willie skittered across the room toward a group of guys gathered by the side wall.

Moe joined us on the other side of the room where Vivian was introducing me to the girls clustered there. Some had greeted me with smiles and handshakes, but others looked me up and down, passing judgment without knowing me. My face flamed as I looked away, startled to realize I was the only white girl in the room.

A girl coming down the steps smiled and waved at me. Iris Brown and I had been volunteer ushers at the auditorium so we kind of knew each other. I smiled and waved back, pleased that I knew at least one girl who belonged there. I wondered if when hers was the only colored face at the auditorium she felt as nervous as I did right then.

Iris strolled over.

"Hi," I said, glad to have someone acknowledge me without staring. "This is my friend, Moe. And Vivian. And—" I looked at the cloud of dark faces and couldn't draw up a single name.

Vivian laughed. "We all know each other."

"Yeah, you're the only outsider," one of the girls sneered.

Just then I was actually saved by a bell. At the front of the room, a tall, thin man with skin as dark as the black keys on a piano stretched his hand up so the cowbell he held brushed against the ceiling. He bent his elbow. The bell clanged as he waved it back and forth, bringing conversations to an end. "Seats, everyone," he ordered.

I looked toward the back of the room, hoping to spot two empty chairs. Vivian and Iris headed toward the front. The pressure of Moe's hand on my back gently pushed me forward. I followed the girls to the second row, right where we'd be in full view of just about everyone in the room. As I sat down next to Iris, Moe whispered, "See you after the meeting."

He gave a slight wave and with a few quick strides was at the front of the room where he took a seat behind a long table facing the audience. The boy who'd made the rude remark in the car, Willie, I later figured out, sat next to him. The tall student sat in the middle seat. Two older men sat on his left. I recognized the white one, Professor Lincoln. He'd given me a C in World History. I didn't know the Negro man, but I figured he was a teacher, too. I slumped in my seat to make myself invisible to the inquisitive stares boring into me from everyone in the room.

"Good turnout tonight," the student leader began. "For those of you who don't know me, my name's G. W. Sloan." He introduced the rest of the people at the table then said, "We'll pass around a sheet for you to sign in. Put your name down and if we don't have it, add your dorm and room number. If you live off campus be sure to give us your address and your phone number if you have a telephone." He pushed a clipboard with several sheets of paper and a pencil across the table. A girl in the front row retrieved them.

"Marla, will you take minutes again?" G. W. asked her. She smiled and nodded then signed her name and passed the clipboard on. I wondered why they hadn't included her at the table.

"First on our agenda," G. W. continued, "we heard from SNCC. They've approved our application for affiliation." There was a smattering of applause and a shrill wolf whistle from somewhere in the back. "We are now officially the western Michigan chapter of the Student Nonviolent Coordinating Committee." More cheers.

When the clipboard reached Iris she boldly scribbled her name on the paper and handed the board and pencil to me. Staring at the names, I didn't recognize any except Iris's. I was here as a guest, not to join the group. Should I pass the board on? Would that offend people? Or would signing my name be more offensive? Iris smiled at me and nodded, a sure indication she expected me to sign. I wrote my name and dorm room on the line below hers and passed the board to Vivian. What had I just committed to?

I heard the tail end of G.W.'s next comments, "the field agent from Atlanta will be here in a couple days." Exuberant applause, foot stomping and whistles met the announcement.

The black professor held up his hands, signaling the crowd to quiet. "More good news," he said. "Second Baptist has agreed to let us meet here every Thursday evening. They've opened their doors to us and offered the use of their mimeograph machine as long as we provide money for ink and paper."

G. W. thanked Professor Moore and added, "We'll try to have the field agent stick around for Thursday's meeting. We've all got work to do before then. We need someone to make fliers advertising the meeting. Any volunteers?" Most of the girls raised their hands. "Marla will you take charge?" Marla smiled and stood so everyone could see who she was, as if we hadn't already figured it out.

G. W. continued, "We need people to distribute them. Volunteers? A few of the guys raised their hands and G. W. appointed a coordinator. "Word of mouth is the best advertisement so everyone should talk up the meeting and recruit as many people as you can. Invite everyone you know, including white people." A murmur grumbled through the crowd. There were only five white people at this meeting, Professor Lincoln, three college-aged guys, and me.

G. W. covered a few more items: preparations for the field agent's visit, meeting formats, news from other SNCC groups. He asked if anyone could afford the time and money to go to the upcoming convention in Atlanta, but there were no volunteers.

Willie Jackson interrupted, "How about we get down to some real business? What we're all here for."

Professor Moore answered, "Setting up the organizational process has to come first. We can't act without clear focus, consistency and solidarity. Once we get everything in place we can become more active."

"We should be doing more than making fliers and holding meetings," Willie complained. A few students called out agreement.

G. W. pulled himself up to his full height. "We *are* working on it. I have copies of the SNCC newsletters you can pick up after the meeting. Groups are arranging boycotts and sit-ins every day in the south. Over the next few weeks, we should have details on how we can help."

Willie shot out of his chair and shouted, "The South! What about right here? I know it's not like it is in the south, but how many of you have been refused service in a restaurant? Or been treated like the clerk in the store thinks you're going to steal something? Who's been called "nigger" or "coon"? Ever been spat on by a white person?"

By the time he'd gotten that far into his tirade almost every person in the room was shouting things like, "Yeah!" "That's right." "Happens all the time." They raised their hands after every form of discrimination he'd mentioned. Some shouted out their own examples.

I shrank lower in my chair. As blind as I'd been to most injustices, I'd heard stories about the things Willie referred to. In some cases, I'd been shocked by the cruelty, but more often I'd chalked it up to ignorance and accepted it as the way things are.

G. W. rang the cowbell. Its clanging didn't stop until the room quieted. Willie and the others who had risen from their seats sat down. Their foreheads wrinkled in anger.

In spite of trying to remain calm, G. W.'s voice wavered. "We will fight discrimination here of course." He turned to Moses Carter.

"Would you be willing to organize a committee on local projects? You can start by compiling a list of incidents. I'll give you what I have on nonviolent strategies for demonstrations. Professor Lincoln, maybe your could work with Moe on this?"

As the professor and Moe indicated their agreement, a groan escaped my lips. What was he getting into? How could we be friends if he was involved in protesting against white people? What if he gets a chip on his shoulder like Willie? More than ever, I regretted finding out what Moe was doing.

Another paper was passed around so volunteers could sign up to make and distribute fliers or join Moe's committee. I suspect I was the only one in the room who didn't put my signature on it.

A coffee can was passed around, too. "Please be as generous as you can," Professor Moore encouraged. Coins, intended for ink and paper, clinked into the can. Of course, Marla volunteered to become treasurer.

The meeting adjourned with G. W. reminding everyone to bring as many others as possible to Thursday's session. A few people straggled out the door, but most stayed to talk about their volunteer jobs or continue discussing discrimination they'd experienced. I sat in my chair feeling every judgmental eye accuse me of three hundred years of injustice to Negroes. I might as well have been wearing a white sheet and carrying a noose.

Excusing himself, Moe made his way through the crowd. "Sorry, I didn't know I'd have all this to take care of. It could take a while."

Iris put her hand on his arm and said, "I'm riding the bus back to campus. Melanie can come with me if she doesn't want to wait."

I jumped at the chance to leave. "Yes, thanks. It's been a long day."

Vivian asked to come along. The bus stopped at the corner and the three of us got on. Half the seats were filled with passengers, a mix of ages and races. We took the first empty seat halfway down the aisle. We didn't go to the back of the bus where, in fact, a white couple sat smooching. No one gave dirty looks, no one expected the group to separate by color. Why had Willie and the others been so bent out of shape? I stared out the window into the darkness while Iris and Vivian chattered about the prospect of meeting a real live Snick leader.

FIVE

Within days, posters advertising the Thursday meeting with the SNCC leader from Georgia decorated every telephone pole, tree, and building on campus. It was more publicity than a Paul Anka concert would have received. Moe met me for coffee only once that week. As he made his way through the student union, he stopped at every table to invite people to the meeting. When he finally sat across from me at our table, our conversation centered on less significant events like whether or not it would rain during Saturday's football game. I was curious about his SNCC activities but afraid of what I might learn, so I didn't ask questions. His reluctance to volunteer information fed my fear.

I scheduled a band rehearsal for Thursday night, but it turned out I didn't need an excuse to miss the SNCC meeting. Moe didn't invite me. He didn't show up for coffee the next morning either and only later that afternoon left a message that he'd been busy meeting with the SNCC leader.

It rained during the Saturday afternoon football game and my sodden band uniform felt like it weighed an extra fifty pounds. Concerns about Moe weighed on me even more.

On Monday morning, waiting for Moe to show up for our coffee date, I looked through the student newspaper. There was a brief article about the meeting, but it wasn't very informative. I overheard one of the students complain that no one from the paper had actually attended, which explained why the article read like a blanket press release from some far off headquarters. No mention of local students.

I finished my coffee, gathered my books and pulled on my sweater getting ready to leave for my next class when Moe rushed up. "Sorry, got caught up with a couple people. Tomorrow?" How could I not forgive him?

By the next day, the SNCC meeting was stale news. Moe didn't even talk about it.

Over the next few weeks, we met for coffee most mornings. He'd become more and more involved with SNCC business and always carried around a stack of folders like a portable file cabinet. Students, mostly Negroes, would stop at our table for information, all the while ignoring me. Extracting brochures from one of the files, Moe would ask the recipients to spread the word.

Our conversations, constantly interrupted, didn't contain much substance. There was an obvious lack of detail about Moses Carter's SNCC activities. I didn't get it. What was going on? Were they planning something they shouldn't? Did he think because I was white, it was none of my business? Maybe he'd found a girlfriend in the group. Probably Marla. She was involved in everything; it wouldn't have surprised me if she thought it was her right to be involved with the sharpest guy on the council board.

As the days passed, I tried to focus on my school work and The Gingersnaps, but a vague uncertainty nagged the edge of my brain. When I was with Moe I measured my words, wary of tripping over my own tongue. I thought I'd gotten past the concern about being different from him, but now I worried that I'd never really understood what he was all about. We were worlds apart.

The drums usually drew me out of my blue funk. Only while playing I felt at ease, but it was not without its problems, too. One evening, as soon as I walked into rehearsal, I could tell something was up. Brad stared at me through squinty eyes, his lips pursed in a severe grimace. "Before we start we want to know what you're doing to get us a gig."

Marv's head bobbed in agreement. Johnny rose from the piano bench, planted his feet and folded his arms across his chest. For a second, I felt like I was about to be executed by a firing squad. But they were only boys intent on intimidating me with their silly bravado.

I pulled myself up straight, looked unflinchingly at them and retorted, "Hey! I'm doing plenty. Sticking notices in every building. Calling sororities and frat houses. I'm getting leads. But, if you don't think I'm doing enough, how about you get out there and try?"

Could they tell I was faking too? I'd put a few notices around and asked a couple girls in my dorm if their sororities were planning dances, but I hadn't done much else.

"It's your job," Brad said with less conviction than before.

"I'm doing what I can. It takes time to get our name out there." I rummaged through my bag for a stack of sheet music. "Here. "You Talk Too Much" is a fun song and it has a neat sax solo," I said hoping my offering would appease them.

Brad snapped the sheets from my hand and muttered, "What's the point of rehearsing when we got no one to play for?"

I glared at him. What was wrong with playing for the joy of making music? Sure, it was nice to play for someone else. To make the audience laugh or cry, tap their feet, move their bodies to whatever tempo we produced. Money and applause were nice, too. But when I was alone with my drums, I could pound away my anger, tap rhythms that matched my laughter, soothe my sorrow with slow steady notes. Music transported me to different times and different places. Africa, the Caribbean, Asia, Bohemia—every culture has its own rhythm. When I played, I imagined myself in grand opera halls, smokey bars, a French cabaret, a paddle-wheel on the Mississippi, at a barn dance, a sock hop or the prom. Maybe other people thought to practice the same notes over and over was a waste of time, but I was euphoric whenever I finally conquered the technique I'd been striving to master. What's the point? No true musician would ask that.

Johnny slunk back to the piano and struck the opening chords. Brad and Marv picked up their instruments. I pulled a stool over to the drums. As we worked through the music the tension eased. Brad gave the saxophone solo a special flourish. By the end of rehearsal, we cracked up as we wailed, "you tawwww awk too much."

"I'll try to have something set up for us by next time," I promised as we left the building. Walking to the dorm, I made up in my head a schedule of calls to make and places to hang posters. Maybe I could rope Diane into drawing the signs. She liked that artsy-fartsy stuff. Maybe I could spring for an ad in the student newspaper. I wanted a gig as bad as the guys did.

Out of habit, I checked my mailbox in the lobby and was surprised a pink message slip was there. The girl who had taken the message tented the slip of paper so I would be sure to see it. Fumbling under my collar, I pulled off the chain that held my keys and opened the box. Big red letters jumped from the pink paper— *URGENT! Call your mother!!*

I rushed to the nearest phone booth as thoughts of every possible disaster ran through my head. Was someone hurt? Had something happened to Gaga or Oompa? Please, no. I gave the operator our home phone number and waited forever for the connection. Mom answered on the first ring and, before the operator had the words out of her mouth, agreed to accept the charges.

"Mom! What's wrong?" I blurted through tears, sure that someone had died or the house had burned down with only the telephone surviving intact.

"For heaven's sake, Melanie, get a hold of yourself." My mother's rebuke instantly replaced my fear with irritation. It bummed me that she always thought I was on the edge of hysteria. Guess I wasn't supposed to have feelings.

"Your dad's in the hospital."

I sucked in my breath. I *was* entitled to hysteria.

"Had his gallbladder out. Had one of his attacks and I had to rush him all the way to the hospital in the middle of the night."

Leave it to her to make Dad's pain all about her inconvenience.

"Anyway," she continued. "I need you to come home and run the store. Tomorrow night's Moonlight Madness Sales after the homecoming game. And of course, Saturday's our busy day. Your dad never did have a good sense of timing."

The air whooshed from my lungs. He was going to be okay. Probably the worst part of his emergency would be that he'd have to put up with her complaints about how inconsiderate he was to get sick at the wrong time.

"How long will he be off work? I can't miss too many classes" As soon as I said it, I realized I was making it about my inconvenience, too. I expected Mom to point out my lack of compassion, but she didn't. We both knew I was the best choice to run the store. I'd filled in plenty of times before and she'd be busy at the hospital. Darlene, of course, was too young, Randy too irresponsible and Junior too far away (it was doubtful the army would give him leave anyway.)

"He should be ready to come home Sunday, he'll have to take it easy for a while. I suppose I can handle things next week. Maybe Gaga can come in to help around the house. Right now I need you for tomorrow and Saturday. Wouldn't you know the Westinghouse salesman in coming at nine tomorrow morning. Of all days."

"Okay. I'll see if there's a bus tonight. Or I'll find some way to get there. I'll call right back and let you know."

I hung up and slumped down in the booth. I had a Current Events exam in the morning. It counted for a fourth of my grade and I'd pulled a C- on the first test. What if my prof wouldn't let me take a make-up?

I called the bus station. The last bus going through Middleton was leaving in twenty minutes. Even if I sprouted wings and flew downtown I couldn't make it in time. The morning bus wouldn't get me home until almost eleven, too late for the Westinghouse Man.

Not that I was eager to see him. The slimy jerk made my skin crawl. With his fat paunch drooping over a belt pulled two notches too tight, double chin, beady eyes, and front teeth that overlapped, he resembled the woodchuck living under Oompa's corncrib. Worse than his grotesque looks, the Westinghouse Man made rude remarks to any female unlucky enough to be in his presence, then brayed like the jackass he was. Even Dad sometimes winced at his crudeness but pretended to be in on the joke. Staying on the good side of the Westinghouse Man meant first choice of appliances, bigger discounts, and quick delivery. My stomach churned at the thought of dealing with him first thing in the morning, but Dad would count on me.

I had to find a way to get home.

Moses Carter had a car.

I called his dorm. In a jumbled rush, I spilled my story begging for his help. His calm voice stilled my jabbering. "Slow down. I understand. I was just about to get in the shower. I'll pick you up in fifteen minutes."

His mention of a shower left me speechless. Was that thumping sound my heart?

I called Mom to tell her a friend would bring me home. "We should be there before midnight."

I heard her relieved exhale. "I'm so glad you found a ride. Your friend shouldn't have to drive back so late. Invite him to stay over. Ask him to stay until Sunday and take you back to school. I'll get on Randy right now to clean up his room."

"Um, I don't think that will work." I hadn't told her who was bringing me home but I was sure she imagined the nice white boyfriend she'd fantasized about as her future son-in-law.

"Don't be silly. Of course he'll stay. What's his name again?"

"M—Mike," I mumbled. It was the name I'd made up for Moe when I mentioned him to my roommate or other girls in the dorm. If I'd said Moses they would guess he wasn't white.

"See you and Mike in a couple hours. And bring something decent to wear for work—a nice skirt and blouse, not bluejeans." Finishing her instructions, my mother hung up without saying goodbye.

I called Moe again and told him he could stay for the weekend if he wanted but he didn't have to.

"That should be interesting," he said. "I'll pack a bag and be right over."

The back of my neck tingled. I'd have a whole weekend with Moe. No distractions. No classes. No homework. No SNCC.

I scurried back to my room and started throwing clothes in my suitcase. I sat on the bed and drew my hand to the back of my neck and squeezed. The tingle had turned to a dull ache. What would I do when Mom threw a hissy about me bringing him home? And that would be only half of it. Everyone in town would be upset and rude. How could I ask Moe to put up with that?

I snapped my suitcase shut, grabbed my jacket, and locked the door behind me. I signed out for the weekend then dashed outside where Moe was already pulling into the parking lot. I ran over and waved. Did he think I'd come out to save time, or did he know that I wasn't ready to have him come into the dorm to ask for me? I wished it was more natural for us to be together. That I didn't worry about what other people thought.

As I climbed into the car, I thanked him and he said he was glad to help. We both lapsed into silence while he drove through campus and onto the highway. Leaning back against the seat, I closed my eyes and imagined that we were going someplace special. Just the two of us for a weekend away from everything. Maybe to a secluded cabin up north where the leaves had already turned and he'd build us a fire in the fireplace while I made hot cocoa and—

"Worried about your father?" I flinched, startled by his voice interrupting the quiet. Even though it was dark in the car I was sure he'd notice my face glowing red as the speedometer dial.

"A little. Mom said he came through the surgery fine and she can bring him home on Sunday."

I told him about the Westinghouse Man and the Moonlight Madness Sale. "I've helped Dad a lot, but this is the first time I've had full responsibility without him there. He knows how to get the best deals from the salesman and which customers to extend credit to and a bunch of other stuff I'm not sure of."

"You'll handle it fine."

I knew I could take care of everything, even put the Westinghouse Man in his place if he got smart with me. What bothered me was how Mom would react when she saw Moe. All summer, she'd been clear about her disapproval of our friendship. I'd really catch it from her for putting her on the spot. Stupid me for not telling her. We could have had our big fight over the telephone. But then she would have made me find another way home. And there were all the other small-minded people in Middleton who thrived on cruel gossip. How was I going to protect myself—and Moe—from them? I couldn't think how to warn him about the hornet's nest we were about to stir up so I rode in miserable silence, fearing the inevitable mess ahead.

As we neared town I transformed from mummy to chatterbox. I pointed out every personal landmark and spewed out its history. "There's the cemetery where Uncle Gus is buried, he was gassed in World War One; down that road is where my friend Pearl lives, she just had a baby; there used to be a big barn over there, but it burned down with six horses inside and people say the farmer set the fire himself; that's the banker's house, a bunch of us cooned watermelons from his patch and lucky he didn't figure out I was one of them because now I work at the bank in the summer."

Moe coughed and shifted in his seat. I was talking too much, as if hearing my running commentary about the place where I grew up would somehow help him fit in. To stall for time I thought of suggesting we go to the Northway Grill, the only place other than the hotel bar that was open that late. Instead, I gave in and said, "Turn here. There's our house over there. The one with the porch light on."

Moe parked the car and as we got out, my mother stepped onto the back stoop. She brought her hand to her forehead, like a soldier's salute, as she drew forward and peered into the nighttime. Moe took his duffle bag and my suitcase from the back seat and turned to join me. Could Mom tell that the silhouette she was trying to make out was dark, not from the shadows but because of the skin color of the tall man she was staring at? We moved into the luminous glow of the porch light.

Her hand dropped to her side and she took a step back, bumping against the storm door, then turned and walked into the kitchen without greeting us. Moe and I followed.

Stiff and pale as a corpse, Mom stood at the kitchen sink staring out the window into the darkness.

"Mom, you remember Moe. My friend from school. You met him last day."

She turned and looked at us. Moe set our bags down and stepped toward her. "It's nice to see you again, Mrs. Sedlak. Although I'm sorry it had to be under these circumstances."

She glanced at his face, then looked past him at the wall. "I am too." she said. The circumstances she was sorry about weren't the ones Moe had referred to.

She quickly recovered, as she usually did in awkward situations. My mother rarely let outsiders know she felt upset, insulted or unsure of herself. She saved her judgmental attitude for home. "Thank you for bringing Melanie. I'll reimburse you for the gas."

"That isn't necessary," he said. "I'm glad I could help."

She stared at our luggage resting next to Moe's feet. She grabbed my arm. "Melanie, I need to speak with you in the other room." Pulling me into the dining room she hissed, "Is he the only one you could get a ride from? You know you can't bring that boy into this town. Everyone will talk You have to tell him to leave!"

"Shhh," I hissed back. We were like two snakes in a pit. "He'll hear you. It's no one's business who I'm friends with and I don't care what anyone has to say. If you want him to leave you'll have to tell him yourself."

She stalked back into the kitchen with me on her heels, quaking over what she would say. Was she angry enough to embarrass herself by revoking her invitation?

With a fake smile plastered on her face she said to Moe, "The boys' room is upstairs, at the end of the hall across from the bathroom. Randy can show you around."

She lead us out of the kitchen, through the dining room to the stairway. Moe started up the steps. Mom grabbed my arm again, keeping me from following. As soon as Moe reached the upstairs hallway, she snarled at me. "I don't want that boy in this house. Tomorrow morning you will see that he is gone."

"He was invited to stay for the weekend and I'm not going to ask him to leave."

Before she could answer, Randy came tearing down the stairs shouting, "I'm not gonna share my room with a nigger!"

"Randy!" Mom snapped. "That boy gave Melanie a ride home. I can't make him drive all the way back in the middle of the night."

"But, Ma," Randy whined, clearly expecting her to side with him against me for bringing an undesirable person into our lily-white home.

"You can sleep on the couch, but you are not to make any impolite comments around him." She turned to me. "And you will get him out of here first thing in the morning."

Somehow I kept my voice calm though anger raged through me, "You told me to invite him to stay the weekend, so you're the one who has to uninvite him." There, let her squirm out of that one.

Her hand flew up and struck me across the cheek. "Don't be smart with me. I have enough problems without worrying about the trouble you cause."

I ran up the stairs. She wanted to control everything all the time so let her handle the store without me. In the upstairs hallway I ran smack into Moses Carter. His shoulders slumped and his eyes cast downward like a dejected puppy who'd just been swatted with a rolled up newspaper. How much had he heard? Had Randy said anything to him? Had he heard Mom's comments about people talking? Did he know she'd told me he had to leave?

"We're leaving," I announced.

He lifted his head and looked me squarely in the eyes. "No, you have to help your Dad. It'll be alright. We'll get things straightened out in the morning."

I stepped back in shock. How could he stay after the way my mother and brother had acted?

As if he'd heard the question, he answered, "I guess you didn't tell your mother who was coming to your house."

I burned with shame for getting Moe into this mess.

"She's right about people talking," he continued. A black man with a white woman doesn't go over in a small town. If talks the worst that happens I can play deaf, but can you put up with it? You have to figure out how much of a problem you'll have with your mother if I stay. And how much you want to put up with from other people. I'll go whenever you say, but you shouldn't leave on my account."

"I'm here to fill in for my dad. And I invited you for the weekend. I don't care what other people think. So, both of us will stay unless you decide you want to go."

He patted me on the shoulder, said goodnight, and retreated to Randy's room.

Mom came up the stairs just then and I figured she'd been listening, but I didn't have the energy to fight with her. She held her clenched hands in front of her waist as if preparing to defend herself in a brawl. "I have a few things to do around here in the morning and then I'll be at the hospital the rest of the day." She gave me instructions as if the argument had never happened. "Darlene and her friend Ann will come into the store after school. They'll want to watch the parade. Keep an eye on them and stick with them at the football game. I'll be home by the time the game's over."

I mumbled, "Alright," and went to my bedroom. Like so many of our battles this one had petered out without any resolution.

Without turning on the light so I wouldn't wake Darlene, I pulled on my pajamas and crawled into bed. After punching the pillow and wiggling around trying to get comfortable, I willed myself to stay still. I stared into the darkness.

A whirlwind of thoughts chased around in my head until it felt like my brain would burst through my skull. How could I ever make it up to Moe for the awful things my mother had said and the terrible words my brother had used? How could he not be hurt? Maybe he thought I was a bigot, too.

The springs creaked as Moe rolled over in Junior's bed. His low cough filtered through the bedroom walls. Was he awake, too? I wanted to get up and go to him. I burned hot with shame. What a foolish thought! There could never be anything more than friendship between us. And now even that had been threatened.

I finally drifted off to sleep. Outlandish dreams, like some weird French cinema, flashed on the screen of my subconscious. Mom telling neighbors Moe was a handyman. Randy in a KKK sheet. The Gingersnaps, in blackface, playing "Nobody Knows the Trouble I've Seen." Moe and I chased by a mob of strange people with huge mouths clacking like claves, their bony hands lacking muscle and flesh grabbing at us. I bolted upright and clamped my hand over my mouth to stifle a scream. Where had that come from?

A few hours later I awoke to the sound of the toilet flushing and water running. It was still dark. I strained to hear Moe move back across the hall and rustle about in the boys' room. I pulled on slacks and a sweater and rushed to the bathroom. Splashing water on my face and running a comb through my hair did little to improve my appearance. I still looked as miserable as I felt—sleep deprived and tense. As I left to go downstairs, Randy plodded down the hallway,

59

ready to exchange the lumpy couch for his own bed now that Moe had vacated the room.

Tying his shoelaces at the kitchen table, Moe looked up at me and flashed a broad smile. "Good morning!" he whispered loud enough to show enthusiasm, but quiet enough to keep from waking the household. He looked refreshed as if nothing unpleasant had ever soiled his life.

The clock radio on the shelf above the stove showed six-twenty. We had plenty of time to get out of the house before anyone was up. "How about some coffee? Would you like eggs for breakfast?" I asked. "They're fresh from my grandparents' farm."

"Sounds good. Thanks."

I put on the pot and took eggs and bacon from the refrigerator. Within a few minutes, the coffee was ready and I poured us each a cup. Moe sat back in the chair, extended his legs, crossing them at the ankle, and sipped his drink. He let out a satisfied sigh. He was the very picture of contentment. I poured orange juice, set the table, fried bacon and eggs, buttered the toast and imagined myself as the picture of contentment, too. Being together that way felt so domestic and almost normal. I served up the meal and sat across from him.

"I had no idea you were such a good little cook," he said as he forked food into his mouth. "What other fine qualities have you hidden from me?"

I felt my heart flip-flop at the intimate tone of his voice. He was such a charmer. But then, he probably said things like that to all the girls. I should've countered with a flirty remark, but I was never good at that sort of thing. I sat there with a goofy smile plastered on my face.

"You two are certainly early birds." My mother's sharp voice made me jump. It's a wonder I didn't hit my head on the ceiling.

Moe had quickly risen from his chair, too. "Good morning, Mrs. Sedlak. I hope we didn't disturb you."

I looked down at a scratch in the formica tabletop so she wouldn't catch my smirk. She was disturbed for sure.

I blurted, "I want to show Moe around town a little before I have to open the store."

Her eyebrows shot up as if the idea that he wasn't leaving immediately was a new concept to her. Pulling herself together, she stuck on her public face and forced a smile. "Thank you again, Moses, for bringing Melanie home. If it isn't too much of an imposition could you pick her up at the bus station when she goes back to school Sunday evening?"

"It's no problem for me to stay, ma'am," Moe said. "I'm sure Melanie could use a hand at the store and I don't mind helping out."

I brought my hand to my mouth to hide the surprised gape. He knew she wanted to get rid of him, but he'd acted as if she'd appreciate his generous offer. Did she see through him?

Then he presented an indisputable argument. "She told me about the salesman from Westinghouse. I'm sure you wouldn't want her to meet with him alone." His concern seemed so sincere even the most hardened heart should soften.

But with the same false sincerity my mother made one last ditch effort to get rid of him. "It isn't necessary for you to stay. I don't want to put you out any. Melanie must have exaggerated her dislike of the Westinghouse man. He's harmless."

Moe kept the see-saw going. "It's no bother. In fact, I insist you let me be of service. And I would be pleased to see Mr. Sedlak when he comes home on Sunday. Maybe Melanie and I could go with you to pick him up."

I would have taken great pleasure in their exchange if I hadn't been afraid he'd push her to the point she'd explode.

She moved to the stove and picked up the percolator. Her deliberate movements created a fear in me. She'd scald us both with hot coffee. Instead, she took a mug from the cupboard and busied herself with the cream and sugar. Even with her back to us, I could tell by the set of her shoulders she was ticked off.

Grabbing a pack of cigarettes from the carton on top of the refrigerator, she stomped into the living room. We heard the snap of the television dial followed by the familiar sound of "Sentimental Journey" and Dave Garroway introducing himself to the *Today Show* audience.

I squeezed Moe's arm and mouthed, "Thank you."

We cleared the table and did the dishes then pulled our jackets on. I called out, "We're leaving. Tell Dad 'hi'. See you tonight." There was no answer.

Sunlight breaking over the horizon offered the promise of a nice day for the high school homecoming. While Moe and I scraped a thin layer of frost from the car windows, I noticed the kitchen window curtains part. Through the gap, Mom gave us the evil eye. My homecoming was as frigid as the October air.

As he backed out of the driveway, Moe asked, "Where to m'lady?"
I pointed left.

We were a half block from home when I started, "You sure put Mom in her place. You know she was trying to get rid of you, don't you?"

He shrugged.

"How can you stay so cool? I wanted to scream at her for acting like that."

He pulled into the Methodist church parking lot and stopped the car. Turning to face me, he said, "The way I'd always seen it before I had two choices when people treated me like I was less than they were. I could keep my mouth shut and put up with it or I could let my anger out with violence. I've tried both in the past. But now I'm learning there's another way. I can stand proud and claim the respect I deserve. That's what I did with your mother. I just acted like I expected her to treat me the way she'd treat any of your other friends. I didn't give her a choice."

"How did you know it would work?"

"She doesn't see herself as racist."

I gasped. Racist was a strong, demeaning word. My mother had her faults, but she didn't deliberately hurt people she didn't know. She just didn't know any better.

"But what if you run into someone who really does hate...Negroes?"

"I'm certain I will. Right here in your little hometown. Probably today. But I've been preparing for that to happen. It'll be a good test of what I've learned."

Was that what this whole trip was about? The reason he was so eager to stay? A chance for Moses Carter to try out his new role as civil rights protester? And what did that make me? Was I just a part of his sociology experiment?

SIX

"So!" my voice squawked like a clarinet with a dry reed. I clenched my fists and shouted, "You offered to drive me home so you could parade around in a white town and see who tries to pick a fight." I'd thought we were friends, but now I saw how he was using me. He'd changed and it was all SNCC's fault.

Moe jerked his head to the side and stared at me wide-eyed. But I had more to say.

"You're just itching for the chance to stand up to white people. You think you can force them to accept you by acting like you belong here. Maybe you even want them to attack you so you can prove you're better than they are. And what about me? Am I your *white* friend—proof to everyone who sees us together that you fit in? That you've gone beyond sitting at Woolworth's lunch counter?"

I turned my back to him and stared out the window so he wouldn't see the tears blinding my eyes. How had I misjudged him for so long? My voice choked, "Maybe you ought to leave."

I heard him shift in the seat and expel a sigh from deep within his chest. Placing his hand gently on my arm he spoke so quietly I could barely hear, "Melanie, you're not some white girl I'm showing off. I drove you home because you needed a ride and I wanted to help you. Because I care about you."

A sob escaped my lips and I became a blubbering mess, swiping at my nose, smearing snot and tears. He cares about me. I wanted to throw my arms around him, tell him I cared about him, too, ask him to forget SNCC and my mother and everything except me. But what did he mean? Did he care the way a guy who wants to spend all his time with a girl does? Or the way people care about a stray puppy or starving children in China?

Moe pulled a clean white handkerchief from his pocket and handed it to me. I wiped my nose and eyes and cheeks and then my nose again, stalling for time. What did he want me to say?

His deep voice broke through the silent air. "I'm sorry you thought I was using you to make a point. Since I've joined SNCC I've realized how out of balance things have always been. And it's never going to change unless people like me take a stand each and every time someone tries to push us down, no matter how small the slight seems. I can't look the other way and pretend it's okay because that's the way things have always been. But this doesn't have anything to do with you, with us."

My palpitating pulse reached a crescendo like the timpani in a Haydn Symphony. He thinks he and I are *us*. If that was true his involvement with SNCC, his standing up to every bigot, his crusade for change, had something to do with me.

"Maybe so," I said, "but I don't see how you can just separate me from the rest of your life. I mean, how do you do that? It's not like when I'm around we're on a deserted island." I looked at him hoping he had the answer that would fix everything so we could be together.

He shook his head. "I guess you're right. I don't want to put you in awkward situations, embarrass you in front of your friends or family. Like last night. I'll leave this morning and come back Sunday afternoon to take you back to school."

"No!" I grabbed his hand. "Don't leave. You didn't embarrass me. You never have. My family, other people, they're the ones who are embarrassing. Don't leave. I want you here no matter what happens."

I let go of his hand, afraid he'd think I was too forward. Maybe I'd said too much, been all gushy when he'd only meant he cared for me like a puppy or a Chinese kid. I couldn't let him go, so I didn't wait for him to decide. "Let's get to the store. I need to get ready for the Westinghouse Man. I'll show you around town later."

Moe restarted the car and drove out of the church lot.

He parked in the wide alley behind the stores bordering Main Street. I sauntered over to my dad's appliance store and took my time unlocking the back door. Let someone see us. Maybe the pharmacist heading to work, or teenagers walking to the high school, the cook from the diner out for a cigarette, or snobby Mrs. Maggelson, owner of Town and Gown and forever my nemesis. Their opinions didn't matter one whit to me.

I showed Moe around the store and looked through the papers

in the office to figure out what Dad had planned to order from Westinghouse.

A stack of posters for the specials he was offering during the Moonlight Madness Sale leaned against the back wall. Moe and I looked through them. I was impressed by how much Darlene's artistic talent had grown. The posters looked almost professionally made. "Want to help me put these up in the windows?" I grabbed the tape dispenser and Moe and I discussed how to display the ads.

The bell above the door jangled. A fleshy middle-aged fellow pushed his way in. Short threads hung from the frayed cuffs of his navy blue jacket, the knees of his slacks were shiny from wear, and a dull brown toupee reposed like a dead muskrat on his head. His plump, pasty face glistened with a sheen of sweat which he swiped at with a rumpled handkerchief. The contemptible Westinghouse Man had arrived.

"Haloo!" he bellowed as he made a beeline toward me. Then, spotting Moe, he took a step back and gulped. "Is Al in? We have an appointment."

"He isn't here." I had no intention of explaining Dad's absence. "I'm his daughter and I'm filling in for him."

Westinghouse Man glanced at Moe. I had no intention of explaining his presence either.

"Oh, well, fine, little lady. I remember meeting you before. You've certainly grown up." His raggedy eyebrows wiggled in a sleazy attempt at seduction.

I wanted to tell him to kiss off, but I forced myself to remain calm as I considered how to handle the jerk. Dad would've gone along with the crude jokes and back slapping, the whole men will be boys thing, even though he never acted that way himself. Even if I could manage to stomach it I definitely wasn't going to play along. I wouldn't employ Mom's technique either. Laughing at innuendo and flirting weren't my style. She could pull it off because she somehow let it be known it was all a tease and she was off limits to anyone who tried to get fresh. It was a charming ploy she'd perfected over years of practice, but had failed to instill in me in spite of her conviction that a friendlier attitude would take me farther in life.

"Shall we go into the office so I can show you the latest catalog?" he cooed. He probably knew the room in back was only big enough for the two of us. I took a step closer to Moe. Moe took a step closer to me.

"There's room right over there by the counter," I said. I moved toward the middle of the store.

As Westinghouse Man showed me the catalog and extolled the virtues of the latest color televisions, he kept one eye on Moe. "This is our deluxe model. Stereo, remote control, comes in French mahogany or dark walnut. I know it's pricey, but worth every penny. You should order at least three of these because they're gonna be big sellers."

Moe leaned over my shoulder for a closer look. Seeing the retail price, he let out a low whistle.

"I'm sure it's too rich for your blood," Westinghouse told him. "But you'd be surprised how many middle-class folks want this set."

I froze. This was just the sort of thing Moe had been talking about. The patronizing salesman making an assumption about a person with dark skin. I was about to tell the creep to leave, that Philco and Magnavox had been after Dad for years to deal in their products, but Moe spoke first.

"I don't see the need for such a fancy set up, but my folks are happy with the two they bought a couple months back."

A florid hue rose to Westinghouse Man's pudgy cheeks. I stifled a laugh.

Shaming the salesman into a two per cent discount which would come out of his commission, I ordered three televisions, but not the deluxe model. I also ordered two fancy new irons with spray steam. To me, that was a more important invention than all the deluxe TVs he offered. Think of the hours housewives would save once they were liberated from dampening clothes.

Tugging his shirt collar, which was soaked with a grimy ring of sweat, Westinghouse Man thanked me for the order and hustled out the door.

Moe and I finished hanging Darlene's posters and straightened the shop. I filed papers, emptied the wastebasket, organized the display shelves. Moe helped and soon the place looked spiffy. While we worked I jabbered about what it had been like growing up in a small town and helping Dad in the store.

"Sounds like a nice childhood," Moe said.

"I guess. But people here judge you by how much money you have. Dad always says if you're Mr. Gotrocks you get away with most anything. Junior Gotrocks has the best chance of being captain of the football team. Rich girls with angora sweaters and a dozen pairs of shoes get voted Homecoming queen."

Moe looked around the store, taking in the merchandise. "Looks like your family is doing all right."

"Yeah, but people still think of Dad as a country bumpkin and Mom as the girl who dropped out of school to get married." I felt my face blaze. I'd said too much.

"Do you really care what people think—especially when it's none of their business?"

"Nope."

My answer wasn't exactly the truth. I ignored most gossip, but sometimes it wasn't just idle talk. Sometimes there were deeper repercussions. Sometimes I did care.

Around 11:30, our first customer walked through the door. I'd known Jeannie Morrow since high school even though she'd graduated three years before me. She was hired by the bank right out of school and had already worked her way up to assistant manager by the time I was hired as summer teller. While some people, herself included I suspect, thought of her as a career woman, she was on the verge of being considered an old maid. Not that I had room to talk. Twenty, with no prospects in sight, I was a prime candidate myself. With increasing frequency my mother had indelicately reminded me of my plight.

The squat heels of Jeannie's shoes tapped the thick-planked floor as she came toward me. "Melanie, I'm so glad the store is open. How's your dad? I heard he's in the hospital."

"Had his gall bladder out. He'll be home Sunday. I'm filling in. Couldn't miss the moonlight sales. How are things at the bank?"

"Good," she answered leaving me to wonder if she meant good for my dad, good of me to help out, or business at the bank was good. She headed for the display of small appliances. "Sorry to be in such a rush. I'm on lunch break. My cousin's getting married in Hastings tomorrow and it completely slipped my mind. I need a wedding gift. Any suggestions?"

"I have just the thing. How about this nice steam iron?" I handed the iron to Jeannie. "It's the latest thing. I was going to use this one for display, but I'll let you have it for nine-ninety-nine, tax included."

She quickly inspected the iron. "Perfect."

We moved to the cash register.

"This is my friend, Moses Carter," I told her as I wrote up the receipt.

Moe dipped his head and smiled. "Nice to meet one of Melanie's friends."

"Likewise," she murmured. She turned away and rustled through her handbag as if it held hidden fortune she didn't want this suspicious character to see. She handed me a ten and I gave her a penny. Rushing toward the door she called over her shoulder, "Have to run to Woolworth's for wrapping paper and a card before lunch hour's over."

Darlene and Ann had just arrived and scooted aside to avoid bumping into her as she scurried out the door.

"Aren't you girls supposed to be in school?" My voice had a snappish quality somewhat like our mother's.

"Lunch," Darlene snapped back. She spotted Moe standing behind the counter and rushed over to him. "Hi! You must be Mel's friend. I'm her sister, Darlene, and this is my friend Ann Stanley."

Moe smiled and extended his hand. "Nice to meet you. Melanie's told me about you, but I have to say you don't look like a pesky pipsqueak to me." He winked at her and laughed.

She punched her fists to her hips and turned toward me, "Mel! What did you tell him?"

"Nothing but the truth."

She stuck her tongue out at me. "Why didn't you wake me up when you got home? Or this morning?"

"That would be like trying to raise the dead," I countered.

"Mom said you're staying 'til Sunday, so you'll get to see Dad." Moe's charm had beaten my mother down and she had given in to letting him stay.

I looked directly into Darlene's eyes, "Oh? What else did she have to say?" I raised my eyebrows a little to signal the real meaning behind my question. My sister picked up on it.

She rolled her eyes. "Oh, you know how she is." She recognized Mom's criticism for what it was; a gust of hot air intended to carry her ego to new heights of superiority, but instead leaving only hurt feelings in its path.

"I see you found the posters," she said.

"We did," Moe said. "I'm impressed with your artistry. Do you take lessons?"

A smile of pleasure beamed from Darlene's face. "Just art class in school. I love to draw." Then she gushed to Moe about her favorite colors (purple and pink) and subjects (rainbows, horses, and angels) until Ann tugged on her sleeve and pointed at the wall clock.

"Yikes, we've gotta get going," Darlene yelped. "Want anything from the diner?"

Without realizing we'd be eating up the morning's profit, I took Jeannie Morrow's ten from the register and handed it to Darlene. "Bring us two grilled cheese sandwiches and French fries. And don't forget to bring back the change."

Later that afternoon business picked up. It seemed like half the people in town came into the store. A few of them bought small items like batteries or light bulbs, but most just looked at the shelves of merchandise.

They all asked, "How's your dad doing?" Thinking that was the real purpose of their visits, I told them about his operation and that I was filling in a couple days.

"This is Moses Carter, my friend from college. He's helping out this weekend." I introduced Moe as if it were natural for a Negro to be staying at my house and helping in my dad's store. He wasn't the only one who could claim his right to be treated the same as any of my friends.

No one offered their hand to Moe and most of them changed the subject and made a hasty exit. I overheard Mrs. King from the bakery whisper to Mrs. Townsend from the flower shop as they left, "Imagine, a colored man. That girl's morals are no better than her mother's."

So, that was what had brought everyone into the store. Jeannie Morrow's tongue had been wagging. When someone's dog barks in the backyard the whole neighborhood fills with the noise of hounds baying over imaginary threats.

At four o'clock, a deep repetitive tone echoed through the town. *Boom, boom, boomity, boom!* People drifted out of storefronts and melded into clusters along the sidewalk. I grabbed Moses by the arm and pulled him toward the door. "Time for the homecoming parade."

As we stepped into the glare of the late afternoon sun, the group in front of our store separated, giving us lots of room. "Thanks," I said to two farmers' wives who had just come from the diner, probably having stopped for coffee and pie. They engaged in busy conversation as if they hadn't heard me. I wondered if Moe thought everyone was discussing the parade and upcoming game instead of the colored man standing on the sidewalk in the middle of town with a local girl.

Wending their way through the crowd of spectators, Darlene and her friend, Ann, finally reached us. They wore green sweaters, had green ribbons tied in their hair and carried pompoms.

"Wow, I've never seen so many people in town," Darlene said. "Thanks for saving us a spot." There had been no saving places involved. Everyone gathered on the sidewalks had stepped away when Moe and I came out of the store. Then they'd stared at us, whispered to each other behind their hands and acted as if they didn't want to get close enough even to prod us with a yardstick.

Attention turned from us to the parade as the first participants, the Middleton High cheerleaders, rounded the corner and pranced down Main Street. A roar of approval from the spectators brought more bounce to the girls' steps and broader smiles to their faces. Halfway down the first block, they stopped and launched into one of their routines. The crowd shouted "Middleton! Middleton! Rah! Rah! Rah!"

The cheers became louder still when the football team surged behind the girls like a determined horde bent on destroying rivals from the next village. The players hopped rhythmically from foot to foot, grunting *huh, huh, huh!* The crowd roared, "Go Marauders!"

Resplendent in new green and gold uniforms, the marching band strutted in place while playing the fight song. The frenzied crowd sang the words with grand enthusiasm. Then the band played the alma mater song and an impressive number of the crowd sang along. Anyone who'd been in Mrs. Huizinga's civics class (which included every Middleton High student over the past thirty-six years) had memorized that song or failed her class. Some of them never forgot.

I waved and called, "Hey, Billy! Denny!" The two drummers I'd given lessons during the summer looked my way. Both sets of eyes raised in surprise. Billy leaned over and said something to Denny who cracked up and lost the beat.

The parade marched forward. A line of four convertibles crept by. In each, a pretty girl in a formal gown waved from the back seat. I felt the heat rush to my face. After all these years I was still embarrassed over my own beauty queen days.

"I love Janie's dress," Darlene sighed.

"The pink one's my favorite. She's only a freshman so she probably won't win," Ann informed me.

I whispered to Moe, "Isn't it cute how eighth graders pretend to be friends with the high school kids who don't have any idea who they are?"

He laughed. "I bet you were the same way."

Most of the high school students who weren't cheerleaders, football players, or band members had assembled by class and followed the band. Arrayed in every style of green clothing and headgear to show their school spirit, most carried pennants or pompoms. Their chants rose to the clouds and excitement sizzled as they paraded by.

An impromptu group of young hot-rodders had attached themselves to the end of the parade. They revved their motors, backing off to get the full effect of the glass packs. The aah-ooga of Petey Wesolowski's '57 Chevy brought a few laughs, but most of the people in the crowd didn't think it was funny. The muttered words, "juvenile delinquents" and "trouble makers" drifted above the onlookers.

Ricky—our local cop, Chief Reichenbacher—hooked his thumbs in his belt and glared toward the cars, ready to jump into action to restore order. The badge on his puffed up chest twinkled with fraudulent authority. His main functions were ticketing cars in no parking zones and hauling weekend drunks out of the pool hall.

A souped up Buick Roadmaster swerved out of line and came to a screeching halt in front of us.

"Hey Randy," Darlene called as our brother flung open the back door and stepped out.

He strode to the sidewalk, flicked his cigarette stub into the gutter, and sneered at me. "Why is your nigger boyfriend still here?"

Darlene and Ann flattened themselves against the store window and cowered.

I couldn't believe my ears. My own brother talking like that. Bitter bile burned my throat. Glowering at him, I shouted, "Get out of here, Randy!"

The car's front doors flew open and two hoods jumped out. I recognized them both, no account dropouts who'd been in skirmishes with the law. The smaller one, Muggs, had even spent several months in county jail for breaking into the motorcycle shop in Whitneyville. The other one was a punk they called Miller. Dad had warned Randy about hanging around with them, but he'd ignored the advice.

They stepped onto the sidewalk. Their menacing looks made me shiver, but I wasn't about to let on that I was scared. "Get lost! All of you!"

The two creeps burst into laughter, slapping their thighs and hooting with phony glee. "Get lost, all of you," Muggs mimicked.

By then a large number of people had turned from watching the parade to become spectators in our drama. I wanted to melt into the sidewalk. My anger welled, not just at the punks, but at Randy, too, for letting them make a scene. I clenched my fists, feeling the nails bite into my palms.

"Get lost," I repeated.

Stepping in front of me, Muggs gave my shoulder a shove. "Watch who you're talking to, bitch. Or we'll run you out of town right along with your nigger." My ears seared at the hateful word.

Miller moved next to Muggs. I stared at my brother, eyes imploring him to step in, to tell his buddies to back off. As soon as his eyes met mine, he jerked his head down and stared at the sidewalk. Darlene was crying. Ann's face was ashen as she stared in fear.

Moe shifted his weight. His voice boomed, "You've gone too far. Leave her alone. Move on."

The two delinquents looked up at him. "Oooh, the boogie can speak English," Muggs cracked.

"But I guess he don't understand it too good," Miller quipped. "We don't allow no coons in this town, so you're the one's gonna move on." His chin jutted upward and his voice took on an even more menacing tone, "That is if you know what's good for you."

From the corner of my eye, I could see everyone along the sidewalk staring. No one stepped forward to help. Some people scurried back into the shops to watch through closed windows. Fearful looks of impending danger crossed many of the faces. Others simply looked disgusted, though I didn't know if they were repulsed by Muggs' and Miller's bullying or by Moe. Worst were the self-satisfied smirks of the men watching as if we were part of the homecoming entertainment.

At the end of the block, Reichenbacher hung back even though he had to know what was going on. How long was he going to let these troublemakers go on before he broke it up? Or maybe he was on their side.

Moe stared into Miller's eyes. "I don't want trouble, but it appears you do."

Miller spat at Moe. "Who said I wanted trouble, boy? You're the one who's where he doesn't belong."

Moe stepped toward Miller disregarding the fact that Miller and

Muggs were scrappy and used to fist fights. He could get hurt. I grabbed his sleeve. "Moe, don't"

In a split second, Miller's hand pulled mine away from Moe's arm. He squeezed and excruciating pain shot through my hand as the bones crushed against each other. "Stay out of this, Melanie," he warned.

Randy rushed forward and clutched Miller's shoulder. With his face as red as a radish and a trembling chin, my brother came to my defense. "Leave her alone, man, she's my sister." Miller shook off Randy's hand and let go of me.

Muggs ran toward the car. "Let's get out of here," he squawked, cocking his head to the left. Chief Ricky had finally made his move toward us. Muggs, Miller, and Randy hopped into the Buick and Muggs peeled out before the policeman reached us.

Darlene and Ann ran to my side, each grabbing one of my hands. "Why was Randy being so mean?" Darlene asked.

Even if I could have figured out how to explain something I didn't understand myself, I didn't have the chance. Reichenbacher stopped in front of us, patted the girls on their heads and asked, "Everything alright?"

"I guess so, now," I said. It wouldn't do any good to tell him what those guys had done.

"Well, we don't want any trouble in our little hometown here." His voice dripped with condescension. He stared at Moe. "Folks all get along here and that's the way I intend to keep it."

I was about to tell him he could start by going after the real troublemakers, but that would mean going after my brother as well as his hoodlum friends. And there was something in the arrogant way he puffed out his chest and spoke to Moe that told me he'd decided the only troublemaker in town was Moses Carter.

I turned my attention to the girls, "I'm closing the store so we can have supper before the game. Ann, are you coming home with us?" The three of us went inside, but Moe stayed behind.

Peeking between the posters on the windows, I watched his interchange with the police chief. Reichenbacher did all the talking, wagging his finger for emphasis. Moe listened and nodded, but didn't say anything. Afterward, he came into the shop.

"What was that about?" I asked.

Moe's brows knit together creating a thick furrow between his eyes. "Nothing of any consequence," he answered.

Maybe he didn't want to say anything in front of the girls.

SEVEN

On the walk home, Darlene and Ann buzzed like cicadas on an August day. They were excited about the homecoming game, but I suspected all their noise was about something else. Maybe they were scared about the fight with Randy's friends. Or they were trying to reassure Moe that they didn't feel the same as all the busybodies and troublemakers. They seemed intrigued—maybe even smitten—with my Negro friend. I half expected one of them to reach out and grab his hand. He ate up the admiration; laughing, teasing, asking questions as if it really made a difference to him which boys they thought were cool and which were gross. People in this town would have even more to gossip about if they'd seen how the three of them were carrying on.

The girls raced into the house ahead of us. Darlene grabbed a note off the kitchen table. "Gaga was here! She left us macaroni and cheese in the fridge and a pint of green beans. She says don't eat all the cookies. Look, Annie, oatmeal raisin and chocolate chip. Yum! Let's take some to the game."

"Oh, no, you don't." I grabbed the treats from her hand. "Gaga made these for customers at tonight's sale." The oaty, chocolatey scent of freshly baked cookies and Darlene's crushed look convinced me to relent. "Okay, we can each have one for dessert. But that's it."

I put supper on to heat. Moe asked what he could do to help, but Ann and Darlene made him sit down and relax while they set the table.

Partway through our meal, a loud shot blasted the quiet.

Darlene dropped her fork. Ann let out a squeak. Moe jumped up and pulled the curtain back from the window over the sink.

"Just a backfire. Looks like you have company."

I ran to the door and out to the street, Moe on my heels. Randy pulled himself out of his friend's Buick and called to Moe, "I guess you didn't get the message."

Then he grabbed me by the arm, yanked me a few feet down the driveway and whispered, "Melanie, these guys are looking to make trouble. You better get that...that fella out of here."

Shaking my arm free, I snapped, "Why are you hanging around with those creeps? Are they more important to you than your own family? What's wrong with you?"

"Please." His face had gone pale and his voice turned whiny. "I don't know what they're gonna do. I don't want anyone to get hurt. Can't you make him leave?"

"Make those hoods leave!"

Moe walked toward us. Randy turned and whispered something to him then ran down the driveway and climbed back into the waiting car. Derisive hoots of laughter mixed with the sound of peeling tires.

"What did he say to you?" I asked Moe.

"We can talk about it later. Let's finish supper."

After dishes, the girls threw on their coats and mittens. "C'mon, let's get going," Darlene urged.

"We'll be right behind you. Save us a seat," I told her as we went out the door.

The chilly autumn air held the smoky smell of burning leaves. We could hear the distant *boom, boom, boom* of a bass drum and the uproar the cheerleaders evoked from the crowd gathered for the game.

As soon as Darlene and Ann were out of earshot I asked Moe, "What did Randy say to you? And what about Reichenbacher?"

"Message was pretty much the same from both of them. They don't want trouble so I should go away."

"So Ricky is on their side."

"Not necessarily. He has to keep the peace."

"But you haven't done anything wrong!"

We walked the next block in silence. Several cars passed on their way to the football field. Some slowed to a crawl so the driver and passengers could get a better look; others sped up so they wouldn't have to see us together. Was everyone against Moe and, by association, me?

Near the gate to the football field, I took one last chance to find out what else had happened. "What did my rotten brother say to you before he left?"

Moe stopped and turned to face me. "He's scared his buddies might do something stupid. He said, 'I don't want anyone to get hurt. Please leave. For my sister.' He's stuck between acting like a big shot in front of his pals and taking care of you."

"He should tell those guys to get lost. They're no good."

Moe snorted. "Hard for a guy to do that." He took my hand in his. "I'll leave right now if you want me to. I can always stand up to racist bigots some place else. I won't have to look for them. They're everywhere. But I don't want to involve you."

I felt the heat surge through my veins. I wanted to pull him to me in a close hug, but the wail of Petey's aah-ooga horn stopped me. Moe dropped my hand. The car sped away, dragging the intimate moment with it.

"Don't go," I whispered

We walked along the front of the home side's bleachers, craning our necks and straining our eyes in search of Darlene and Ann. Enthusiastic spectators of every age crammed together on the seats creating a mountain slope of green and white. Hundreds of eyes bored into us from above. Elbows nudged sides, and voices dropped the chant "Go, Marauders, Fight!" replacing it with disturbing murmurs. My thoughts burgeoned like weeds in a neglected flower bed. Everyone in Middleton harbored hostile feelings toward us.

An exuberant shout broke through the crowd, "Mellie! Up here!" Moe pointed out Darlene and Ann jumping and waving like marionettes manipulated by a crazed puppeteer. We climbed the steps. Moe held my elbow to steady me as we made our way down the row toward the girls. As we settled on the bleachers, the couple behind us got up and left. The girl sitting next to Moe pulled close to her friend so her coat wouldn't brush up against his. Humiliation burned within me as I took on everyone else's shame and let myself become the scapegoat for their cruel behavior.

Darlene shot a scowl in the girl's direction and asked, "Mellie, would you trade places with Moe? I want to sit by him so I can tell him who the players are."

"I know them better than you do. I should sit by him," Ann argued.

We rearranged ourselves so we sat Ann, Moses, Darlene, me. The arrangement sheltered other people from having to sit next to someone they thought would contaminate them, so it seemed to satisfy everyone. Except me. I didn't care who the players were and Moe probably didn't either, but the girls chattered his ears off, leaving me out of their cozy threesome.

The Marauders ran out onto the field. Everyone's condemning eyes turned from the scandalous appearance of a colored man in their town. The raucous crowd rose to their feet and focused on the game. Passes, fumbles, touchdowns, referee whistles, cheerleaders, roars of the crowd merged together in one grand frenzy of excitement dispelling all thought of the intruder.

Halfway through the second quarter the Marauders, who were drubbing the Wildcats, called a timeout. Darlene proclaimed it a good time to go to the concession stand. Ann offered to hold our seats if we'd buy her a Holloway sucker. As Darlene, Moe and I made our way down the steps and along the sidelines, the whispers followed us. There was no mistaking that the low boooo was not aimed at the Wildcats. My muscles tensed and I shook with anger and embarrassment. How does Moe stay so calm when he hears this hateful stuff?

After we walked behind the end zone, away from the noise, he said, "You know this isn't your battle. I know it's hard for you. I'll leave if you want."

"Don't be silly." My voice squeaked an octave higher than normal. "Those are just teenagers showing off for their buddies." It wasn't true. I'd noticed men old enough to know better and some women, too, express their disapproval.

The concession stand volunteer, a student's parent I didn't recognize, ducked his head to peer at us out the low window. He backed away and busied himself at the popcorn machine. The other parents occupied themselves with tasks and no one came forward to wait on us.

Darlene planted her elbows on the counter in front of the window and yelled, "Hey! How about some service here."

One of the moms looked up from the Rice Krispie Squares she was wrapping in waxed paper. Seeing no one else moving to help, she bustled over to the window. "Hi, Darlene," she said. "What can I get for you?"

"Hi, Mrs. Brocker," Darlene said to her classmate's mother. "I'd like two Cokes, M & Ms and a Holloway sucker." She stepped aside. I took her place and ordered chips and a Coke. I moved over and Moe ducked his head and looked at Mrs. Brocker through the concession stand window. I held my breath.

"May I have a hot dog and a Coke, please," he said.

Someone behind the woman placed the candy and chips on the counter. Another person fished three bottles from the cooler and set them next to the candy. Mrs. Brocker grabbed a towel and wiped at the cold water puddling on the countertop. She scribbled the prices on a paper napkin and checked our order then turned to the other parents and said, "I need a hot dog and another Coke."

The man at the cooler reached in for another bottle, but everyone else looked away. Mrs. Brocker pursed her lips in an apologetic grimace. She stalked over to the warmer, grabbed a hot dog, slapped it into a bun and wrapped it in a napkin. She handed it to Moe. "That'll be a dollar seventy-five."

Moe pulled his wallet from his back pocket. "No," I said. "My treat." But he already had two dollars in his hand and I didn't want to embarrass him by paying, even though we weren't really on a date.

Mrs. Brocker took the bills and gave him a quarter. I saw one of the men grab her by the wrist and take the money so she wouldn't put it in the cash box.

We were about twenty feet from the concession stand on our way back to the game when a snarling voice called out, "You still in town, nigger?"

"Yeah," sneered another. "We told you to get lost."

Muggs and Miller stood wide-stanced before us, their feet anchored firmly to the ground. Their nostrils flared with disgust, their chins jutted in defiance and their fists threatened to strike. Randy slumped in the shadows a few feet behind them.

Moe put his left hand on my arm and his right on Darlene's shoulder and attempted to steer us around the thugs. They stepped in front of us.

"Not so fast," Muggs threatened.

Randy moved forward and Darlene ran to him. He grabbed her by the arms.

I shouted. "Darlene, go back to the game."

Randy let go of her and nodded. She took off running.

Muggs laughed. "Are you gonna run away like a little girl, too? Or is your big black spade gonna save you?"

Moses took a step toward Muggs. He looked a foot taller and a foot wider than the scrawny troublemaker. "You owe the lady an apology," he said. Muggs didn't budge.

Miller dodged around Muggs and leapt onto Moe's back. Moe staggered to stay upright. The hot dog flew from his hand and Coke oozed from the fallen bottle like blood from a wound. He fell to the ground. Miller landed on top of him with an "ooof."

Muggs piled on. The thugs pummeled Moe's back and head.

The sickening thuds of fist hitting skin and muscle caused my stomach to cramp with nausea. "Stop!" I screamed.

Randy rushed forward and tugged at Miller's arm. He shook Randy off like a dust rag.

Two men appeared out of nowhere. They hauled Muggs and Miller off Moe and helped him to his feet. My eyes gushed tears of relief while Muggs' and Miller's bulged with rage.

One of the strangers pulled back his arm. His fist slammed into Moe's jaw. Moe crumpled to the ground.

The other man threw his arm around me, pinning me to his side. Nausea returned at the stench of stale beer filling my nostrils as he spat, "Whore! How dare you bring this piece of scum into our town." My pulse pounded in my ears muffling the sound of Muggs' and Miller's scornful jeers.

A small crowd gathered around us. Most were looking at Moe, but no one made a move to help him. Someone yelled, "Get out of town." Other voices joined the shouting. Confused and frightened, I couldn't decipher their insults.

Moe straggled to his feet. He lunged forward and wrapped his arm around the neck of the man who held me. "Let go of her!" he shouted. In spite of the neck hold, the man refused to loosen his grip.

The sound of Moe's command penetrated the fright that had dulled my senses and prompted me to act. I bit the man's arm. Hard. A high-pitched yelp rose from his throat and he dropped his hold on me. Moe kept a stranglehold on the drunk.

Randy shouted. "Run! Get out of here."

"No!" I screamed. "Moe!"

Muggs and Miller stepped toward Randy. The other drunk stood to the side, running his fingers through his hair as if he couldn't decide whether to help his friend or run.

"Let it go, Sedlak," Muggs warned my brother.

"You let it go!" The waver in Randy's voice exposed his courage as a fraud.

The man in the headlock scuffled at Moe's shins and clawed his arm. Moe released his grip.

The two drunks moved next to Muggs and Miller. The four of them became a menacing wall in front of Randy, Moe and me. Three men stepped from the crowd and took places behind them.

A woman shrieked, "Someone get Reichenbacher!"

Our assailants turned to assess the crowd and in that split second Randy grabbed my hand. "Run!" He took off, dragging me along. Moe ran, too and grabbed my other hand. The three of us sped behind the concession stand and out the exit gate. Still holding hands we raced toward home.

Next to the house, we stopped to catch our breath, then clumped up the back steps and into the kitchen. We squinted as our eyes adjusted to the glare of the overhead light. Still gasping, Moe and I hung our coats on hooks next to the door. Randy plopped into the nearest chair, propped his elbows on the table and held his drooping head.

Mom rushed in from the living room where she'd been watching *77 Sunset Strip*. "What happened?" she demanded, her voice a mixture of concern and accusation. "You all look like you've been in a fight. Where's Darlene?"

Wondering how she'd come so close to guessing what had happened, I glanced at Randy. His hair looked like it'd been styled with an egg beater and his jacket was covered in mud. I turned to Moe who stood by the door, hands clasped behind his back. Blood trickled from a cut above his left eye. A bruise on his upper lip ballooned. I rushed to the cabinet beside the sink and pulled out a clean dish towel.

Mom shrieked, "Where's Darlene?"

"She's still at the game with Ann," I answered. I turned on the faucet. "Moe, sit down, you've got a cut."

Moe sat across from Randy. I ran the warm water through the towel and squeezed it out, then pressed the damp cloth to his forehead.

Mom stepped toward me. Her eyes blazed with anger.

"Those hoodlums Randy hangs out with started it," I said. "They jumped Moe and then two drunks joined in and tried to hurt me, too."

My mother's hand flew to her mouth and I heard her inhale as if she was trying to keep from suffocating.

"Darlene and Ann are okay they weren't there they're watching the game with friends there are lots of parents around they're okay," I said in a rush, bending the truth to keep my mother from imagining the worst.

"Randy!" Mom ordered. "In the other room, now!"

Head down like a puppy who'd just been given a good scolding, he followed her as she stomped out of the kitchen.

I rinsed the bloodied dish towel and pressed it on Moe's cut again. "Hold this here. I'll put a band-aid on it when it stops bleeding." I wrapped some ice cubes in another dish towel and held it to Moe's lip.

"Shanks," he slurred. "Sorry I'm sho much trouble."

"I'm the one who's sorry. Sorry people are such jerks." I checked his lip to see if the ice was taking down the swelling. "Oh no, your shirt. There's blood on it. Let me soak it in cold water before it sets."

Reaching down I unbuttoned the first two buttons. My heart thumped like a bass drum. I dropped my hand. Moe finished with the buttons, shrugged off his shirt and handed it to me. I ran it under the faucet's cold water then filled the sink and put the shirt in to soak.

As I worked, the chair legs scraped along the kitchen floor and I heard Moe move toward me. His bare arm brushed against mine. The hair on the back of my neck prickled.

"There's a little blood on my undershirt, too."

I turned. Before me stood a muscular black Adonis holding a bloodstained undershirt. I had always imagined a perfectly formed physique hidden under his clothing and now I saw it was true. Forcing my gaze from his impressive torso, I slowly raised my head and looked into his eyes. In spite of the ghastly gash on his forehead and a fat lip, he was better looking than any man I'd ever seen, even in my dreams. His eyes shone as he stared into mine. Maybe it was the reflection from the overhead light. Would his eyes still shine if I turned off the light?

A grunt shattered the scene into a million pieces. My mother stood in the doorway looking the way she had when I was eight and she'd found out I'd taken that spoiled Judy Morgan's Cinderella doll because even Santa couldn't afford to give me one.

"I'm soaking Moe's shirt. There was blood on it." Why did my explanation sound like a lie?

She stepped forward and glanced in the sink. "You should put a little bleach in it."

She looked directly at Moe as if really seeing him for the first time, then said to me, "There are band-aids under the sink in the bathroom. And find one of your Dad's shirts for Moses."

Moe's voice was choked and distorted by the bruised lip. "Thank you, ma'am. I have another shirt in my duffle." He dashed out of the kitchen like a rabbit with a hound in hot pursuit.

Mom's critical eyes turned to me. "You better clean yourself up, too. Your hair is a mess. You can't take care of the store looking like that. I told Randy to go with you. There could be more trouble, so your friend better stay here."

I gaped at her like an imbecile. I'd forgotten about the store. Considering the prejudices of everyone in town someone would surely cause more trouble. Maybe we should forget the Moonlight Madness Sale. We probably wouldn't have any customers anyway.

"Are you sure we should open tonight?" I asked.

"Your dad expects you to take care of things, Melanie. Just be careful. Leave Moses here and stick with Randy. I'm going to look for Darlene at the football game. We'll come by later." She tied a wool scarf on her head, pulled on coat and gloves and was out the door before I could argue.

I ran upstairs. Moe stepped out of the bathroom. He was already dressed and held a large square band-aid. He bent down so I could position it over the cut on his forehead. He winced as I pressed it into place and I wanted to kiss him and make it all better. He straightened and said, "Thanks." His voice sounded husky and sweet. I looked up and smiled.

Against his dark skin, the pink square broadcast an advertisement. Attention: This Negro has been hurt. I wondered if there was such a thing as band-aids for different colors of skin, or was it like the crayon in Darlene's crayola box—flesh was the name, but it didn't look like the skin color of anyone I knew.

I ran to my room to change clothes and make myself presentable for the store. Coming back down the stairs, I heard Moe and Randy in the living room.

"It won't happen again," Randy promised.

I leaned over the banister to catch Moe's response but his voice was too low. I crept down a few steps and craned my neck. Moe jumped up. He'd seen me.

I skipped down the rest of the steps and called out, "Let's get to the store. The game'll be letting out any minute."

Randy rose from the couch. "Mom said Moe should stay here in case there's more trouble."

"You can if you want to," I said, "but you don't have to."

Moe pulled himself up tall and my mind conjured the muscles under his shirt. "Punks and drunks don't scare me. I came here to help Melanie and I intend to do just that."

Randy laughed. "Punks and drunks! But there is someone you should be scared of."

A spot of blood blemished the bandage as Moe's brow wrinkled in distress. He must have thought Randy believed he wasn't man enough to take care of himself.

Together Randy and I clarified Randy's statement. "Our mother!"

Moe laughed with us. "She is formidable, I'll admit. But I think I may be winning her over."

Randy grew serious. "Well, if you've got her figured out maybe you can teach me."

I smiled as I pulled on my mittens. I'd bet Moe could win my mother over, and it looked like he had a good start on winning Randy, too.

Walking toward town, we again heard the roar of the fans echo from the football field. There were few people downtown: those who'd left the game early to reopen their businesses and a handful of housewives who had no interest in football but anticipated the bargains offered by the Moonlight Madness Sales.

Mrs. Maggelson stood in the alley outside the Town and Gown a few buildings down from our store. She dug through her handbag, pulled out a wad of keys on a ring as big as a jailer's. Stepping out of the building's shadow, she moved into the glare of the mercury lamp and flipped through the keys, hunting for the one to unlock her store. Her head rose as she craned her neck. Her piercing eyes gave us the once over. She'd been mean and spiteful to me years before and I still considered her my arch enemy. I waved to make her think she no longer bothered me. She turned on her heel, stuck her snoot in the air and marched through her back door. Moe and I would provide juicy morsels for the banquet of slanderous prattle she served to anyone willing to partake.

Within a few minutes, we were ready for the sale. Randy had turned on televisions, adjusting pictures and sound. The showroom was filled with bright screens, the buzz of talk and canned laughter, and the smell of freshly brewed coffee. I placed napkins and paper cups next to the coffee pot on a table Randy and Moe had set up at the front of the store. Moe arranged Gaga's cookies in neat rows on a tray. I smiled. Would customers refuse homemade goodies if they knew a Negro had touched them? But how would they know? I wouldn't tell.

A blast of car horns and screech of tires announced the arrival of jubilant boosters of the football heroes. We rushed out the front door to add our cheers to the celebration, then stopped short. The triumphant clamor came from Wildcats' fans flaunting their victory over their biggest rival, our Marauders.

"What happened?" I asked a group of forlorn teens slinking past the store. "We were ahead by four touchdowns!"

One of the girls turned to me. "They came back in the second half and won."

"Walloped us, is more like it," a boy added. "42-28. It's like we threw the game or sumthin'."

The boisterous victors raced their motors, threw disparaging remarks at the vanquished, laughed with disdain and pride. Then they sped on their way to boast in their own hometown.

Gloomy teens headed toward the Rexall to drown their sorrow with Cokes or phosphates and rock and roll from the jukebox. Men clustered in front of the stores to replay the game and shake their heads over the nit-witted errors the Marauders had committed. Their wives wandered in and out of stores searching for bargains and friends to chat with. Admonishing their children to behave, they let them run free.

A gang of little squirts dashed into our store and each hand snatched up a cookie. At the sound of Moe's deep laugh, the little thieves looked up. Mouths flew open, a cookie fell to the floor and one brave soul spoke with a quavering voice, "Wow, you sure are black."

Moe bent in half to look the child in the eye. "You sure are white!" he boomed.

The kids screamed and ran from the store. A woman grabbed the frank little shaver by the nape of his neck and marched him down the sidewalk. The others dragged their feet as they followed. After a brief lecture from the boy's mother, the gang obediently threw the cookies into the trash can on the corner and ran off in search of treats from a more acceptable source.

"Oops," Moe said. "I guess I sent those rascals from the dark demon to the white witch."

"You're hardly a demon," I said. "And that woman isn't exactly a witch. You need to change the 'w' to a 'b'."

We watched people drift along the sidewalks checking sales posters in the store windows. A few of them stopped to admire Darlene's handiwork, but no one was enticed to enter even though our prices were the lowest we'd offered all year.

At last, the bell above the door jangled and Randy, Moe and I put on dazzling smiles preparing to greet our first real customers. Mom, Darlene, and Ann walked in. Mom scanned the store assessing the situation. It didn't take an Einstein to figure out we were the targets of a boycott.

She pulled me into the office, slammed the door and attacked. "I told you not to bring him here. Look at the business we're losing. You always have to prove your point! Honestly, Melanie, are you ever going to learn?"

"I didn't do anything wrong!" My voice rose along with the temperature of my face. "Who wants their business anyway? Racist bigots. Who are they to judge me and my friends!"

"Watch your tongue, young lady. You can't bring a colored person here and expect everyone to accept him. And you know it! I'm going home. Tell him to stay in back. If no one comes in in the next half hour, close up shop. The two of you can go back to school tonight."

"What about tomorrow? Are you going to run the store? And besides, I want to see Dad when he comes home."

"I can manage without you. Who knows if the customers will ever come back? Your father just had an operation. He doesn't need this mess you've created." She marched out of the office and called to Darlene and Ann, "Home. Now."

I slumped at the desk, my hand bracing my forehead, too furious to cry. Moe stepped in and cleared his throat. I looked up and asked, "Did you hear?"

He nodded. "Couldn't help it. You two were really going at it."

"I'm sorry. She's worried about Dad and about business and she always gets worked up over what other people think. It's not as bad as she makes it out to be."

"Your mother understands better than you do, Melanie."

It was like a slap to my face. I couldn't believe he'd take her side. She'd just said she wanted him gone.

He put his hand on my shoulder. "It happens all the time. People don't want me here. I told you before I wouldn't make this your fight. Talk your mother into letting you stay. I'll leave tonight."

EIGHT

I opened my mouth to argue but before any words came out I was jolted to my feet by a loud crash.

"What the hell?" Randy shouted as he flew past the office.

Moe and I raced after him to the back door. Shards of glass crunched under our feet, cold air blew through the shattered window opening, a hefty rock lay on the tile floor.

Randy pulled open the door, careful not to jar the bits of glass that remained in the frame. We peered into the dim alley at the silhouettes of two males, one a scrawny stretch, the other a fireplug. Unmistakably, Miller and Muggs. They moved out of the shadows, Miller casually tossing a baseball a few inches into the air and catching it. They stepped closer.

Muggs' menacing voice cut through me. "Nigger lover!"

Randy slammed the door with such force the remaining glass crashed to the floor. "Melanie, call the cop."

Before I could move, the hoods pushed their way in. Muggs grabbed me, his nails biting into my arm. I smelled his sour breath as he snarled, "Not so fast, sister. We're just here for a friendly visit. Maybe I'll buy me a new TV."

I shook my arm free. Moe lunged toward Muggs. Miller dropped the baseball on Moe's foot and grinned. "Oops, looky what just happened."

Moe grabbed Miller forcing him into a headlock. Miller's flailing legs barely missed Moe's shins. Moe squeezed tighter. The punk's face turned red and gagging sounds struggled to loose themselves from his throat.

Randy snatched the ball off the floor and held it overhead. Cocking his arm back for a better aim at Muggs, he yelled, "Get out or

I'll clock you."

Muggs rushed forward and threw his arms around Randy's waist. The baseball fell with a thud. My brother and the fireplug scrambled into the showroom, jabbing at each other with their fists.

I screamed and reached for the ball then bolted after them. Jerking my arm into position, I threw with all my might. The baseball hit Muggs square in the thigh.

"You bitch!" he yelped, clutching his leg.

Moe dropped the chokehold on Miller, who hightailed to the back door and flung it open.

Red flashes flickered against the wall like lights of a pinball machine. The blare of a siren announced the arrival of a patrol car which screeched to a stop behind the store.

A sheriff's deputy hopped out and shouted to Miller, "Stop right there."

A great gulp of air, built up from holding my breath, burst from my lungs and left me limp with relief.

The deputy, tugging Miller along by the shirt collar, yelled through the window frame, "Everybody! Outside!"

Moe, Randy and I scurried out the door and stood shivering next to the building. Muggs followed with a defiant smirk. Another police vehicle crept down the alley and stopped. Officer Reichenbacher emerged and tipped his hat to the deputy. "Looks like these boys are trying to finish what they started at the game. How 'bout we go inside and straighten this out."

The deputy deferred to Ricky and we were soon standing in the back of the showroom. A small group of late night shoppers gathered on the sidewalk in front of the store, then drifted away like actors in a grade B movie who'd just been told "Nothin' to see here, folks. Move along."

"Okay, boys," Ricky addressed the fellows while ignoring me. "What's this all about?"

Randy, Muggs and Miller blurted jumbled accusations. Moe and I, trying to sound like the calm word of reason, added our voices to the clamor. The deputy held up his hands. "Stop! I'm taking all of you in for disturbing the peace."

Officer Ricky chimed in, "Excuse me, sir. I'd like to keep this here in my jurisdiction. How 'bout we take them to my station and hear each of their stories before you haul anyone off to county?"

The deputy shoved Miller and Muggs out the door to the alley and into the back seat of his patrol car.

Moe and I unplugged the coffee, wrapped the cookies in waxed paper, and locked the store while Randy swept up the broken glass and nailed a piece of plywood over the window frame. Outside, Officer Ricky and the deputy leaned against the fender of the chief's car and jawed while they waited for us to finish.

Huddled between Moe and Randy in the back seat of Officer Reichenbacher's car, I felt tears of anger and fright well in my eyes. Ricky drove around the deputy and led the way through town to the police station. Neither turned on their flashing lights and sirens, but I still felt everyone gawking as we rode past.

The Middleton police station sat on the main drag just barely inside the village limits. Pea-green paint flecked off the squat structure's concrete blocks. Rectangular windows, lined up just below the eaves, allowed little light to enter even on the brightest days. A sign over the double door read "Middleton Police Department." In the center of a strip of dry grass, a large American flag fluttered at the top of a tall pole. Illuminated by a light from below, it gave importance to the small plain building.

Officer Reichenbacher eased the patrol car into a spot marked with a hand painted sign that said "Chief Parking Only." The deputy wedged his car between Ricky's and a scrubby shrub encroaching on the meager parking lot.

Perfectly synchronized, the cops got out of their cars and opened the back doors. We detainees scrambled out in a cluster. Following Officer Ricky, Muggs and Miller swaggered toward the building in a show of bravado. Randy, Moe and I slunk behind like outlaws about to face the hanging judge. The deputy followed close; his cupped hand hovered above the pistol in a holster hanging from his belt.

I glanced at Moe. He stared ahead, his jaw tight, his spine straight as a ramrod. Was he feeling as composed as he looked or was he worried there were lynch mobs in the north, too?

We walked into a reception area, barely large enough for the desk cluttered with pencils, notepads, scraps of paper, a telephone, a typewriter, and an account ledger. An oak chair squeezed between the desk and the wall. Apparently meant to keep visitors from lingering, it was the only seat in the room.

Ricky led us through a door and down a narrow hallway. On one side, two jail cells with bunked cots, portable toilets, and thick iron bars stood ready to imprison anyone who fell into Officer

Reichenbacher's clutches. No amount of scrubbing with soap and bleach could cover the foul odor of sweat and urine, though someone had certainly tried. Earlier jailbirds had decorated the walls with crude drawings and words that made my stomach churn with disgust. This was no scene out of Jailhouse Rock. No hip-swiveling Elvis had ever resided here. I imagined a disheveled drunk leaning against the wall, blowing a mournful tune on a harmonica while his fellow inmate clanged a tin cup along the bars and shouted for his daily ration of bread and water.

The police chief unlatched a ring of keys from his belt and unlocked the cell doors. "We'd best keep these hoodlums separated," he told the deputy. Muggs and Miller were shoved into a cell, and with a twist of the key were shut away—no longer a threat to society.

Ricky nodded toward the other cell. "And those are your new accommodations."

Randy stepped into the cell. Moe grabbed my hand and moved to join him.

Officer Ricky shook his head. "Not you, Miss. Come with me."

I tightened my grip on Moe's hand. Why weren't they sticking me in the cell, too? Where were they going to take me?

The deputy grabbed my arm, "C'mon."

Moe unloosed my hand and nodded. "Go ahead." He stepped into the cell. The clank of the door reverberated as I followed the cops across the hall.

The chief's office had a desk more impressive in size and no less cluttered than the one in the reception area. Posters and notes were tacked willy-nilly to a set of bulletin boards hanging above the desk on the wall it faced. I couldn't make sense of it. Detective work must be sloppy and involved.

In the middle of the room, a metal light fixture hung from a chain above a rectangular table. Mismatched sets of two chairs flanked each of the longer sides. This must be the interrogation area where criminals were berated, threatened and tricked, under the sharp glare of the overhead light, until they were broken and sobbed out their confessions.

Reichenbacher cocked his thumb toward the table. "Sit there," he growled. I perched on the edge of the seat, so tense my shoulders ached. The sheriff's deputy pulled out a chair across from me and plunked into it. He leaned forward, forearms pressed against the oak tabletop. The other chair scraped along the floor and creaked as

Chief Reichenbacher settled in next to the deputy.

"We don't mix females with males in the cells," the chief explained.

I wanted to argue that it shouldn't matter—Randy's my brother, and Moe's my friend—but I was too scared to speak up. It'd probably get me in worse trouble.

The deputy glanced at the chief and snorted. "Maybe we should put that bunch of hooligans in together and let 'em duke it out. Save you the trouble."

Reichenbacher's lips pressed together like a door slammed shut to keep words from escaping. Even I thought since he was the chief and this was his town he shouldn't have to put up with such insolence.

Maybe a county sheriff's deputy has more authority than a town cop. Still, Reichenbacher was considerably older and surely had more experience. Then it dawned on me that although he was the chief, he really wasn't treated with much respect by anyone. The older folks in town thought of him as a glorified crossing guard or dog catcher. When there was real trouble they called the county sheriff. Taking their cue from the adults, all the kids in town referred to our chief as Uncle Ricky. A cozy nickname indicating the genial relationship we had with our local law enforcement. Truthfully, everyone regarded him as a buffoon. And I think he knew it. Maybe he'd be especially rough on Randy, Moe and me just to prove his authority.

"So," the chief continued, looking directly at me, "we'll interrogate you first. If we have to hold you we'll figure something out."

I half-expected the light above the table to drop down and glare in my face while the cops wrested a confession from me.

The questioning started out mildly. Name? Address? Age? Occupation? I tried to appear confident and cooperative, but answered only what I was asked. My voice cracked as my dread grew. I couldn't let myself cry like a scared little girl.

The deputy surprised me by smiling and asking about school. What was I majoring in? Did I like my classes? He seemed interested in my band and wanted to know what kind of music we played, and what our future plans were.

I relaxed a little. This isn't so bad. They're just trying to put a scare in us. Once they talk to Randy and Moe they'll let us go. Who knows what they'll do about Muggs and Miller, but at least they'll know who had started this mess. And that my brother, my friend and I are innocent.

"So, tell us," Reichenbacher interrupted. "Just what is your connection to that colored feller in there?" His lips tightened in the same grimace I'd seen before.

The deputy's mouth was set in a similar frown and his stare pierced right through me. The abrupt change of topic and demeanor of my interrogators set my heart thumping. I shouldn't have let my guard down. My palms suddenly covered with sweat.

I swallowed the phlegm clogging my throat and croaked, "He's a student, too. He's a friend."

"And why did you bring him to our town? Especially now—when your father is in the hospital and your mother has enough to contend with?" The chief knew exactly who I was and he even knew that Dad was in the hospital. I should have figured as much. Most everyone in town knows everyone else's business and it stands to reason the local cop would be privy to all the information.

"My mother asked me to come home and take care of the store. Homecoming is one of our biggest weekends. Moe gave me a ride and stayed to help."

"Was that the only way you could get here?" the deputy barked.

Reichenbacher added, "Last I knew there's a bus stops here three times a day. And I know your daddy can afford bus fare. Don't you think he'd rather you got here that way than with some colored stranger?"

Words spewed from my mouth as I tried to make them understand. "It was too late for the bus and when we got here it was after eleven and Moe shouldn't have to drive all that way back at night and besides he was a big help getting things ready for the sale and it was better for me to not be alone when the Westinghouse man came and—" I was jabbering like a fool. I felt my face redden. Taking a deep breath, I stared at the two men across from me. I didn't owe them an explanation.

"Well now," the deputy drawled. "Didn't it occur to you that bringing a nigra to a quiet little white town would raise a few eyebrows? Maybe even stir up some trouble?"

Reichenbacher shifted in his seat, then quietly examined his fingernails. The clock on the other side of the room ticked patiently as if waiting for my answer.

A burst of air expelled from my lungs and I slumped like a fallen cake. How should I answer that question? Yes, I knew this town was full of bigots, but I'll bring whoever I want to here because I don't care. Or no, I didn't have any idea that people would be bothered. I'm so sorry and I'll never bring an offensive person here again.

"I don't understand why it should matter to people," I began. "It isn't as if he's moving here or is even trying to associate with anyone here. Moe is a person, just like you and me." I bit my tongue to keep from adding, "actually he's better than you and most everyone else in this town."

Reichenbacher leaned forward and twisted in his chair blocking the deputy from my view. He was in charge of the questioning now. He cleared his throat and ordered, "Tell me about the encounter you and—" He hesitated. I heard the clock tick. "you and your friend had with those other punks after the parade." He nodded in the direction of the cells. "I saw some of it and I'm not clear whose side your brother was on. What exactly happened?"

Finally, the questioning was back on track. I could give them the real story. The one I'd rehearsed in my head while we were in the squad car. "My little sister and her friend and Moe and I were on the sidewalk outside the store watching the parade. Some hot rods were at the back and one of them stopped and dropped my brother off. Muggs was driving." I skipped over what Randy had said about Moe. "Then those two, Muggs and Miller, got out of the car and started calling Moe names. I told them to leave but they grabbed me and threatened him."

"Do you recall just what that threat entailed?" the chief asked.

"I don't remember the exact words but they said he'd better leave town or, or there would be trouble."

"Hmmm, that doesn't necessarily mean they were planning something. Could be they were just giving you a friendly warning, a piece of advice."

"There was nothing friendly about it," I snapped. "You saw them. And when they saw you coming, they split."

"And your brother went with them." The chief drew his finger and thumb across his chin and nodded as if confirming a fact I'd neglected to add. "And as I recall, your friend and I had a little chat and I suggested, just as those two young men had, to avoid trouble perhaps he ought move on. Not that I necessarily agree with everyone's opinions about colored people, but I do have a duty to keep the peace. I've found it best to nip things in the bud before we have a full-blown problem on our hands."

He waited a moment to let his words sink in, then leaned forward and continued. "Let's move on. Instead of leaving, your friend went to the football game. I understand there was some sort of ruckus there. Could we hear your version of that?"

I was never much of a student of government and not so sure how the law worked, but I knew a person was supposed to be considered innocent until proven guilty. His comments seemed contrary to that notion. The chief and the deputy nodded and exchanged knowing glances. My "version" of events was highly suspect.

"We were leaving the concession stand when Muggs and Miller came up and called us names. Miller jumped Moe and a couple of drunks joined in. I don't know who they were. Randy and Moe and I ran home." I emphasized Randy's name so they would know he was innocent, unlike those creeps who'd tried to lure him into their criminal ways.

A sly grin crossed the deputy's lips. In my effort to keep the story short and leave no room for error, I'd made the fight sound like a childish schoolyard spat.

Before I could add anything, Reichenbacher asked, "And what happened later at your dad's store?"

"Those hoods threw a rock through the window and came in through the back and Miller threw a baseball at Moe and tried to hurt me. Muggs started beating on Randy. Then you showed up." There! Was that plain enough about who had broken the law?

Reichenbacher pushed his chair back and stood. "Okay, I think we've got enough information from you. You can go."

Relieved at the abrupt change of opinion, I stood and pulled on my coat. "Thank you." The chief and the deputy remained stuck to their chairs.

"What about Randy and Moe?" I asked.

"We'll get to them soon enough," the chief answered.

"Yeah," the deputy added. "We've got four more stories to hear before we decide who to lock up and who, if anyone, we let go."

I brushed my hand roughly against my cheek hoping neither of them saw the tear. "I'm not leaving without my brother and my friend," I announced in a voice surer than I felt.

A perturbed look crossed Reichenbacher's face. "I suppose you can wait in the outer office. Don't touch anything on the desk." The gruff warning startled me. What was on that desk that would be of the least interest to me?

I followed the chief to the front. He pulled the chair from behind the desk and set it beneath the window on the far wall. I wondered how long I'd have to endure the hard wood numbing my butt before they set Randy and Moe free.

The walls were thin and I heard the clink of keys, the clank of the cell door, the shuffling of feet moving across the hallway. "Sit there," the chief ordered. After murmurs I couldn't decipher, chair feet scraping the floor and a long silence, I heard the chief's voice again.

"Your full name?"

"Moses Demarcus Carter."

My ears perked. I leaned forward straining to hear every word.

The chief didn't waste time getting to the point. "Suppose you tell us how you ended up in Middleton."

"Melanie asked me to give her a ride home so she could help her parents."

Silence followed. I couldn't stand it. Deciding to sneak down the hallway and see what was going on, I jumped up. Reichenbacher's voice stopped me.

"How is it you are acquainted with Miss Sedlak?"

"We're both students at Western."

" You in music, too?"

"No."

The deputy took over. "What you there for?"

"Business with a finance minor."

I sat again and listened.

"Is that right? Well, then, how is it you know that young lady?"

My mind flashed to the night we'd met. I'd played every detail in my head over and over like a well-worn record. What he wore, what he said, how he smiled. The music.

Moe's voice was calm in spite of the accusatory tone of his interrogators. "We met at a sorority dance last winter. Her band was playing."

"I see," the deputy said although he probably had never set foot on a college campus and had no idea what life was like there. "So, is it usual for the band and the guests to mingle with each other? Maybe things have changed since I was your age but I still don't think it's common for colored boys and white girls to associate with each other. Is it?"

I clenched the chair's seat to keep from jumping up again. What did that jerk's questions have to do with anything?

"Is she your girlfriend?" Reichenbacher's voice came out all slimy like he was hoping to hear a dirty story.

I held my breath. Would Moe say yes? Of course not. He'd never asked me on a real date or said that he liked me.

"We are friends. There's nothing between us."

The words rang against my brain like the crash of a cymbal. Nothing between us. Nothing. Is that what I am? Nothing?

Moe was taken back to the cell and locked in. He hadn't even been asked about the fight with Muggs and Miller.

The next round of questioning began like the others. "Name?" I hoped my brother would stay as calm as Moe without giving some wiseacre answer. Instead, I heard a voice I wasn't expecting.

"Malvern Quiddly."

I clapped my hand over my mouth to stifle a giggle. Malvern? What kind of name was that? No wonder he went by Muggs.

The deputy began, "So we hear you told that nigra boy to leave town. Tell us about that."

"It wasn't my idea. I mean, I dint even know about him til Randy told us. Said his sister brought a spook home and he didn't like it one bit and he was gonna tell him to get lost. We dropped him off after the parade so he could do just that. Then his sister got all bent outa shape about it. We was just trying to keep scum out of our fine village here."

I bit my lip to keep from shouting, "Liar! It wasn't like that at all."

Reichenbacher spoke next. "Nice to see you're trying to stay on the right side of the law. Be a shame if you end up in county again. Tell us about the scuffle at the football field."

"There weren't nuthin' to that neither. Just tried again to tell that coon to leave town. Then some other jokers got into it. It's pretty easy to tell how folks here feel about coloreds. Anyway, Melanie and that darkie ran off. Randy went with them. Chickenshit."

The men snickered like this was all some big joke. My stomach did a flip-flop. Hadn't they noticed the bruises on Moe's face?

The chief continued, "And the problem at the TV store? The broken window and fist fight?"

"Again, I didn't have nuthin' to do with it."

"You were there."

"Yeah, but that don't mean I broke no window. Randy asked us to come in the store and then he freaked out and started pounding on me. You saw how he was actin'."

"Okay, I think we've got a pretty good handle on what happened."

I couldn't believe it. They'd agreed with every word that came out of that punk's filthy mouth. They took him back to the cell and brought out Miller, whose story was pretty much the same. Like Muggs, he laid the blame squarely on Randy's shoulders and claimed to be acting in the best interest of the town. It made me retch.

When it was his turn, Randy's story matched mine but the deputy and the chief brushed it off. There was nothing he could say to change our fate. We were doomed.

I couldn't stand it anymore. I rushed to the doorway of the chief's office and said, "Excuse me. I have to use the bathroom."

"You still here?" the chief asked.

"Yes, I'm not leaving without Randy and Moe," I said, forgetting the excuse I'd used to interrupt them.

The chief handed the keys to the deputy and said, "Bring that colored feller in here."

Randy and I silently stared at each other trying to send signals on what to do next. I got nothing from him and I'm sure he got the same from me.

The deputy gave a rough shove and Moe tripped through the doorway. Expressionless, he stood next to me.

"Okay," Reichenbacher started. "I'm tired and I don't want to stay up all night babysitting you so here's what I'm gonna do. I'm charging both you guys with disturbing the peace." A demented grin spread crookedly across his mouth and I noticed he was missing his left canine tooth. "But," He paused a moment like an actor in a bad play. "I'm going to go easy on you. As soon as you pay the fine you can go."

"We have to pay a fine? To you?" I asked.

Randy gave a slight shake of his head warning me to shut up.

"Yep. Saves you court costs and saves the judge's time. It's only a misdemeanor. Like I said, I'm going easy on you." The chief's grin broadened as if he was proud of bestowing such a generous favor. "Randy, your fine is twenty dollars." He turned to Moe. "Yours is forty. And as soon as you pay it I'll let you go. With one stipulation. Get out of our town and don't come back. Hear me, boy?"

The deputy stepped next to the chief, his hand resting on the butt of his pistol. A menacing smirk crossed his face.

Before Moe or I could speak Randy blurted, "Sir, could I talk to my sister a minute about getting the money?"

Cupping his chin with his hand, the chief considered Randy's request. The deputy gave a slight nod and Reichenbacher said, "Okay, figure it out. We'll be in the front office."

As soon as they left the room, I grabbed Randy's arm and whispered, "He can't do that. You didn't do anything. Why should we pay him? And why is Moe's fine double?"

"Melanie," Moe interrupted. "He's not supposed to take money, but he can because he's the one who has the key to the cell. Our choices are to pay him or to stay here. If Randy wants to pay, I'm okay with that. But I'm going to let that cop lock me up."

My stomach tightened. "What? No! I'll get the money."

Moe put his hands on my shoulders and looked at me as if I were a child. "I want you to call G. W. Sloan. He's the one you met at the SNCC meeting. We've put together a group to protest when stuff like this happens. When they show up the weight will shift to our side."

"No!" I shouted. Then, remembering the two men in the front office, I lowered my voice. "You can't let them lock you up. It isn't fair!"

A sigh rose from Moe's lungs and exited his lips. "That's exactly why I'm letting it happen. As long as they can impose fines and lock up black people without a legitimate reason things aren't going to change. You'll find G. W.'s phone number in the side pocket of my bag."

"You told me you weren't here to take a stand. It's my hometown, these people all know me and—"

"And you said I should stay, no matter what happened."

I sucked in my breath. Moe had just thrown my own words back at me.

Randy interrupted, "Melanie, just get the money and get back here. They'll let us both go and it'll be done with."

I turned to my brother thankful he'd agreed that Moe should be let go. But it wasn't that simple.

"Where am I going to get sixty dollars in the middle of the night? Do you have any money?"

"I've got a few bucks stashed in a cigar box under my bed. You can get the rest from the Tide box in the cabinet above the washer."

"What? The Tide box?"

"A couple people heard about Dad and came in to pay off the stuff they're buying on payments. Mom didn't have time to go to the bank so she hid it in the Tide box. It'll be enough."

"But when she finds out—"

"I'll figure something out, just get going."

I turned to Moe. "It's settled. I'm going to get the money. I'll be right back." I fled from the room before he could answer.

The chief and the deputy stared at me as I bolted into the reception area. Grabbing my coat from the chair, I told them I would bring the money as soon as I could get home and back with it.

"How 'bout I give you a ride?" the deputy offered. "Pretty late at night for a girl to be out by herself." He cocked his head toward the clock on the wall. It was well past midnight. I nodded. Agreeing to accept a favor from that creep was as bad as spending Sunday afternoon with my mother, but sometimes you choose what's practical no matter how nasty it is.

Once we were underway he asked, "So, how do you like being away at college? Big city a lot different from little ol' Middleton?"

I shrugged. Engaging in small talk with the captor of my brother and my friend was the last thing I felt like doing. Maybe it was a ploy to get me to confess something. He turned onto Maple Street without asking where I lived. I guess the police know those things. At least he didn't turn on the flashing lights and sirens. I felt enough like a criminal as it was.

He pulled into the driveway and said, "Do you want me to come in with you or wait in the car?

"You can go. I'll drive myself back." I hopped out of the car and fled to the house.

NINE

I slid through the back door and slipped off my shoes then silently cut across the kitchen. Slower than a sad ballad, I advanced in the dark through the dining room to the stairway. Halfway up the stairs I hesitated. Distracted by worry, I'd forgotten to count the steps. Which was the one with the telltale squeak? The one Junior had taught me to skip over so the sound wouldn't wake our parents. I guessed and raised my knee high to skip over the next step.

Squeak! I froze. My nails dug into the banister as I held my breath and listened. After what seemed an eternity, sure no one had stirred, I shifted slightly trying to make myself as light as a balloon. I slowly brought my foot to the next step. On tiptoes, I made it up the rest of the stairs. Running my hand along the wall, I groped my way down the dark hallway.

In Randy's room, with the door closed, I could finally turn on a light without risking discovery. I fell to my knees and reached under his bed. I felt a crusty sock, some wrinkled comic books, and a dried up banana peel before my hand finally landed on the cigar box. I sat on Randy's disheveled bed counting the bills, impressed that he had squirreled away thirty-two dollars. Too bad his motorcycle fund was going to be wasted on a bribe.

Stuffing the money in my coat pocket, I moved to the other bed. Moe had made it with neat hospital corners, something my brothers had never cared to master. His duffel bag rested squarely on the foot of the bed. I unzipped the side pocket and reached in, then smiled at my good fortune. His keys were in the first place I looked. I shoved them in my pocket with Randy's money. As I started to zip the bag shut, a folded piece of paper caught my eye. I shouldn't snoop I told myself as I pulled the paper out. I made out the scratchy writing: G. W. Sloan's name and phone number. Cramming the paper into the deep corner of the bag's pocket, I quickly pulled the zipper to shut away what I'd found.

In the dark hallway, I tiptoed past my parent's bedroom. Mom was a light sleeper, especially when any of us kids was out. It was a miracle the thump of my heart banging against my ribcage didn't wake her.

I crept back to the kitchen and clicked the light switch at the top of the basement stairs. I scurried down, opened the cupboard above the washer and pulled the Tide box off the shelf. The money was there, just as Randy had said. I counted out twenty-eight dollars and added it to the stash from his cigar box. There were a few bills left so maybe Mom wouldn't notice the theft before we could replace what I'd taken. I placed the box back on the shelf trying to remember the exact position it had been in.

Then I ran up the stairs, shut off the light, slid into my shoes, ran out the door and jumped into Moe's car. I fumbled around searching for the headlights' switch, adjusting the seat and rear view mirror, and trying out the gear shift. The quicker I moved the longer things seemed to take. Finally, I took a deep breath, turned the key in the ignition and backed out of the driveway. My hands gripped the steering wheel and I hunched forward as tense as a piano wire.

As I pulled past the house, a light flashed through an upstairs window.

There wasn't time to wonder what Mom had heard or knew. I sped down the street. At least I didn't have to worry about getting a ticket—our local cop couldn't be bothered to patrol traffic when he had a jail full of hardened criminals to keep under control.

I rushed into the chief's office. Reichenbacher leaned back in his chair, feet on his desk, a cup of coffee in his hand. The deputy slouched in another chair. A cigarette dangled from the side of his mouth; the long gray ash threatened to drop to his chest. They stared at me as I stood trembling in the doorway, but neither made an effort to get up or to speak.

What had happened while I was gone? A vision flashed before me of Randy and Moe being carted off to Jackson prison. My imagination exploded. Randy strapped into an electric chair. Moses standing on a platform with a noose around his neck. Shaking my head to sweep away the images and restore my mind to reality, I bleated, "Where are Randy and Moe?"

Officer Reichenbacher pulled his feet off the desk and set down his cup. "Locked 'em back up 'til the fine's paid."

I stepped into the room. "Let me see my brother. I have the money."

The deputy snuffed out his cigarette on the sole of his boot and tossed the butt into the wastebasket next to the chief's desk. He grabbed the keyring, and brushed past me. A few moments later he was back, pushing Randy and Moe into the room.

Pulling the money from my coat pocket, I handed it to Randy. Moe leaned close to me and whispered, "Did you get a hold of G. W.?"

I shook my head. Moe's teeth clenched. I couldn't tell if he was angry, disappointed or worried. Whatever, the look definitely conveyed negative feelings. And they were directed at me.

Randy counted out twenty dollars and handed it to the chief. "Here's for my fine." He stretched out the i and cut the word off with a sharp edge of sarcasm. I stepped closer and put my hand on his arm. He handed over another forty dollars and mumbled, "This is for him." His eyes shifted toward Moe who stood, hands clasped in front of himself, eyes focused on the floor.

The police chief counted the money. The corners of his mouth turned up in an insincere smile. "I don't want to see you here again, Randy. Next time I won't be so generous so there better not be a next time. We'll just keep this little incident between us. No need to tell your daddy about the trouble you caused."

He looked at me. I nodded in agreement even though I knew his warning to keep our mouths shut wasn't to protect us from our father's wrath, but to protect his own hide.

He sneered at Moe, "And you—not only do I not want to see you in this station again, I don't want to see you anywhere near this town. That's the deal. Understand, boy?"

The veins in Moe's neck bulged as his jaw clenched tighter, but he remained silent. The chief stared at him for a long moment, then shrugged and said, "Get lost, all three of you!"

We scrambled out the door. I pulled Moe's keys from my jacket pocket. "I hope it's okay I drove your car."

He snatched the keys from my hand and got in behind the wheel. Randy opened the passenger door and pulled the seat forward so I could get in the back. I didn't argue. It was only a few minutes drive home. Time for all of us to cool down before we talked about what had happened.

When Moe turned down our street, Randy let out a long, low whistle. Our house was lit from top to bottom. "Holy Cow!" he said.

"The queen of saving on the electric bill must be hoppin' mad. She's got the house lit up like an airport landing strip. We better get our story straight before we go in."

"We have to tell her about the broken window," I said. "Let's say we went to the police station to report it." It wasn't that much of a lie. "What did they do to those hoods?"

Randy snorted. "Let 'em go as soon as you left. Guess they figured Muggs and Miller didn't have money—and anyways it's no big deal to those two if word gets out. Happened before." He was out of the car and halfway up the steps when he stopped and said, "Let me do the talking."

Moe and I followed Randy into the house to face what would surely be a harsher inquisition than we'd just endured.

Mom, in robe and curlers, stood in the middle of the kitchen. I'd never noticed before how old she looked without makeup. She clasped her arms tight across her chest. The fire in her eyes was all the warning I needed to keep my mouth shut. Randy stood in front of her. I noticed the hair on the back of his neck bristle and his arms tremble. Moe hung back, standing by the door like he was ready to bolt any second.

"Where have you been? It's almost 2 o'clock," she shrieked.

My head snapped up so I had a good view of the clock on the wall. It was 1:20. Just like her to make it a bigger deal than it already was. But I'd learned years before not to correct her when she was in a mood.

"We didn't know it was this late," Randy began, to soften her up. It was as close to an apology he would ever muster. "Trouble at the store. Somebody threw a rock through the back window. We had to board it up and close early so we could report it." He put on a remorseful face, shoulders slumping with relief that Mom had started to calm down. But I could tell from the suspicion in her eyes that she wasn't buying his story.

"Who broke the window?" Her voice was surprisingly calm. It was the same tone she'd used many times to question me when I was little. Somehow it always worked and I'd end up confessing the truth.

Randy didn't hesitate. "Well, no one saw it happen, so we can't prove anything, but I have a pretty good idea it was those two guys you and Dad told me to quit running around with. I guess you were right." Oh, he was a smooth one. I'd never be able to lie like that. My face would be so red you might as well carve a big L for liar on my forehead.

"And you went to the police?"

"Yeah," Randy answered. "Uncle Ricky said he'd look into it, but you know he won't do nothin'. Anyway, after that, we went out to the Northway for a cuppa coffee. Guess we were just putting off telling you. I'll fix the window tomorrow. Good thing they didn't steal anything." He prattled on buttering her up. If he didn't shut his mouth, he'd trip up and say something he shouldn't.

Mom glared at us. "Let's go in the other room and sit down and get the real story." She tromped out of the kitchen. Randy, Moe and I looked at each other. I'm sure the shadow of dread showed as deeply on my face as theirs. We didn't dare take time to come up with a better explanation.

In the living room, Mom sat in the recliner. It's was Dad's chair and I suspected she sat there to remind us of her authority. Randy and I slunk to the couch and perched on the cushions. Moe stood in the archway between the dining room and living room. I motioned him to join us.

He shook his head and said, "This is a family matter. I'll wait in the kitchen."

"You were with us. She should know your side of it, too," I insisted. He sat beside me. His reluctance and discomfort broadcast from him like names on a theater marquee.

Randy squirmed as our mother's eyes bore into him. Her voice was cool and accusing. "That was an interesting tale you fabricated. Maybe you should write a book."

Then she turned her attention to me. "Suppose you tell me what really happened."

Randy's knee pressed against my thigh in warning. I stammered, "It, it was like Randy said. Somebody broke the window. We were at the police station." By telling a half truth I'd committed a sin of omission Could she see my nose growing?

Mom leaned forward, her hands clutching the chair arms. "You can both stop dancing around. I know what happened."

"What?" we both asked, my tone one of shock, Randy's of curiosity.

"The town's busybody, Mrs. Maggelson, couldn't wait to call and report the details. Her version doesn't match yours."

I'd been the victim of that battle-axe's gossip years before and I still felt the sting and stigma. I had to say it. "You know she makes things up."

"Yes, I know, but she didn't have to make up anything this time. The three of you acted like hoodlums at a rumble. You were hauled off to the police station. I was going to let you stay there and stew a while, but," She sighed as if the burden of motherhood was too much for a mere mortal. "When I heard Melanie come home to get the car you can't even imagine what went through my mind. Now how about filling in the blanks?"

Randy began "There's nothing—"

She held up her hand to silence him. "Melanie, you tell me what happened at the police station." Her stare pierced my conscience like a scalpel used to autopsy our lame excuses.

"It was Muggs and Miller. They tried to pick a fight after the parade and then they attacked us at the football game and then they threw a rock through the window and then they came in and then they started beating up Moe and Randy." I was babbling but I couldn't stop myself. "Then Reichenbacher and a sheriff's deputy came and they took all of us to the police station. And then the other guys lied and the dumb police believed them and let them go, but they made Randy and Moe pay a fine or they'd keep them in jail. I know they just pocketed it. They said Moe had to get out of town because he was a troublemaker, but none of it was his fault."

"How much was the fine?" The calmness in her voice sent a chill through my veins.

"You mean the bribe," Randy corrected. "Or maybe we could call it extortion. Twenty from me and forty for Moe. Nobody wants coloreds in this town."

I slapped Randy on the thigh. "Shut up!"

"Where did you get the money?" Mom asked.

I slapped Randy again. I wasn't going to let him make up a cockamamie story. She'd find out sooner or later. "I came home and got the money Randy was saving for a motorcycle and I took twenty-eight dollars from the Tide box."

"Wait a minute," Randy interrupted. "You took all my money? I paid for part of his?" He pointed at Moe.

"Excuse me," Moe said. "I'll pay both of you back. Even though I didn't do anything to create a problem here, Randy is right. People in this town don't want a person with dark skin here. I've been ordered to leave and if you'll excuse me, I'll get my things now and go." He stood.

Mom stood, too, and said, "Yes, that would be best. You can send us a money order."

I jumped up and grabbed Moe's arm. "Wait! I'll go with you."

Mom stiffened. "Melanie, that isn't necessary. You can go back on the bus Sunday afternoon."

"No! I'm not letting Moe drive back alone in the middle of the night. You told me before that we both should leave."

Through gritted teeth, she said, "I changed my mind. The two of you shouldn't see each other any more. Not here and not at school. It only causes trouble."

Moe pried my fingers off his sleeve. "It's okay, Mel. Besides, your father's coming home. You'll want to see him."

In three long strides, he was at the stairway. By the time he'd reached the top I was right behind him.

"I'm going with you!" I scurried down the hall and into my old bedroom.

Darlene sat up on her bed, rubbing her eyes. "What?"

"Go back to sleep," I hissed as I grabbed my suitcase and began throwing things into it. I ran back down the stairs.

My mother shouted at me, "Melanie, stop this nonsense right now! Let him go."

Brushing past her I ran out of the house. Moe had already started the car and shifted into reverse. I grabbed the door handle and wrenched the door open. Throwing my suitcase in back, I clamored into the front seat and said, "Okay, let's go."

He turned in the seat and faced me. "Where you planning on going? The dorm's locked at one on Friday nights."

He had me there, but I couldn't let him go back alone. And I couldn't go back in the house and spend another minute with my mother. She might not say I told you so, but those words would reverberate through my head for a long time.

"Just go, I'll think of something."

As he turned onto Main Street and headed south out of town, a car sped up behind us, sticking close to the back bumper. Moe adjusted the rearview mirror to cut the glare from its headlights. A few miles down the road, the car pulled alongside us. The large emblem on the door was clearly visible—Martin County Sheriff Department. The deputy stuck up his middle finger, laughed and sped away.

Moe muttered something, but I couldn't make it out.

In the silence that followed, my mind roiled with worry. Where could I go until the dorm opened at seven? How could I ever go home again? What would Mom tell Dad? When would I see him again? Was Moe mad at me for this mess? Did he blame me for bringing him to Middleton?

I jumped when Moe interrupted my thoughts. "Why didn't you call G. W. like I asked?"

I shivered at the tinge of anger in his voice. "I couldn't find his phone number," I lied.

"You found my keys. His number was right there."

"I, I guess I didn't see it. Besides, I got the money. You didn't need G. W.'s help."

"It wasn't about the money."

I sat in the dark silence for nearly two hours worried that Moe and my mother would never forgive me. What had he expected from me? I had no idea what I could have done other than pay the police to let him go. Surely, he didn't blame me for everyone else's attitudes. I couldn't change things and I was afraid of what would happen if he tried.

And Mom? Why was she so against someone she didn't know anything about. Moe was a wonderful person. If he'd been white she would have been thrilled that we were friends. She'd want me to fall in love with him and make him a part of our family. Instead, she didn't want me to ever see him again. Ever. Why did he have to be black and me white?

Neither of us spoke until we were a few blocks from the university. Then Moe asked, "Where am I supposed to take you?"

I started to cry. "I don't know. I'm sorry. I made such a big mess of everything. Can I stay in your car until the dorm opens?"

"Then what? Are you going to sneak in and pretend you'd been there all night? Don't you have to sign in or something?"

He was right. I'd signed out for the weekend and it wouldn't make sense that I came back at seven on Saturday morning. I'd have to stay away until some time in the afternoon and then make up an excuse for coming back a day early.

"It's after three. It's too cold to stay in the car. Do you know anyone who lives off campus you could stay with?"

I shook my head and sobbed. "Maybe you could drop me at the bus station. I could stay there like I'm waiting for a bus."

"No, I'm not leaving you alone in a place like that. I'll go back to the dorm and see if any of the guys are up and maybe borrow enough for you to stay in a hotel." It was a generous offer considering he probably felt like dumping me in the middle of town, leaving me to fend for myself.

He left me in his car in the parking lot while he went into the dorm where most of the Negro men lived. As I waited I thought about how different it was to be a male—even a colored one. They could come and go as they pleased. The dorms were left open all night and they didn't have to account for where they were spending their time. If the girls' dorms weren't so strict, like another set of overanxious parents, I wouldn't be in this spot.

A few minutes later Moe was back. "C'mon. No one's up. My roommate went home for the weekend. You'll stay in my room tonight."

Spend the night in his room? A sizzle pulsed through my body leaving me sweltry and lightheaded. I remembered feeling the same the night before when we'd slept a room apart. The possibility of what might happen caused me to tremble. What if he wants me to—? No, he's too much of a gentleman. The realization of the risk we were taking, jolted me out of my anticipation. I asked, "But, what if we get caught?"

"Keep quiet and move fast. No one should see us." He grabbed my hand and we stealthily ran to the dormitory door. Once inside, I pressed close to his back trying to hide, while he scanned the lobby. We ran to the stairwell and up two flights to his floor. He opened the door, pulled me through and down the hallway to the third room on the left. While Moe fumbled with his key and finally threw open the door, I jerked my head back and forth fearing suspicious eyes watching us.

His room was a monk's' cell. Unadorned walls and floor. Two beds, two desks, two chairs, two built in sets of drawers, two closets —all of the same light ash. The plaid bedspreads had the same precise hospital corners Moe had made on my brother's bed. The desktops were also neat; books and papers in squared off piles, pencils and pens points down in metal cups, lamps precisely poised in the right hand corners. Except for the saxophone case near the window and the poster of Cannonball Adderley on the wall, the room gave no clue to the personality of its occupants.

I shrugged off my coat and Moe placed it over the back of his desk chair. He hung his in a closet. "Here's an extra blanket if you need it." He pulled a green army blanket from the shelf and placed it on the end of his bed. "I'll be back in a few hours and we'll figure out what to do with you. Don't open the door for anyone."

"What? Where are you going?"

"You didn't think I'd stay here with you, did you? You've caused me a helluva lotta trouble as it is. Don't make it worse." He walked out and locked the door.

I sat on the bed and wallowed in the ooze of my own misery. He was so mad at me. How was I going to get out of here in the morning? Once he was done helping would he be done with me?

I'd left my suitcase in the car, so I pulled off my shoes and lie down fully dressed on Moe's bed. It seemed sacrilegious to muss up the sheets. Pulling the blanket over me, I tried to sleep. It was no use, thoughts spun around in my brain like clothes in a washing machine. Then I had to pee. Bad.

I tried to will my bladder into submission, but it wouldn't cooperate. I squirmed and held my breath and sucked in my gut and crossed my legs. The urge only grew more intense. Unable to stand it any longer, I shot off the bed, dashed to the door and opened it a crack. Seeing and hearing no one, I made a run for the bathroom at the far end of the hall.

As I scurried into the place that had held such mystery in my imagination, curiosity stopped me. I glanced at the walls and floor both covered in pale green tiles. A row of mirrors was anchored to the left wall, each above a white porcelain sink. It was like the bathrooms in my dorm except for the lack of counter space. And across from the sinks, a group of urinals lined up in a U-shaped formation. There were only four toilet stalls. At the end of the room two open showers, each with six shower heads, stood bare of curtains or other means of aiding modesty. How icky that boys think nothing of being naked in front of each other. They don't care the least about privacy. And the odd smell—a mixture of Lysol and Old Spice didn't quite mask the hint of urine.

I danced to the first stall making it just in time.

I was washing my hands when a slender, dark-skinned guy stumbled into the room. He stopped short, then grinned. "Well, looky here. Who's fox are you?"

Inspired by the slur in his voice I seized on a plan that might save me. Forcing a confused look, I hiccuped and said, "What ish this place? I was jus' tryin' to go home and I guess I kinda got los'." I forced a giggle for added effect.

He guffawed and said, "Aw, you don't have to pretend with me. If one of my brothers is entertainin' in his room, I'm cool with it. I won't tell."

"It isn't like that. I was in a jam and needed a place to stay," I argued with newly restored sobriety.

"I said I wouldn't tell. 'Specially if your friend don't mind sharing." He lurched toward me.

"Stay away," I warned.

"C'mon woman, don't get uppity now. I just want me a lil taste of white sugar." He grabbed my shoulder.

The reek of alcohol assaulted my nostrils. I couldn't scream and risk waking up the whole dorm. Shutting my eyes, I summoned the courage to act. Quick as a grasshopper, I lifted my bent leg and kneed him in the nuts. Cursing he fell to the floor, clutching his offended privates.

I ran down the hallway to Moe's room and grabbed the doorknob. It wouldn't budge. Stupid me, I had let the door lock behind me when I'd left. I dashed through the door at the end of the hall and slumped onto the first step in the stairwell, gasping for breath. What if that creep came looking for me? I had to find Moe.

The girl's dorms all had television lounges in the basements, maybe this one did too. I crept down three flights of stairs until the steps ended in a small windowless space. I could just make out the words on the dirt smudged door across from me. "Maintenance Employees Only." I tried the door but it was locked, too.

I trudged back up the steps to the main floor, pushed the door open a crack and peeked into the lobby. As far as I could tell there was no one there. Opening the door to get a wider view I noticed a short hallway past the reception desk. A red exit sign hung crookedly at the end. Maybe there was another stairway there. Crouching down to make myself as small as possible, I slipped across the lobby and down the hallway. As I flung open the stairway door, I heard someone.

A woman's voice came from near the front door in the lobby. "Glad you pulled weekend shift with me, Marty. Help doesn't show up half the time. You'd think they didn't need the job."

"Most of 'em don't get up for breakfast anyway," the other one answered.

I slipped onto the landing and pushed against the door with my back. That was close. How early do the cooks get here in the morning?

Their laughter stopped. "Did you hear that?" one of the women asked.

I held my breath and strained my ears to hear if they were approaching my hiding place. Though only a moment, the time passed as slowly as thick glue. Finally, I heard pans clattering in the kitchen and I knew I'd again escaped. But how would Moe and I get out of the building now? If I ever found him.

I crept down the flight of stairs and ended up in a large, low-ceilinged room. The odor of stale cigarettes and burnt popcorn mingled with the distinct smell I recognized from my brothers' bedroom, a male smell of sweat and dirty socks. Past the ping pong table a cluster of overstuffed chairs and couches straggled in front of a television. The test pattern on the screen cast a muted glow. Please let that lump on the sofa be Moses Carter. I stepped closer.

He bolted up from the couch. "What are you doing here? I told you to stay in my room."

"I'm sorry. I had to use the bathroom and the door locked and I didn't know what else to do."

Rousing strains of "Stars and Stripes Forever" blared at us from the TV. In another time, I would have laughed at how ridiculous it all seemed. Moe in his skivvies, me talking about having to pee, both of us trapped in the basement of the men's dormitory, all accompanied by the U S Army Band. But there was no laughter. The music meant it was six o'clock, early enough for some people to be up. A greater chance we might be discovered.

Moe pulled his pants on. I turned away, but I'd already seen far more than I should have. Long dark legs, slender hips, the outline of his, his. I'd seen my brothers prance around in their underwear and even in their all togethers, but seeing Moe like this made my stomach flip flop. It felt almost the same as the time I'd stolen a box of Snicker's bars off the shelf in Woolworth's just to see if I could. The taste of that forbidden fruit had been bitter and, for a long time after, the guilt had been unbearable.

Moe moved to the stairway. "We hafta get out of here."
I followed, afraid to ask what he planned to do.

A cold blast of autumn air hit us as we stepped out the exit door at the top of the stairs. I hugged myself and clenched my teeth to stop them from chattering. The ground was hard and cold beneath my stockinged feet.

"Quick, to the car." Moe's harsh whisper startled me into action.

Shivering, I stood next to the passenger door while he unlocked the driver's side, got in and reached over to pull up the lock.

He started the car. "It'll take a few minutes to warm up," he said as I plopped into the seat. "I'll go get your coat and shoes. Don't get out of the car."

The warning held an ominous threat which I was in no way going to test.

"Wait! I don't think you better go back in there." I told him about the fellow who'd found me in the bathroom. "If he sees you he'll figure it out."

Moe crossed his arms and tilted his head back. He stared at the dome light, his lips pursed in exasperation. I'd have been relieved if he'd called me stupid. I would have agreed with him and hoped he could forgive me because I was careless and dumb. I wanted to confess and pay penance and get back in his good graces if he'd give me a chance.

He put the car in gear and started driving. The silence was killing me. I wanted him to yell at me, let me know how angry he was about this whole mess I'd created. Say something! Anything! Just don't shut me out.

He leaned forward and turned a knob on the dashboard. Lukewarm air wafted over me, but his silence left me cold as sin. We were off campus and all the way downtown before he finally spoke, "Do you have another pair of shoes in your suitcase?"

I'd been worried he was going to dump me in a deserted alley and instead he was worried about my feet. That simple act of kindness humiliated me. So many times I'd felt I was getting what I didn't deserve. I believed people should treat me better. I didn't know receiving kindness I didn't deserve could be painful, too. A shroud of shame fell over me.

Finding my voice, I choked, "My slippers."

Moe stopped the car in front of the diner we'd gone to the first week of school. He reached into the back, lifted my suitcase and put it on the seat between us. "Fish them out and we'll see if the service here has improved.

TEN

We must have been quite a sight—a scrawny blonde girl wearing two sweaters and fuzzy pink slippers, and a tall man with skin like the finely burnished maple of an aged bass fiddle. Rather than looking slovenly, the hint of dark stubble shadowing his cheeks and chin enhanced his manliness. The Ugly Duckling and Prince Charming.

The middle-aged waitress didn't seem to notice my disheveled appearance or his dazzling presence. She slumped over to the booth we'd chosen and muttered, "Coffee?"

I nodded and Moe, turning his cup upright, answered, "Please."

Steam rose as she filled the mugs, bringing a welcoming aroma that promised the warmth and comfort she withheld. The woman pulled two large laminated menus from under her arm, placed them on the table in front of us and walked away. After doctoring his drink, Moe replaced the creamer next to the wall, knowing I liked mine black. We picked up the menus and looked beyond the ketchup stains and syrup goop for something appetizing.

"I guess I left my purse in your room," I said. One more complication he'd have to fix.

"I've got enough for breakfast." His curt answer left me wondering if he meant he had money for his meal or for both of us. I was starved so I chose to think he was offering to pay for mine.

"Thanks," I squeaked.

The waitress returned with water glasses and flatware wrapped in paper napkins. She pulled an order pad from her apron pocket and flipped the pages, placing a slip of carbon paper between them, then stood before us with pencil poised and a bored look on her face. Her indifferent attitude suited me fine. I'd rather be invisible than the center of controversy.

We both ordered the Saturday Morning Special—two eggs, bacon, and toast for $1.25, free refills on coffee included. I looked

114

past the tables through the window at the front of the diner. The sidewalk was empty, the street lights cast long shadows on the building across the way. I glimpsed a brief patch of sky in the distance. The sun's attempt to creep over the horizon lent it a dull gray shade like the patina of unpolished pewter.

"Figuring out what comes next?" Moe asked.

My chin dropped to my chest and I let out a defeated sigh. I wanted to be rescued like Snow White but Moe didn't seem to comprehend what his role should be in my scenario. I hadn't created the dilemma by biting into an apple offered by the Wicked Queen, though my mother fit that description. Rather, it was more like I'd accepted one from a serpent. My downfall was a product of my own free will.

Moe remained silent, unwilling to rescue me from me.

The lethargic waitress plunked plates of food in front of us, shifting the focus away from the unanswered question. She sloshed coffee into our cups and muttered, "Anything else I can getcha?" Without waiting for an answer, she ripped the ticket from the order pad, slapped it onto the table and skedaddled to the kitchen.

I plunged the tines of my fork into the eggs and watched the yolk ooze out. Wiping my toast across the plate to staunch the flow, I wished it was as easy to clean up the mess of my own life. The faint *clink* of his fork against plate signaled Moe had given up staring at me.

The bell over the door jangled. The waitress perked up and dashed, coffee pot in hand, to the table in the middle of the room where three men seated themselves. With the arrival of several more breakfast seekers the room filled with good-natured joshing and laughter. I relaxed, even dared to look up at Moe. He looked up, too, and shrugged. As we ate, we listened to the banter around us and exchanged eye rolls and grins over the convivial chatter.

As soon as we'd cleaned our plates, Moe picked up the bill, reached into his pocket and tossed a quarter on the table. "Guess we better go, there are people waiting to sit."

I didn't want to leave. It was cold out. The sun was barely up. It wasn't even eight o'clock. I'd have to tell Moe my plan. I didn't have a plan.

While he paid the bill, I stood under the heat vent near the cash register absorbing the last bit of warmth before we stepped into the cold, cruel world. The sun had found its way above the lowest buildings promising a nice fall day, but I wasn't convinced of it.

With long strides, Moe moved down the sidewalk in the opposite direction of his parked car. Puzzled, I caught up with him and attempted to match his pace, but had to take a step and a half to his one. Crossing the intersection we followed the sidewalk to the fountain in the center of Mansard Park. The water had been shut off weeks before revealing a shabby concrete bowl half filled with dirt, leaves, gum wrappers, and a lone dime long left behind by a well-wisher. The maples along the park's perimeter had shed their flaming red foliage leaving limbs brown and bare. Likewise, the peeling paper-thin-barked trunks of the birches rose naked branches which had recently lost their brilliant yellow leaves.

We sat on a bench and I closed my eyes to shut out the bleak view. In just two days my life had lost its luster, too, blown away like the leaves. If only Moe would put his arm around me to ward off the cold. But he was distant and distracted. Why was it so hard for us to talk about what had happened, to figure out what to do next?

He stood and his voice came down like a pronouncement from on high, "You should go back home. I'll take you to the bus station."

So, he'd decided to decide since I wouldn't. But it was the wrong solution. "No, I can't. I won't."

"What are you going to do? Make up a lie to explain why you're back early? Not see your father? Not fix things between you and your mother?"

"You don't understand. My mother and I have never gotten along. I can't go back there with my tail between my legs and beg her forgiveness. And she won't let me come back any other way."

"Running away isn't the answer. Don't you want to set things right?"

I stood and kicked at a pile of leaves bunched on the edge of the sidewalk. What could I say to make him understand that I wasn't going back there for a long time? Not until things blew over, until a new crisis blew in to take the place of this one. What else could I do, it was too much for me to face on my own. I wasn't good at placating people and I wasn't good at standing my ground. What's in the middle of those two things other than avoidance?

"When the time is right, we can both go back together. Just not right now." My voice didn't carry quite the finality I'd counted on.

"You want me to go back with you? Melanie, this is between you and your family."

"But it's about you, too. Nobody has the right to say who I can be friends with."

Moe grabbed my arm. "Aren't you doing what you accused me of? Using me to show how liberal-minded and tolerant you are? That you can be friends with a black man and everyone else has to put up with it, because you don't give a damn about how they feel?"

I shook my arm free. "I guess you just don't understand," I mumbled half hoping he'd mistake what I'd said for something profoundly brilliant.

"No, I guess I don't. And you don't seem to understand that my issue isn't about who I choose as friends."

"Just what is your issue?" I blurted, half wanting to get to the bottom of things and half scared to find out who Moses Carter really was.

"It's something bigger. It's every racist who ever called a black person a filthy name, or denied him a job, or made him sit in the back of the bus, or hanged him from a tree, or hauled him off to jail when he'd committed no crime. But you don't understand or you would have done what I asked. You would have called G. W."

The accusation stung. I'd failed to do the only thing he'd ever asked of me.

"I'm sorry. I couldn't. I was afraid." The truth spilled from my heart. "I didn't want you to get into bigger trouble. I just wanted to get both of us out of there. Please don't hate me. I thought you cared about me." The words had flown from my mouth before I could stop them. More followed, equally uncontrolled.

"Don't you see? I don't want to go home. I want to stay here. With you. Because I care. I care about you. I love you."

How had those words, buried so deep in my heart I didn't even know they were there, escaped through my mouth? How would I ever get them back? Did I even want to?

Moe backed away and gaped at me like I'd run away from the local asylum. His words confirmed the opinion, "You're crazy, Melanie. You don't know what you're saying. You can't have those feelings for me. It would never work."

The bite of his words forced me to throw back harsh words of my own. "You accuse me of using you because it's what you're guilty of yourself!" Fists on hips, I jeered, "Look at me, everyone. I've got a nice little white girl as a friend. See, I don't have to take the back seat to anyone. White people like me. But they better not like me too much."

What strange force had invaded my body, taken over my vocal chords, commandeered my tongue? What was I saying?

"You think that?" he shouted.

"Yes!" I shouted in return. "And I was a fool to think you cared about me. It was all an act. Well, the curtain comes down right now. You can forget about me. I've already forgotten about you."

I turned and stomped away. The hard sidewalk drubbed against my feet through my thin slippers. Tears slid down my cheeks. Only two things could create the rage rising in me, love and hate. At that moment, I felt them both.

As I neared the far edge of the park, I slowed so Moe could call after me or run and catch up to enfold me in his arms and beg for forgiveness. He did neither. I turned to take the sidewalk to the left and slid my eyes to the side hoping to catch sight of him and hoping he wouldn't notice I was looking.

He was gone.

Shivering with cold, I trooped on. Soon I was in the rough part of town still two miles from campus. I picked up my pace and hurried past trash-strewn yards—tiny patches of dirt and weeds that bordered unkempt homes. The front porches housed an odd assortment of over-stuffed couches, rusty charcoal grills, flat-tired bicycles, broken bottles, a wash tub, worn out shoes. What's the saying, "One man's junk...?" Did anyone actually think they'd use that stuff someday?

Except for an occasional car slowing so the driver could get a better look at the out-of-place white girl, there was no one about. Sometimes I heard noises drifting from inside those disheveled houses and I pictured the families inside. Little dark-skinned kids in too-small pajamas mesmerized by Saturday morning cartoons while they munched on dry corn flakes straight from the box. A neglected dog scratching at the door. A baby bawling to have its diaper changed. Mom and Dad, still in bed, sleeping off the effects of a hard night of drinking.

I trekked through the neighborhood keeping eyes straight ahead (though tears still blurred them.) An old man standing on his porch stared at me and scratched his groin. I jogged down the sidewalk, stumbling over uneven concrete until I came to a main intersection where I stopped to catch my breath.

The little grocery store on the corner was closed, an iron grate bolted tight against its entrance. Windows across the front were plastered inside with paper signs announcing in big red handwritten letters: *Spare Ribs 29 cents, Pork Feet 10 cents a pound, Spry 3 lb can 89 cents.* Customers must have needed that much grease to fry those ribs and feet.

A more permanent sign of thin plywood warned in big bold letters, *NO CREDIT.* Looking at the locked grate, I wondered what would keep someone from gaining entrance simply by throwing a rock through the window. Credit not needed.

A light came on in the house across from the store and eyes peered at me from behind a torn curtain. I crossed to the opposite corner. A black cat ran out from behind an abandoned service station, scaring me half out of my wits. I rushed past a few more houses and a Baptist church with a neatly trimmed yard. It was where Moe had taken me for the SNCC meeting. Now it looked small, serene, innocent. How could this place of peace and mercy possibly have hosted that raucous, militant group?

I reached the main drag. Traffic zipped past, people headed downtown, women going to the supermarket, men to the hardware, parents toting children to the library. The Saturday morning busyness felt more familiar and comfortable than the neighborhood I'd just left behind. The sun had climbed higher overhead and the temperature had risen to a pleasant fifty degrees or so. A bright crisp fall day—Indian summer. I still pulled my sweaters close and my feet were numb, but I was beginning to thaw.

At last campus was just ahead. Trudging to my dorm, I was determined to get to my room without explaining myself to anyone nosy enough to ask why I was back a day early. I walked across the lobby to the message boxes on the wall next to the reception desk. I could see through the little glass window that my box was empty. I slipped the chain which held my keys from around my neck, opened the box and moved my hand along the sides, bottom and top even though it was foolish to think a memo slip might cling there. Moe hadn't called. Neither had my mother. I was unloved, an orphan.

At the sign-out desk, I found my card where I'd marked that I was going to my parents' for the weekend and expected to return Sunday evening. Checking the wall clock, I wrote in the time-of-return space Saturday, 10:12 a.m. and replaced the card in the box. Did they even check those things? Of course. They monitored us like inmates at Jackson prison.

I plodded up to my room, stumbled over to my bed, and collapsed in a torrent of tears. I was sure the numbness of my feet and the anguish in my heart would forever keep me from rest, but eventually I slipped into a fitful sleep and finally a state of catatonia.

Tap, tap, tap, boom, boom boom, Melanie, Melanie! The banging and shouting forced me out of my stupor. "Leave me alone," I wanted to shout. "She died and went to hell. Go away." I pulled myself up from the bed and trudged to the door. Opening it a crack, I peered into eyes shrouded with impatience. The Residence Assistant snarled at me, "Open the door."

It was her job to provide us with guidance, support and friendship while maintaining order, but the power had gone to her head and she wielded it with disturbing fervor. Miss Dictator insisted on weekly scrutiny of our rooms where she ran her white-gloved finger over the light bulbs in our desk lamps and gave out demerits for undumped waste baskets. A gleeful smirk graced her face whenever she caught one of us committing crimes like using a popcorn popper in our room, leaving drapes open after dark thus enticing boys into a life of hardened window peeping, or (gasp!) forgetting to sign out after seven p m. She loved to watch the demerits pile up so that once the magic number had been reached the scofflaw would be sentenced to a weekend grounded in the dorm. Miss Dictator's only social life consisted of supervising those convicts.

What did she want now? Fear gripped my very soul as I slid the chain from the door guard to let her in.

With her foot, she pushed my suitcase through the door. Dumping my coat, shoes and purse into my arms she announced, "A man dropped these off. House Mother wants you in her apartment right away." She stood before me, arms crossed, toe tapping, as if she intended to deliver me herself to Mrs. Ebert.

Somehow I managed a civil, "Thank you. I'll freshen up and go right down." I gave her a gentle shove.

"No need for you to wait," I said, shutting her out.

Her skirt caught in the door so I had to open it again to release her. When she turned to face me, all she saw was the flat surface of the door an inch from her nose as I again pulled it shut.

Rummaging through my suitcase, I discovered everything was the same as when I'd snapped it closed that morning. I frantically searched my coat pockets and purse and even felt around inside my shoes. Moe hadn't left me a note.

I wanted to sit and cry or break something or call my mother and shout at her for raising me in a town full of bigots. Instead, I changed into my plaid skirt and blue sweater. After I stopped at the bathroom to splash water on my face and comb my hair, I hurried down the stairs and knocked on Mrs. Ebert's door.

I barely knew the housemother. On the first day of my freshman year, she'd welcomed all the residents. Dressed in a trim plum colored suit and sensible shoes she looked more like a grandmother headed to Easter services, minus the hat, than any of our mothers. Sixtyish, widowed and bland faced, she addressed us with a condescending tone, "Your Residence Assistants are here to help you, but should you feel the need for the comfort or counsel of an older woman, I am available. A cup of tea in a homey atmosphere is often all that's needed to relieve homesickness. An encouraging word can alleviate schoolwork jitters. A listening ear frequently leads to solutions to a myriad of problems."

A cup of tea? An encouraging word? A listening ear? My mother never provided any of those. Only the passage of time made me feel better when I was left out. The encouraging words I'd heard growing up were, "Stop crying or I'll give you something to cry about. You made your bed, lie in it. You can do better than this." In our family usually a shouting match worked to clear the air so we could move on. Could Mrs. Ebert really become my substitute mother?

During that first semester, she invited each new girl to tea. Her apartment on the first floor of the dorm was small and smelled of lavender. It was stuffy with more heat than our rooms enjoyed. The mahogany coffee table, matching love seats, silver tea service, dainty bone china cups and bouquets of fresh flowers made it feel like the home of a dowager of a former eastern European duchy. I'd perched on the edge of the love seat, sipping my tea with pinkie finger extended and answered her questions about my background and aspirations. Though she feigned interest, I didn't impress her with my history or my intended future. Within a few minutes, she'd sent me on my way.

A few girls with cultured, wealthy lineages were invited to join her privileged circle. Those who committed egregious violations of school policy were also summoned, though I doubt tea was offered. Since I didn't fall into either category, I'd never been invited by Mrs. Ebert again.

Why now? Nothing had changed in my background and I certainly hadn't achieved any stellar accomplishments in school. Had she found out I'd been in the men's dorm? Was there a network of spies recording every move I made? Had the waitress at the diner ratted me out? Was that grubby old man on the porch an undercover informant? Maybe he'd been adjusting a hidden camera. Could it be that my own mother called to report my transgressions? That's crazy. She'd never tell on me if it meant a black mark on her own reputation.

What did Mrs. Ebert know? And what would it cost me?

The chain slid along the lock on the opposite side of the door, a shiver slid down my spine. Time to face the music. Mrs. Ebert beckoned me in and indicated a chair near her desk. Trying to portray the picture of pure innocence I sat with hands primly folded in my lap. My eyes lowered in a humble gaze and fixated on a tuft of wool snagged from the carpet. She didn't offer me a homey cup of tea. There were no calming words of encouragement. She didn't appear ready to lend a listening ear to assure me I could solve the as yet undefined problem.

Settling into the imposing chair on the opposite side of the desk, the housemother picked up a manila file folder and opened it. My name was penned in neat red letters on the tab. She set the folder down, folded her hands on top of it and looked directly at me. Her owlish eyes widened behind the lenses of her glasses.

"According to the sign-out sheet, you went home late on Thursday evening with plans to return tomorrow evening." The lack of a smile matched her matter-of-fact voice.

I lifted my head and gave a slight nod. When I was going to be out of the dorm after seven p. m. I signed out, listing the time and where I was going, and signed in when I returned. As long as I was back by eleven on week-nights and one on Friday and Saturday there should be no problem. As for overnight sign-outs, I was supposed to give an estimated time of return. But that was it—an estimate. If plans changed and I came back early it shouldn't be a problem. I'd followed the rules. Why was she grilling me?

Her stare bore into me like a drill trying to penetrate hard rock. "It's unusual for someone to leave so late in the evening, and on a Thursday. I see by your schedule you have classes on Friday. Was there a problem?" Her lack of empathy, or her mistrust, kept her from sounding sincere.

I clenched my hands until the nails bit into my palms. The pain served as a reminder that I shouldn't say, "What business is it of yours, you old bat."

Instead, I tried to keep the annoyance out of my voice as I answered, "My father had emergency surgery and I was needed at home to manage his business."

There, bat, aren't you sorry to accuse a poor girl whose father is practically on death's door? A girl who sacrificed her time, to say nothing of imperiling her grade point average, to come to her parents' aid. Without her help, the business would fail, the family would fall into dire destitution and the girl would have to drop out of school permanently. Live out the rest of her years laboring as a charwoman to support them.

"I'm sorry to hear about your father," she said without a glimmer of warmth. "But if you were needed at home, why did you come back this morning?"

I lowered my head like a sad puppy dog in hopes of conjuring at least a drop of sympathy from her. The sad act bought me a few seconds. Why hadn't I come up with a feasible explanation instead of wasting time fretting over Moe? He had a big part in bringing me to this mortifying interview and where was he now? I was on my own.

I swept through my brain to come up with an acceptable answer. Keeping my head down to hide the blush that consistently betrayed my attempts at deception, I said, "I handled an important interview on Friday morning and filled in the rest of the day. My mother knew I have a big paper due on Monday so she insisted I come back. She said since I organized everything so well, she and my brother could manage the business."

I looked up at Mrs. Ebert's expressionless face. Had she bought my story? Should I elaborate? No. I'd learned from years of parrying with my mother that keeping my mouth shut was the most effective defense.

Mrs. Ebert let out a bored sigh which I thought signaled the end of the interrogation. Certainly my explanation was plausible and cast me in a good light. If anything it should have earned me brownie points.

"Who was the young man who brought your suitcase and coat and shoes this afternoon?" It sounded like an offhand, by-the-way, type of question, but her rigid posture and the tight set of her jaw betrayed her accusatory intent. This was the real reason I was hauled up before the seat of judgment.

Refusing to be intimidated, I retorted, "Well, I didn't see who brought my things. The RA delivered them to my door."

Her scowl deepened the creases on the sides of her mouth like a set of parentheses. I immediately retreated. "However, I had left them in the car of the acquaintance who provided me with transportation. I'm sure he, or someone he asked, kindly returned my things."

She picked up her pen and pulled a scratch pad close. "And his name would be?"

I stood up. "As I said, I'm not sure who brought my things. Now I'm sorry, I really must get back to my room and work on my paper."

She gave me the evil eye "Sit down, Melanie. We're not quite finished. Your mother called me this morning. Early this morning."

I plopped into the chair, putting on a blank expression to mask how horrified those words made me feel. When my mother was mad who knew what vindictive retribution she would inflict?

"She called at eight this morning. When you didn't answer the intercom, she refused to leave a message but asked to speak with me instead. She told me you'd left very early and she wanted to know if you'd made it back. I checked. You hadn't signed in." Mrs. Ebert sat back in her chair, folded her arms over her ample bosom, and waited for my response.

I tried to outwait her, but just like in the staring game my friend Pearl and I used to play, I gave in first. "I'm sorry. I forgot to call her when I got back." As if I'd bother letting my mother know anything after the way she'd treated me. Did she tell Mrs. Ebert I had stormed out of the house and who I was with? Did she say we'd left six hours before her call?

With pursed lips and a slight shake of her head, Mrs. Ebert relayed a silent tsk. "She was concerned of course. We must learn to be more considerate." Her buttery voice oozed rancidness.

Concerned? More like steamed as a pressure cooker. But by the tone of her voice and choice of words, my mother could act all sweety-sweety if she didn't want someone to know she was angry. And that someone was just about anyone outside our family. Heaven forbid they would think her life was less than perfect.

"I'm curious," Mrs. Ebert continued with brows pulled together as if trying to reason out an elaborate riddle. "If your mother was sure you'd be back before eight, and you didn't arrive until after ten, how do you account for your time?"

Who did she think she was? Joe Friday? Should I tell her we had a flat tire? Ran out of gas? Spent the night together in his dorm?

I cleared my throat and said, "We stopped for breakfast. My mother is a worrier. I'm sure she thought we left earlier than we actually did. And she doesn't realize how long the drive is." Instead of catching in my throat the way they always had before, the lies slid off my tongue.

Mrs. Ebert stood. She must have figured she wasn't going to get me to crack. "It's unclear which school policies you have violated. I'll take this issue up with dormitory council when they meet Thursday evening. We'll decide whether this should be taken further or handled in-house. For the time being, you are campused. You must remain in the dorm except for attending class or work. You will need special permission for any other activities."

Campused! It was the school's version of grounding except more humiliating because I was twenty years old. And that was just the beginning. What excessive punishment would the dorm council come up with? Miss Dictator would relish the chance to keep me imprisoned until graduation.

I swallowed the bile that has risen to my throat and mumbled, "I have band rehearsal Monday evening."

"I'll put a note in your file that you are excused for rehearsal on Monday night. Now, I suggest you call your mother and apologize for causing her worry."

"Yes, ma'am," I said like a good girl. I knew full well I wouldn't call my mother, but I would figure out how to convince the guys we needed to rehearse every night next week.

I actually did have a paper due on Monday and I tried for the rest of the day and all of Sunday to work on it, but I couldn't concentrate. *Effect of Castro's Policies on U S-Cuban Relations*—why had I chosen a subject so foreign? The only thing I knew about Cuba was that it was Ricky Ricardo's birthplace, and he wasn't even a real person. Why worry about that dot in the ocean?

As I plugged away at the confusing facts, a hurricane roared through my brain. Its mad swirl left my thoughts a wide swath of debris. Moses Carter, my mother, Randy, Muggs and Miller, Moe, Chief Reichenbacher, Moe, Mrs. Ebert, the deputy, Moe, the Dictator, Moe all made their appearance and not one of them was on my side.

Around four o'clock on Sunday, my roommate returned from her visit home. "Hi!" Her voice always sounded like champagne bubbles celebrating a good time. "I didn't think you'd be back this soon. How's your dad?"

A flood of regret surged through me. I hadn't even seen him. "He's better, thanks. I came back a little early because I have a ton of work this week."

"Oh, well don't let me bother you." Diane didn't make a sound as she unpacked her things and put them in their proper places. "Catch you later," she whispered. She left the room in search of more interesting company.

Several hours later she returned carrying a pizza box. "Did you get supper? We had some pizza left. You're welcome to it."

The dorm didn't serve Sunday evening meals and the smell of onions and pepperoni made my empty stomach gurgle. I devoured the leftovers in record time, then headed to the bathroom to get ready for bed. By the time I returned to our room, Diane was already asleep. It was hours before my mind finally shut down enough to let me doze off, too.

On Monday, a nasty rain spit from drab clouds blown in by frigid Canadian wind. I handed in my paper, embarrassed by my lack of scholarly effort and fearful of a failing grade.

Not wanting to face Mrs. Ebert again, I had decided not to ask if returning to the dorm between classes was part of being campused. It was only an hour break so surely I could go to the library to study or even the student union for a snack without reporting in. I followed my usual routine of stopping for coffee after my nine o'clock.

Paper cup in one hand, textbooks in the other, I took my time walking through the crowded room. Our table was empty. I sat down and sipped my coffee. Maybe Moe was running late. After fifteen minutes of sipping, watching every person who walked in and pretending to read the student paper, I couldn't delude myself any longer. He wasn't going to show. He had said he cared for me, but when I declared my love for him he'd called me crazy. He'd ditched me faster than a pianist could play "Flight of the Bumblebee." And he hadn't stopped his flight. As far from me as possible.

I left and wandered around campus, tears and rain wetting my face. During my next class, I was a soggy mess shivering at the back of the room. The professor announced, "Today we'll listen to and discuss Tchaikovsky's overture to Romeo and Juliet. Could someone briefly retell the story, in case anyone here has been living on Mars where I presume they aren't familiar with the fine works of The

Bard?"

Naturally, the fluffy harpist volunteered. She recounted the story with dramatic flair, plucking at our heartstrings as nimbly as she tweaked notes from her instrument. The professor put needle to record and we settled to listen. From the first tones of the violins to the end of the piece, I wallowed deeper in my puddle of misery. Not even the pounding of the kettle drums and clashing of the cymbals at the end could cheer me.

After dinner, I presented Miss Dictator with my pass and escaped the confines of the dormitory. On the way to the music hall, I decided my only hope for happiness was to go back to my original plan of becoming a rock and roll star. I should quit school, hit the road, maybe go to Memphis and see if my old friend, Jerry Lee, would help me find a band in need of a drummer. When I was famous I would forget everyone else.

I walked into the practice room and was confronted by Johnny, Brad, and Marv who were already set up for rehearsal.

"Pick up any gigs?" Johnny demanded, always the first to make me feel like I wasn't holding up my part of the deal.

"No, I've been busy. My dad's in the hospital." The three of them looked at me with as much sympathy as you'd expect from guys, but at least they shut up. I should have used the excuse with my Current Events prof. It might get me a better grade on my paper.

We ran through a few songs. My spirits were so low even the music couldn't lift me. The notes fell flat, Brad's sax reed squawked, the piano was out of tune, and we all needed a shot of inspiration. Stardom wasn't going to fall from the sky. I'd have to work harder on making a name for myself or I'd always be stuck with my miserable life. The little energy I had had drained away and I was ready to call everything quits.

In a valiant effort to draw us into a more optimistic mood, Brad hauled some papers out of his saxophone case. "Here's the sheet music to "Goodbye Cruel World." Too bad we don't have a calliope but you can fake it, Johnny." He handed the sheet music to each of us and we looked it over. The lyrics could have been written by me, only it was a mean, fickle *man* who'd turned my world upside down. My voice choked. "Maybe we ought to each practice this on our own and go over it later." I put on my jacket and left. Being imprisoned in the dorm was not as hard as being held captive by my own thoughts.

The week dragged on, slow and dreary as a funeral dirge. No

matter where I was, despondency shrouded me. I'd lost something I'd never had, which made me want it all the more. Moses Carter, wherefore art thou?

Eventually, Thursday evening came. The dorm council meeting was scheduled for seven p.m. I decided to arrive a few minutes late. The meeting would be underway and I wouldn't have to make small talk with the RAs and Mrs. Ebert. I rapped on the housemother's door and the RA from fourth floor answered. A puzzled look crossed her face as she stepped aside to let me in. Just inside the doorway, I felt everyone staring in judgment. This was going to be one tough jury.

Mrs. Ebert looked up from her chair and said, "Melanie, this is a closed meeting. You are not allowed to attend."

"Oh!" I yelped. "I didn't, I thought, I'm sorry." I backed through the doorway, turned and ran up the three flights to my floor. How could I have been so stupid? Wait! How could they decide my fate without hearing from me? I spent the next hour repeating those questions over and over to myself. Then I was summoned to the housemother's lair.

I stood before her desk, silent, head bowed, like the convicted waiting for sentencing. "The council discussed your case. They determined that you did not break any dorm policy and therefore you will not be punished," Mrs. Ebert said. "However, young lady, I must caution you to use more discretion in the company you keep. One mustn't create even a modicum of speculation about the choices she makes."

She picked up her pen and began writing in my file, a sure signal that the meeting was over.

"Thank you," I murmured. Thank you? I'd already been punished. Five days and nights of being campused, with every girl in the dorm thinking I'd done something wrong. Even in my trance, I'd been aware of the whispering tongues and pointing fingers. Snippets of conversation like "stayed out all night" "*said* she was home" "Negro man."

I returned to my room, free, yet trapped in the clutches of a dilemma of my own making.

ELEVEN

On Saturday morning, intense rays of sunshine glittering through the slats of the window blinds roused me from a dark sleep. I rolled over, forced my eyelids open and checked the alarm clock. It was nearly eleven. After an agonizing week of nights filled with tossing and turning and loopy dreams, this was the first I'd had undisturbed sleep. Why didn't I feel more rested?

I slithered from my bed like a slug, inhaled and stretched trying to replace my weariness with energy. As I opened the blinds, brilliant sunlight filled the room. Ordinarily I would have taken this as an omen forecasting a brighter future, but dispelling my despondency wasn't that simple. Just a week ago, I'd created a bigger than usual rift with my mother and I'd lost someone I'd only just discovered I loved. My reputation in my hometown and at school was in shambles. Things couldn't get much bleaker and I couldn't see how they'd ever get brighter.

At least I had something to take my mind off my troubles. In less than an hour, I was with the pep band in the stands at the football field. Even in my depressed state, I acknowledged it was a perfect day for a game. The sky was a sharp clear blue, the sun warmed the air, the students were out in full force. The cheerleaders jumped and pranced as if their chants and acrobatics were the team's sole source of victory.

At first, as I muddled through the fight song, usual fanfares and pep cheers, I did my best to pretend enthusiasm. But within minutes our team scored two touchdowns, shouts rose from the jubilant spectators and I was caught up in the emotion. I furiously pounded my drums giving an all out performance. Alternating between snare and bass, I beat out riffs that advanced and retreated. I exploded around my drum kit bashing out a barrage of notes. With increasing intensity I performed buzz rolls and rimshots interrupted with the explosive crash of the cymbal. Everyone else in the pep band stopped playing and let me forge on.

When I finally stopped, I clenched my fists tight around my sticks to quell the shaking. My arms ached, my face was burning, and my heart continued to echo the solo I'd just finished. A roar of approval was flung into the air above the student section. And it all came back to me. This, not Moses Carter, not my mother, not the narrow-minded judgments of others, this was my destiny.

Exhilaration carried me through the halftime performance where I rat-a-tat-tatted the snare in perfect cadence and lifted my knees high in precise marching formation. During the second half of the game, my fellow pep banders encouraged me to perform another solo. Or maybe they simply allowed me. I was dazzled by thoughts of stardom and needed no encouragement.

As I walked back to the dorm after the game, the elation hissed out of me like air seeping from a punctured tire. Dreaming about stardom was easy, achieving it was not.

Like a butterfly blown off its migratory course, I'd been trying for years and getting nowhere. And even if I could figure it out, I needed someone to share it with. Someone to talk to about my plans, to help me sort out details, to keep me on the flight pattern. Someone who understood how I felt. I needed Moses Carter.

I went to my room, sat on the bed and gave myself a good talking to. *Get a hold of yourself, Melanie.* Ouch! Those words sounded like they came straight from my mother's mouth. *Wanting that boy is foolish. Being involved with him will only cause grief.* How was it that I was thinking the same things my mother had warned me about?

Banishing her from my head, I started thinking for myself. *Don't let him distract you from important things.*

The door flew open and Diane bounced in. She ricocheted around the room like an eight ball. "Wasn't that a great game? We really drubbed them. Did you see Lonnie catch that pass?" she croaked. "I screamed so much I'm losing my voice." Her caroming finally stopped and she looked at me.

She immediately turned on the sympathy. "Hey, are you okay? Is something wrong?" She sat next to me on the bed. "Is it boyfriend trouble? I noticed you haven't been with your fella at the student union lately. It isn't because of all that stupid talk about last weekend is it?"

I felt myself stiffen next to her. How did she know about that? I hadn't said a word to her. I didn't think she even knew I'd been campused all week.

She patted me on the arm. I pulled away, afraid she was about to hug me. We weren't pals. I didn't want to confide in her. I willed myself to keep from letting the tears spill. I took a deep breath.

"No, it's nothing like that. He and I are just friends. I'm a little upset because the guys in my band are pressuring me to find us some work. We're new this year and I've been pretty busy with classes and I haven't had the time to get our name out there."

I stood up and moved to my desk. "It's no big deal. I'll work it out."

Diane stood and put her arm around my shoulder. Oh no, here was the girlfriend hug I was dreading. Would I be able to hold it together?

Even though her voice was raspy from an afternoon of yelling, it still sounded as soothing as a mother bandaging her child's skinned knee. "I'm sorry."

Then the bubbly champagne voice came back and she squeaked, "What you need is a fun night out! I know I'm just a freshman and you're a junior, but I think you'd have a good time with my friends. We just goof around and have fun and laugh a lot. C'mon we'll cheer you right up."

I definitely wasn't in the mood for giggly. "Thanks, but I'm turning in early. Maybe some other time."

"Okay, if you're sure," she answered. And within minutes, she was out the door. Thankfully.

As the evening wore on, my resolve wore out. I'd done my laundry, taken a shower, dried my hair, ironed my clothes, anything to keep busy. Unfortunately, my hands weren't the only things that weren't idle. My brain cells had taken off on a journey of their own.

It started slow and quiet—almost a whisper. "Melanie, you miss Moe," its mournful score began. I shook my head trying to chase away the notes but the chorus droned its doleful tune like a Mozart Requiem. "Melanie, you miss him." The theme repeated itself, imitated itself, constructing layer upon layer as it moved onward. The unrelenting canon stormed on faster and louder until it ran at a prestissimo pace and boomed a thunderous fortissimo."You miss him. You want him. You need him He misses you. He misses you!"

I clapped my hands over my ears to block the noise. But it was no use. There was only one thing that could calm the commotion.

I fled to the phone booth and ordered the desk girl to call Moe's dorm. Trembling like a guitar string, I waited to hear his voice.

Instead, the desk boy said, "He's not answering. Must be out. Wanna leave a message?"

Of course he wasn't sitting in his room on a Saturday night. Probably on a date. The only music in his ears would be a movie score, something from the jukebox, or a pretty girl's laughter.

"No, no message." I hung up the phone and the cacophony swelled to a deafening pitch, reverberating in my head as if my skull were hollow as a drum.

Grabbing the receiver, I called again, This time I left a message. *Please call Melanie*. What would he think when he read those words on the pink slip? I didn't care, as long as he called.

The raucous performance in my head suddenly stopped.

The next morning the soft *swish, swish, swish* of rustling paper pulled me from my sleep. I sat up, leaned over the edge of the lower bunk and forced my eyes to focus. Diane sat cross-legged on her bed, sheets of notebook paper scattered about her. A leg and one furry ear of her favorite stuffed animal stuck out from beneath the paper as if a freak snow storm had surprised the Teddy Bear Picnic.

"Oh," she gasped. "I'm sorry. I didn't want to wake you. You tossed and turned a lot last night so you're probably still tired."

I yawned and rubbed the sleep from my eyes. Diane's fingers, sticking out from the too-long sleeves of her flannel pjs, riffled through papers she held in her lap. She'd tilted the lampshade to aim the light her way, creating an enormous shadow on the wall. Her giant fuzzy ball of unruly hair reminded me of a huge halo like the nimbus surrounding a Madonna in a Renaissance painting.

"It's okay," I mumbled. "I guess I'll get up now anyway. If I hurry I can make it to nine-thirty Mass." I pulled myself from my bed and searched for something to wear.

"Good!" Diane bubbled, shifting herself over the edge of the bed and letting her feet reach the floor. "I've come up with some ideas for your band. If you're not busy we can get a lot done today."

Had I missed something? When had we decided she was going to help the band? There was no time to figure it out now. Maybe she had some good ideas. Wouldn't hurt to listen.

Before I left, I checked my message box. I'd been in all night so I knew I hadn't missed any calls, but still I'd hoped there had been one while I was down the hall in the bathroom. The box was as empty as a popcorn bag at the end of a double feature.

As I rushed to church I pondered whether or not my state of grace was sufficient enough for me to take communion. Had I created false idols of the two things I wanted most: my music and Moses Carter? And honor your father and mother. I'd really blown that one. I'd let Dad down, didn't take care of the store for him. I hadn't even talked to him since his operation.

And Mom. She was the source of every sin I committed as a child. Every lie, every anger, every disrespect stemmed from our clashes. Once, when we'd stopped at Rexall for her cold cream, she wouldn't buy me a candy bar so I stole a dollar from her purse and bought a whole fistful of Baby Ruths. I gobbled them all before she could find them, and buried the wrappers deep in the wastebasket. I had diarrhea for three days. Hundreds of times I'd confessed to our priest my sins against my mother but God never cared enough to keep me from going right back and doing the same things all over again.

Over the past week, I'd done my share of false witnessing. I'd told lies left and right to save my own hide.

Then there was that business about coveting. Our catechism teacher had always harped about impure thoughts like we were some craven sex-obsessed morons. I suppose some of the boys were, and maybe even Suzie Young, but it hadn't been much of a problem for me.

I felt sweat dampen my armpits and I opened my coat to let the bitter November air cool me. Was the weird feeling I'd experienced when Moe slept in my brother's bed, with just a wall separating us, impure? And what about my disappointment when he'd left me alone in his room? A woozy feeling overcame me as I remembered the wave of desire I'd felt when Moe stood before me dressed only in underwear. When we were in the park and I'd blurted out my feelings was it really love or was it an impetuous, wanton passion?

The bell in the church tower bonged and I hastened through the door. Too late for confession. I slid into a pew and knelt to pray. The church was nearly full, mostly with college kids. Some looked like they were still asleep, their hair and clothes disheveled, their eyes mere slits. A faint beery odor from the boy next to me teased my nostrils. I noticed a girl from Botany class. Her lips were swollen and raw, a bruised hickey decorated her neck like a tacky tattoo. She hadn't even had the decency to cover it with her scarf.

When the time came, I had no qualms about following my fellow parishioners to the communion rail. Their transgressions were undoubtedly graver than mine. Father Mike wouldn't know which of us had done our penance anyway. I'd been attending St. Martin's for over two years, but whenever I shook his clammy, limp hand after Mass he always gave a vacant smile and said, "And what is your name?" Attentive he was not.

When I got back to the dorm, my message box was still barren. I imagined having to fight my way through cobwebs if there was ever a letter or message to retrieve from it.

I walked into our room. Diane leaped from her bed and waved a sheaf of papers in my face. "Wait til you see all my ideas!"

While I took my coat off and hung it up, she continued, "I sketched an idea for posters. It would be neato if we could take a picture of the band and get copies to attach. Or maybe have business cards made up."

I looked at the poster she'd thrust in my hand. Across the top, in bright letters, she'd crayoned *The Gingerbreads*. I winced. She'd left space for a picture and our names and other information.

Diane was good at remembering details, she could repeat entire conversations she'd had with girlfriends, noticed the smallest facts expounded by her teachers, and never forgot anyone's name. It was my fault I hadn't told her anything about the band. She hadn't even gotten the name right. I'd closed myself off from her, ignoring her many overtures toward friendship, and here she was offering to help. How was I going to tell her she had made a mistake about our name without sounding ungrateful?

At the bottom of the poster she'd printed in block letters: For booking information contact Melanie or Diane in Dunbar Dormitory, Room 322. I caught myself before I could accuse her of being presumptuous. If she was willing to handle requests who was I to object?

"I've started a list of places to put posters and people to contact." She snatched the prototype from my hand and replaced it with several sheets of notebook paper. "I'm sure you and the band can think of lots more," she added.

The list was impressive. I doubted I could add to it. Maybe Diane was on to something. The more she chattered, the more I began to believe in the possibilities.

"How about we go to dinner and then we can finish developing these posters," I suggested after a while. We hadn't eaten a meal together since the second week of school when I noticed she had made lots of friends and didn't need me to show her around.

"Cool!" She grabbed her brush and ran it through her hair in a futile attempt to calm the frizz.

In the cafeteria, several of Diane's friends beckoned her to join them. "Oh, thank you." she squealed. "We'd love to sit with you, but Melanie and I are working on a project and we have so much to discuss. I'll catch up with you later. I promise." She oozed sweetness and fun topped off with a brilliant smile. Even set her tray down a couple of times to dispense hugs. I marveled at the ease with which she made everyone feel important and pleased even as she refused their invitations.

Once we were settled at a table on the far end of the room, Diane said, "I've been jabbering about my ideas without giving you a chance to say a thing. Maybe we should start with you telling me everything about the band. I'm embarrassed to say I don't know much and I should have asked you long ago."

I felt the heat rise to my neck and face. She was apologizing but I was the one who'd been standoffish. I mumbled something that was meant to be an apology, but it didn't come out anywhere as smoothly as hers.

"Don't be silly," she said. You're so busy, and I'm just a freshman. Don't feel like you had to include me in everything. I understand."

What a gem this girl was.

By the time we licked the last crumbs of chocolate cake from our forks we were chattering and laughing like best friends. I'd told her all about the band, even how I'd wanted Moe for my saxophone player. I tried to imply I was only interested in his musical talent, but her cocked head and knowing smile made me suspect she knew my feelings ran deeper.

She apologized over and over for calling the band The Gingerbreads instead of The Gingersnaps, especially after I'd told her the tragic story of my friend Ginger in whose honor I'd chosen the name.

"Maybe you could change the name to Ginger. It sounds more grown up, kinda spicy even," she suggested. It was an idea worth considering.

I was surprised to learn Diane knew more about music than the average teen. And she'd sung in her church choir back home. I'd never seen her go to church even though I went to Mass every Sunday.

"I know, I'm a heathen." She crooked her index fingers on either side of her head and wiggled them. Her voice deepened to a sinister tone. "I'm here to take your soul in exchange for rock and roll stardom." She let out a wicked laugh. I cracked up.

At her suggestion, I called Bob, Louie, and Marvin and asked them to meet us for pizza at Bruno's at six. Reluctant at first, the mention of food tipped the scales and they agreed.

Diane and I arrived early at Bruno's but the booths along the walls were already filled with students so we commandeered a table in the center of the room. The yeasty aroma of fresh dough reminded me of my grandmother's homemade bread. The smell of spicy tomato sauce, rich with garlic and onions, made my mouth water. A young waitress wiped the red and white checked oilcloth and brought us Cokes.

Students arrived to pick up takeout orders or cluster around the other tables. Their laughter drowned the sounds from the jukebox in the corner. Several kids stopped to exchange hellos with Diane. "I'd ask you to join us," she said, "but we're expecting some fellows."

After a while, I apologized to her. "Looks like those deadbeats aren't going to show. I'm sorry. Let's order. We can take the pizza back to our room if you want."

She grabbed my hand and stared at me with wide eyes. "I hope nothing happened. Maybe we should go look for them."

I pulled my hand away and slowly shook my head. She always thought the best of people and when they failed to behave well, she refused to believe it was their fault. Something must have gone wrong.

"No. They're just being rude. They weren't all that excited to meet with us in the first place."

"They were probably busy and lost track of time. Let's wait a little longer."

I sighed. "We can give them a few more minutes." I bit my tongue to keep from adding, "and they better have a good explanation."

While I seethed she eyeballed every one of the growing number of students crowding the pizza parlor. She was having a good time. I slumped down in my chair, crossed my arms and watched the fellow behind the counter toss circles of pizza dough in the air. It seemed like half the campus was in that little joint and, other than Diane, I didn't know anyone.

Brad, Louie and Marvin strolled into Bruno's laughing and punching at each other like they had all the time in the world even though they were twenty minutes late. Diane and I hastened to remove our coats and purses from the chairs we'd been saving. We'd suffered muttered remarks and the occasional evil eye from customers who were forced to stand while we'd hoarded the seats. It had gotten to the point I was afraid if we didn't relinquish them soon we'd be forced out by management or rampaging students.

The guys ambled over, turned the chairs around and straddled the seats. Resting their folded arms over the chair backs, they mugged at us like a trio of chimpanzees.

"You're late," I scowled.

"Hi, I'm Diane." My roommate lit up like a birthday candle. "I'm so glad to finally meet you in person. Melanie told me what great musicians you are. I'm so excited to get to know you."

I'd told her no such thing, but the boys swallowed the compliment and puffed up like blowfish. With one sentence in her bubbly voice, Diane had wiped away their reluctance and made three more new friends.

After we ordered pizza and refills of our Cokes, Diane launched into her plans for the band. "I know you're all busy and, of course, your real job is to dazzle the crowd with your playing, but it will take all of us to get your name out there. By the way, what do you think about changing the band's name? To Ginger. Spicy, huh? "

"We always wanted something less girly," Louie said. "You know, like The Imperials or The Commodores, or The Champions or something. Melanie was the one hung up on The Gingersnaps."

Brad and Marvin nodded.

"I understand," Diane said in a hushed, sincere voice like a psychiatrist who had just probed the very depths of Louie's psyche. "But Melanie has good reason to want to honor her friend and someday when she's ready to share the story with the world, people will have even more admiration for the band. And, well, Ginger is a good name. It's spicy, flavorful, peppy. And I like the idea of a one-word name, don't you? I can see it in big letters on a marquee." She raised her hand and swept it across in front of her. "Ginger."

The boys' eyes glazed over and I knew they were imagining themselves on a stage before an audience of screaming fans. I'd had the same vision hundreds of times.

The pizzas arrived, the guys turned their chairs around, and we committed to a new name.

"We'll need loads of posters and flyers," Diane said. "Before you know it, everyone on campus will know about Ginger." She showed the boys the snazzy poster she'd made.

Brad snatched the pizza from his plate and blew at the glitter that had drifted to the table and everything on it. "Did you make this sign? It's pretty good, but what's this space for? He pointed to a large blank spot in the center.

"That's for a picture of the band. You know, an eight by ten glossy."

They pursed their lips and furrowed their brows in skepticism, but she kept right on talking. "I have a friend who's taking photography. He has a really nice camera and I'm sure he'll be glad to take the pictures. Maybe as a class assignment. He might even develop them for us."

Of course she knew someone who had a camera. Someone who would do a favor for her. She knew everyone.

"How many of these are you planning to make?" Marv asked. "Looks like a lot of work,"

"I'm thinking just a few, maybe five, to post in places where they can't be missed. Then we'll have a bunch of handbills printed up." She pushed a sample flyer across the table. "I have a list of places to hand them out. If you have enough money we could give out pictures, too, or maybe have them printed on the flyers."

"Wait!" Louie sputtered. Bits of pepperoni and tomato sauce sprayed from his mouth and landed on my blouse. "You expect us to come up with the money for all the printing and pictures?"

She smiled. "You have to invest in this if you want people to hire you."

They all blurted questions at once, "Where would we get money? How much is this gonna cost? What if it doesn't work and we're out all that dough? Do we hafta do this?"

She let them natter on. When they finally wore down she smiled and said, "It has to be done. I'll get us the best deals I can." Then she cooed, "C'mon fellas, crack open your piggy banks. I'm sure you have a bit of cash stashed away. The money you invest will be a pittance compared to what you're going to make."

As soon as she elicited agreements from them to contribute, she moved on to the next part of her plan. "What do you wear when you perform? Do you have a costume or uniform?"

Brad slapped his thigh. "Hah! That's a good one. Do you think we should wear our marching band uniforms? The spats are especially stylish. I just wear whatever happens to be clean."

The other boys guffawed and admitted the least dirty shirt and pants were what they wore, too.

Diane giggled. "You boys are such goofs. Well, there isn't time to put together a wardrobe, so tell me what you already have."

She persuaded them to tell her about all their clothes, what their mothers thought they should wear, the stuff they felt comfortable in, their biggest fashion blunders. Before long Diane determined they each had a pair of navy blue slacks and a gray crewneck sweater. No one had asked about my clothes. Did they think I should wear slacks and a sweater, too, or maybe just whatever was cleanest?

Diane turned to me. "This is perfect. You have that cute gray skirt and the navy crewneck your Mom gave you last Christmas. That'll look really sharp. The guys with navy pants and gray sweaters, and you with a gray skirt and navy sweater. Cool."

Now that we had a new name and a coordinated look, we were a real band. Diane offered to check into the pictures and handbills, the boys agreed to crack open their piggy banks and I volunteered to type up her list of people to give flyers. We left Bruno's on a high note.

A jillion stars twinkled and winked in the cloudless sky above, more dazzling than the glitter on Diane's posters. I laughed.

"What?" Diane asked.

"Nothing." I linked my arm through hers. "It's been awhile since I've felt this good."

Arm in arm, we walked back to the dorm in silence, keeping words from interrupting the mood.

As we entered the lobby I asked, "Would you sign me in?"

I unlocked my mailbox and ran my hand around the inside. It was devoid even of dust.

Later, in pajamas and robe, I toddled down the hall to the phone booths. Whispering into the phone, I asked the desk girl for Moe's dormitory. The desk boy there answered with a voice so loud I had to hold the receiver away from my, ear hoping no one would overhear. Pulling the phone back to my ear I whispered, "Moses Carter, please."

A few heartpounding moments later the desk boy shouted,

"Moses Carter isn't answering. Want to leave a message?"

Dictator RA was lurking nearby and stared down her nose at me. Had she heard? Would she rat me out to Mrs. Ebert? She was probably waiting to trap me so I'd be grounded again. I spoke into the phone with such confidence she couldn't possibly think I was making a call I shouldn't. "Yes, please leave a message to call Melanie. Thank you." I hung up before the desk boy could boom an implicating response.

The next morning, I stayed after Botany to pick up the extra credit paper my prof had accepted in place of the test I'd missed. To my relief and surprise, he'd given me a B minus. It was probably better than I would have done on the test. I'd worked really hard on it, but my mind had been in such turmoil I wasn't sure if what I'd handed in was gibberish or a brilliant report. Neither, but good enough.

I dashed through the front doors of the student union and wended my way through the mass of tables looking like someone on an important mission—as long as no one noticed my eyes darting all over the place. Once again the search was fruitless. No sign of Moe. I left through the side door and kicked at a stone on the sidewalk. How would we ever resolve things if we didn't see each other? Crossing the street, I headed toward the library.

A tall man in a tan jacket walked out of the business building a few feet ahead of me. It was him. At least, it looked like him. Same broad shoulders, same long strides. He wasn't wearing a hat and I could see the hair wasn't quite right. Instead of the meticulous close cut, it was too long, frizzy, mussed looking. Maybe it was Moe. Maybe he hadn't had time for a haircut. Maybe he'd let himself go, too distraught about what had happened between us to care. His head turned slightly and I knew by the profile it was him.

"Moe!" I called. "Moses Carter!"

He rushed on, not turning to look. Stunned, I hesitated and watched as he fled from me. I couldn't let him get away.

"Wait!" I shouted, running to catch up.

He ran into Morgan Hall, a men's dormitory. I followed into the lobby but he had already gone through the doors to the stairwell. Females weren't allowed beyond the lobby. I turned and left, tears blurring my vision. I wasn't sure if the rejection had created anguish or anger. All I knew is that it hurt more than anything I'd felt before.

I don't remember how I made it through my next class and back to the dorm. Like the bad habit of a heroin addict, I succumbed to the craving and plodded over to the mailboxes. A slim paper leaned against the inside of my box. In an instant my shattered heart reassembled itself. Maybe Moe hadn't heard me. Maybe it had been my imagination that he was running away. With hands trembling like an old man's, I turned the key and reached in.

Clutching the letter from my mother with one hand, I splayed the other across my chest to keep my heart from bursting again.

I ran up to my room and sank onto the bed. Might as well read it now. Whatever she had to say couldn't cause me any more hurt than I already felt.

Melanie,

Len and Colleen are having Thanksgiving dinner this year. Do you have money for bus fare? If you don't, call and I'll pay for your ticket here.

Don't get any crazy ideas about inviting someone to come home with you. It only leads to trouble.

I received a money order—forty dollars—from Moses Carter. We are done with him and can put it all behind us. You should too if you haven't already.

I'll expect you on the 4:15 bus. Come to the store when you get here.

Mom

I crumpled the heartfelt epistle and tossed it into the wastebasket. The cold war between us had resumed. Thank goodness my uncle and aunt were hosting the holiday dinner. At least we'd spend one day in neutral territory.

In the cafeteria, while picking at my lunch, I tried to decide if the pleasure I'd derive from scamming my mother out of three dollars bus fare outweighed the annoyance of talking to her on the phone. Figuring I might as well get a little of Moe's money from her—it might be the only thing I'd ever get that was his—I called.

"Hello?" Dad's voice echoed through the phone. It bugged Mom that he never answered, "Al's Television and Appliance."

I smiled. Talking to him would be no problem. The operator asked him to accept the charges, then connected us.

"Hi, Dad! I only have a minute. Mom asked me to call if I needed bus money for Wednesday. I'm a little short."

"Oh sweetie, don't put yourself down like that. Five-six is actually tall for a girl." He guffawed into the phone and I laughed even though he'd used that silly joke on me a dozen times before.

"Your ma just ran home to put a roast in for supper. Sorry you missed her."

"It's okay. I'm glad I got you. How are you feeling?" A wave of guilt washed over me. I hadn't talked to him since before his operation.

"I'm doin' good. How 'bout you? That was quite a ruckus you and Randy and your friend got into. You'll have to tell me your side of the story when you're home. I suspect your ma exaggerated some like only she can."

I wanted to forget the whole incident like it was ancient history, but I was glad he wanted the true facts. "Okay, tell Mom to pay for my ticket—I'll be on the 4:15 bus Wednesday. See you then."

"I'm looking forward to it more than the pumpkin pie!" What a declaration of love from my father who could, and often did, down a half a pie in one sitting.

When I got back to my room, my gray skirt, white blouse and navy sweater were laid out on the bed along with a note. *Ginger photo session in room 112 arts building. Marv will be here at 3:30 to help you carry your drums. Bring your makeup!*

Diane could get more things done in less time than anyone I knew. Already she was off and running on to something else. I packed my drum kit and changed my clothes. Bring makeup? All I had was two tubes of lipstick, an eyebrow pencil and a bottle of half dried up nail polish. Who did she think I was? Marilyn Monroe?

As Marv and I struggled down the sidewalk with my drums I grumbled, "What a pain,"

Marv laughed. "You think we've got it bad, think of poor Johnny pushing a piano over here."

"She wouldn't make him do that, would she?" Picturing Johnny trying to get a piano down the lumpy sidewalks cracked me up. My drums seemed lighter and so did my mood.

Diane ran up behind us just as we reached the arts building. "Good! We have plenty of time to fix your hair and makeup."

She held the door while Marv and I wrestled our instruments through.

As soon as I set my snare down in room 112, Diane grabbed my arm and spun me around. "Sit there and I'll see what I can do with your hair. Did you bring bobby pins?"

I plopped down in the chair and rummaged through my purse

retrieving a few stray pins.

Diane started fussing, brushing my hair this way and that like she was trying to tame the fur on a wild cat. What made her think she could make my mop look better when she couldn't fix the bird's nest on the top of her own head? She brushed and sighed and pinned, then sprayed a half can of AquaNet to glue everything in place. Finally, she pulled a mirror from her small train case which contained an impressive array of potions and lotions and other girly stuff. I gazed at my reflection, amazed that the new hairdo framed my face in soft waves making me look a little like Sandra Dee.

"Now for some makeup," Diane exclaimed. "What did you bring?"

"I don't wear that stuff," I answered. I tried to stand, but Diane pushed me back onto the chair.

"You'll look all washed out in the pictures without makeup. We're not the same coloring, but I think I can make something work." She rifled through her case pulling out bottles and compacts and tubes and examining their contents. She slathered flesh-toned goo over my face and stepped back to appraise her artistry.

"Your brows could use a good plucking, but we don't have time." Using a tiny brush she smoothed the hairs into place, then penciled my eyebrows into arches.

The longer she worked on me, applying eye shadow, mascara, blush, lip liner and lipstick, the more nauseated I became. At first, I thought it was from the smell of all those concoctions, but then I realized the awful feeling was the memory of my mother and all the pretty baby contests she'd forced me to enter. She didn't make up my face, of course, just a little light color on my lips and a pinch of my cheeks to make them rosy, but the contestants in the teen portions of the pageants painted their faces in gaudy parodies of movie starlets. I hated the smell and the look, but mostly I hated the feeling that I would never be pretty enough to please my mother.

Diane thrust the mirror at me again. It was a lot of makeup for me, but she'd used lighter colors that looked more natural than painted. Johnny and Brad and the photographer had arrived by then and, along with Marv, confirmed that I looked good.

Diane's friend, Frank, set up a tripod for his camera and sent the boys down the hall to fetch a piano from the props department. I wondered if they had a set of drums. Diane pulled a giant letter *G*, covered in an inch of sparkly glitter, from her book bag. She attached circles of scotch tape to the back and stuck the cardboard monogram in the middle of my bass drum without even asking.

"Hey! You'll get glue on my drum!" I reached over to pull off the offending initial before it could damage my precious instrument.

"It'll be fine," Diane argued. "You've got to have a logo so everyone recognizes the band and thinks of you whenever they see that *G.*

Frank interrupted, ordering us to take our places. Diane shoved a stool behind my drum kit and I sat, outshone by the garish letter.

As the photo shoot progressed my roommate rearranged us, positioned our bodies and our instruments, straightened our collars, ordered up smiles and gave her opinion on every pose. When she was finally satisfied we'd done all we could, Frank promised to have the proofs by the following Monday.

"I'll be using some of the photographs for my term project so I need your permission. Here are the release forms." He handed us each a half sheet of paper and we signed our names, not sure what we were agreeing to.

Diane asked Frank to drive us to the dorm. I was glad I wouldn't have to tote my drum kit all the way back. Marv was relieved, too. Looking at Frank, I could tell he wasn't that hot on the idea, but he agreed. Diane had that effect on people.

Later that evening she told me she'd thought of several more places for our posters. "I hope those 8 x ten glossies turn out and Frank doesn't charge too much. We'll need at least ten. I guess I'll be spending all of Thanksgiving break doing the artwork."

"My sister is a really good artist and she loves making posters. She could do some of them for us." It was a brilliant idea, the perfect way to lighten Diane's workload and thrill my sister with a serious project. Maybe I'd even pay her a little.

"No, I know exactly how these should be done. They have to look professional."

I looked at Diane's prototype. Crayons and glitter didn't spell professional to me. Darlene did just as good a job. But the finality in Diane's voice told me if there was an argument I'd lose.

TWELVE

I settled back in the seat of the Trailways bus and stared out the window. The sun appeared overhead like a hazy disk trying to cast its light through the bloated clouds. The sky's ominous mood matched my own. Snow seemed a likely probability for Thanksgiving. Over the river and through the woods...

The thrum of the bus tires on pavement droned Moe Moe Moe. With a great show of willpower, I'd resisted calling him again. Asking for a ride to the bus station seemed like such a plausible excuse. Instead, grappling with my suitcase and book bag, I'd walked to the opposite side of campus, stood shivering in the cold and taken the city bus to the terminal downtown. Mom would be so pleased.

At 4:15 the hiss of air brakes announced the arrival in Middleton. I plodded down the sidewalk to Al's Television and Appliance Sales and Service. Long ago, I'd lobbied for a shorter name but Dad was proud that his shop had grown from Al's Radio Repair to a real business. Everyone called it Al's or the TV store so the moniker was only a problem for Darlene who had to spell it out on the posters she made.

I pulled open the door and the bell overhead jangled. Mom looked up from the counter, gave a slight wave and returned to her accounting ledger. Dad rushed forward calling, "There she is!"

I grabbed him and gave a bear hug. Then remembering his gall bladder operation, I released my grip. "Oh, I didn't hurt you, did I? Are you okay?"

He chuckled. "Little slice 'em and dice 'em can't keep me down. Wanna see my scar?" He tugged his shirt up and displayed the nasty red incision railroad tracking across his belly.

"Gross!" I squealed. It was just the reaction he'd wanted.

Stepping from behind the counter, Mom scolded, "For Pete's sake, Al, pull your shirt down. You two are such clowns." She was laughing. Dad wiggled his ears bringing both Mom and me to a fit of warm giggles that thawed the frosty feeling between us.

Later that evening, after Darlene and I had finished supper dishes and Mom was busy making a lime jello salad, I wandered down to Dad's workshop in the basement. He was tinkering with an old radio. He liked fixing up the models that had tubes. Called his projects a "busman's holiday."

I sidled up to him and whispered, "I suppose Mom told you all sorts of dreadful things about what happened when I brought Moses Carter home."

He set down his screwdriver and grinned at me. "She gave me an earful alright. Told me every last detail, plus a whole lot more. I pretty much deciphered what really happened, though it ain't easy to sort out when she's on her high horse. Anyway, I figured it was a whole lot of fussing about nothing."

"Frog farts," I giggled. It was our code for something insignificant that someone (usually Mom) made into a big deal.

"She was pretty upset for a while on accounta what people were saying about you. But they've moved on to other business. Something about the Congregational minister showing too much interest in the organ player."

That sounded like an interesting story, but I knew Dad wouldn't have any of the dirt. It probably wasn't even about a minister or an organist. The gossip could have been provoked by anything from someone's 'female problems' to the disgrace of a woman donating a store-bought cake to a bake sale. Mom would probably fill me in on the juicy details later.

"But the part that gets my goat is the way old Reichenbacher extorted money from Randy and your friend. I was about to go down there and clean his clock, but your ma warned me against it. Said I'd probably end up in jail or back in the hospital."

"I'm sorry about all the trouble. Why do people have to be so hateful?"

Dad draped his arm over my shoulder. "I don't know, little girl. Guess it makes them feel like they're better than somebody else."

"But they aren't. Moses Carter is a good man. Way nicer than most people in this town."

"I'm sure he is. You wouldn't be friends with him otherwise. But, you need to be careful, Melanie. I'm with your ma on this. I don't want to see you get hurt."

I pulled away too shocked to speak, then bolted up the basement steps, threw on my coat and ran out the door. Shivering under the cloud-draped sky I fumed over the betrayal by my father. How could he side with her? He knew she thought I could never do anything right. Now he thought I was wrong, too, for caring about Moe. He's prejudiced just like her, or he wouldn't have said what he did. "I don't want to see you get hurt." Well, look again, blind man, I am hurt. Hurt that you don't care about my feelings, just your own.

I hugged myself and put my hands in my armpits to warm them. Mom's silhouette moved back and forth behind the kitchen curtain as she prepared her contribution to Thanksgiving dinner. Worried that the jello salad might not unmold properly, while I stood outside—my whole life a lumpy mess. I hurried down the driveway and onto the sidewalk, my mind racing as fast as my feet.

I'm old enough to figure out whether or not to take a chance with Moe. I'm the one who has to put up with the garbage ignorant people dump on me, on us. What business is it of theirs if he's black, or yellow, or green?

My throat tightened. Would serve them right if I strangled to death right there on the sidewalk.

I sobbed. Daddy, I thought you'd understand. If I love Moe will you stop loving me? Don't you care that I'm not happy without him?

As I stomped down the sidewalk, thoughts of Moe marched along trampling over everything else in my head. It's not like I set out to fall in love with him. But he is the man I've always dreamed of. Mom would love him too if she only gave him a chance. It's not fair!

I know it won't be easy. Just being friends had been hard. Half the time I had to backpedal because I'd blurted something stupid—cooning apples, working like a slave—I'd even referred to one of my professors as master. I didn't even realize I was saying anything wrong until I was with Moe.

Why do I let what other people think bother me? Afraid of being seen with him. Afraid people will talk. Why can't I ask him to meet me at my dorm or go out for pizza or to a movie? I can't even say his name because someone might disapprove. If being his friend is so hard, how can I ever be his girlfriend? Maybe I am in over my head.

My rambling had brought me to the Pet Milk Factory near the railroad tracks. What would happen if I just kept walking? Would anyone care?

I turned around and headed toward home.

The last time I'd been with Moe I love you had spewed from my mouth like stormwater gushing through a downspout. That had been the moment I knew I do love him.

But why had Moe run away? Maybe, like Mom and Dad, he didn't love me either. Trudging up the steps and into the dark kitchen I resisted the urge to shout, "I'm home and I hurt."

The next morning the distant ring of the telephone roused me. I peeked at the alarm clock and groaned. Who was calling at this hour?

Dad's off-key singing "Home on the Range" in the shower filtered through the thin walls. Groggy from lack of sleep, I pulled myself from my bed, wrapped up in a robe and went downstairs.

Mom was in the kitchen arguing with someone on the phone. Stopping outside the doorway, I leaned against the dining room wall to listen.

"Of course she's here—

"My daughter does not lie—

"What do you mean 'in light of her past behavior?'" My mother's voice became angrier, more defensive.

"That was a misunderstanding—

"I don't care if you are the house mother, you are not Melanie's mother. I am!"

Sweat dampened my face even though the room was chilly. Mrs. Ebert had called here? What was she telling my mother? I held my breath and strained to hear.

Mom's voice rose a half-octave. "We don't need your nosy interference. I raised my daughter right and she is perfectly capable of behaving properly. Your job is to help girls who need it. Not to think you are their mother. Keep your big nose out of *my* daughter's business. Or you will regret it."

Then she regained her composure and calmly told Mrs. Ebert off. "No, I'm not threatening you. I'm warning you. If you call here again with your preposterous stories and unfounded accusations, I will report you to the college president."

Bang! The phone receiver hit the cradle. A cup slammed against the countertop and coffee gurgled from the percolator.

I crept through the dining room and tiptoed up the stairs. Mama Bear had protected her cub and eased a little of last night's hurt. Maybe I'd been wrong about my mother.

I crawled back into bed and fell asleep.

"Melanie! Mel! Wake Up!" Darlene's harsh whisper pulled me

from the steep stairway I'd been trying to climb in my sleep. Whenever I got near the top, I'd slipped and slid down the steps frantically grabbing for the handrail. Sometimes I'd caught myself and clung on for dear life. Other times I slid all the way to the bottom. I gathered strength and began the long crawl back up. I didn't know what was at the top, or why I so desperately wanted it, but whenever I got near I lost my footing and tumbled back down.

"Mel! Get up! It snowed last night!" Darlene ran to the window and yanked on the bottom of the shade, sending it rolling upward. It hit the top of the window frame with a sharp snap and my eyes flew open. Blazing sunlight flooded the room.

"Okay, okay," I moaned.

"Hurry up! We have to make snow angels." Darlene pulled her boots from the back of the closet and rummaged for mine.

Within a few minutes, we were flat on our backs in the backyard. The cold snow jolted the last of the sleep from me. We swished our arms and legs back and forth like DaVinci's Vitruvian Man. I turned my head to look at Darlene. She was in ecstasy as if she'd been transformed by the snow into a real angel.

I remembered when I'd taught her to make snow angels. She was about two and a half. The idea came to me after reading her the story of the first Christmas and explaining about angels. We bundled up and I helped her move her arms and legs, then lifted her and we appraised her snow art. Every winter after, we filled the backyard with a host of heavenly angels. She decorated them with halos of stones gleaned from the driveway. I thought she'd give up the tradition, especially now that she'd turned thirteen.

We pulled ourselves up, careful not to disturb our masterpieces any more than needed.

"That has to be the best one yet," I declared over her angel.

She pressed her hands together and bowed her head. "Thank you," she murmured. I wasn't sure if she was thanking me for the compliment or praying over the icon. Either way, I realized my little sister, bratty pest that she could be, was quite angelic herself.

We brushed the snow from each other's backs and went into the house for toast and jam. Mom stood at the kitchen sink, drinking coffee and smoking a cigarette. She pulled the curtain aside and peered into the back yard. "Only two angels this year?"

Darlene mugged at her. "When you've reached perfection, who needs more? Isn't that why I'm your last born child?"

Mom laughed. "Don't eat too much, you know how much food there'll be for dinner."

She was right. Stepping into Aunt Colleen's kitchen at noon, I inhaled the wonderful aroma of roasting turkey and sage stuffing. The slight scent of burnt marshmallows made my mouth water and reminded Gaga to check the candied sweet potatoes.

Even though it was Colleen's kitchen, she deferred to Gaga who briskly directed the final meal preparations with the precision of General Eisenhower conducting the D-Day invasion. Colleen mashed the potatoes, Mom unmolded her jello salad, Gaga made the gravy. Darlene filled water glasses and I supervised the little cousins in setting the table.

"Remember, the spoon and the knife had a fight, they both thought they were RIGHT. The fork got mad and LEFT," I told the children. The little boys brandished the knives like swords to reenact the clash of the silverware.

In the living room Oompa, Dad, Randy, and Uncle Len debated the Lions-Packers game and whether or not the Lions would redeem themselves over the previous year's surprising defeat.

Dad's voice rose and I imagined the red glow of his ears as he argued, "Shoulda never traded away Bobby Lane. Earl Morrall is no wheres near the quarterback." After two years he still hadn't forgiven the Lions for trading his favorite player to the Steelers.

"What we need is some of those black apes like Jim Brown. Big dumb guys who hit hard," Uncle Len suggested. "Those spades can really throw the ball. Their arms are strong from swinging through the trees." He alone guffawed.

My body stiffened. How could Uncle Len talk like that? And what was wrong with Dad and Oompa for letting him get away with it? The hurt my parents wanted to spare me came from right there in my grandparents' living room.

"Dinner," Gaga announced. We gathered and bowed our heads for grace. I glanced across the table at my uncle. I'd often overheard him complain about being discriminated against because he'd lost an arm in the war. How could he make jokes about someone different? Skin color was sometimes a handicap, too.

As Oompa carved the turkey, which weighed more than the littlest cousin, Aunt Colleen asked me about school. I told her about Ginger. Everyone wanted to know more, especially Mom and Dad though they acted like it wasn't the first they'd heard the details. The more I talked, the more I was convinced the band was headed for stardom.

"That's so cool," Darlene said. "You can play at my Junior Prom and everyone will be jealous because you'll be famous by then."

"Yeah," Randy piped in. "Darlene's gonna charge her friends for your autograph and make a killing."

While everyone laughed I wondered if it was over Darlene's money-making scheme or the improbability of my success.

Uncle Len leaned forward and asked, "Got a special fella, Melanie?"

My mother's eyes bore into me. My face grew warm.

Like a big chicken I said, "No, school and the band take up all my time," as if I didn't care one bit about having a love life. My heart kicked my chest and my conscience yelled inside my head, tell him you're in love with a black man. A man who is honest, smart, kind, intelligent, and does not swing from trees.

"She's too young to be involved with anyone," Dad said, even though lots of girls my age were married and already had a baby or two.

Mom interjected, "We're proud of Melanie working so hard to graduate from college. And doing something she enjoys."

She's proud of me? I was always sure she was ashamed of me. I'd never measured up. I made all the wrong choices. I picked all the wrong friends. Her words echoed in my brain, "proud of Melanie, proud." I felt as if Darlene's snow angel had swooped in and flown away with a part of my pain. There was something to be thankful for after all.

The next morning Gaga came to town to take Darlene and me to IGA for baking supplies. Then we picked up the little cousins and went to the farm to make Christmas cookies for her freezer.

At supper, we picked at our macaroni and cheese.

"You spuntiks," Gaga said, calling us the familiar Bohemian nickname. "Too many samples of cookies, too much licking of spoons and bowls. I should have known better than to think you'd want supper."

Later, Darlene and the little cousins and I clamored into the beds in the big upstairs bedroom and I read stories until each had drifted off into a sugar induced coma. I laid awake wondering how Moe celebrated holidays with his family. If we were married would his mother make cookies with her half-white grandchildren? Would mine?

The next day we spent hours elaborately decorating the cutout cookies—stars, bells, Santas, and trees. We saved the gingerbread men and women for last. I spread each figure with frosting then the littlest cousins diligently applied raisin eyes and cinnamon-red-hots buttons. Darlene piped the frosting into swirly hairdos and fancy embroidered clothing. She was so artistic I wished I'd pushed harder to let her make Ginger posters.

Later that evening, Mr. and Mrs. Strahn dropped by. They were good friends of my Aunt Celeste even though they were closer to my grandparents' ages. Years ago, Aunt Celeste told me Michael Strahn had been a priest and Gladys a high school teacher when they fell in love. Eventually, they could not stay apart and they were married. It was quite a scandal and it took a long time for people to forgive them. Even Gaga had judged them.

After Gaga served coffee and pie, Darlene took the cousins upstairs leaving us to visit with the Strahns. An air of tranquility and tenderness surrounded the sweet couple. They seemed like two parts of a whole as if one could not exist without the other.

"You've grown into such a lovely, intelligent young woman," Mr. Stahn said to me. "I'm sure your future will be more than you can imagine." He reached over and placed his hand on his wife's and continued, "Just remember to follow your heart, no matter what obstacles you encounter." His words sounded like a command and a promise.

Long after the Strahns said goodnight and left for home, his words repeated themselves to me, "Follow your heart, no matter what obstacles you encounter."

The next afternoon I hugged everyone goodbye—even Randy. No matter how many troubles we had, we were family. Was I on a path that would take all that away?

As the bus rolled down the highway the thump of its wheels sang, "follow your heart, follow your heart." Dad's words answered, "don't want to see you get hurt, don't want to see you get hurt." What should I do?

When I turned the key to unlock my dorm room, relief spread through me. It would never feel like a home but it was a refuge from the turmoil I'd tried to leave behind. Maybe here I'd find enough peace to sort things out. Maybe time really would heal my wounded heart.

Diane looked up from where she sat on the floor. "Hi," she squealed. "Look at the pictures. Aren't they cool?"

Eight by ten photos were strewn across my bed and a pile of 3½ x5s was stacked on the desk.

I picked up each photo from my bed and scrutinized it. There were four different poses. The pictures were in clear focus, no one's head was cut off, no shadows blocked our faces, we were centered properly, there was a good balance of dark and light; only the subjects were the problem. In one picture, Marv was scratching his nose. In another, Louie's mouth gaped like a door on a broken hinge. And, in every one, even behind my drums I looked fat. The boxy crewneck sweater had to go.

"They look good," I said, afraid that if I complained Diane would arrange another photo session. I doubted the results would be any better.

Diane stuck her tongue out the side of her mouth to aid her concentration as she applied glue to the edges of a photograph and stuck it on a poster. She held it up and smiled. "There! You each owe six dollars. I need the money by tomorrow afternoon."

The following day, the boys groused as we forked over the cash to cover expenses. Diane handed us posters, handbills, and the smaller photos, along with a list of contacts. She issued orders to complete our distribution of advertisements by Wednesday evening.

"Complaining isn't going to get the job done," she chided. "This is the only way people will know about Ginger. If you want to play for some of the Christmas dances, you've got to do this now!"

She scheduled rehearsals for every Monday, Wednesday, and Thursday evening reserving the last half hour to audition for any group interested in hiring us.

Her plan worked. Several people dropped in to hear us play and we were hired for a children's Christmas party put on by the Honorary Accounting Society, and a fraternity dance. One evening Diane threw her arms wide and announced her major coup. "Ta da! We have a date to play during Snow Carnival in February! And I've got a bunch of other gigs in the works."

As I scurried about campus to classes and rehearsals and contacts with potential employers, I occasionally caught sight of Moses Carter. His hair had grown longer, looking a little like Diane's nest, and he no longer wore ear muffs. There were always several other Negro students with him. Necks bent, they trudged down the sidewalk engaged in serious discussion, unlike the other colored fellows who ambled by loose-jointed, finger-snapping, wide-grinned, loud-voiced.

One morning, between classes, I saw him sitting at "our" table in the student union. This was my chance! I'd sit across from him and ask if we could clear the air. I'd tell him I hadn't meant to scare him off. I'd ask how he felt about me. Assure him I wanted nothing more than friendship. There would be time to figure out the rest later.

As I approached the table, voices around me grew quiet. Then I saw her. Marla across from him. In my seat. She leaned over the table, head close to his. Her hand reached forward and rested on his arm. She murmured something only Moe could hear. He smiled.

My heart fell to the soles of my feet, cementing them to the floor. Moe glanced up. A startled look flashed across his face. I turned my head away, pulled my foot up, pivoted, and ran.

How could he? Just like that he'd found a girlfriend. Or maybe he was seeing her all along. Maybe that's why he'd never talked about the SNCC meetings. I felt betrayed. Humiliated. Crushed. I skipped my class and ran back to my room.

"Was your class called?" Diane chirped as soon as I walked in.

Saying yes would've been the easiest way to squelch her curiosity, but the lie stuck in my throat. A great agonizing sob came out instead.

Diane jumped from her bunk and reached for me. "What happened? Are you okay?"

I don't know how she did it, but pretty soon we were sitting together on my bed and I was pouring my heart out. She listened with sympathy, gently asking questions and I told her everything. Every Thing. How we met, how much time we spent together, the disastrous trip to my hometown, the night in his dorm, my declaration of love, how everyone was against us and now Moe was too. "He's already dating Marla, that's how little I mean to him," I wailed.

"Don't worry," she cooed. "I know everything will work out. You just wait." She handed me another tissue then got up and dug through the bottom drawer of her desk. "Here we are." She waved a big Hershey bar at me. "This is what you need right now to make you feel better."

I took a bite but the sugary sweetness made my stomach lurch. I shook my head and handed the candy back to her.

"Wow, you do have it bad," she said. "Chocolate always makes me feel better."

That explained the various candy wrappers I found in the wastebasket most days. I wondered what her disposition would be like if she ran out of treats. Not that she couldn't stand to lose a few pounds.

"I'll be okay. Now I have more time for the band. I've let Moses Carter distract me from my music long enough," It wasn't Diane I was trying to convince. I wanted to believe I could let go of Moe, and music could fill the hole in my life.

She gave me a quick hug. "Good for you. We're going to go far."

A few days later, Diane coerced the boys and me into shopping for new outfits. "You can't make it big looking like a group of kids who wear clothes pulled out of their closets. You have to look like a real band."

"We can't afford this stuff," the boys complained. They dumped everything they'd tried on into our arms and marched out of Montgomery Ward.

"C'mon," Diane ordered. She trounced to the service desk and put over eighty dollars worth of clothing on layaway.

"You know the boys won't buy those sports coats," I warned as we left the store. "And I sure can't afford that dress. It's divine, but I'm broke."

"Don't worry. I'm keeping the money you earn until it's paid for."

"You can't do that. You didn't even ask us."

"If I did everything the way the four of you say it should be done, we'd get nowhere. I've been right so far, haven't I?"

"I suppose," I mumbled.

Diane arranged more dates for Ginger. Sometimes we played for free. She said we needed the exposure and had to take every offer we got until we became well known. When we complained about being broke, she dribbled a little cash our way. None of us knew which jobs had paid and which hadn't. I was the only one who knew she withheld our money.

My heart still felt heavy as lead. I ached to see Moe but I was afraid Marla would be with him. I avoided the student union like it was under quarantine. I even took different routes to some of my classes. What would I do if I saw them together? I imagined tearing her hair out and screaming, "he's mine!" Then he would take me in his arms and swear he'd never cared for her, only went out with her

155

to try to ease the pain of being without me.

For the first time since I'd started college, I looked forward to going home. At least there I wouldn't have continual reminders of Moe. Christmas was a time of peace and love, surely my family would be happy to have me with them. How bad could it be?

The first few days were fine. I helped decorate the tree and wrapped the meager gifts I'd bought. Junior was home on leave. The army had matured him. He didn't pick on us and he spent most of his time with his buddies. Mrs. Costanich asked me to play the bells during the carol sing before Midnight Mass.

It was Mom's turn to host Christmas dinner. She was so glad to have my help she forgot to criticize me. Aunt Celeste and Uncle George and their three boys came all the way from Washington D. C. The aroma of ham and squash and homemade pie wafted through the house.

A dozen of us crowded around the dining room table and five of the cousins sat at the kids' table presided over by Darlene. The adults' nostalgic chatter singing round the table warmed the older folks, but it was the children's giggles dancing across the room that lightened my heart. Through it all, I wondered what chatter and laughter Moe was hearing.

Once the holiday was past and Mom, Darlene and I had put the house back in order, I drooped like the pine tree in our living room. It needed water and I needed something to quench the indescribable thirst afflicting me. We were both fading fast. Maybe my dreams of a future with Moe should be thrown out along with the dead tree.

"Stop that," Mom yelled.

"What? I'm not doing anything," I retorted.

"You're so fidgety. Constantly tapping your foot, thumping your fingers on the table, you're as noisy as a one man band. Get out of the house and burn off some of that restlessness."

I took a walk around the block, hoping the fresh air would bring my brain fresh thoughts. Instead it deepened the numbness.

Inside the kitchen, I pulled off my coat and boots and started for the stairway. Might as well take a nap. I halted in the dining room. Junior and Mom were in the living room.

"What about Roy Calkins? He's a nice boy. Couldn't you have him ask Melanie out for New Year's Eve?" Mom's request sounded like an order.

"Why do I hafta fix her up? Maybe if she wasn't moping around all the time, she could get her own date."

I felt the corners of my eyes grow damp. Was he right? Was I so unpleasant I'd never have a boyfriend? I'd messed up with Moe, the only one I'd ever cared about. I was destined to be alone my whole life!

I sneaked back to the kitchen, slammed the back door and stomped on the floor. I stalked through the dining room calling "Going up to study," and scurried up the stairs.

That evening, Roy Calkins called and invited me to a New Year's Eve party at his cousin's house.

"Thanks for asking, but I already have plans," I said, not making much effort to let him down easy.

He sounded relieved rather than disappointed.

Mom was furious. "Why did you turn him down? What plans do you have? He's a nice boy. You need to start thinking about your future."

Her words stung. All I'd been able to think about was how miserable my future would be.

I spent New Year's Eve babysitting so Pearl and her husband could go out. As I snuggled little Larry in my arms, my heart twinged with pain. I'd never have a little baby of my own. The only children I wanted were Moe's. Maybe my parents and Moe were right. If I had his baby everyone would treat it like a bad mistake. I couldn't bear seeing our children shunned and made fun of. I didn't want to see them get hurt.

The next day we gathered for one last reunion at Gaga's. The house was teeming with relatives. The Strahns were there, too. My head throbbed. I escaped the clamor by retreating to the porch where I watched Darlene and the cousins in the front yard. She was instructing them in the proper technique for making snow angels.

"Just like the putti on the Sistine Chapel," Mr. Strahn commented as he stepped next to me. "Only with a lot more clothing."

I laughed. His sense of humor surprised me more than his sudden appearance.

"Mind if I join you? It was getting a little stuffy in there." He pulled a pipe from his pocket and lit it. I hoped he'd tell me about the Sistine Chapel, but instead he asked "Things going okay?"

Ordinarily I might have taken that as a rhetorical question, like when people ask how are you but they really don't want to hear about your sour stomach or your broken heart. Instead, I said, "Not really. I remember you said follow your heart, but so far that hasn't worked out."

"Too many obstacles? Care to tell me about it? I'm a pretty good listener."

I barely knew the man, so what was the risk if I told him my problems? The only one I'd talked to about Moe was Diane and once I'd spilled everything to her I regretted it. He'd been a priest, he knew to keep things to himself. Desperate to figure things out, I took the risk.

"Okay. Obstacle one: I'm in love but he doesn't love me. Obstacle two: He won't give us a chance. He won't even talk to me. Obstacle three: He's a Negro."

I glanced at Mr. Strahn, expecting to see shock register on his face. His expression hadn't changed. He nodded encouraging me to continue.

"He says things can't work between us. I know most people are racists and we'd have a hard time. My own parents don't want me to see him. Don't want me to get hurt. On top of that, I've always wanted to play drums in a rock and roll band. I still think that could work. Only now I just don't know what I want."

If Mr. Strahn had put his arms around me I would have bawled like a baby. Instead, he said, "I understand. My experience wasn't that different from yours. People condemned me for the choice I made. It's possible you can work things out with your young man, but you have to decide what you're willing to sacrifice because there will be losses. Don't give up your music. But you're at a crossroads now. Will the music be enough?"

I wanted him to tell me what to do. How to make everything work without all this pain. "What should I do? It's too hard," I whimpered.

"Follow your heart."

He tapped the bowl of his pipe against the porch column and ashes flew across the yard, blowing in the wind.

THIRTEEN

In the weeks before final exams, the campus sounded like a junior high orchestra tuning up for its first public performance. Freshman girls, who'd barely conquered their homesickness before Christmas break, whined like violins at having to leave home again. Negligent students, worrying too late about their classes, mourned like bassoons over the impending doom of failing grades. Less serious types, with devil-may-care attitudes, tootled like flutes tossing their notes in the air. The dissonance was deafening.

Like a Tchaikovsky symphony, my mood covered the whole range of emotions. Relieved to be away from home, thrilled with Ginger, worried about finals, despondent over Moe. The underlying theme was exhaustion.

"How about cutting out some of the rehearsals, I need time to study," I complained to Diane.

"We can't change our schedule now. Look at all the people who are coming to hear us audition. We're getting new work all the time." She pulled a bottle out of her desk drawer and handed it to me.

"Here, take a Dexie. It'll give you extra energy."

"Yeah, it gives extra energy all right, but not for me." I handed the bottle back to her. "It might keep me awake, but I'm not good for anything. Makes me feel like I'm gonna jump out of my skin. I'll stick to coffee."

"Okay, but if you change your mind I can get more at the health center. They give this stuff out like candy on Halloween." Diane popped a pill in her mouth. Now she'd be up all night chattering.

I needed a break from her. "You don't have to come to our rehearsals," I told her.

She hadn't missed a single one since she'd become our promoter. Three evenings every week she sat in the classroom and listened. Sometimes she'd applaud or offer other encouragement. Sometimes she'd offer advice like, "That's good, but I think it should be a little faster" or "A little shorter solo for the drums." She suggested songs and told us which ones to eliminate. Often she sat in the corner mouthing the lyrics to our instrumental renditions of pop tunes.

Whenever someone she'd talked to about hiring us appeared, Diane sprang into action, asking what type of event they were hosting and what music they liked. She prompted us to play our best songs and promised we could play whatever they wanted. She'd had us learn a couple polkas, some tunes from the forties and even Hava Nagila in case a Jewish client came knocking. She laid on the charm, lied about our resume', badgered and bargained. And she got us a respectable number of gigs.

At one of our rehearsals, she pulled out several copies of sheet music, purchased no doubt with the earnings she was holding hostage. "This is a dreamy song, very current, and perfect for a slow dance. Everyone's gonna love it," she told us as she handed out the music.

"Elvis! That's great. The chicks really dig him," Brad agreed.

Johnny played the opening bars and the others joined in. I would have been okay, but then Diane stood and sang along. "Are You Lonesome Tonight" had just hit number one and I'd heard it dozens of times. Each time, my heart felt like it was being squeezed and twisted until every drop of feeling had been wrung from me. When I could, I turned off the music or left the room, but sometimes I bawled like a wounded lamb, unable to help myself. Late at night, as I lie in my bed, listening to Diane's arrhythmic snore, I thought of Moe. Yes, Elvis, I am lonesome every night. Of all the songs she could have picked why had Diane chosen this one?

When exams were over, every campus organization sponsored a celebratory event. Some students worried their grades would be disappointing, some knew they had flunked out, but everyone was relieved to have reached semester's end and rushed off to party. Our band had four gigs in three days. We were ecstatic.

Things had barely settled down when fluffy flakes drifted from the sky transforming campus into a giant snow globe. Trays heisted from dormitory cafeterias became makeshift sleds flying down snow-packed slopes. Snowball fights broke out, frequently reaching epic proportions as students banded together to defend their dorms' reputations. Snowmen appeared all over campus. The timing couldn't have been better. It was Snow Carnival Week.

The theme was Carnival of the Decades although most everyone called it Carnival of the Decadent. Competition to create the most impressive snow sculpture inspired brigades of students from every dormitory, sorority and fraternity. I opted out of helping my dorm mates. The decade they'd chosen was the Gay Nineties and I was sure their snow figures of bustled women in fancy hats would topple long before Saturday's judging. Instead, I bundled up and trundled over to the music hall to help sculpt the saxophone, trombone, banjo, drums and musical note for the music society's Roaring Twenties jazz combo.

That week Diane paid the ransom on the clothes she'd laid away at Monkey Wards and surprised the band with new outfits.

The boys griped at me, "She's been holding our money and you didn't tell us. What a couple cheaters. What else are you keeping from us?"

"It was the only way we could afford this. You wouldn't save up the money. Now we look like a real band. She isn't doing anything wrong and from here on out we'll get our pay as soon as it comes in."

I was ready to put the deception and the guilt it invoked behind us. I promised the boys Diane wouldn't do anything like that again. They settled down and admitted they looked sharp in the new clothes. My dress, royal blue with a sequined neckline and twirly skirt, was perfect. I vowed to never wear the bulky crewneck sweater again.

That evening, Diane helped us set up our instruments in the smaller ballroom of the student center. We weren't playing for the formal Snow Carnival Ball, which was for the Greeks, but the Snowball Dance for the independents was almost as special.

Once Diane was sure that we all looked our best with every hair in place and shoes so shiny they reflected the slightest glimmer, and the lights and microphone were adjusted just right, she said, "I'll be back." She left us scratching our heads as she waltzed out the door. This was our biggest gig and she wasn't staying?

"Well, that's a relief," I said. "She hovers over us like a mother hawk. Aren't you all sick of it? We need to tell her to back off."

Marv and Brad laughed. "Go ahead," Marv said. "You tell her and see how much good it does."

Johnny sat at the piano and examined the sheet music as if he'd just discovered a long lost Beethoven sonata. I doubted the bright pink emblazoning his face was from the heat of the spotlights. Did he think Diane was a better manager than I was?

Girls in frilly gowns entered the ballroom arm in arm with young men in rented tuxedos. The cummerbunds matched the color of their dates' dresses. Like pack hunters, the fellows stalked toward the refreshment table to snare paper cups brimming with punch. Meanwhile, the co-eds gathered to admire or envy each other's' attire and hairstyles. A stodgy professor of anthropology called for quiet and dug into a long welcome. Finally he wore down and nodded to us.

Johnny struck the opening chords of "Let It Snow!" and couples drifted to the dance floor.

Near the end of our set, the floor was packed with bodies gyrating to "The Twist." I finished my drum solo and looked up expecting to see admiration on every face. Instead, I spotted Diane moving along the outside of the crowd toward our stage. Stunned, I dropped the beat.

She wore a tight red dress and must have had on industrial strength foundation garments because instead of looking chubby she looked voluptuous. Her waist appeared slim over ample hips swaying sensuously as she walked toward us on stiletto heels. Above her gown's plunging neckline, her breasts were like two sand dunes rising from the Red Sea. She'd used everything from her makeup case to turn her face into a work of art. Lipstick, vibrant red as her dress, painted her lips into a kissable pout. Her skin tone was powdered smooth. Pink colored her cheeks a contradictory blush of innocence. Eyelids were coated in slate gray shadow. Thick mascara caked her lashes; she could have used them for paintbrushes. She had somehow tamed the bird's nest on her head into a tight French twist secured in place with a rhinestone barrette.

She stepped onto the platform, wobbling to keep her balance. We played the last downbeat and stared at her. Everyone on the dance floor stared, too. She pulled the microphone from its stand and cooed into it.

"We're going to take a break in just a few minutes, but first, Ginger has a special song for you."

She nodded to Johnny. He played the intro while Brad, Marv, and I looked on, frozen with shock. His finger glided across the keys, as he played the intro again. I picked up my sticks and set the beat. Marv and Brad joined in.

Diane began to sing, "Are You Lonesome Tonight?"

For the first time, the song didn't yank longing for Moe from my heart. While I tapped my foot on the bass drum's pedal I imagined pounding the tempo with my fists in Diane's face. I wanted to cram my drumsticks down her throat until she spewed blood all over that shameful red dress. Who did she think she was? Strutting on our stage like she was part of our band. And how dare her sing that song? No one should sing Elvis, especially a chick with a wimpy voice. Why hadn't the crowd booed her off the stage? How did she rope Johnny into helping her? Conniving bitch!

Diane warbled the last "tonight" probably thinking the waver in her voice was sexy instead of off key. She bowed deeply giving everyone a good look at the fleshy mounds protruding over the top of her dress. The crowd offered a smattering of lukewarm applause. A couple guys whistled. The date of one admirer punched his arm.

Diane sighed breathily into the mic, "Thank you. We'll be back after a ten-minute break."

As she strutted through the audience acting as if she didn't notice the leering, a big shot senior called to her, "Nice singing, Ginger."

That did it! I vaulted off my stool and rushed after her. My momentum was so forceful that as she pushed through the restroom door I smacked right into her back.

"Oh," she gasped.

I shoved her as hard as I could into the nearest stall. Trembling, I latched the lock and turned. We faced each other, crammed between the toilet and the metal door.

"Let me out!" She tried to lift her arms, but I pinned them to her sides with strength I didn't know I had.

"You're not getting away with this," I snarled. "No one said you could be our singer. Do you think this slutty dress is enough to keep the crowd entertained? Because your voice sure isn't!"

"I was just trying to help," she whimpered. "I wanted to surprise you. I thought you'd be happy."

"Happy? You made us look like fools. And then, and then..." I felt hot tears sting my eyes. "You wanted everyone to think you're Ginger. I'm sorry I ever told you about her. She sang like an angel, but you, you're the devil!"

I let go of her wrist and pulled her hair from its carefully styled twist. The rhinestone barrette skittered through the air and plunged into the toilet.

"Stop!" Diane screamed. "Help!"

Someone knocked on the other side of the door. "What's going on in there? Are you okay? Somebody, go get help."

I grabbed Diane by the shoulders. Her face had turned red as her dress, her lips trembled and sweat rimmed the hairline of her forehead. I relished the look. I had taken control and it scared her. Just to be sure she got the message, I said, "I don't want you coming anywhere near my band ever again. Got that straight?"

I unlatched the door, shoving it against the girl on the other side, then rushed out of the restroom leaving disheveled Diane to the crowd of meddlesome co-eds. I didn't care what explanation she gave them. Let them think what they will. I was done with her.

I fled to the stairwell at the far end of the building and slumped on the top step. Anger overwhelmed the hurt. I pounded my fists against the floor, a poor substitute for the evil Diane and her accomplice, Johnny. At least I didn't cry.

Gulping deep breaths and exhaling slowly, I calmed myself. There was no way Diane would interfere again. I'd deal with Johnny later. People had paid for tickets and dressed in their best. It was time to give them music.

Diane didn't reappear and, to my relief, no one mentioned her. After the crowd had left and the band had packed up their instruments, I couldn't stall any longer.

"Before we go," I said, "we have to clear something up."

Brad and Marv exchanged nervous glances. Johnny plopped down on the piano bench. His eyebrows drew together creating furrows in the flesh.

"I should have figured out what Diane was planning," I started.

"I didn't know, either," Brad said.

Marv nodded.

I continued, "She took over, all the while acting like she was helping us, but she went too far. She won't bother us anymore. I told her to butt out."

Johnny drew in a sharp breath. My head snapped in his direction. He didn't return my stare.

"It was pretty obvious you were in on her little stunt," I accused.

Brad and Marv both snorted. Idiots. Thinking the betrayal was something to laugh about. I'd intended to ask them whether or not we should oust Johnny, too, but obviously, they didn't think it was such a big deal. Besides, we had quite a few dates lined up. He was in all those pictures of Ginger. Breaking in a new piano player would be no easy task. Keeping Johnny was the only way.

Still, I wanted to see him squirm. I'd been a fool to let Diane weasel her way in, and I'd make sure no one took over my band again.

"From now on," I said, "I'm the only leader. No one does anything without my okay. Especially you, Johnny. I don't know why you let Diane make the band look like fools. Or how she talked you into keeping it from the rest of us. But if you screw up again, you're out."

Johnny squirmed and lowered his head. His hand shielded his eyes to deflect the sharp shards of accusation my stare cast at him.

"Sorry." He mumbled so quietly we could barely make out the apology—or was it regret that he'd been caught?

Marv and Brad giggled like little girls. I turned and scowled. "What's so funny?"

Restoring sober looks, they muttered, "sorry, nothing."

I pulled on my coat. "We'll keep the same rehearsal schedule. Bring all your sheet music so we can plan our sets for the Tri Sig's Valentine's Dance."

I walked out into the cold starlit night, glad to be alone for the short trek to my dorm. Would Diane be there? Would she attack me or try to wheedle her way back into my good graces? I wasn't falling into that trap again. Not even going to worry about it. I said I was done with her, and I was. The band would go on without her. We'd be an even bigger success. We already had dates for the Kappa Phi tea and two Valentine's dances. One song we wouldn't be playing was "Are you Lonesome Tonight?"

Had a year passed since I'd met Moe at a Valentine's dance? Clarity suddenly engulfed me. I meant it when I said I was done with Diane and just as surely I meant it when I said "I love you" to Moe.

In some ways, it seemed like we'd shared only a brief moment, but still it felt like I'd known him my entire life, maybe even in a past life. Maybe we had been lovers or an old married couple with a dozen children. Maybe we'd lived in another country, another century. Maybe we'd shared several past lives. Maybe he'd been white.

"Melanie," Brad called from behind, interrupting my fantasy.

He rushed to catch up. "I'm sorry about what happened tonight. Diane's a real pain in the ass. Good riddance. Marv and I didn't know what she and Johnny were cooking up, but, well, I guess we shoulda suspected. She's been putting out for him a while now."

"What? Diane's been? What are you saying? They had sex?"

"Yeah. You know how she is. She'll do whatever she needs to if she's after something. "

"Do you think Johnny likes her? Will he quit Ginger?"

"Nah. I'm sure he liked the hanky panky, but he was using her just like she used him."

"Thanks for telling me. I shouldn't have let her take over the band like that. We're better off without her. Let's just move on."

I thanked Brad for walking me back to the dorm and trudged up the steps to the third floor.

I let myself into our room, afraid of what would happen if Diane was there. Her red dress lie in a crumpled heap on the floor, her stilettos carelessly flung alongside. I undressed and flopped onto my bed and immediately fell asleep. In the morning, I was surprised to see Diane sleeping in the top bunk like an innocent child.

She was gone when I got back from Sunday Mass and after that stayed away most of the time. When we both happened to be in our room we didn't speak. I pretended she didn't exist and hoped she felt as awkward as I did.

The band didn't mention her again. I was used to acting like nothing had happened. I'd grown up that way. In my family once the yelling was over, even if nothing had been resolved and feelings were still raw, we just didn't talk about it anymore. Eventually, the problem was forgotten, or at least buried in some deep part of our hearts. It would be the same with the band, but I vowed it would never be that way with Diane. I'd never trust her again.

I asked the boys to track down all the posters and flyers we'd stuck around campus and black out her name. If anyone contacted her, I had no idea what she told them. One evening a couple sorority girls came by to see about hiring us. I didn't ask who had given them our rehearsal schedule.

The cold war between Diane and me was as intense as the relationship between Kennedy and Khrushchev. Whenever I slipped and thought about her I named her Nikita or Fidel or even Adolph Hitler. Traitor! There were times I wanted to break the silence, to throw it in her face that the band was getting gigs without her help. We'd even raised our price and still people wanted us. But an entire month passed without a word spoken between us.

On the first Wednesday of March, I had just returned from lunch when the intercom buzzed and the desk girl told me I had a call on third floor. I rushed to the phone booth hoping it was confirmation of another job.

"This is Melanie," I spoke into the phone attempting to sound professional.

"Melanie. It's Moses Carter. We need to talk."

I clutched the phone with one hand and my heart with the other. I hadn't spoken to Moses Carter since the day I'd run away from him in the park. Every day of those nineteen weeks I had thought about him, devastated over losing the man I loved. Every day I tried to figure out how to win him back. I'd imagined this moment hundreds of times. I'd rehearsed what I would say, but now my brain was as empty as church on Tuesday.

"Uhk," I croaked.

"I'll pick you up in fifteen minutes." *Thunk!* He slammed the receiver into its cradle.

Legs twitching with excitement and fear, I wobbled back to my room. My brain was suddenly populated with so many thoughts I had to shake my head to think straight. With all the twitching and shaking I must have looked like a real spaz.

Why had it taken him so long to call? Maybe he felt the same way I did and figured it was useless to resist. Finally, he was ready to admit he loved me.

I changed into my blue sweater, the one that brought out the color of my eyes, and my plaid skirt. I wished the snow was gone so I could wear my Capezios. I gazed down at the fur-lined numbers on my big feet. Maybe if I made my hair and face more attractive he wouldn't notice the clunky boots. My hair, as usual, was a disaster so I tied it back into a ponytail and pulled a few strands out to frame my face with tendrils. Unfortunately, they came out scraggly rather than wispy.

After making sure our door was locked, I lugged Diane's makeup case from her closet and grabbed several lipsticks. Streaking samples across the back of my hand, I chose Stormy Pink. I carefully applied the color then practiced a coy, pouty look in the mirror. Pawing through her eye shadow collection I decided to pass, figuring I'd end up looking like a raccoon. Carefully replacing the lipstick tubes in the exact spots I'd found them, I worried Diane would notice I'd used her stuff. I'd deny it, of course, and accuse her of accusing me just so she could get me talking again.

Pulling on my good wool coat and the leather gloves Gaga had given me for Christmas I stepped out to face my destiny.

Moe's car was idling in front of the dorm. I waved. He leaned across the front seat and opened the passenger side door.

"Hi," I said trying to sound perky. I slid into the seat and turned toward him. He stared straight ahead as he put the car in gear and pulled away from the curb. If he was trying to appear impassive, the slight twitch of his jaw betrayed him. Still, I couldn't tell if he was excited, nervous, angry. I stared out the windshield, too, wondering where he was taking me. He drove off campus a few blocks to Greenwood Cemetery and stopped the car at the back in a wooded area behind a large mausoleum.

His hands gripped the steering wheel as if he were afraid it would get away from him. Eyes riveted on something in the distance, he spoke through gritted teeth, "What the hell got into you, pestering Marla and spreading those lies." He turned and glowered at me.

My eyes opened so wide it felt like they could fall out of my head.

"What? I don't. What? What are you talking about?"

"Don't, Melanie. Don't act that way. It's time we got it all out. No lies."

I had no idea what he was accusing me of but I saw red. He'd avoided me for months, wouldn't even talk to me, and now he calls me a liar.

"You're right!" I bellowed. "It's time to get it all out. You're the one who's been hiding. Remember?"

His shoulders slumped with the burden of guilt. "I stayed away because things weren't going to work out the way you wanted them to."

"How do you know what I wanted? You never gave me the chance to tell you."

"That's no excuse for going after Marla."

"What does she have to do with anything?"

"Nothing. That's the point. You sent her all those crazy letters telling her to break up with me. Even threatening her."

"Letters? I don't even know her last name or where she lives. How could I send her letters?"

"Thanks to your meddling, she got so she believed we were a couple. Even told me she wouldn't break up with me no matter how crazy you are." His answer made me wonder if he'd heard what I'd said.

"Wait a minute. I don't get this at all. I never had anything to do with her." I couldn't make sense of any of it, but I did grab onto one thing he'd said—the most important thing. "You mean Marla isn't your girlfriend?"

"No, she isn't. But she thinks she is because of you."

"Okay. Let's get this straight. I never said one word to her. I didn't send any letters. I don't even know what you're talking about."

"She showed them to me."

"Was it my handwriting?"

"They were typed."

I shook my head. Slowly the truth dawned on me. "I can't believe she did that to me!"

"You've got it backward. Marla never did anything to you."

"No, not Marla. Those letters were from Diane."

Moe's look of anger turned to one of confusion. "Diane? Your roommate? Why would she send Marla those letters?"

I told Moe everything about Diane including that we hadn't spoken to each other in a month. "She's been out to get me all along and now she's really done it."

"I'll be dipped," he said. "She sounds like a real witch. We've got to straighten this mess out so Marla quits glomming on to me like I'm the love of her life."

I stiffened, wanting to cry out, "No! You're the love of *my* life! Can't you see?" He'd said we've got to fix this. We. Was there still a chance? "I'll do whatever you want."

"The only thing that will convince her is if both you and Diane tell her the truth."

It was a tall order. First, I'd have to break the silence with Diane. I was so frosted, I certainly would talk to her. If she thought I'd given her a piece of my mind when she'd pulled her stunt at the Snow Ball, wait til she heard what I had to say about this. She wouldn't have any choice except to confess to Marla.

The hard part would be for me to face Marla. From the moment I'd seen her with Moe in the student union, I'd thought of her as my arch rival for his affection. Could I keep from making a complete fool of myself? If I didn't handle things right I'd destroy any chance of seeing him again.

"I'll take care of it," I vowed.

He started the car and said, "See that you do." His voice was as cold as the frost forming on the windshield. As we rode back to campus I didn't dare restart the conversation. The saying 'silence is deafening' was never more true.

There was no time to build my courage or plan my attack. Diane was in our room when Moe dropped me off. I shrieked at her, called her names and told her I knew about the letters.

She tried denying it at first, but finally spat at me, "Yes, I did it! I've worked my butt off to help you and you've given me nothing in return. You think you're so much better than me, you won't even talk to me. The worst of it is, I was trying to help you. You've been mooning over that guy ever since I've known you. I was getting rid of his girlfriend so you could get him back."

Shocked at her revelation, I plopped onto my bed, bumping my head on her bunk on the way down. She was trying to help me? After the way I'd treated her? I rubbed my head. A lump was rising and so was my suspicion. There was a diabolical glint in her eyes. Brad's words came to me, "She'll do whatever she needs to if she's after something." She was after revenge.

I ducked my head and jumped up. "Hah! You don't fool me. You've stooped as low as you could this time. You won't get away with it."

We threw angry accusations at each other until our yelling was interrupted by loud thumps on the door. We both froze. Diane straightened herself, plastered a fake smile on her face and opened the door.

Dictator RA's eyes shot daggers at us. "You could be heard all over the dorm. I'm giving you both ten demerits." She thrust slips of paper toward Diane.

Diane took the demerit slips and said in a soothing voice, "Jenny, it wasn't me. Melanie was making all the noise. She's upset about her boyfriend and she was taking it out on me. I tried to get her to calm down, but you know how touchy she is." She handed the demerit slip with her name on it back to the RA.

"That's a lie!" I shrieked, adding credibility to Diane's appraisal of my temperament.

"Calm down or I'll have to send you to Mrs. Ebert."

At the RA's threat, I broke into a cold sweat. I couldn't face the housemother again. She'd probably believe Diane. I'd be grounded for life or expelled.

I ripped my demerit slip from Diane's hand. "What about her? She was yelling, too."

Dictator grimaced at me and I recognized the same diabolical look in her eyes. Were they part of some evil cult? Even her raspy voice sounded satanic, "You are the only one I heard screeching."

As soon as she left, I grabbed Diane's arm and whispered, "You won't deceive me again. I've seen how you manipulate everyone. How about I tell the dean the papers you've been handing in were written by someone else?"

Diane's face turned pale and she stammered, "You, you can't."

I squeezed her arm tighter. "Oh yes, I can. I've seen you copy word for word the papers your cousin wrote for her English classes at State."

"No, please. I'll do whatever you want."

"You're darn right you will. You'll go with me and tell Marla the truth."

She nodded. Tears streaked her cheeks.

I released her. "You better watch yourself. You know how touchy I am."

She fled from the room.

The demerits meant I was campused for the weekend. It gave me time to catch up on laundry and schoolwork and to plan our meeting with Marla. Diane stayed away from our room, but whenever I saw her in the cafeteria, I sidled up to her and whispered in an ominous tone, "I'm making arrangements to meet with Marla so you can confess." The fear on her face was almost worth the trouble she'd caused.

When I'd done my time, I collared Diane at lunch.

"We're meeting Marla in the library at one forty-five. Don't even think of ducking out."

A few minutes later, she scraped her uneaten lunch into the trash bin at the dishwashing station and flung her tray onto the counter. I followed her out of the cafeteria.

"Let's go to our room and get ready." I made it sound like we were about to go out for a fun time, but inside I quaked as much as she did.

In our room, I reminded her that she was to tell Marla she had written the letters and to apologize.

"You might as well be truthful and tell her you did it to get revenge for my firing you as our band promoter. And if you say one word about my feelings for Moe, you will regret it. Behave or pay the consequences."

When we arrived at the library, Marla was pacing in the lobby with a wary look on her face. I marched up to her with Diane in tow.

"Thank you for meeting us," I said. "Diane is here to explain."

I shot Diane a warning glance and stepped aside so the two girls faced each other. Diane looked at me with fear in her eyes, then back at Marla.

She began, "The letters were from me, not Melanie. She had nothing to do with it."

I hoped Marla hadn't noticed it wasn't really an apology and that would be the end of it. But she wasn't letting either of us off the hook. The girl wanted details.

"Why did you send those letters? What did she tell you about me? And about Moe?"

I held my breath. Would Diane's wicked tongue spew out a bunch of lies? Or even the truth I'd made her promise to keep secret?

"Look," she said. "I did it because I was mad at her. It didn't really have anything to do with you. She never told me anything about you. I just figured if I made something up it would get her in trouble. That's all."

Still no apology. It was time for me to remind Diane of that part of the bargain.

"I'm sorry this happened," I told Marla, "even though I didn't know what Diane was doing and it wasn't my fault. Right, Diane?"

Diane sneered at me and my heart thumped like it was trying to burst through my ribcage. Finally, she mumbled, "Yeah, sorry."

Marla sniffed and turned to me. "I still don't believe you had nothing to do with it. You'd love to see me and Moe break up, wouldn't you? Probably think if you can't have him, no one should."

"No! I didn't try to break you up. I mean, there was nothing to break up. Moe never was your boyfriend. He told me so himself."

Oops, now I'd done it. She'll tell him what I said. The plan was for Diane to apologize and for Marla to accept it and when she'd tell Moe about it he would let her down gently, tell her she was his friend and that's all. I was sure he'd come back to me.

"You're pathetic," Marla snarled. She stomped away.

That evening Diane switched rooms with another freshman. My new roommate was a quiet mouse, probably terrorized by Diane's fabrications about my monstrous ways. I attempted cordiality, asked her about her classes, her family, her interests and shared a few mundane details about myself so she wouldn't be afraid of me. Still, we shared a peaceful co-existence based on mutual evasion of each others' space.

I called Moe. Not knowing if Marla had reported her version of our meeting, I forged ahead with mine.

"Diane and I met with Marla. Diane admitted she sent the letters and she sort of apologized. I hope that helps you with Marla."

"I'm working on it."

Not even a 'thanks, see you around.'

FOURTEEN

A few nights later, a fitting accompaniment for my misery drifted from the radio. Ray Charles' mournful wail, "I Can't Stop Loving You" brought wrenching sobs. I hadn't had a really good cry in weeks and holding my feelings in had been like trying to contain Lake Michigan in a bathtub. Now the great rush of relief was like water bursting through a weak dam.

I pulled myself together and resolved to go on. I wouldn't give up. Moe and I could work things out. We could be a real couple if he'd only listen. I called Moe.

"We have to talk," I said. "Pick me up in fifteen minutes." It wasn't as effective as when he'd said, "I'll pick you up," but I prayed he'd come to me. I hung up before he could give an answer I didn't want to hear.

I splashed cold water on my face to wash away the tear stains and cool some of the redness. Staring in the mirror at the drowned rat I'd become, I knew if I won him back it wouldn't be because of my good looks.

On the sidewalk in front of the dorm I shook with the cold, the fear of rejection, the excitement over the possibilities. This was my last chance. Headlights broke through the dark. A car glided up the hill to the dorm. My pulse pounded in my ears. The car stopped. A girl flew out of the lobby and hopped in, greeting her date "Hi honey!" The driver leaned in and pecked her on the lips.

I pressed my lips together to keep from blurting out my disappointment. When Moe gets here I'll hop into his car and say "hi honey" just like that girl. Another car pulled up. And another. The crush of rejection weighed on me like a heavy stone resting on my heart. I'd been an idiot to think he'd show up.

My head jerked up at the toot of a car horn. Moe reached across the seat, opened the passenger side door and I slipped in. Neither of us spoke as he drove through campus and to the secluded cemetery. How had he discovered this place? Certainly other students had found it, too. It was the perfect place to park and make out, but we were the only ones there.

Moe turned off the engine and doused the lights. The darkness covered me like a comfortable blanket. I had things to say, questions to ask, feelings to reveal. Seeing his face and the look in his eyes would surely distract me.

I didn't know where to begin so I decided to ask about our most recent problem and work back from there.

"Did you work things out with Marla?"

I could hear his soft breathing and his hands drop from the steering wheel to his lap. "Yes. She knew all along I wasn't interested. We're still friends."

"And what about us?" I whispered.

I felt him turn in the seat to face me but I saw only a vague silhouette. Would he let me down, too, telling me the way he had Marla that he'd never been interested? Would he withhold even friendship?

"Melanie, when I met you I was intrigued. A girl drummer in a rock and roll band. A spunky chick who liked the same music I did. Who didn't care I was a different color. And when I got to know you, you were easy to talk to. I liked your goofy sense of humor and that you had dreams. It meant a lot that you didn't care what other people thought when they saw us together."

A whirlwind swirled in my head. Could he see the red glow of embarrassment heating my face? It wasn't true that I didn't care what other people thought. I'd worried about it all the time. Even wondered if I shouldn't see him anymore. But something kept tugging me closer until it was hopeless and no one else mattered.

I hoped he'd say more but a long moment passed and I had to break the silence.

"I felt the same about you," I choked. "What happened?"

"When we were apart last summer, I missed you. But I don't think you have any idea how different we are. How hard it would be. I even hoped when we got back in the fall, you'd moved on to someone else. Problem solved. But the minute I saw you, I knew."

"Knew what?" Please say you love me.

"I wanted more than friendship."

My mouth opened but all I could force out was "oh." I moved closer so he could put his arms around me. He didn't.

He said, "I knew it couldn't work between us. We're from different backgrounds. Other people get in the way."

"But you said you liked that I didn't care what other people think."

"Strangers, maybe, but not family. You care about them."

I squirmed. Did I care? Mom and Dad warned I would get hurt. But they were the ones hurting me by not accepting Moe. How could other people decide what hurts and what makes me happy?

"We could make it work. Even if they don't think so. Even if—"

"After what happened when you took me to your home I knew being together could never work for us."

"You're wrong," I argued. "It doesn't matter that some bigots don't like us. We can ignore them. And my family will come around. You know they will." I grabbed his hand. An electric shock coursed through me. Had he felt it too?

He pulled his hand away and turned the ignition key. "Melanie, your life and mine are too different. Every day is a struggle for a black person and even harder for a white woman with a black man. I realized you didn't get it when you made the choice to pay my way out of jail instead of calling G. W. like I asked."

"But I couldn't leave you in jail. Who knows what they would have done to you? What could G. W. do so far away? How can you be mad at me for helping you?"

Moe's mind was set and my arguments didn't penetrate his reasoning or his heart. He drove back to school without answering. Had I been mistaken? Was he the kind of man who demanded total obedience from a woman?

He pulled in front of the dorm and reached across me to open the car door. I tried one more time to salvage whatever I could from the ruins of our disastrous relationship.

"Moe, I'm sorry I didn't do what you asked, but I had to help you."

"You don't help a man by deciding what you think is best for him. A man has to take care of himself instead of letting others do it. Especially a black man."

I crept from the car feeling more beaten down than ever. Was this really the end? There should be something more.

Late that night, I lie awake stewing over what Moe had said. He admitted he's attracted to me. I'm not crazy after all. He kept saying we're different from each other. Opposites attract, isn't that what they say? Who wants to marry their twin? Okay, I am crazy. It isn't about city boy versus small town girl. Tomatoes, tomahtoes. It's about growing up in black skin. What do I know about that? What is the difference? Or is it about the last thing he said, "A man has to take care of himself?"

My dad takes care of himself and all the rest of us, too, but he always lets Mom put in her two cents. Sometimes she gets her way. Sometimes it isn't even clear who wears the pants, but her haranguing and bossing never makes him less of a man.

Some men don't let their wives drive or have their own money or even talk to other people without permission. Is that how black men think it should be? Sounds like slavery to me.

And why does Moe have to stand up to everyone over every little thing? Is that the kind of man he is?

Torrents of confusion cascaded in my brain keeping me from sleep. I rolled and twisted in my bed until, curled into a ball like a wounded animal, I finally dropped off.

After two days of torment, I made a decision. I would find out just what Moses Carter was about. Then I would know how to win him back. Or if I should try.

I rode the city bus to Second Baptist. The SNCC meeting had been moved from the basement to the main part of the church but, even with the extra space, the place was packed. I stood at the back trying to figure out if there was a specific seating order. I couldn't tell because Negro and white, male and female, old and young shared the pews.

"Melanie?" a voice behind me asked. I turned. I hadn't seen Iris Brown since last semester when we'd ushered together at the auditorium. She flashed a warm smile.

"Iris! Hi, how are you?"

She suggested we sit together and led me to a pew a few rows back from the front. It was an ideal spot to see and hear what was going on and, surrounded by people, I wouldn't be noticed.

The front of the church looked bare compared to St. Theresa's back home. Instead of a crucifix, a plain wood cross hung on the wall. There was no altar, just a couple rows of chairs facing the congregation and, to the side, a big lectern called the pulpit. I'd only been in a protestant church a couple times because it's a big no-no for Catholics. It shocked me to see ordinary people sitting where the altar should be.

They were the same people who had been leaders at the meeting I'd gone to with Moe back in October. This time, Marla was allowed to sit with them. A stack of books and papers rested at her feet. She balanced a large board on her lap as a desk so she could take notes.

Moe sat a few chairs away. G. W. Sloan stood in front of him. His long, lean body bent forward to catch what Moe was saying. Then G. W. checked his watch, approached the lectern and raised his hand. I expected to see the cowbell, but the audience quieted without it.

The meeting proceeded like any organization's—introductions, minutes and financial reports (presented by Marla and unanimously approved), information from some far away national office. Then G. W. called for local activity reports.

One by one, people came to the pulpit and related their experiences: called names while walking in a white neighborhood, ignored by store clerks, followed through the store as if they intended to shoplift, received a lower grade than the white student in the next seat, passed over for a promotion at work. Weren't these things white people put up with, too? Especially teen-agers. A lot of people treat them like they're either dumb or up to no good. The Negroes blamed everything, no matter how petty, on racial discrimination.

I checked the crowd to see if the other white people felt the finger of blame pointing at them. Some grimaced in pain over the injustices, others nodded in empathy. There were angry white faces, too. Everyone agreed the Negroes were poorly treated and something had to be done about it.

Finally, a white student came forward to speak. "I called College Square Apartments about renting for the summer term. The manager was hep to rent to me. Said they have lots of places empty in the summer so I'd have my pick. I made an appointment to look at a couple of them with my roommate." He nodded and his roommate stood up.

The crowd hooted, stomped their feet and whistled. The roommate was a very dark Negro.

The white guy grinned and continued, "The manager's face turned whiter than mine when we showed up. And, of course, you know the rest of the story. Suddenly, all the apartments had been rented. No room for us at the inn."

My muscles tensed til I was afraid I was permanently paralyzed. That was clearly wrong. And I'd heard of it before. It was no secret that in Middleton realtors would never show property to a Negro. Since it didn't affect me I hadn't given it much thought. But now I thought about when I'd walked through the neighborhood a couple blocks from this church. I'd seen Negro families crowd into small houses with broken windows and peeling paint. It wasn't hard to imagine the interiors: old furnaces that couldn't keep up with cold drafts, leaky plumbing, and linoleum so worn it couldn't be cleaned no matter how much you scrubbed. I'd wondered why anyone would choose to live like that. Now I understood. They didn't have another choice.

G. W. returned to the lectern. "We need black and white, male and female to pose as applicants for rental properties. If you want to sign up, see Marla after the meeting. Once we have enough evidence we'll work on the city commission to pass a fair housing law. And enforce it."

"Finally, it's something I can do to help," Iris whispered. "Want to sign up with me?"

I was on a fact-finding mission, not there to get involved. But it was time I crossed the color line and became friends with a black girl. Maybe it would help me understand Moe's life.

"Sure," I said. Oops! I'd have to face Marla when we signed up. Would she say something nasty?

G. W. closed the meeting with, "If you're thinking of joining the voter registration project in the south this summer, we're having a special meeting tomorrow night. Let's get involved."

The church filled with loud chatter as small groups collected to discuss the meeting, their own tribulations, and how to volunteer. Iris and I waited in line to give Marla our names.

"Out slumming?" I didn't have to look behind me to see who had said it. I would recognize Moe's voice inside a roaring wind tunnel or a raging volcano.

"Hello. Um, you know Iris, don't you?" It was a pathetic excuse to avoid explaining why I was there.

"Nice to see you again," he said to her. "Are both of you signing up for the housing thing?"

Iris nodded and we stepped toward Marla.

Talk about being caught between the devil and the deep. Marla looked me up and down like I was a bug under a microscope. Moe smiled at her, then at me. "Gotta take care of a couple things." He walked over to a group clustered around G. W.

Iris and I gave Marla our information. She wrote it all down and said, "Quite a few have signed up. We'll have to figure out the assignments. Do you want to work together?"

Iris looked at me. I nodded and we were a team.

Marla smiled. "Thanks for helping." I couldn't have been more shocked if she'd stood on her head. Moe must have done some smooth talking to convince her I wasn't a vicious fiend

When Iris and I were getting our coats she said, "Let me write down my dorm room so we can get in touch when we have our assignment."

I wrote down my room number for her, too and suggested, "If we don't hear anything in a week or so, maybe we could get together for a Coke or something."

I rushed ahead of her to the doorway where Moe was saying good-bye to someone. "Oh, hi!" I said hoping he wouldn't catch on that I wasn't there by chance.

He smiled at me and then at Iris and asked, "Did you two get signed up?"

I told him what Marla had said about contacting us and that Iris and I were partners.

"Do you need a ride back to the dorm?" He looked directly into my astonished eyes.

"Thank you. That would be nice." I felt as awkward as a fat, gawky adolescent being asked out by the star basketball player. I looked at Iris.

Her mouth formed an O. She shook her head. "Thanks, but I'm all set. I have a ride. You two go ahead. See you later."

She rushed out the door before I could protest. Not that I would. I wanted to hug her. She'd done the very thing any best friend would do. Her ride was the city bus but she pretended she had other plans.

As we walked to the car, Moe asked, "Did Iris invite you to tonight's meeting?"

I swallowed to ease the lump pressing against my windpipe. Should I pretend that was why I was there? He'd guess the only reason I'd go to a SNCC meeting on my own was to spy on him. For such a long time I'd hated the silence between us, but hearing lies was worse. If I wanted the truth, I'd have to give it.

"No. I came to find out more about you. I need to know who you really are."

He didn't say anything until we were driving down the street. "I guess no one really knows another person, but you can try if that's what you want." It sounded more like a challenge than an invitation.

He turned onto Maple Street heading in the opposite direction of campus. My heart leaped. I was unable to speak. He pulled into the cemetery and parked in back.

Turning on the dome light and looking at me he asked, "What do you want to know?"

How do you feel about me?, I wanted to ask. Instead, I risked bringing everything out in the open. Maybe things I'd rather not know.

"Do you hate me for not calling G. W. Sloan when you were in jail?"

He expelled a breath and slumped back in the seat.

"Melanie, I don't hate you. I couldn't. I was angry that you didn't do what I asked, but I know you did what you thought was right."

"I couldn't leave you in jail. And if I called G. W. wouldn't he bring a lot of people to Middleton and there'd be even worse trouble."

"Yes. I was counting on it."

"You—"

"You can't know how I felt." His abrupt voice was cold, his eyes narrowed. "I was being punished for something someone else did. Because I'm a black man. I was angry and humiliated and I wanted the whole damn town to know it. I wanted to make trouble."

His anger frightened me. Would he hear a rational comment? I had to try. "But that would make things worse not better. People would use it as an excuse to hate Negroes even more."

"I know." He sighed and the tenseness left his body. He looked into my eyes. "It's just as well you didn't call G. W. SNCC can change things but we weren't ready. It'll take time and hard work. And it will probably get worse for all of us before it gets better. Black people want change and some of us are ready to do whatever it takes. A lot of white people are just as willing to fight to keep us down. It's going to be a series of battles in a never-ending war. I have to believe some day things will be different."

I already sensed that things were changing. At the meeting, I'd seen people of both races talking and laughing and working together. Maybe someday it would be like that everywhere. But I'd also heard anger and restless calls for violent action. Moe was right, things might get worse.

"I think things will change, too. I came to the meeting to find out more about you, but when Iris asked me if I'd help, I knew I wanted to. Is it okay with you?"

He laughed and I savored the deep, cheery sound I hadn't heard in months.

"Woman, you've never asked my permission before, don't start now."

His laugh, how he called me woman, the teasing all felt familiar, comfortable, the way we'd been before.

But he broke the spell. "Be careful about getting involved. It could get ugly. I don't want you to get hurt."

Stunned to hear my parents' words thrown at me, I blurted, "Why does everyone worry about me getting hurt, but think it's okay for them to do the hurting?"

"Sorry," he said. "Just trying to warn you."

I felt anger surge through me. It was more about my parents than him, but he was the closest target so I hit him with stinging words.

"A woman has to take care of herself instead of letting others do it."

"Ouch!" he yelped. "Do you think I deserved that?"

"Oh! No! I'm sorry. It's my parents I'm mad at. They keep telling me what they think is good for me. They don't listen to what I want. I shouldn't have said that."

"Maybe I shouldn't have said that about me, either. I didn't do a very good job of explaining so you'd get it."

He checked his watch. "Wow! It's almost eleven. I don't want to have to put you up for the night again." I heard his soft chuckle as he started the car.

The street lights allowed me a good look at Moe as we sped toward campus. His relaxed, assured smile reinforced my affection. I wasn't sure where we stood, and I wasn't going to miss this chance to find out.

"When will I see you again?"

"Coffee, tomorrow?"

I floated to my room. I would win Moses Carter back.

The next day I dressed in my most flattering skirt and sweater and took extra time with my hair. Strong March Wind pushed me to class and greeted me afterward bringing its brother, Late Winter Sleet. I slid into the student union, a soggy, wind-blown mess.

Dropping my books and purse on the table, I settled into the chair and wrapped my hands around the cup to warm them. Several minutes passed before I admitted to myself that Moe wasn't going to show up. What the heck was going on with him? Had he changed his mind about me again? I seethed through my next class and trudged back to the dorm.

There was a message: *Sorry, couldn't make it. Will call.*

I waited all day and considered skipping rehearsal, but in the end, the music drew me and got me going. I had my coat on and my hand on the doorknob when the intercom buzzed. I should ignore him. That would show him. Desire won out over vengeance. I rushed to the phone on third floor.

"Hi Melanie, it's Iris."

My anticipation was smashed like a stomped grape. I croaked out a hello.

"Will you be at SNCC tonight? Marla wants to do a training afterward. She has our assignment."

"I have band rehearsal, but I'll try to cut it short and get there by the end of the meeting." I hung up, excited that we had an assignment already. Moe would be at the meeting. I should ignore him for standing me up.

The boys of Ginger agreed to cut our rehearsal short. Brad said, "I don't think we need to rehearse so much anyway. We have plenty of work now and I need time for other stuff."

"We can drop meetings to one night a week. Go over our schedule and arrange sets, maybe practice a little," I offered. We settled on Tuesdays. Other evenings would be free to spend with Moe. I rushed off to the catch the bus.

The SNCC meeting was winding down as I squeezed next to Iris in the pew. I mouthed, "I made it." Craning my neck I sought out Moe. He was in his usual seat. His eyes caught mine and he smiled. Okay, I wouldn't ignore him. He probably had a good reason for not calling. I smiled back.

Immediately after G. W. closed the meeting, Marla led a group of us to a room in the basement. She handed out several mimeographed sheets and proceeded to go over them point by point. My foot tapped restlessly. She asked if anyone had questions and a hand shot up. The question was about something she'd already covered more than once. I groaned as she launched into a long-winded answer. People shifted in their seats, yawned, made remarks to each other like asides in a Shakespearean play.

Finally, she said, "You can see me after the meeting if you still don't understand. If any of you decide you can't or don't want to go on with the project, let me know so we can assign someone else. Good luck!"

She stepped over to talk to another student.

The rest of us fled like a stampede of buffalo.

I charged up the stairs. Moe was gone.

On the bus to campus, Iris chattered about the assignment but my brain overflowed with thoughts of Moe. I didn't hear a word she said.

The next morning Moe called as soon as the switchboard opened. "Sorry, I had to cancel our coffee. I can't make it today, either. Things at SNCC are really heating up."

A few months before I would have teased him or pouted to get him to find time for me. But because of the strain between us, I forced myself to act graciously. "I understand. I'm swamped myself. Percussion has extra rehearsal today, Ginger's playing a sock hop tonight and a White Rose dance tomorrow night. And Iris and I are apartment hunting tomorrow afternoon."

Rattling off my schedule, it dawned on me that I had filled my life doing what I loved most—playing drums. The only missing piece was him. It was a gap that rivaled the Grand Canyon.

"How about going out for pizza Sunday? Pick you up at five?"

Cool! That peace offering was unreal! An actual, true date. The anticipation would sustain me for the next fifty-eight hours.

I dashed to classes, met Iris for coffee in between, and played my part with perfection at percussion practice. At the sock hop, everyone danced and sang along to our music. During intermission, I signed us up for another gig. Our calendar was almost full for the rest of the semester.

Brad's enthusiasm matched mine as he walked me back to the dorm. "Mel, I think we're ready to cut a record."

"Great idea. We might have to go to Detroit or Chicago to find a studio. I'll ask around."

Finally, everything was falling into place. I had followed my heart and soon I'd have both my music and Moe.

Iris came by my dorm at ten on Saturday. We crammed into the phone booth and I called the name Marla had given us. Yes, they had apartments available, no pets, one year lease, only two tenants allowed.

I said, "We'll be there at two to look at it. We're very interested. Thank you."

Iris helped me choose clothes for our appointment. SNCC had a very particular dress code. Everything clean, neatly pressed or polished. No blue jeans, mature clothing only. No gaudy jewelry or bizarre hairstyles. Nothing to draw undue attention or criticism.

When I walked her to the lobby to say goodbye, we got a few looks, but nothing as appalling as I'd imagined. More like curiosity rather than condemnation.

After lunch, I went to the Negro girls' dorm and asked the girl at the reception desk to alert Iris I was coming to her room. "You have a guest," I heard the girl say, using the same code the desk girls in my dorm used. Iris greeted me at the top of the stairs and showed me her room. It looked very much like mine. Why had I thought her dorm would be different?

She wore a loden green wool dress and black flats. She'd pomaded her hair and topped it with a felt pillbox hat. I'd never interviewed for an apartment so I didn't know if wearing Sunday best was expected. In my plaid skirt and navy sweater, I felt like a real slouch.

"I have an idea," Iris said.

I wasn't sure we should veer from Marla's plan on our very first time out, but what Iris had thought of made so much sense I agreed. We got off the bus a block from the Maple Glen Apartments. Iris stayed on the corner. Propelled by nervousness I hustled to the agent's office.

"I'm sorry, my roommate had something come up, so she'll be here a little later. We didn't want to change our appointment." I hoped the rental agent would think I was blushing because I was shy. Could he tell I was lying? Did my blazing face signal that I was a phony only pretending to look for an apartment?

The agent, a short, balding man with bad teeth, rolled his eyes. Maybe having me arrive separately wasn't such a good idea. Maybe he already had a bad opinion of Iris for not showing up. He went over the terms of the lease and gave me a long list of rules, emphasizing promptness in paying rent.

"Do you want to wait or look at the apartment by yourself?" His voice held a tinge of annoyance.

"Oh, I'd love to see it now. I'm sure if I like it, Iris will, too. And I don't want to keep you waiting," I gushed with too much enthusiasm.

He grabbed a set of keys from a rack on the wall and led me up two flights of stairs. The apartment was neat enough, but the sparse furnishings were shabby. A dirty path on the carpet meandered from the doorway to the kitchen and through the living room. The acrid smell of stale cigarettes hung in the air like a mushroom cloud. Still a little elbow grease would fix the problem. I liked Iris, she and I could have fun as roommates. I'd almost forgotten this was make-believe. I was confident I could fool the man.

"This is really nice. It's perfect for Iris and me. Can we sign a lease today?"

The little man grinned like a monkey and rubbed his hands together. What if I had to sign papers? Could he force me to move in? Where was Iris?

Back in his office, the agent filled out the lease form and slid it across his desk.

"If you'll sign here. Your roommate can sign when she gets here. Then all I'll need is your fifty dollar deposit to hold the place. If you aren't moving in until June, I'll only charge you half price for April and May. Rent's due on the first of the month."

I had no idea about all this. If I signed his paper could I get out of it later? Where was Iris? I lifted the pen, desperate to think of a way to stall.

The door opened, the agent and I looked up. Thank heavens, it was Iris.

"Sorry I'm late," she gasped.

I jumped up and, like Audrey Hepburn, resumed my role.

"Iris, the apartment is perfect! I already said we'd take it."

The agent cleared his throat. "Oh, well, um, I need your deposits and also the half rent for April and May, and then your first month's rent. And I forgot to mention the damage deposit. Let's see, that comes to two hundred each. I need it today because I have other people interested in the apartment." His fingers ran along the edge of the contract, teasing it as if he were about to rip it up.

"Will you take a check?" Iris asked.

"No, no, no, strictly cash. And, and. Oh, wait. I'm sorry I didn't notice this note from my boss."

He picked up a scrap of paper and scrutinized it. I leaned

forward and peeked. Nothing there but meaningless doodles.

He squinched the paper in his hand and said, "Oh dear, it seems my boss rented the last apartment yesterday. Heh heh, egg on my face." He stood. "I'll let you know if anything else comes up."

Without asking for a phone number, he ushered us out the door

On the bus ride back to the dorm, I relayed to Iris every word the man had told me before she arrived. I promised to write it all down. We had definitive proof that he withdrew the apartment once he'd seen her.

"We've got him!" I said with glee.

Iris pulled a hanky from her purse and dabbed at her face.

"Sorry," she said. "That was so humiliating."

"Oh, Iris, I'm sorry." I put my arm around her shoulder, worried she might shake it off because I was white. "But you shouldn't feel that way. That creep should crawl into a deep hole. Don't even think another thought about him."

"Don't you see, Melanie? He was more than willing to rent an apartment to you. But it's not that way for black people. Couldn't you see how he hated me?"

"I'm sure he didn't hate you. He just doesn't understand."

"He understands alright. He understands that because he's white he can treat me and everyone like me as if we're filthy vermin. Even you don't understand that. You don't know what it's like to be treated like that."

"Iris! You don't think I'm like that jerk, do you? I'm your friend. I'd never act that way around you or any other, other—"

She shook her head. "You don't even know what you should call us."

I stared at her and bit my bottom lip to stop the quiver of my chin. Why had she suddenly become so cruel? I thought we were friends, but she'd turned on me like the racists she was talking about.

She shook her head. "I'm sorry, Melanie. I want to be friends and I know you do too. It's hard sometimes to understand each other because we're different."

She moved to the front of the bus and got off near her dorm.

FIFTEEN

All that evening, Iris's words pealed through my brain like a church bell, echoing what Moe had said, "We're different. You don't understand." My drumming couldn't stifle the sound as I gazed at the students gliding across the dance floor. Every face was white—even the name of the formal was White Rose. Did anyone realize how segregated they were? Did they care?

At Mass the next morning I prayed for understanding, but the vague feeling I would never achieve it haunted me like a tune I couldn't get out of my head. I called Iris that afternoon. She wasn't in.

Moe picked me up in front of my dorm promptly at five.

I'd barely settled in the car when I blurted, "Iris and I went to the apartment and it was horrible! I can't stop thinking about how that awful man treated her."

As I related every detail, Moe didn't say a word. Before I realized we were there he'd stopped the car in the lot behind the pizza shop. How long had I been ranting?

"I'm sorry Iris had to go through that." He opened his door and got out of the car.

The hair on the back of my neck prickled at the eerily calm tenor of his voice. Did he get riled up only when things like that happened to him?

Bruno's was crowded and noisy. Every spot was taken, but a group of students from SNCC waved us over, inviting us to sit at their table. Everyone in the place stared as if I'd escaped from the circus. In high school I'd developed a pretty thick hide over the judgment of people who jumped to conclusions about me, but this felt different. This was about the color of my skin and how it didn't match my friends'. I was beginning to realize the roots of racism were rampant and deep.

As for the kids we'd joined at the table, each was unique. Different sizes, different ages, different interests. Some were talkative and funny, some shy and serious. Some brilliant, some average. Each one had dreams and fears, successes and failures. To me, some of them were more likable than some white people. And some weren't. Shouldn't you get to know a person before deciding what their character is?

I asked about Iris, but everyone shrugged. Why hadn't I tried calling her again? I should have invited her to meet us at Bruno's. Was she mad at me?

Two fellows and two girls in the group had gone on apartment hunting assignments, but though they'd had similar experiences, Iris and I had been the only mixed pair. Stumbling over the words, I related what had happened to us.

"Nice to be white, huh?" Willie sneered at me.

Then I remembered he was the one who'd called me whitey at the first SNCC meeting. He liked to stir up trouble, to bait people so he could accuse them of being racist.

Struggling to remain calm, I answered, "This isn't about me. I'm as upset as the rest of you about how Iris was treated."

"Sure!" Willie snorted. "I'll bet your granddaddy felt the same way sittin' on the veranda of his plantation."

I wanted to set him straight. My grandfather came from Bohemia and people had discriminated against him, too. He was a peaceful man who had worked hard to buy his farm. It was no plantation.

G. W. interrupted, "That was uncalled for, Will."

Will slammed his Coke bottle on the tabletop, but at least he shut up.

The manager of the pizza shop looked over at our table and frowned.

"I don't think he likes us," one of the fellows whispered. "What should we do if he tells us to leave?"

"We've got as much right to be here as anyone else," another student said loud enough to be heard at the neighboring tables.

I felt a subtle shift as the students bristled at the idea of being thrown out. Lips tightened and fists clenched, preparing for battle. Should I speak up? Tell them, "this is ridiculous. We're done eating. We've been sitting here for over two hours. He wants us to leave so someone else can have our table. Why do you always make everything about race?" My lips remained as tight as everyone else's, but my anger wasn't toward the restaurant manager.

Moe stared directly at Will and said, "We should leave. There are people standing around who'd like our table."

"Well, they can wait. We've had to wait for whitey for a hundred years. None of them ever gave up their table for us. I say we stay." Willie's belligerence shook me. He was a powder keg about to explode.

Two fellows at the table crossed their arms and nodded indicating their intention to stay put. The others pulled away, averted their eyes, toyed with their drinks. The divide was as great as the gap SNCC had been trying to repair.

G. W. stood and towered over us. "Moe's right. We haven't been treated any differently than any other customers. Let's go. Don't forget to clear the table and push in the chairs."

Most of us pulled on our coats, preparing to leave.

Willie tossed his chair aside and stormed out with his two cohorts close on his heels.

The rest of us cleared the tables, someone mumbled an apology to the restaurant manager and we quietly left.

"Well," Moe said as he opened the car door for me. "Quite a lot of discussion tonight." I climbed in and he shut the door, giving me a momentary reprieve before I had to respond.

Once he'd put the car in gear, I found my voice, "I'm learning a lot. After what happened to Iris and hearing everyone else's stories, I can see why people are upset. But Willie makes a big deal about stuff that happens to everybody. Seems like he's just itching for trouble."

Moe shook his head and looked upward as if it was hopeless to believe I'd ever understand. He pulled out of the parking lot and headed in the opposite direction of campus. At last, we'd have time alone. But how could I steer the conversation away from all this race talk? I'd told him I wanted to know what makes him tick, but I didn't want another lesson about discrimination. I'd already gotten that point even if I didn't understand Willie's reaction.

Moe parked in the secluded area at the back of the cemetery and reached for my hand. "You wanted to know me. I think you're getting a good idea of where I come from. Disappointed?"

I scooched along the seat so I was right next to him. "No. I want to know everything there is to know about you. I hope I don't scare you away again, but I've been wanting to say this for a long time, ever since I said it before. I love you."

He let go of my hand, pulled me close and kissed me. Suddenly I understood what it meant in those old movies where the damsel fell in a faint to her couch. The kiss made me swoon. I went limp, my head was full of air, my body flushed with heat. It was the most wonderful feeling I'd ever experienced.

"If I recall correctly," Moe said, lifting my chin with his finger, "you were the one who ran away that day."

"But, but, you let me."

"Yes, I did. Not because I wanted to. I think I knew before you that we were falling for each other. I told myself it was okay for me to love you as long as you didn't love me back. Melanie, you heard those kids tonight. You're beginning to see what life is like for a black person. Don't you see what it would be like if we were a couple?"

I reached up, placing my hands on the sides of his face. As I kissed him, I felt him relax. His arms went around me and his lips pressed harder against mine.

When we finally released each other I said, "We can't give up without giving it a try. For months, we've acted like anything but a couple. I want to be your girlfriend. I want you to be my boyfriend. We have to try. I'll do whatever it takes. And if we can't make it work —which won't happen—at least we'll never regret not giving us a chance."

Moe laughed. "Woman, you speak with wisdom." I suspected he believed his words and he believed in us.

Suddenly we were like two awestruck greenhorns who'd just discovered love, as if we were the only ones who'd ever enjoyed such exhilaration. We giggled and kissed and said sweet things and planned how to spend every minute possible together.

Time stood still and flew away like a rocket.

We finally pulled ourselves apart and Moe drove back to my dorm.

"Park in the lot, Mr. Carter," I instructed. "You're going to escort your girlfriend in like a proper gentleman."

As we walked hand in hand into the lobby my courage faltered. Couples stood along every wall, wrapped in each other's arms, shamelessly making out in full view. I'd made my way through that hormonal mass many a time at closing and swore I'd never act that way. Now I had a boyfriend and I sure wasn't going to shake his hand to say goodnight.

I pulled him over by the mailboxes and leaned against him. Startled by my brazen behavior, he stared wide-eyed. I stood on tiptoe, my face upturned for a kiss. His lips brushed mine lightly and he whispered, "I don't really like public displays of affection. And I don't mean because you're a white girl. It just makes me uncomfortable to see all this necking in front of everyone."

I gave him a quick hug and said, "I agree. We should save that for when we're alone."

Mrs. Ebert walked through the lobby creating a chill that brought a halt to the most serious romantic activity. Couples held hands, hugged, or pecked their lips at each other, but there were no more hands on breasts, open mouthed kisses or hickey suctioning.

She nodded to a girl at the reception desk. The girl jumped up and swung a mallet at a metal disk suspended from a pole next to the switchboard. The clang of the gong signaled the five-minute warning before girls would be locked up and boys locked out.

Moe and I held hands and walked toward the lobby doors. I jutted my chin out a little as we moved past Mrs. Ebert. Moe kissed my cheek and whispered, "I'll see you tomorrow."

He left and I floated up to my room.

After that night, we spent as much time together as we could steal from the everyday duties that tugged at us. The forty-five minutes for coffee between morning classes flew by like "The Minute Waltz." I wanted to skip my next class, but Moe wouldn't let me.

On Monday and Wednesday's, right after supper, we went on study dates. In the most secluded corner of the library, we opened our books but I couldn't concentrate. The words were worms crawling across the page. I felt Moe's leg brush against mine. Within an hour after he picked me up at the dorm, we were parked behind the cemetery. Sometimes we'd have to crack open the car windows because it was so hot, even though it was still March and Moe had turned off the engine.

Ginger continued rehearsals on Tuesday evenings. "What's wrong with you?" the boys groused. "You keep losing the beat, you forgot your sheet music, you haven't checked into recording." I apologized and tried harder, but dreams of Moses Carter were a constant distraction.

On Thursdays, we went to SNCC meetings. It didn't take long for everyone to recognize we were a couple. Several SNCC members openly shunned us. One tried to explain, "It's just better to stick to your own race. We aren't trying to mix, we just want the same rights and opportunities." Another accused Moe of being a sellout. Harsher words were whispered about me. But most of SNCC accepted our relationship, some even welcomed it.

Another mixed couple invited us to double date. My band had gigs every Friday and Saturday night so Moe and I had to pass. I wanted to be seen in public with him. To go places other couples went. I knew we'd be sneered at and called names, maybe even refused service, but I didn't care. I wanted a life with Moe and I'd proudly accept all of it.

Marla had made fair housing her personal mission and asked if Moe and I would pose as husband and wife searching for an apartment.

"Probably not a good idea," he told me. "Remember what happened to Iris? You'll be treated even worse."

"I can take it." I argued that we would be instrumental in making real change and I didn't stop badgering until I convinced him. I couldn't wait to pretend we were married. Now I'd have a chance to almost experience my dream of being his wife.

I called Regency Apartments pretending my husband had received a job transfer to First National Bank's local branch and we would be moving in a few weeks. The rental agent, a pleasant sounding woman, assured me they had several new apartments for lease.

"We've only been married two months, but we expect to start a family. Are children allowed?" I said it with such ease it felt as if it were actually true.

"Yes," the woman said. "These apartments are perfect for young couples. You'll make friends right away and we have lots of babies here."

She scheduled an appointment for the next day.

We arrived on Saturday precisely at two o'clock. Several two-story brick buildings, surrounded by neat yards, faced the parking lot. The office was at the far end of the first building. A sign in the window advertised one and two bedroom apartments, several immediately available. I shivered with excitement. Maybe someday Moe and I would live in a place like this.

Moe held the door as I stepped into the office. The walls were bright, the furniture neatly arranged and the aroma of freshly brewed coffee and new carpet teased my nose. A sharp looking woman in an expensive tailored suit looked up from the desk and smiled. She stood and stepped toward me. "You must be—" She stopped, the smile frozen on her face.

Moe stepped from behind me and extended his hand. "Moses Carter. And this is my wife, Melanie Carter."

Deep lines etched a harsh look of disapproval on her face. The joy I'd felt hearing his words shattered like a glass thrown in anguish against a wall.

Ignoring Moe's hand the woman rushed back to her desk and picked up a file.

She turned, looked down her nose and said, "We don't seem to have anything for you. I'm sure you'll find something. There are rentals on the north side of town."

"You told my wife you have several apartments available. And there's a sign in the window stating the same thing." How could Moe remain unruffled after that insult?

"I, I was mistaken." She rushed to the window, pulled up the blind and ripped the sign from the pane. "Now please leave. I don't want any trouble."

"We'd like to see the model," Moe insisted.

"I told you there is nothing here for you." The woman's voice became shrill, rising toward hysteria. "Now leave or I'll call the police."

"The police!" I shouted. "We haven't done anything wrong."

Moe put his arm around my shoulder. The woman's lips pinched together, turning her mouth into a withered apple. I returned her look of disgust with one of my own.

"Get out!" she yelped. "There is no law that says I have to rent to people like you. This is a nice area and I won't have it contaminated by your kind!"

She grabbed the doorknob and flung the door wide. "Go!"

Moe took my hand and led me out. By the time we were speeding down the street, I was crying so hard I thought I'd drown. He slowed as we neared the entrance to the cemetery. A cluster of people was brushing snow from the stones marking the graves. Moe drove past.

He parked on campus in the bookstore parking lot. Reaching into his back pocket, he pulled out a clean handkerchief and wiped my face. "I'm sorry I put you through that. I know you think we should have done more, but we did what we were assigned."

"You didn't put me through anything. That evil woman did."

"She's no different from a million other people. If we're going to be together, this is what will happen. Now maybe you understand why I can't ask you to share my life."

"No," I sobbed. "I won't let anyone stop us. I love you. I don't care how those people treat us. We belong together."

Moe started the car and drove to the north side of town where the broken sidewalks were strewn with debris left behind by melting snow. Ramshackle houses huddled forlornly along the streets. We passed a scruffy playground where a group of young Negro boys took turns throwing trick shots with a basketball at a netless hoop, trying to earn the letters to HORSE.

He stopped in front of a group of fourplex apartment buildings and led me into a tiny disheveled office. He pushed the bell button on the wall next to the doorway.

Soon a large black woman hustled down the hall calling, "Hello, welcome, can I help you?"

Moe asked if there were any available rentals.

Her wide smile beamed at us and I'd never seen eyes shine with so much delight. "Yes, we have one left. A really nice place and I can see you're the really nice couple it's meant for. Come with me, Babies."

We followed her out the back door and to another building.

"This is quieter than the ones right on the street," she said. "And there's a parking spot right by the door."

A child's sled and a tricycle were recklessly parked in the hallway, ready in case of either a late snowstorm or a spring warm-up. The commingled odor of fried fish and stale cigarette smoke made me want to leave the outer door open.

The one-bedroom, ground-floor apartment was small but spotless. I suspected the woman had spend hours scrubbing every inch. The carpet was worn and the kitchen tiles were chipped. The mismatched refrigerator and stove were old, things my dad would not have taken in on trade though he was apt to accept most anything. The woman turned the kitchen faucet on and off, opened the refrigerator door, and lit the stove with a match to show everything was in working order. Even with the door closed, we could hear a couple in an upper apartment arguing and the blare of a television across the hall.

"This is about the nicest apartment you'll find this side of town," the woman bragged. "Rent's a hundred twenty a month, includes heat and electric." The price was the same as the new unit the woman across town had refused to show us. This lady, eager to have us as tenants, offered us a lease.

Moe thanked her, said we'd get back to her, and we left.

"She was nice," I said as we drove toward campus. "It's terrible how white people act."

"Mel, it isn't just white people. She was a nice person, yes, but you've seen how some of the black kids act toward you. They can be biased, too."

He pulled in front of my dorm and reached over to open my door.

"I didn't take you there so you could see that black people are nicer than white ones. I wanted you to see the kind of place a mixed couple could rent. Would you want to live there?"

I wanted to say, "I'd live in a cardboard box if you were with me," but the words stuck in my throat.

SIXTEEN

The rest of the afternoon Moe's words played a relentless beat in my skull. Would you want to live there? Of course, I would. With him. My folks' house was nice enough but nothing grand. They hadn't started out that way and I didn't expect to start married life in a nice house either. Living in the apartment we looked at would be fine. I could fix it up real cute—sew matching curtains and bedspread. Buy some second-hand furniture and paint it in cheerful colors. It would be fun. Where we lived didn't matter. Nothing mattered except being with him.

Ginger was playing a dorm mixer that night. I'd asked Moe to come by to see first hand how much my music meant, but he'd refused. "Graduation will be here before you know it. I can't risk getting poor grades at this stage."

That was one more thing to add to my list of worries. What were we going to do when the semester was over and he'd finished school? Time wouldn't stand still no matter how much I willed it to.

When the guys and I had put together the lineup of songs for the mixer, we included two new ones Johnny and Marv had written. We'd tinkered with them until they sounded right and told their stories. "Crazy Time" was a frenetic instrumental with solos for each of us. It sounded like something The Ventures would play. "I Won't Forget," a tearjerker like "Teen Angel" and "Tell Laura I Love Her," was sappy and none of us was a strong singer, but Johnny thought it was good enough for a B side. He was still pushing me to arrange a recording session.

The dance was a good choice for the debut, a minor event with low attendance, kids who craved pop tunes and fantasized about being on American Bandstand. "I give it an 85 because it's got a good beat and it's easy to dance to, Mr. Clark." They were the kids who buy records and there was no accounting for what would become a hit. The reaction of the test audience would let us know if we were on to something.

I put together my drum kit and we set up at the far end of Maxwell Dormitory's cafeteria. Tables had been moved to the side creating a small dance floor. Students filtered in and out, some staying all evening, others moving on to more exciting adventures. The makeshift dance floor was always full—proof that our band played music the crowd liked. When we played our new numbers, the applause was a few degrees above lukewarm. "We give it a 64, Mr. Clark." But Johnny had heard a raucous reception and cued us to play an encore. Afterward, he pushed me even harder to set up a recording date. As if I didn't have enough to do.

The next afternoon, Moe and I joined G.W., Marla, and a few other SNCC folks at Bruno's Pizza. I sat next to Iris, glad that she'd forgiven me for being insensitive about how hurt she'd been.

As soon as Cokes were brought to the table and we'd all grabbed our pieces of pizza, I blurted, "Wait 'til you hear what happened to us." Everyone's eyes focused on me and the heat of embarrassment crept to my face. "I, we, we had an assignment to pose as husband and wife."

Vivian leaned forward, her wide-eyed stare searching Marla's face. She seemed upset or maybe worried about Marla's feelings. But Marla wasn't bothered. The whole thing had been her idea. Or had she set us up so I'd find out how mean people would be to Moe and me? Did she think I couldn't take it? Was it a ploy to get him back?

Will, whose perpetual sullen look challenged anyone in his space, leaned back in his chair and crossed his arms. His eyebrows pulled together creating a deep wrinkle at the bridge of his wide nose. His lips compressed as if holding back a spate of venomous words. He glared, daring me to continue.

I turned to Moe. Oblivious to the tension, he nodded. I had to forge ahead on my own.

"I made an appointment to look at Regency Apartments—those brand new places—and when we got there the woman said they didn't have anything available, even though she'd told me on the phone they had a bunch of openings, and there was a sign in the window that said the same thing. And Moe asked to see the model and she ripped the sign off the window and told us we had to leave or she'd call the police."

My blathering had botched the story. I hadn't told them what she'd said when I called or what the place looked like, or how she looked when she saw Moe. I'd barely even mentioned the threat to call the police. Was I clear how horrible it felt, how bigoted and evil that woman was? I wanted everyone to see what we had been subjected to, to understand how it hurt, to know that something had to be done. Why wasn't Moe saying anything?

A couple of heads nodded in recognition; others bowed, eyes studying crumbs littered on the table. Will's threatening stare remained fixed on me. Why wasn't anyone speaking? Did my words sound to them like meaningless syllables spoken in a foreign tongue? I swiped at my cheeks with the back of my hand and blinked back the tears.

Will jerked forward, sitting tall, nostrils flaring. He bared his teeth like a rabid dog.

"What the hell did you expect? Welcome to your new apartment, Whitey. Your nigger husband can live here, too, because you're a rich white bitch."

Iris and I gasped as the words flowed from his mouth like caustic foam. Vivian inched her chair closer to Will's. Moe jumped up. G.W.'s hand reached forward and grasped Moe's arm just above the wrist.

Will bolted from his chair, stabbing his finger at me as he ranted, "Who invited your white ass here to make things all nice for us? We don't need you trying to fix the things you people broke. Haul your damn self-righteous white guilt out of here and leave us alone."

Moe lunged forward and I thought he was going to punch Will, but instead he put his arm around me to protect me from the onslaught. G. W. dropped Moe's other arm and stood.

"Let's step outside, Will." He reached over and placed a calming hand on Will's shoulder.

Will shook him off and barked at Moe, "Traitor. You're the one who's trying to hide behind a white woman's skirts. You think that's all it takes to wrangle your way into a white man's world?"

The din of chatter from the surrounding tables hushed. The only sounds outside our circle came from the jukebox—Connie Francis belting out "Everybody's Somebody's Fool."

The restaurant manager shouted, "Hey!" and hustled to our table warning, "No fighting. Either pipe down or leave."

G. W. had a tight grasp of Will's jacket collar and pushed him forward toward the door. Scowls deepened both of their faces.

Vivian screeched "Let go of him!"

She and several others rose and pulled on their coats, preparing to follow.

Moe leaned toward Iris and said, "Take Melanie back to the dorm."

Iris thrust my coat and gloves into my arms and pulled me toward the door. "C'mon, you've gotta get out of here."

As we walked out of Bruno's, Vivian rushed toward me. Her wool scarf, caught by a gust of wind, blew from around her neck and skittered across the parking lot. She kept coming.

"You!" she screamed arms waving like a windmill. "Get your skinny flat ass out of here. And keep your hands off our men! White Slut!"

Iris gave me a shove that started my feet churning toward the bus stop at the end of the next block. When we reached the stop, I bent over, hands on thighs, gasping to collect my breath so I could speak.

"Why? I don't understand. I need to go back and find Moe."

The bus pulled up and Iris stepped aside. "Get on. You're going back to your dorm."

I climbed the steps, dug into my pocket, and deposited change for both of us in the coin box.

Iris opened her purse and pulled out fifteen cents. "I can pay my own way."

I told her it was no big deal but she insisted I take the money. Her refusal to accept such a small thing felt like a rejection of our friendship.

The bus was full of students so Iris and I stood in the aisle. There were so many things I wanted to say, things I didn't want overheard. Busybodies had always stuck their noses in my business, so I kept quiet. Iris didn't even attempt small talk.

We got off, along with several other students, at the main stop on campus. Iris turned in the direction of her dorm without saying good-bye. I grabbed her arm.

"Iris, what's going to happen to Moe? And why does everyone hate me?"

"It's complicated."

"Please, can we go someplace and talk about this?"

"Talking won't fix anything. Moe'll be alright. Willie might try roughing him up, and there'll be some nasty words, but it'll blow over."

"I didn't know—why are they against him being with me."

Iris shook her head. "You don't get it, do you?" She sounded as if she had given up drumming the periodic table of elements into a dull student's thick skull. She sighed and made one last attempt.

"You think they are against you because you're white? It's more than that. We don't think the races should mix any more than you whites do."

"What? Iris, how? I thought we were friends."

A slight smirk touched her lips. "We're friends. As much as we can be. But, what do you know about me? We're only friends because of SNCC. It isn't like we're going to invite each other over for Easter dinner."

I couldn't invite Iris home with me even if we became best friends. Just like I couldn't invite Moe. Is it possible to have a friend that everyone else you care about refuses to accept? Do I have to make a choice?

"Isn't that the purpose of SNCC? So people can get to know each other and become friends?"

Iris' eyes grew wide. "Is that what you think? SNCC isn't anything about being friends. We don't want to live in your lily-white apartments so we can be happy little neighbors. We want to live where the roof doesn't leak and there aren't cockroaches and the rent's the same you pay. We want to go into stores and not be followed like we're planning to stuff bottles of whiskey in our underwear. We want jobs. We want people to stop treating us like we're stupid or dirty or immoral just because of the color of our skin. We don't care about being friends."

"Why are you accusing me?" I sputtered.

"I'm not, but I'll tell you why Will is so angry. Every mixed couple means one of us is trying to join your world. You and Moe want Moe to be white like you. It's time to stop trying to make us what we aren't. We have to fight to be treated the way every human being deserves, but we aren't going to stop being black to make it happen. I'm through straightening my hair and bleaching my skin and trying to act like you." She turned and stomped off toward her dorm.

A sick feeling welled up threatening to spew forth like a volcano as I watched Iris move away, taking with her my only chance for friendship with a Negro girl. How had we so sorely misunderstood each other?

I slunk back to my dorm, closed myself in my room and stretched out on my bunk, too shocked and hurt to cry. After a few minutes, I marched to the telephone booth at the end of the hall and asked the operator to place a call.

"Sorry, Moses Carter isn't answering, want to leave a message?" The desk boy's chipper voice threw me into an even deeper funk. I choked back tears and hung up.

My mind whirled with visions of Moe lying in Bruno's parking lot, skin slashed by a switchblade pulled from Willie's back pocket, tomato-sauce-red blood oozing onto the crusty asphalt. My Moe abandoned by those he'd called brothers, left to die. All because he loved me. A white girl. And there I sat, doing nothing about it. Was I that weak? Afraid to stand up for him?

I pulled on my coat and boots, rushed out of my room and pounded down the three flights of stairs, determined to be by his side.

As I crossed the lobby, a voice called "Melanie! There's a call for you."

I turned toward the front desk. Had I heard right or was my imagination playing tricks on me?

"What?" I squeaked.

"You have a call. I'll put them through to second floor."

I flew up the steps, feet barely touching the treads and grabbed the receiver.

"Hello!" I gasped. I plunked down on the seat and pulled the door shut.

"It's Moe. Are you okay?"

"Silly, I know it's you," I blubbered, laughing and crying and talking all at once. "What happened? Are you okay?"

"Got pushed around a little. Biggest damage was to my jacket. Lost a button and ripped my sleeve. I'm sorry. Those people aren't as open-minded as I thought. Will wants trouble. G. W.'s talked to him quite a bit, trying to get him to back down, but he thinks SNCC is too passive. He sees every incident as an excuse to agitate. Now we're the target."

"It isn't just Will," I said. "Everyone took his side. Even Iris."

"They just got caught up in the heat of the moment."

"I guess so," I answered, not having the energy or desire to discuss the dilemma over the telephone. "If you bring your jacket over, I'll sew it for you. Do you have the button?"

"It's getting late. I'll see you tomorrow after class." He hung up without saying 'I love you' or 'I miss you' or any of the other sweet words he'd been using the past few weeks. Was I losing him?

All night, dreams of Iris, skin turned black as an oboe, hair a dark, kinky cloud dwarfing her face, ran in an endless loop like a bewitched film reel.

A rustling noise pulled me from my sleep. Through puffy eyes, I saw my roommate bundling into her coat and mittens.

"What time is it?" I whispered through parched lips. I struggled to sit up.

"Sorry. You were zonked and I figured you needed your sleep because you didn't set your alarm. It's 8:30." She left for class.

I pulled on clothes, ran a brush through my hair and, after a quick stop in the bathroom, ran off to class, too. I was a few minutes late and so rattled, I probably should have skipped.

"What happened to you?" Carol mouthed, confirming I looked like a wreck.

"Overslept," I muttered.

The professor kept us over to finish his lecture on "Wagner's Ring Cycle" which felt longer than the musical piece itself. I couldn't risk stopping in the restroom to repair the destruction sleep deprivation and bad dreams had wrought on my face. I had to meet Moe.

I bolted out of the music hall, sprinted down the sidewalk, and dashed into the student union. Without stopping to catch my breath, I wended my way through the mass of students, unceremoniously bumping one of them and not even apologizing for the hot coffee splashed on his shirt.

I slid into the chair across from Moe and appraised the damage to his face. A fist-sized shiner puffed the skin around his right eye, the dark flesh purple as an eggplant. There were no other signs of injury and I suspect, in my disheveled state, I looked worse for wear than he did.

We assured each other we were okay, keeping the deeper wounds inflicted by racist hatred hidden. Eventually, we would have to examine them and determine a course of healing. If there could be such a thing. For now, I wanted to continue pretending all that mattered was the two of us. The rest of the world didn't exist.

He asked about Iris. I glossed over it telling him that she brought me back to campus and that was all there was to it. He knew me too well and eventually elicited the whole story.

I asked, "Is it true? Do people bleach their skin and straighten their hair because they are pretending to be white?"

He laughed. "I don't think so. They're just trying to be fashionable. You should take it as a compliment, not competition."

"But she seemed so angry."

"Who knows what she meant? But think of it this way, what musicians do you like best? Chuck Berry, Little Richard, Ray Charles. You play their music. Are you trying to be black?"

I wanted to believe his argument, but I knew the comparison was off. If only Iris would talk to me, to help me understand.

Moe looked at his watch. "Time to get going. I'm busy until tomorrow evening. I want to take you someplace special for dinner. Pick you up at six?"

"Of course," I said covering the disappointment of not seeing him for such a long stretch and wondering over the mystery of what occupied his time.

SEVENTEEN

The next afternoon, as I walked from class, I lifted my face to the sky and inhaled the fresh air. Harsh winds that had accompanied me that morning had blown themselves out, leaving the atmosphere calm and humid. The sun, a yoke freshly broken from the shell of clouds, sizzled at me from above. Bitterly cold rain had recently washed the earth leaving the pungent odor of loamy dirt to fill my nose and evoke sweet thoughts. Spring always brought promise and this year I sensed it stronger than ever. I took one last deep breath before pulling open the dormitory door and entering the lobby.

As usual I stopped at the mailboxes, but this time I knew mine would contain more than dust and cobwebs. I pulled a stack of envelopes from the small box and flipped through them. Mom, both grandmothers, Aunt Celeste, Aunt Colleen, and my friend Pearl had all sent me cards. There was even an envelope from Darlene, addressed with a purple pen in flourishing handwriting, a heart dotting each i. Glitter drifted like fairy dust from the envelope to my jacket sleeve. I smiled. Although the first official day of spring had passed unnoticed three weeks earlier, for me this was the real beginning of a new season. I tucked the cards inside my notebook and started across the lobby.

Several girls, clustered in front of the reception desk, admired a delivery from the florist shop and clamored to learn the lucky recipient. Probably a sorority girl. Those rich girls always received flowers for special occasions, from boyfriends, or, when one became engaged, from her sorority sisters. As if flashing a big diamond wasn't enough to inform the rest of us that she had secured her future with the man of her dreams.

Melanie," the desk girl called. "These are for you."

I rushed over to claim my prize. Certainly my parents hadn't sent me flowers. Although Mom grew tulips and hyacinths in spring; zinnia and begonias, and always a tall stand of sunflowers boarding the back fence in summer; plus asters and mums in fall, she was opposed to "hothouse flowers."

"Why waste good money on something that's going to die and be thrown out in a few days?" she always asked. She'd even made it clear for her funeral her coffin should be nothing more than a plain pine box and the only flowers should be blooms from her garden or wildflowers from a field. As if any of us would be inclined to cut flowers and arrange bouquets at the time of her death. Who did she think would go trouncing about the county looking for wildflowers among the corn stalks and hay fields?

"What if you die in winter?" I asked to show her the fallacy of her instructions.

"If you insist on decorating my grave a pine branch will do," she retorted beating me in yet another argument.

As I approached the desk, I blushed with shame. I should have spent more time with my grandmother Moroskavich over Christmas break. I'd barely stayed an hour when I dropped in and now she was sending me flowers for my birthday.

On the counter, a gorgeous bouquet of cheery yellow jonquils filled a tall clear, cut-glass vase. Slender green stalks topped with round purple floral heads were interspersed among the shorter flowers. I recognized them as the same variety Gaga had planted in her garden just for me. Drumstick allium. Sprigs of dainty lily of the valley provided delicate balance to the arrangement.

I lifted the flowers to my nose and inhaled the heady sweet fragrance of the tiny bell shaped lilies. Slipping the card from the envelope attached to the vase, I read, *Happy Birthday. I love you! Moses Carter.*

My heart vibrated with joy.

"Who are they from?" all the girls wanted to know.

"My boyfriend," I answered, lifting my chin with pride. They'd have a fun time chewing on that, especially the ones who knew who my boyfriend was, but I didn't care. The rest of the world didn't matter.

In my room, I opened the cards and read the messages inside. Even Mom's contained a sweet sentiment:

*Dear Melanie, I remember the love I felt the first time I
held you twenty-one years ago. Happy birthday, may
all your dreams come true. Love, Mom*

I brushed tears from my cheek and reread her message. Did she really wish all my dreams would come true, even those that didn't match hers? I knew better.

When I opened Pearl's card a smaller card slipped out and fell to the floor. I bent down and picked up the picture of her sweet baby boy. A note from Pearl confided she'd splurged at Sears for the photo of little Larry on his six month birthday. The picture of health and glee, his mouth wide open in laughter displayed two tiny teeth glistening behind his bottom lip. I gently ran my finger over the photo. Larry's plump arms and legs and cheeks were the very essences of a bouncing baby boy.

I was charmed that my best friend had found such contentment in housewifery and mothering. I hadn't understood her feelings before, but now I imagined being married and giving my husband a child, too. I glowed with warmth, brushing away all thoughts of the pain Moe and I would face.

I tacked Larry's picture on my bulletin board and lined the cards up next to the flowers on the desk. The yellow, purple, white and green bouquet presented a cheery combination, fresh and whispering of spring. The lilies infused the air with their sweet scent. Had Moe selected these flowers, or left it up to the florist?

Something clicked in my brain. The teacher of last semester's dreaded botany class had focused on boring rather than beauty— plant structure and the functions of each part: roots, stems, shoots, leaves. We were supposed to learn about plant reproduction, but I didn't remember any of it except there were sepals and stamens. Studying all that lessened my appreciation for flowers although the knowledge increased my awe for the intricacies of nature. Sensing the lack of enthusiasm from his students, the teacher spent one class period presenting a slideshow of pretty flowers.

He'd told us many cultures attributed special meanings to them. "Just for fun," he dryly commented, "here's a list of their supposed meanings." I'd given the handout a cursory glance and tucked it in my notebook. At the end of the semester, I tossed my botany notes but decided to keep the list. It would be fun to share with Gaga as we interpreted the flowers in her garden the following summer.

I pulled a tattered cardboard box from under my bed, rummaged through notebooks and retrieved the list. Smoothing the wrinkled paper, I skipped through the alphabetical list caring only about the flowers from Moe. I loved the drumstick allium, a tribute to my music, but I was even more delighted to learn that allium stood for unity and patience. It would take every bit of patience I could muster to wait for the unity between Moe and me to come to fruition. Jonquil represented desire and meant 'you're the only one.' Lily of the Valley expressed devotion and said 'you've made my life complete.'

As I stared from flowers to words and back again, desire coupled with apprehension overwhelmed me. Did Moe know the message he had sent? Should I tell him? Would it risk denial? Why were those promises, so direct and simple on the sheet of paper, so complicated in real life? Why couldn't we share desire, unity, and devotion and complete each others' lives? Why did everyone get in the way of our happiness?

Pulling myself away from the flowers I trudged down the hall to the bathroom to get ready for our date.

Instead of Bruno's or Bill Knapp's Moe took me to The Embers, a restaurant downtown. The walls were paneled in rich dark wood; plush red carpet covered the floor, the color matching the cushioned chair seats. Crisp white linen cloths and napkins folded into crowns dressed each table. Light reflected from the crystal chandeliers hanging overhead made the silverware twinkle. I gasped at the elegance.

A gentleman in a black suit hesitated a brief moment when Moe gave his name, then made check marks with a grease pencil on his seating chart. He led us to a small table next to the kitchen's swinging doors.

A waiter in a white shirt and black bowtie filled our water glasses, handed us menus and left. I glanced around the room. Moe was the only black person. The waiter poured water and handed menus to a couple who had been seated just after us. He smiled at them and pointed out items on the menu and took their drink orders. Moe crooked his arm and pulled his fingers forward signaling the waiter to return.

"Was there something I could get you? Are you ready to order?" the man asked in a flat voice.

"It's the young lady's twenty-first birthday and I would like to be the first to share a drink with her." Moe looked at me and asked, "Do you know what you'd like or should I order for you?"

My folks were beer drinkers. At family get-togethers, Dad and Oompa and my uncles would go to the basement and drink boilermakers—beer followed by a shot of whiskey. Once in a while Mom and Dad went dancing and she'd have a cocktail. That was as fancy as it got. I wasn't even sure what was in a cocktail. I nodded and Moe ordered us rum and Coke.

I opened the menu's leather cover and stared at the list of food selections.

"There aren't any prices," I whispered.

Was this a trick? Did they have special menus so they could set higher prices for Negroes?

Moe smiled, "Don't worry about it. Order whatever you want, birthday woman."

The waiter soon returned to the dining room with a tray of drinks. He placed fancy, stemmed glasses in front of the other couple. The man's drink was clear. Olives, bigger than I'd ever seen, skewered on a toothpick, had been placed across the top of the glass. The woman's drink, a frothy pale yellow concoction was garnished with a bright red cherry and a vibrant orange slice stuck to a tiny paper umbrella. The couple lifted their glasses, clinked the edges together in a wordless toast and took delicate sips.

The waiter brought us tall straight sided glasses of dark bubbly cola, rum, and ice. Each held a straw and a slice of lime wedged over the rim. Moe twisted the straw in his drink and smiled at me.

"Cheers," he said and waited for me to sample my first legal drink.

I took a sip. The rum left an odd, oily taste in my mouth and a warmth in my belly. I took a bigger gulp and started coughing. My face grew as warm as the pit of my stomach. Moe smiled. My uncouth behavior, a constant source of embarrassment to me, never seemed to bother him.

The menu contained an abundance of beef choices. I was used to Sunday dinner pot roast and hamburger in all its many forms: patties, meatloaf, Spanish rice, goulash, chili, and a zillion other dishes Mom served us. None of those were offered. I didn't know the difference between a New York Strip and a Delmonico. The seafood choices were just as puzzling, more exotic than the bluegills and bass my dad caught at the lake. I was sure the lobster tail was the most expensive item on the menu and I didn't know what kind of fish fillet of sole was. The name made me think of the cartoon of a fisherman with an old boot on the end of his hook.

I ordered the Breast of Chicken Kiev suspecting it would be nothing like Gaga's fried chicken. Wasn't Kiev a part of Russia? How far was that from Bohemia? Was their food anything alike? Moe ordered prime rib, it's very name meaning it would be special and pricey. Maybe I should offer some of the birthday money from my grandmothers to help pay.

The waiter brought us a basket of warm bread, and lettuce wedges with tomatoes and Thousand Island dressing. Although he visited other tables, replenishing the bread, refilling water glasses, taking re-orders on drinks, and asking if everything was satisfactory, he didn't return to us until long after we'd finished the bread and salads. He set the entrees before us, asked if we wanted anything else and turned to leave.

"We'd like two more rum and Cokes," Moe said to his back.

The waiter turned, nodded slightly and said, "Of course." He took our drink glasses and left.

The chicken Kiev was round and covered with a golden brown crust. Except for the butter it was swimming in, it looked a lot like Gaga's fried chicken fancied up with a big sprig of parsley. I pierced the meat with my fork and stuck the knife in. An oily mix of butter and garlic squirted in a long stream hitting me just above my left breast.

Moe jumped up, dipped his napkin in his water glass and reached over to help. Just as he was about to wipe my blouse with the napkin, his hand recoiled. The look on my face must have matched the mortified look on his. The couple at the next table stared with mouths open. I grabbed the napkin from Moe, he plunked back into his chair.

"Maybe I should try to fix this mess in the bathroom," I mumbled.

Stumbling away from the table, I fled to privacy. I dabbed at my blouse and then at my eyes, neither of which improved with my ministrations. I would have stayed in the bathroom the rest of the evening nursing my injured ego, but I couldn't leave Moe alone with all those white people staring at him.

I summoned what false dignity I could and marched back to the table, pretending the soiled blouse and blotched face were nothing to be concerned about. I took large gulps of the rum drink the waiter had brought in my absence, fortifying myself against the humiliation.

The chicken was delicious. Moe shared a taste of his prime rib, and soon we were laughing and cooing like love birds. Our fancy date was a success.

Arms wrapped around each other, we walked unsteadily down the sidewalk. Was it love or rum that caused my lightheadedness? When we reached Moe's car, he pulled me close. Desire rushed through me. Bodies pressed together, we shared a long, deep kiss. I shuddered with pleasure.

As Moe drove, I sat plastered to his side and caressed his arm. Within a few minutes we were parked behind the cemetery. His knee hit the dash as he turned to pull me into his arms. I shifted to accommodate his long legs. He moved to fit even closer to me; his knee banged against the steering wheel. Frustrated, he grabbed the lever and pushed the seat back as far as possible.

I leaned back against the door, luxuriating in the feel of Moe's hands on my face, my neck, my arms, my breast. My dress rode up and he touched my bare thigh. He quickly withdrew his hand and sat up as if startled to realize what he had done. I pulled him back to me and guided his hand to my leg. A moan drifted from his lips like the deep, mellow note of a bassoon. I trilled "I love you" in response.

I slid along the seat and felt the exquisite pressure of his body on top of me. We fumbled with each others' clothing, eagerly touching, kissing, ignoring the awkward positions we had contorted into in order to share our love. I was delirious, willing the moment to last forever.

Too soon, we were sitting up, readjusting our clothing, too self-conscious to disturb the spell with words.

A deplorable thought shook my brain. Could he tell I wasn't a virgin? This wasn't the time to explain, to tell him I had been raped on a date at the drive-in when I was sixteen. I should have confided in him before this. But how could I? It had been horrific, so different from what Moe and I had just done. I had been ashamed then, but now I was thrilled to give myself to the man I loved. Would he understand? Or would I lose him?

"Wow," he whispered his voice raspy. "It's almost eleven. We have to get back before curfew."

He drove past the rows of tombstones and out of the cemetery before turning on his headlights. I wanted to beg him to take me someplace else, anywhere but the dorm. How could we separate for even one minute after we had just joined together?

Moe sped through the streets, eyes darting from speedometer to rear view mirror. His car careened around the corner and sped up the hill to the dorm.

Through the glass doors, I could see Mrs. Ebert moving rapidly across the lobby, intent on performing her last duty of the night. Keys, suspended on a cord around her neck, bounced against her ample chest.

Moe slammed on the brakes, I jumped from the car, yelled, "I love you!" and dashed through the dormitory doors.

Mrs. Ebert emitted a loud harrumph, probably disappointed that she hadn't been quick enough to lock me out and surely appalled that I had been on a date with a Negro.

Did it show that we had made love? I felt as if I'd magically changed into someone else, a woman who was loved by a man. If the other girls drifting off to their rooms didn't notice they must be mooning over their silly boyfriends. And sour Mrs. Ebert was too bitter to recognize joy when it was right in front of her.

The next morning, I ran out of the music hall greedy to be with Moe, to tell him all the things that had tied my tongue in knots the night before. I was thrilled to see him standing on the sidewalk just outside the door. He must have missed me as much as I had missed him. I rushed into his arms.

He kissed my forehead and said, "Could we skip coffee? We should talk." His face was expressionless. Was he going to dump me after what we had done? Because of what we had done?

"I drove over. I'm in B lot," he said still giving no indication of his feelings. He took my hand and led me to his car like a child.

I sat on the passenger side, not moving from near the door, and stared straight ahead. Blinking, I willed tears to keep from straying down my cheeks.

Neither of us spoke as he drove beyond the outskirts of the city and finally turned down a gravel road.

"Hopefully, we can talk here without anyone coming along."

He shut off the car and turned toward me.

I looked up, afraid of what I might see on his face. Still nothing. His eyes blank, like two dark stones, his lips slightly pursed. What was going on?

"Melanie," he began. "I didn't mean to hurt you last night. I shouldn't have done what I did. We can't. I can't ask you to."

"Hurt me?" I gasped. "You didn't hurt me, you didn't ask me to do anything I didn't want to do. I love you. And you love me, don't you?"

I blubbered the last, not sure he could decipher what I had said.

"Yes, but look at all the trouble we've had. No one wants us to be together. I can't let you go through all that. To give up your family. To have no friends. To—"

I grabbed Moe's face between my hands. "Is it because I wasn't a virgin?"

His eyes grew wide. "No. I mean. No, I didn't know."

The secret I'd kept locked inside spewed from my lips and my heart like red hot lava. As I told him how I'd suffered when my reputation was ruined by lies, the humiliation returned as raw and painful as it had been five years earlier. Great wracking sobs threatened to split me in two. Moe put his arms around me and let me cry. I don't know how long I bawled, but finally the torrent subsided and I slumped against him like a rag doll. Shifting in the seat, he pulled a handkerchief from his back pocket and gently wiped my face.

"I'm sorry," he said. "I didn't want to hurt you again."

I bolted up, startled by his misinterpretation of what had happened between us. I grabbed his hand.

"You didn't hurt me. I just now realized that I have been afraid of ever getting close to anyone until you. What we shared last night was the best thing that has ever happened to me."

A grim look shadowed his face.

"Melanie, we shouldn't have let things go this far. You're going to be hurt again and again if you stay with me. We have to stop seeing each other."

I stared through the windshield unable to respond. This wasn't happening.

Moe cleared his throat, "I should have told you before. I've signed up to join SNCC on the voter registration project. I leave right after graduation for Mississippi."

"Mississippi? I don't understand. Is it because we—?"

"I've been thinking about it for a long time. I've applied for dozens of jobs. With a name like Moses they figure I'm either black or Jewish so I'm not even considered. Most of them don't even answer and the ones who do all say the same thing, 'Sorry, we don't need you.' Mississippi is a start, a chance to change things."

"Isn't there anything closer? Couldn't you stay here and work with G.W.?"

"He's going, too. I have to do this. Things will never change if people don't act. I have to be a part of it so someday people like us can be together. I don't want to regret not trying."

His words hit like a blast from a foghorn. Hadn't we made a promise to make things work for us so we'd never regret not having tried? Now he was willing to give me up for people he didn't even know.

"Didn't you think about me?"

"Melanie, you're all I thought about. Every job I applied for, I thought if only I'd get hired, I could spend next year starting a career, saving money, making plans for us to be together. I even dared hope we could convince people it was a good idea for us to get married. But it's foolish to think it would work."

Bitterness filled my throat and tinged my words. "Maybe I'm a fool for believing you when you said you'd try."

An old pickup crawling down the road slowed as it passed. The driver, a craggy-faced coot in a beat up straw hat, stared at us then sped up splaying mud and gravel against the side of Moe's car. The interruption shifted the tension and gave me time to compose a better response.

"You said we should try and now you're giving up? Why did you say you love me if you didn't mean it?"

"I mean it." A sob caught in his throat making his answer sound sincere, but I knew it wasn't.

"Love is forever." I countered.

"My feelings for you won't change," he said. "But the timing is all wrong. You need to finish school, work on your music, pursue those dreams, not have to fight for everything because of me."

"So that's it! You've made this big decision about what my life should be and I don't have a say in the matter. You have a lot of nerve saying you love me and don't want to hurt me."

"Melanie, don't"

"Don't, yourself! Unless you figure out how I fit into your life there's nothing left to say."

I crossed my arms and pushed back against the seat. Anger and hurt muddled my brain. Had I just shoved Moe away for good?

A red glow whirled through the back window and a police car pulled next to us. Moe reached over, putting his hand on my arm and whispered, "Don't say anything unless you're asked."

He rolled down the window as two officers approached. We were ordered out of the car. Moe's arm was twisted behind his back and he was pushed against his car's fender. One of the policemen pressed his hand against Moe's back while the other frisked and handcuffed him.

Then one of the cops ordered me into the back seat of the squad car. He sat in the front and turned to face me. After looking at me a long moment, as if trying to decipher what kind of girl I was, he said, "You're safe here. You can answer my questions without being afraid. Was that man holding you against your will?"

"No!" I shrieked. I took a deep breath to regain my composure. I didn't want to give him reason to suspect I was afraid to tell the truth. "He's my friend. We were just talking. He isn't doing anything wrong. Neither of us is."

My voice remained calm as I assured him I was there voluntarily and Moe and I were simply having a conversation. I felt anything but calm. If I'd been on that lonely country road with a white boy, they wouldn't have even stopped or, at most, would have told us to move along. Because of his skin, Moe was always suspected of doing something wrong. Why would he choose to go to Mississippi and put himself in the thick of the battle when there were enough fights for him in every day life?

I finally convinced the cop everything was okay. Warning us we should only use a car for transportation, he let us go. The police followed us a few miles as we drove toward town, then veered away at the city limits.

Moe parked on a side street a few blocks from campus and said, "I don't want that to keep happening to you. Now, do you understand?"

"I understand that this is the way things are, that those things will keep happening when we're together, but it just made me mad, not ready to give up. I haven't given up on my music either. I'm not the one who's a quitter." I grabbed the latch and swung the car door wide.

"Wait!" I had never heard Moe sound so desperate. "I want to work things out. We have 'til graduation and after that I'll write to you every day. You'll have time for your music and to finish school. But I have to do this, Melanie. It won't be forever. Next year I'll get a real job and we'll make it work. I know we will. Because you believe in me."

I pulled the door shut and smiled at him.

"Because I believe in us."

EIGHTEEN

Over the next few weeks, time sped like a runaway train toward its destination, our last moment together. Moe labored over final assignments, studied for exams, and prepared for the Voter Education Project in Mississippi.

My drumming took on a fresher, sharper, more frenzied style as I banged out my scattered emotions. Ginger was booked every weekend and for the first time we turned down jobs. I renewed my pursuit of a recording gig.

As often as possible Moe and I stole away, holding tight to the racing hours and each other. The cemetery's solitude was often interrupted by funeral processions or visitors spiffing up their loved ones' graves so Moe found an alternate secluded spot. The narrow road which dead ended at the railroad tracks was off a street called Lovers Lane.

Sometimes a train stalled alongside our parking spot and men in grease-splattered coveralls hooted catcalls at us. But mostly we were afforded the luxuriant pleasure of time alone. As we kissed and touched each other, I sensed Moe fighting to resist going all the way. The more he held back the more desirable he became. We always gave in. I never felt guilt, only pleasure. Memories of those intimate moments sustained me when we were apart.

Dreading the time away, I went home the weekend of Dad's birthday. When we returned from Sunday dinner at Gaga's, Mom called me into her bedroom.

"Are you dating that colored boy?" she demanded.

The question had pressed between us all weekend, pushing so insistently I was relieved it had finally exploded like a popped balloon.

I should have had a more civil answer prepared, but I confronted her as bluntly as she'd confronted me.

"I'm twenty-one now. You have no say over who I date or anything else I do."

"You are headed for big trouble, Missy. No one approves of coloreds mixing with whites."

"Not everyone is a bigot. You want me to be just like you. Well, I'm not! I'm going to do what I want. I'm going to be a drummer and I'm going to be with Moe and there is nothing you can do about it."

"I will never have that boy in this house," she hissed.

"Fine! You won't have me in this house either!"

Shaking with anger, I ran from the room. Darlene watched as I sorted through all my stuff in our bedroom. I told her she could have what I was leaving behind.

"You're never coming back?" she asked. "Can I have the boots Mom gave you for Christmas?"

I trudged outside lugging a box that held the few items still linking me to home and family. Randy drove me downtown to catch the Greyhound at Rexall's.

"Are you sure you want to do this?" he asked. "You know she'll get over her snit eventually."

"No, she won't. She hates me. I'm not coming back." I wanted to hug Randy to preserve some connection with family, but I couldn't trust that she wouldn't brainwash him, too.

Without good-byes I left Middleton and my family behind.

Moe picked me up at the bus station curious to know why I'd come back early. He mutely listened to my tirade against my mother and my vow to never return home. When I ran out of steam and sputtered my last complaint, he put his arm around me and said, "I'm sorry."

"Stop apologizing! She forced me to make a choice. I won't regret never seeing her again."

"She's your mother. You'll work things out with her this summer."

"She's my mother; she'll never change. I'm not going back there."

By mid-May, I still wasn't sure where I'd spend the summer. Certainly my grandparents would take me in, but with the stipulation I make up with my mother. That wouldn't happen unless she apologized and changed her mind about Moe. Fat chance! She was too stubborn.

I pleaded with Moe to take me to Mississippi but he was emphatic. "It's too dangerous. They do terrible things to interracial couples."

"How much worse could it be than it is here?

"Down there they do more than hurt your feelings and your dignity. It gets brutal."

"But nothing could be worse than being apart."

He shook his head and gave me that look, like I was too dumb to get it. I gave up rather than let arguments ruin our last few days together.

Still trying to figure it out, I visited the registration office and picked up information on summer school. Back at the dorm, I moved trance-like to my mailbox and with dread and curiosity retrieved an important looking envelope. It was from Fortune Records in Detroit, one of several recording companies I'd sent tapes of Ginger's best songs. I ripped open the envelope, read the letter and let it slip from my fingers to the floor. Fortune wanted us to audition! They might offer to record and promote a forty-five. I swept up the papers and ran to the phone to call the boys.

Moe offered us a ride and picked everyone up by 7:00 on Saturday morning. It was unusually warm for May and the car was crammed with instruments and musicians cranky from too little sleep and too much anxiety. Our bickering over song choices threatened to become a large-scale battle. By the time we arrived we were bedraggled, sweaty, wrinkly-clothed and tense as piano wires.

The guys and I straggled through the door of the square cinder-block building and stopped short. In the small room, several people leafed through stacks of records crammed together on tables and shelves

"What the hell? This is nothin' but a record shop," Johnny complained.

"The studio's in back," I whispered pointing to a small neon sign above the door. "Follow me."

The studio was much smaller and more primitive than Sun Studios in Memphis where I'd long ago cut a record. There were only two microphones, the control room was stuck in a tiny closet and the studio piano was an antique. Johnny's brow wrinkled with skepticism, but when he played the F sharp scale he declared the piano in tune. Brad and Marv jittered with excitement. I didn't let on to the guys how disappointed I was. How could this place turn us into rock and roll stars?

By one o'clock, we had made a recording and signed a contract giving Fortune Records seventy percent of profits after recovered costs and exclusive rights to our music for the next two years. Moe tried to persuade us to think it over before signing but all we saw were our names in bright lights like the Milky Way spreading across the sky .

Afterward, we went to a Coney Island for lunch and committed to the rest of our future as Ginger. We agreed to go on the road for the summer. I was relieved to have a plan, no matter how indefinite. My music was consolation for being without Moe. None of us had a car, we had no gigs lined up, and no surplus funds to support us, but we had optimism. We were a rock and roll band on the verge of making it big. The rest was just details.

Moe dropped the boys at Wayne State to spend the night with one of Marv's buddies. I told them I would be staying with a friend in St. Clair Shores, though no such friend existed. Instead, Moe and I drove to Flint.

I chattered all the way, so nervous I thought my heart would burst and splatter my emotions all over the highway letting my empty body float into outer space.

Moe smiled. "Settle down. You're so jumpy, you'll never be able to keep Mama's cookin' down. You'll hurt her feelings if you don't stuff yourself and ask for seconds."

I stopped talking out loud, but my mind rattled on. What if Moe's family didn't like me?

He pointed out the massive Buick factory complex where he'd worked the summer before, then drove across the river and through a neighborhood of modest homes, finally pulling into the gravel driveway of a neat two story house. It looked smaller than my parents' and had a tiny front yard edged with a cracked cement sidewalk. Similar houses snuggled close on either side. I imagined Moe sticking his arm out the bedroom window upstairs and tagging someone in the room next door.

A plumpish black woman stepped onto the side stoop and waved the hem of the faded apron she wore over a floral housedress. Moe jumped from the car, bounded up the step, swept the woman off her feet and twirled her around. Her face bloomed like a flower and, laughing, she swatted at his arm to set her down. My mother always said, "You can tell a good man by the way he treats his mother." If only she had seen this she would know Moe was right for me.

"C'mon Mama, I want you to meet Melanie." He led her to the car and flung open the door. I looked up with a timid smile, unable to speak. Moe reached in and pulled me from the car.

Mama pushed him aside and grabbed me in a hug. She smelled of fried food, lilac cologne and a slight hint of Lysol. "Miss Melanie, you are a skinny one. Come inside and Mama will feed you right now."

I laughed. "Thank you, Mrs. Carter. My mother always says I'm too fat."

Within a few minutes a feast had appeared on the kitchen table —biscuits and gravy, fried chicken and something that looked like cooked spinach, but wasn't.

Moe's mother heaped my plate. "Just a little something to hold you over to supper. Naomi pulled a weekend shift at the hospital. She'll be home by seven and we'll eat then."

In between bites of crispy chicken and fluffy biscuits I answered her questions about school and the band and my family. Her voice sang with pleasure over my mother's good fortune.

"Your mama must be real proud of you. Such a talented, sweet little thing."

I could never let this dear woman know what a horrible mother I had.

I ate up every bit of what she offered—her food and her kindness—except for the lemon pie which I promised to have after supper. As I washed dishes, she dried and told me about Moe's childhood.

A few minutes before seven, Naomi burst through the door calling, "I'm home. Little brother!"

She flew into the living room where Moe and I sat on the overstuffed couch looking through family albums. She stopped in mid-flight and gasped. Moe stood and took a step toward his sister.

Naomi squawked an accusation of betrayal. "Mama didn't tell me she was white."

I was stuck to the couch cushion, my face turning from pale white to crimson. Naomi turned and fled from the room.

Moe raced after her, calling, "Naomi!"

Silverware clattered to the linoleum floor in the kitchen and Moe's mother rushed through the door. She hustled up the stairs after Moe and his sister. Their voices rose and fell in tones of argument, apology, soothing and anger. I couldn't make out the words but I didn't want to hear them anyway. I pressed my hands against my ears shutting out all but the sound of my pounding pulse.

A while later Moe gently held my hands and whispered, "We have to go."

We stumbled to the car and drove away. We'd crossed the river before he explained.

"All through high school white kids made fun of Naomi. Girls spread lies about her. Boys called her dirty names and touched her when they walked by her locker. It got so bad she almost dropped out. I tried to protect her, but I couldn't be there all the time." Moe's jaw tightened at the memory.

I wanted to defend my race, to remind him not all white people act that way, but what could I say? I'd been teased, shunned and lied about in high school, too. But it hadn't colored my judgment. Or had it? After a while, things had simmered down, but they had only gotten worse for Naomi.

"She has trouble at work, too. Sometimes white people ask for a different nurse when they see she's black. She's passed over for promotions and given all the scut work by white supervisors. I didn't realize how badly it affected her."

I reached over and caressed his hand. "I'm sorry."

He grasped the steering wheel so tightly the veins in his wrist bulged. After a long silence, he said, "Mama asked me to tell you she's sorry she couldn't have you stay. She has to back my sister in this. Maybe someday Naomi will see things differently."

"Yeah, my mother, too," I said, knowing it would never happen.

I finally understood how hurt Moe felt when my mother had rejected him. He had worried I wouldn't have the strength to give up my family to be with him. Could he give up his?

Around ten that night Moe parked in the lot behind Detroit Memorial Hospital. "This should be safe and with traffic in and out all night we won't draw attention. You can sleep in the back seat, I'll stay in front in case someone comes along."

As I crawled in back and stretched out over the wide seat I longed to ask Moe to join me, but it was too risky. Thoughts of all that had happened kept me awake. Ginger was on its way to success, I had a plan however sketchy for the summer, Moe was leaving, everyone was against us. Occasionally I heard him shifting about. I listened for the slow steady breaths of slumber, but I didn't hear them. I think he was awake the entire night. Only a few inches from each other, the distance felt insurmountable.

As soon as the sun came up, Moe drove to a small grocery store near Wayne State and bought us coffee and donuts. We sat on a bench in a neighborhood park, too tired, physically and emotionally to talk about anything other than the weather which threatened rain. At 10:30 we picked up Johnny, Marv and Brad and headed back to school.

I didn't protest when Moe dropped me at my dorm. I crawled into bed, pulled the sheet over my head and slept fourteen hours straight. At four in the morning, I took a shower, hit the books, and tried to convince myself life would eventually work out.

There was no need to discuss what had happened. Naomi felt about me the way my mother felt about Moe. As long as we were together, people would reject us but no one would inflict as much pain as family. Sadness weighed me down like an elephant on my shoulders. We were leaving in two weeks. Moe for Mississippi, me for the unknown world of small town taverns and county fairs, separated from our families and from each other.

One afternoon, driving to our parking spot Moe looked particularly down. As soon as he shut off the engine I put my arms around his neck and drew him toward me.

He pulled my hands down and held them. "Mama called. Naomi won't come to my graduation if you're there. Mama won't leave Naomi. My sister Lydia can't travel, too close to her due date. And Ruthie said she and Mack won't come unless Mama and Naomi will."

What should I say? He was leaving for Mississippi right after graduation. How could I give up my last few hours with him?

"Maybe I should skip the ceremony," he said.

It sounded like a question. Did he expect me to give the answer? To tell him, 'yes let's spend the time alone together,' or 'no, you should be with your family.' No matter what I chose, someone would be hurt and Moe and I would both be unhappy.

"You've worked so hard," I said. "It's your special day. What do you think you should do?"

He slammed his fist against the steering wheel. "Damn! Why does it have to be this way? I want you there. I want my family there. I want my family to want you there. Hell, I even want your family there."

I laughed at his bitter joke. My chin quivered and I held my breath to keep from crying. Everyone was being so unreasonable and I wanted to be unreasonable too—to demand he choose me to sit in the front row of the field house and cheer when he received his diploma. To go out afterward for dinner and champagne, to spend the night together, to live happily ever after.

Instead, I forced myself to sound mature. "Call your mother and tell her to come. I'll stay away."

Air escaped from Moe's lungs with a great whoosh. The look of relief on his face was unbearable. I turned away so he couldn't see how he'd hurt me. Maybe it was unreasonable and immature of me to regret the gift I'd offered, but I hadn't expected him to accept it so eagerly.

On the morning of graduation day, Moe came by and gave me his saxophone and the keys to his car. He'd have no use for a horn or a car in Mississippi and had offered them to Ginger, who surely had a need.

The night before we'd said little, cried and made love. There was nothing left.

He hugged me and walked away, back to his dorm on the other side of campus to wait for his mother and sisters. He and G.W. would leave right after the graduation ceremony for Columbus, Ohio, where they would join the others going to Mississippi.

I loaded all my possessions in the trunk of the car, turned in my room key and left to pick up Johnny, Marv and Brad.

Brad offered to drive. In no condition to navigate the highway I willingly gave up the wheel. Withering in the backseat, I was deaf to everything the boys said, blind to everything we passed.

A few hours later, when we arrived in Sparta, Brad's hometown, I was forced to pull myself back to reality. His parents welcomed us into their home and fed us an early supper. We set up our instruments at the VFW hall and played a crowd fairly sizable for a Sunday night in a small town. I barely made it through the gig, numb with loneliness for Moe. Afterward, the guys bunked in Brad's childhood bedroom and I slept on the living room couch.

The next morning, I called Fortune Records and learned they had sent copies of our record to a couple dozen radio stations. We'd even received a little airplay. The receptionist who gave me the information said she had a list of clubs and events we could audition for. After I'd written everything down she said, "The pay varies, but the going rate for new groups is around fifty dollars a night—four forty-five minute sets."

Although math wasn't my strong suit, I calculated each of us would take home a little over twelve dollars if, like the VFW, they paid cash. We wouldn't get rich but we'd survive.

Her voice lowered like a spy passing secrets in a dark alley, "Anything you sign up for through us has a fee—twenty dollars per event." Our wages dropped to seven-fifty a piece.

"Ohhh," My reaction was more an exhale of shock than a statement of agreement.

"Of course, if you set up your own dates, you don't have to pay us..." Her voice trailed off as if she intended to add "do you get what I'm telling you?"

I did get it and so did the fellas. Certain we could create our own fortune, we agreed to find work without the record company's help. I kept the list in case we got desperate, but by noon we'd come up with a long list of our own.

We spent the summer crisscrossing the state, playing at country fairs, local festivals, clubs and every hick bar in the region. Sometimes our pay was as measly as five bucks a player, a couple times fifty dollar bills crossed our palms, but like the Fortune Records' receptionist had said, twelve-fifty per was standard. We quickly learned to set out a tip jar, but few people contributed no matter how much beer they'd drunk.

Whenever we had a gig within driving distance, we stayed with Brad's family. Other times we bummed off friends and relatives until we sensed we'd worn out our welcome. I steered us away from accepting gigs within a twenty-five mile radius of Middleton.

Brad hauled out a pup tent from his scouting days and some nights the guys slept in it while I took the back seat of Moe's car. Now and then we stayed in cheap roadside cabins. I suggested we split the cost equally, but the boys disagreed because the three of them shared a cabin while I had one to myself.

"How'd you feel if we had to split the cost of meals even up?" Johnny asked. "Marv eats like a horse."

It was a valid argument. Most of the bars we played gave us free meals, but we still had to eat breakfast or lunch out. Marv's tab was always the largest. Mine was the least. Being tired from the odd hours and worrying about Moe worked better than Ayds Candy, my mother's favorite appetite suppressant.

While Moe and I were on the road neither of us had a phone number or mailing address. Before he'd left he came up with a plan to keep in touch.

"In two weeks, call Professor Lincoln. By then I should have a phone number where you can reach me or an address to write. I'll leave a message with him."

Two weeks after we left campus, I called the number Moe had given me, but there was no answer. I tried several more times and with each unanswered call my frustration grew like a weed in an untended garden. Then I remembered it was Sunday. Of course, Professor Lincoln wouldn't be in his office.

The next morning I found a pay phone and tried again.

"He comes in at one," a sparkly voiced student secretary informed me. After several agonizing hours, I finally reached Professor Lincoln.

"I did hear from the boys," the professor droned, then paused as if winding up to deliver a long, dull lecture.

I shifted from foot to foot wanting to scream.

"They made it to Mississippi. They're having quite a time traveling through those backwoods to register folks to vote."

"Did Moe leave a phone number?" I demanded. I didn't want to hear the old codger's tales. I wanted to hear Moe.

"Moe?" The professor sounded as if he had no idea what I was asking.

"Moses Carter. He said he'd give you a number so I could call him."

"Oh, oh that's right. Let me see. I think I have it here someplace." The receiver thunked on the desk, followed by the rustling of papers. Those gags about absent-minded professors had been written with him in mind.

Finally, he was back on the line. "Says here, oops can hardly read my own handwriting." He chuckled and I imagined grabbing his bobbing Adam's apple and squeezing the life out of him.

"Nope, sorry. No phone number. They're on the move too much to light in any one place. They'll be checking in with me again sometime this week. I could give him a message from you if you want."

The thought of having that dusty old goat relay my love to Moe made my stomach queasy. I had no phone number or address to give him.

"No, no message. Can I call you later to see if there's a message for me?"

"Of course, young lady. I have office hours from 1 to 3 Monday through Thursday."

Did Moe know that? If he couldn't get to a phone during that time—or I couldn't—how would we ever connect with each other?

I called Professor Lincoln every day he had office hours. At first, he sounded sympathetic as he repeated that he hadn't heard from Moe, but as time passed his voice took on an edge of exasperation. "No, no word," he said. Or "Mississippi is the deep south. They have to keep on the move. Folks they stay with don't have telephones." Although the words "I can't help you. Stop calling" didn't leave his tongue I sensed they dwelt in his mind.

As Moe moved through Mississippi, I roamed through Michigan with the band. We played every night, slept late in the day and contacted potential employers. We billed ourselves as the band with the new hit single, "Crazy Time," hoping someone had heard it on the radio. We'd only heard it twice ourselves and we'd whooped and carried on as if we'd just made *Billboard's Honor Roll of Hits.* Only my drumming or images of future stardom relieved me from my longing for Moe.

Over two weeks passed before Professor Lincoln finally gave me the number of a pay phone and instructions to call on Wednesday evening at eight-thirty. That night we were scheduled to play at the Prairie Schooner, a little bar out in the boondocks. The closest pay phone was in town eight miles away.

"Sorry," Brad said. "We have to set up at eight-thirty. We can't screw up and lose this job. It's two weeks' work."

"I don't care," I scowled. He stepped toward me. My voice reached banshee pitch. "I'm not missing my call."

Marv backed away holding up his hands in surrender while Brad pushed his angry face even closer to mine.

"You're crabby all the time. You gotta give up weepin' over that guy or you'll never make it in this business."

Johnny stepped between Brad and me. "It's okay. You can drop us off early and go make your call. We'll set up your kit. Just be ready to play at nine." Since the ugly incident with Diane, Johnny had continually done penance and had become my best advocate in the band.

I dropped the boys at the bar at eight and sped to town. Settled in the phone booth, I spread the coins I'd exchanged for a five at the bar onto the narrow shelf below the phone. I didn't know how much a call to Mississippi was but no matter how much money I had it wouldn't be enough to cover the amount of time I wanted to stay on the line with Moe.

A deep drawl answered on the fourth ring, "Jammie Leez, who yawl callin' on?"

A din of voices, clattering dishes, and thumping music blared through the phone.

"Moses Carter! Moe Carter!" I shouted.

"Carta" the voice boomed above the noise. Then came back at me, "Sor' ma'am, ain't no Carta here."

"But he said he'd be there. Moses Carter. He's with the voter registration people. G. W. Sloan, Moses Carter. Please. Try again."

A woman's voice, gravelly and annoyed, came over the phone lines. "You lookin' for them vota fellas from the noeth?"

"Yes, please. Moses Carter. He said he'd be there."

"Dem boys in a heapa trouble. Done got run clear outta town. Dey ain't comin' back. Least til things git settled down."

"Who should I call?"

"Sorry, honey, don't know." She hung up.

I stared at the phone willing it to transport Moe's voice from a thousand miles away.

A half-hour later, as the crowd looked on in wonder I beat so furiously on the drum head I broke one of my sticks. A long haired yokel lifted his fingers to his mouth and forced a shrill whistle from between his yellowed teeth. The thick heels of cowboy boots stomped and applause threatened to shake the walls. I slumped over my snare and cried.

The next day I called the professor. He'd heard from SNCC that Moe and G.W. had been threatened by the local sheriff. They knew that CORE workers had been severely beaten in that town—one lost hearing in his left ear, another was in the hospital for twenty-six days. The whole county was on CORE's list of places to leave if confronted. Moe and G.W. had moved on.

It wasn't until July 13th that the Professor had another phone number for me. At the designated time I called the pay phone in Pelahatchie, Mississippi. Moe answered on the first ring. I slipped to my knees at the sound of his voice. We babbled how much we missed each other. When he tried to assure me he wasn't in danger, I detected hesitancy in his voice. Moe was lying.

I told him things were good with me, but I don't think he believed me either.

"The band is busy every night," I told him. "Our record's getting some play and we even got a royalty check. Not much, but it's a start."

I didn't admit how truly miserable I was. How each moment I felt emptiness that couldn't be filled, fears that couldn't be dispelled, questions without answers.

"When are you coming home?" I croaked, my vocal chords compressed tight against my throat.

"I don't know. There's so much to do here. I miss you. I want to be there. We're going to try to make it back for the first meeting on campus in September."

I clung to that promise ignoring the warning that it wasn't a sure thing.

Over the next month, we connected sporadically on the phone and I wrote letters every day, never sure Moe would be able to pick them up.

His infrequent notes, mailed to Brad's parents' house, were short, but horrifying. He downplayed the danger, but only an idiot wouldn't pick up on how violent it was in Mississippi. He mentioned church burnings, beatings of Negroes and how difficult his work was.

"It's going to take a long time. People here are frozen with fear. Whites run everything and blacks are too paralyzed to stand up to them. They live under constant threat. They're afraid to register to vote."

SNCC's meeting place was bombed, Moe and G. W. were accosted on a back country road by a pistol-wielding man who ordered them to leave the area. Moe made light of the incident, "Can you believe it? We thought he was just some hick, but he was the mayor and most prominent citizen of the town." I sensed the danger and his discouragement.

During our infrequent phone calls, I begged him to come home. I cried, wheedled and tried to manipulate him with sweet words of love, but he could not be moved.

"I miss you, too, but there's too much to do here. I can't leave."

"But it's dangerous." My voice wavered. I'd meant my words to shame him into giving in, but they truly expressed my fear.

"I'll be okay. SNCC is taking care of us. They share all their connections; let us know every person who supports us. They tell us who runs the towns and what places to keep away from."

Moe's trust in SNCC didn't still my fears.

With each brief phone call, I experienced every emotion, even some I'd never felt before—anxiety and relief, misery and pleasure, despair and euphoria, rage and calmness. They say absence makes the heart grow fonder, but my heart ached with weariness and longing.

Music was my only source of comfort and often our work was so trying even that failed. Ginger continued to travel throughout Michigan and sometimes into Indiana or Ohio, playing wherever we could find work. By the second week of August, all of us were especially snappish. The outside temperature was in the nineties and our distemper added several degrees to the car's interior. I gritted my teeth and gulped to suppress the carsickness welling in my stomach. The radiator overheated and we were stuck in Owosso for a couple hours making us late for our next gig. The club was a dirty dive with few customers. They heckled us, rudely belly aching about our music. We left during break without collecting our pay. It was the only thing we'd agreed on all day.

We checked into a cheap motel whose sign falsely advertised air conditioning. Ignoring the cockroaches in the bathroom and the dusty cobwebs in the corner, I cried myself to sleep. My band mates had long ago made it clear they didn't want to deal with female romance problems. I was alone. All that kept me from giving up was the thought that the next day I would call Moe.

I deposited the coins in the pay phone slot and listened to the persistent ring on the other end of the line. The operator cut in, "There's no answer. Please try your call later." I hung up, collected the change from the coin return, and rummaged through my purse for Moe's letter to confirm the time and number. Why hadn't he answered?

I tried several times over the next few hours with the same result. Digging through my purse again, I found Professor Lincoln's home phone number. I'd wheedled it from him a few weeks before with the promise to use it only in a dire emergency. I was certain he would think my concerns did not qualify as a dire emergency, but as soon as I identified myself, he said, "I'm glad you called." Then added,

"G. W. Sloan and Moses Carter are in Parchman prison."

NINETEEN

Professor Lincoln told me Moe, G.W. and six other SNCC workers had been arrested and hauled off to the worst prison in Mississippi.

"Parchman has a reputation for trying to break civil rights activists," he said.

My mind pitched about in a quagmire of confusion.

"How will they get out?" I asked, surprised to sound so calm while the question shrieked in my head.

"We've got people on the way. I'm sure they'll be released in no time. Do you know how I can reach Moe's family? I should let them know."

He doesn't have family, except me, I wanted to say. Besides, hadn't he told me that SNCC kept track of everyone? Wouldn't they have contacted his family? I gave him Mrs. Carter's Flint address which I'd memorized from all the letters I'd written the summer before. Maybe Professor Lincoln would mention to her how helpful I was.

Dazed, I wandered to the diner where Johnny, Brad and Marv were having a late lunch. I told them about Moe and for once they didn't brush me off.

"Guys, I can't play tonight. Maybe there'll be some kid in the audience itching to fill in."

It wasn't such an odd suggestion. We'd been approached dozens of times by fellas, young and old, who wanted to be in a band, to join the glamorous life they imagined we led.

Seeing the tears glisten my eyes, the boys agreed to give me a break.

"How about we spring for the motel again tonight?" Johnny offered. His hand gently patted my shoulder.

In the dreary motel room, I reviewed my life since Moe. I'd been so naive when we met, thinking I was so sophisticated and open-minded to befriend a black man. How unaware I'd been of what being black means. Probably I would never fully understand. But I saw in him kindness, intelligence, caring and ambition, all the things I'd dreamed of in a husband, the same things my mother wanted for me. Why couldn't people see past our skin tones?

Moe and I would have to give up our families to be together. He wouldn't fit in my world, I wouldn't fit in his. We'd have to forge our own world. And every way we turned there would be obstacles. He had warned me, afraid I wasn't strong enough. A few months ago he would have been right.

Now I was ready to forego whatever I had to, to be with him. I'd stand up for him when he needed me and stand behind him when he chose to stand on his own. I'd been advised to follow my heart no matter the obstacles. I knew what I had to do.

Early the next morning I left the car key at the desk for Johnny, Brad and Marv, then walked three blocks to the Greyhound Station. In twenty hours, after layovers in Chicago and Memphis, I'd arrive in Parchman, Mississippi. I'd find Moe.

The bus rumbled down the two-lane highways of southern Michigan. I pressed my forehead against the window and stared at the silos, barns, and farmhouses rushing by. We passed acres of brittle cornstalks, ears drying to maturity before harvesting. Tractors, pulling hulking balers up and down the rows of dried hay, kicked up dust storms. Old farm trucks with flat trailers followed behind. A boy who reminded me of Randy paused to wipe sweat from his neck with a dull red bandana before hoisting a bale and tossing it on the flatbed. I thought of the summers I'd spent at my grandparents' farm absorbing, without realizing it, the cycle of sowing and harvesting.

My mother had been planting, too, malicious seeds fertilized with poisonous words tattled to everyone I cared about. Telling them I was wild and unstable, involved with a colored man.

The letter Gaga had written to me the last week of school revealed the power of my mother's tales.

You're young and far from home, on your own for the first time. Girls your age sometimes make bad choices. Life is hard enough without adding problems you don't need. Always remember, you reap what you sow... Stick to your own kind—a nice Catholic boy.

My anger welled at the words, only to be pushed down by

overwhelming grief. Would I ever see Gaga and Oompa again? For the first time, I couldn't count on my grandparents to soften the harsh edges of my relationship with my mother. Instead, they had become a grinding stone sharpening the knife she used to stab me. That letter was my last contact with them.

Grandmother Moroskavich had written that week, too. I found it hard to believe that my mother had even spoken to the woman she despised, but I held the written evidence in my hand. Shock waves ran through me as I read her words.

As you approach your senior year, I will not pay your school expenses without assurance that it is money well spent. You can continue playing in your little band as a hobby, but now you must concentrate on earning a teaching degree. It is a career suitable for a young woman. You must live in the dormitory and give up the foolish relationship that has given rise to scandalous speculation...

I couldn't imagine a worse fate than trying to teach kids how to turn squawks on rented clarinets or weak whistles spit into flutes into real music. The past few months on the road hadn't been easy, scrabbling for gigs, sleeping in the car, skipping meals or eating in scroungy diners, putting up with loud-mouthed drunks, getting stiffed on wages. But none of that mattered when compared to the exhilaration of making music. Would being with Moe mean my music would become a mere hobby? No, I could make marriage and my music work together. I didn't need a degree or Grandmother Moroskavich's money. I'd drop out of school.

Near noon, the bus rolled into another drab town and stopped in an alley where a small, spare room attached to a diner served as bus station. "Thirty minutes," the driver announced.

Most of the passengers entered the diner but I followed a small group into the station and joined the line waiting for the restroom.

After using the toilet and wiping my face, neck, and hands with a damp paper towel, I crossed the street to the A&P on the corner. I bought a jar of Skippy peanut butter, a box of Saltines, and two bottles of Coke from the cooler, then walked two blocks down the street and stood under a large maple. It was a few degrees cooler in the shade, but the breeze I'd hoped for didn't stir. Leaning against the tree, I guzzled a Coke. My stomach churned when the cold liquid hit.

As passengers filed out of the diner and boarded the bus, I trudged back down the street. The sun scorched my neck, perspiration greased my face.

The bus was sweltering in spite of the ads promising air-conditioned comfort. The farther one sat from the driver, the hotter it was and my seat was two-thirds of the way back. "Leave the windows shut," the driver warned. A librarian-faced woman in the second row turned and scowled at those of us behind her as if our actions would cast her into the same hell we suffered.

I opened the peanut butter and dipped a cracker to scoop the thick brown paste. It crumbled in a jillion pieces. I replaced the lid and ate an entire sleeve of crackers, washing them down with lukewarm Coke. A pair of flies practiced dive bombing me, the humid air left me sticky, the rough fabric of the seat prickled my skin, but the drone of the wheels thrumming over the pavement lulled me to sleep.

It was late afternoon when the bus pulled into Chicago's Randolph Street terminal. Crowds of sailors, businessmen, old ladies, and families wrangling restless kids bustled about. The noise made my head ache. I looked for a seat near the area of my transfer. People fanning themselves with newspapers or wiping their faces with rumpled hankies filled every bench. Dropping my suitcase to my feet I leaned against the wall. After a while, I fished the peanut butter from the grocery bag. It had melted to a thick goo. I pulled a Saltine through it and wolfed down the sticky snack. My stomach revolted and I barely made it to the restroom to throw up. Queasy from the close heat, I didn't dare eat anything more.

Finally, my transfer was announced and I boarded the bus.

Traveling south we passed through miles of flat farmland with parched and forlorn crops. Darkness descended, passengers quieted and I fell into a restless sleep. It seemed only a few minutes passed and we were in Memphis. It was 3:30 in the morning.

As I stepped off the bus and entered the terminal a flood of memories overwhelmed me. How naive and frightened I had been when I'd run away and ended up here five years ago. Was this time much different? My plans were almost as vague. Even though I'd convinced myself I was running toward my goal to be with Moe, wasn't I running away from my home, my family, school? Again? Maybe I should stay here and regroup. Look up the guys in my first band and the people at Sun Studio. Would they even remember me?

In the end, I decided to press on. I had to help Moe, make a life with him. Maybe he and I could start over in Memphis. We could form a new band and play on Beale Street. But the memory of what had happened when I'd lived with my friend Ginger in Memphis tore away any desire to live there now, even with Moe.

At six in the morning, the call to board the bus to Parchman (and all spots in between) sounded over the intercom. As I stepped up next to the driver, a crowd of dark faces stared from the back seats. I stuck my suitcase on the rack above and sat next to a grandmotherly looking woman in the third row. The brakes hissed, the bus pulled onto the highway and in a few minutes crossed into Mississippi.

At every small crossroads, the bus rumbled to a stop to let people off or take on new passengers. Most towns consisted of a huddle of scrappy dilapidated buildings with few people stirring. From the bus window, I spotted "whites only" and "colored only" signs over doorways and in storefront windows. Not once did I witness a black person and white person talking together. Why would Moe want to come here when Michigan had so many more opportunities?

The woman next to me got off the bus in Clarksdale and a dozen or so black people got on. Last in line, a girl who looked to be two or three years younger than me carried a fretful infant. A little boy, no more than three, in a starched white shirt and polka dotted bowtie, clutched the girl's skirt and followed with wide eyes. I looked behind me and saw one empty seat. I rose, smiled at the trio, and offered them my seat and the one next to it. The girl froze, confused by my gesture, then returned the smile, unclutched the boy's hand and prodded him into the seat by the window. She sat next to him and let out the weary sigh of an overwhelmed mother.

Everyone's eyes bore into me as I moved toward the back. Among the seats filled with Negroes, I squeezed into a spot next to an oversized woman.

The bus driver scowled in the rear view mirror at a black man in the seat straddling the line between white and colored. Quickly unfolding his long legs to stand, the man stepped toward me and offered to exchange seats.

I shook my head and mumbled, "Thanks, but this is fine. You don't have to switch."

He returned to the middle of the bus and sat, pulling himself together trying to shrink into invisibility.

The driver shrugged, threw the bus into gear and lurched into the street. A low, persistent buzz of whispers filled the air. I wasn't surprised the white people in the front thought what I'd done was wrong, but I hadn't expected the people I sat among to feel that way, too. I slumped cross-armed in the seat and kept my head down. Would it always be like this for me? Never fitting in? Shunned by both whites and blacks? Could Moe and I find a place where we could be together without being confronted with everyone's hatred?

After a few hours, people rustled in their seats, collecting their bags, combing their hair, attempting to brush dust and wrinkles from their clothes. I sensed their excitement, anticipation, happiness and sadness. Those same feelings churned within me.

The Parchman drop off was at the dusty intersection of a pair of narrow two-lane roads. I followed the crowd off the bus, stretched and looked around.

A rusty gas pump, abandoned in a patch of weeds, looked like it hadn't been operable since before I was born. The only building, a small general store with sparse chips of paint clinging to rough pine siding, had a front porch with a roof that slumped like a worn mattress. The doors were slung open wide letting in fat, slow moving flies along with equally lethargic customers.

The woman I'd silently sat next to for the past hour got off the bus and spoke in low tones to a young man waiting there. He had a knapsack slung over his shoulder. His neck was bent, his eyes focused on the dirt his restless foot kicked. I guessed she was his mother come to retrieve her son who would forever carry the brand of ex-con. They got on the bus for the return trip home. I wondered how long and what it would take to repair the fracture between them. They were family and she had come for him so there surely was hope for them.

Having no idea how to get to the prison, I followed the crowd trudging down the dirt road. We passed fields of corn, hay, and wheat and several large vegetable gardens. Cows grazed in other fields. Spotting a barn in the distance, I thought this seemed more like my grandparents' farm than a prison. Except dozens of men, dressed in striped pants, wielded hoes and pitchforks and toiled under the sharp eyes of gunslinging overseers.

The men, mostly Negroes, had stripped off their shirts and their skin glistened with sweat. Chains shackled some together and I thought of pictures I'd seen in history books of slaves working on southern plantations. Horrified that he might be suffering like this, I strained my eyes searching for Moe.

After we walked through a large iron gate into an area of buildings, my fellow visitors scattered in all directions. They seemed to know where to go to find their loved ones. I tried asking a few of them, but most brushed past me as if I were a clump of weeds. Others shrugged or said, "don't know." One less-than-helpful fellow pointed vaguely in the direction of the largest building. I stomped over, angry that no one cared to help me. How ungrateful. Moe had come all the way down here and was in prison because he tried to help those people.

A sign over the door read "Unregistered Visitors." I guessed that would be me. Inside, a uniformed man perched on a stool behind a long counter. I squirmed as he ogled my body. I clenched my fists willing the pinch of nails pushed into palms to toughen my courage.

Staring defiantly at the clerk I announced, "I'm here to get Moses Carter freed."

"Oh, you are?" The man taunted and I felt my resolve wither. "Well, little girl, let me see if I can find out who this Moses Carter is and what dastardly crime he's committed."

He swiveled around on the stool and scooted across the floor to a file cabinet like the one with Dewey Decimal cards in the library.

He stood, pulled out a long drawer, set it on the nearest table and thumbed through the cards.

"Moses Carter you say?" he asked, turning toward me. I nodded and he thumbed some more.

"Yep, here we are." He waved two cards at me like tickets to the circus. "Two of 'em named Moses Carter here. Wait, this ain't right."

He stepped toward me. "Both these punks are niggers. You wouldn't be here for one of them, would you?" His upper lip curled in an evil sneer.

"Moses Carter. He's twenty-two years old and he's from Michigan," I offered.

"Well, now, that would be this bastard. One of them rabble rousers from the north. Stirring up a mess a trouble where they don't belong." His eyelids lowered and he peered at me like a serpent ready to strike. "You one of them, too?"

"No!" I shrieked. Realizing my denial as betrayal, I backed up and said, "I mean, I'm not officially with the group, but I'm here for Moses Carter so yes, I'm in support of, of...please, just let me see him."

"Nope. Ain't his visiting day. No visitors 'til Sunday."

"But, I came all this way and I don't have anywhere to go and I can't wait until Sunday." My eyes burned with tears.

"Well, little girl, why don't you just go on back home to your mama and daddy where you belong? You're too purty to be caught up with some dirty nigger jailbird."

He leaned forward and I felt his hot breath on my face. "Unless you want to stay with me. Got me a real nice trailer out by the woods, nice and private. I could use some company. Get's kinda lonely these sweltering nights." A wicked grin spread across his jaw.

My skin crawled and I wanted to run, but I forced myself to stand my ground. "You filthy creep!" I screamed. "I am not leaving here until I see Moses Carter. And I'll report you if you don't take me to him immediately."

Alerted by my screeches, two guards rushed into the room.

"Get this crazy bitch outta here," the clerk sputtered. "She's makin' threats."

The guards moved to either side of me and each grabbed an arm.

"Let me go," I yelled. "I need to see Moses Carter. Now!" Completely bonkers, I kicked and screamed as the guards wrestled me out of the building.

They held my arms to my sides until I calmed down. I tried to explain why I was at Parchman but they said I had to leave or they would arrest me. If I was thrown in prison would I have a better chance of finding Moe? Probably not.

I decided I would have to work out a plan and come back later. The younger guard, not more than a year or two older than Moe, offered to escort me out and send me on my way.

As we walked toward the gate, I pleaded with him, "Please, I came all this way. I have no place to go. I need to see Moses Carter. Please help me."

We reached the gate and he continued walking with me down the road past the fields. "Is Moses Carter one of them civil rights fellas that came down here? Is he from Flint, Michigan?"

"Yes," I whimpered, afraid to let my hopes soar.

"My auntie lives in Flint. I could get in real big trouble for this, so don't let on what I'm tellin' you. Moses Carter is working in that big field of peas to the left of the cornfields. Should be there a couple more hours til supper. Be careful the guards don't catch you."

He turned and rushed back toward the gate.

I hustled down the road past acres of cornfields which ended abruptly at a scraggly row of spindly pines. Was this the "woods" where the slimy clerk kept his trailer? The trees wouldn't provide much cover, but if I was careful I might be able to get through them without being seen. I moved among the trees, startled by the snap of dead branches and rustle of pine needles resounding as if magnified a hundred times. The thump of my heart added to the clamor.

The tree row continued beyond the cornfield and bordered a gigantic field of peas. I slipped behind the thickest tree and stood sideways hoping its girth would conceal me. Every few seconds I darted my head out and scanned the pea field where a dozen or so men bent to pick the crop. A lone guard meandered among the rows, occasionally prodding one of the men with a thick stick before moving on. I blew out a long puff of air as the guard turned and walked in the direction opposite my hiding place.

I stepped closer to the field, my hand to my forehead to block the sun's glare, and searched for Moe. The physical closeness we'd shared had imprinted his physique in my mind, creating an image I'd clung to during those lonely months we'd been apart. Surely I'd recognize him immediately. A dozen dark bodies bent over the rows, moving slowly back and forth as the prisoners harvested the peas. Was Moe even among them?

A slender man rose and arched his back to relieve the tight muscles. He jerked like a startled deer. I stepped back and ducked behind the tree knowing it was too late.

The man hesitated, craned his neck, then dropped to the ground. He scrabbled along the rows making his way toward me. I should run. My heart pounded triple time, but I remained cemented to the dirt. By the time I'd decided to act, he was next to me still squatting low to avoid being seen by the guard.

His voice was deep and scratchy, dry as field dust, "You gotta git. Ain't safe here."

"I'm looking for Moses Carter," I whispered.

"Git down in the shadows and head back to that corn. I'll send him if I don't get caught. Careful now. Git goin'."

He skittered off and, watching the overseer, pretended to pick peas as he made his way through the rows. I crawled behind the tree row back to the cornfield and hid among the tall stalks. Crouching low and staying still, I watched the prisoners.

They had an undetectable way of communicating and, although it appeared they were working as if nothing had happened, each one glanced toward the corn field. I sensed they knew I was there.

At last I saw Moe. He stood to stretch his back and casually turned, looking toward my hiding place. I wrapped my arms tightly around me to keep from jumping out and running to him. Taking a chance I waved, but Moe acted so nonchalant I couldn't tell if he'd seen me. Then he dropped to the ground and belly crawled, arms pulling him toward me.

A few prisoners strolled over to the overseer resting on the gate of a pickup truck. They distracted him by taking a water break. One by one they slowly dipped the tin cup into a galvanized tub in the truck bed and took a long, slow drink, risking reprimand for dawdling. As the overseer picked up his stick and threatened them, two other prisoners came forward lugging gunny sacks full of peapods.

Moe crawled closer. I moved along the rows of corn until I was directly across from him. He rose to a crouch and hustled over to me. As he stood, I grabbed his hand and pulled him deeper into the field where we couldn't be seen. Then I threw my arms around him and cried.

"How did you get here? Why?" he asked.

"I came to get you out."

He gripped my arms and pushed me away. He was filthy with a coating of dust and sweat; his hair was matted and messy, a dark bruise covered the left side of his face.

"You're crazy!" he spat. "You can't do anything about this—even if I wanted you to—which I don't."

His bitter words jolted me.

"But, you don't belong here. You have to get out and come home and forget—"

"Don't you understand? I could have had SNCC pay my way out of here, but the deal would mean I'd have to leave Mississippi. I've been through too much and there's more to be done. I'm gonna do my time and go back to work."

"No, I don't understand." I gestured toward the field and argued, "How can you think of staying?

"I won't stop until people are not afraid to stand up for themselves. Every battle we win is a victory for all of us. I belong here."

I babbled on pleading for him to come to his senses. Finally, I gasped, "What about us? You promised you'd come home. We'd be together."

"Stop! There can't be any us. My life is here now or wherever I have to be to help my people. I can't go back. I tried to tell you all along. Forget about me. Go back to school, stay in the band, find someone else. Make the life you want."

I wanted to tell him he was all I wanted. To let him know we could make everything work. To tell him we had to. But the overseer's shouts interrupted us as he stomped along the edge of the field yelling for Moe.

Shoving me to the ground, Moe whispered, "Quick! Move to the other side of the field. Stay down. Don't leave until we're gone. Then get out of here and go home. I'm sorry."

He stepped out of the cornfield. As I crawled deeper into the jungle of cornstalks I heard him shout, "Sorry sir, had to piss, sir. Sorry."

The *thwack* of a thick stick hitting flesh followed.

I sat in the dirt and cried, clutching my chest to keep my heart from shattering.

It was over. Moe had made his choice and I was no longer a part of his life.

Once the prisoners had quit for the day, I found my way to the bus stop and began the long trip back to Michigan. I had turned my back on family and school. And now I'd lost Moe. Where would I go? What would I do? My mind played over a hundred possibilities like a musician running his fingers over the piano keys. Every note out of tune.

Late that night, I felt a flutter, like a dozen butterflies, low in my belly. And I knew. Moses Carter had given me a gift and a part of him would always be mine. I would go on without him. I'd find a way to survive. A way to keep the marching band of every challenge and every person who opposed me from trampling my dreams.

Leaning back, I rested my hands on my stomach.

Determination, hope and peace filled me.

My heart would find a new path to follow and new music to play.